The Bridge of a Hundred Dragons

Also by Emma Drummond:

FORGET THE GLORY
BEYOND ALL FRONTIERS

Emma Drummond

St. Martin's Press
New York

 For information, address St. Martin's Press, 175 Fifth Avenue, New York, N.Y. 10010.

Library of Congress Cataloging in Publication Data

Drummond, Emma, 1931–
The bridge of a hundred dragons.

1. China—History—1912–1937—Fiction. I. Title.
PR6054.R785B75 1986 823'.914 86-3967
ISBN 0-312-09549-X

First published in Great Britain by Victor Gollancz Ltd.

First U.S. Edition

10 9 8 7 6 5 4 3 2 1

AUTHOR'S NOTE

At the time in which this novel is set, it was widely believed that Chiang Kai-Shek was a Communist. The Nationalist party in China appeared so revolutionary in aim, so closely allied to and advised by Soviet Russians from Moscow, it was viewed as a dangerous extension of the Red Menace. Time has proved those beliefs to be mistaken, but they are reflected in the attitudes of the characters in this book, all of whom are fictional, apart from well-known personalities.

The village of Lu-Seng has never existed, but the events in Nanking are based on what truly happened to foreign residents. Details of the emergency in Shanghai are strengthened by the personal reminiscences of two of my uncles, who were amongst those rushed out from England to defend British residents and their property.

I should like to thank those gentlemen who gave me their valuable time and knowledge to assist in the writing of this book.

The Bridge of a Hundred Dragons

CHAPTER ONE

Hong Kong in December. The low, leaden clouds hung like a blanket of fog over the barracks, the chill dampness of the accompanying rain reaching into the bones of those used to the sweltering summer heat. Mark shivered as he stood in front of the immobile ranks awaiting an official inspection by a visiting British statesman. They had all formed up half an hour before they need have done—eight hundred and thirty men with expressionless, sun-tanned faces that now had a beading of moisture on eyebrows and moustaches.

They could have been isolated from the rest of the world on that parade ground. Cloud obscured all but the stone barrack-blocks straight ahead, giving no impression of the view to be found from that site halfway up Victoria Peak. The weather also rendered the colony eerily silent from where Mark stood. Even the regimental band sounded as if it were corked up in a bottle.

That simile led Mark on to thoughts of the stiff brandy he would have when the parade was over. He shivered again, but carried out the necessary ritual when the inspecting party marched briskly past, intent on getting out of the drenching rain as soon as possible. However, drenched or not, the officers were obliged to gather in the Mess for the luncheon, none being too enthusiastic about the duty. Even less so was Mark: it was not his regiment playing host. As an Engineer with various detachments under his command scattered all over the colony, it was often necessary for him to be present when his men paraded with their host regiment. Always onerous, to him, it was particularly so when the visitor was a civilian who had no interest in or was completely unimpressed by military ceremonial . . . and in weather like this it was a damned waste of his own time.

Although he knew most of the officers present Mark stood aside for a short while as he drank the brandy he had promised himself, then ordered another. The room smelt of damp uniforms, scented hair-oil, and sweat. The two large overhead fans were silent and unmoving that morning: a small token fire had even been lit in the grate at the far end of the room. The visiting statesman was standing before it, of course, toasting his behind. Above him hung the portraits of King George and

Queen Mary. On the wall at Mark's end of the room was a vast painting of the Battle of Waterloo. The occupying regiment had distinguished itself on that occasion. The painting had replaced one of the Charge of the Light Brigade, in which the previous regiment had featured most gallantly.

Mark thought of his own war. No one sported vast canvases of Ypres or Passchendaele! He supposed that mud and blood and khaki did not look impressive enough to inspire artists, even though the dying was as real and terrible as at Waterloo. He sighed and tossed back his second brandy. It was 1926 and the fashion was to forget those four years —except that he did not seem able to. Not entirely.

The windows began to steam up. Since the trenches Mark had had an aversion to enclosed spaces that allowed him no sight of outside and beyond. In an effort to counteract the feeling he turned to a nearby group, his third brandy in his hand. The men greeted him genially, and they all chatted of military matters together until Mark found himself isolated in conversation with a newly-arrived young officer and asked the man how he liked his new posting.

"Can't say I'm frightfully impressed with the place, so far," he complained in an affected drawl. "The bally sun hasn't shone since I arrived, the streets smell like latrines, and I've been given a Chink for a servant. Can't understand a bally word the blighter says. It's most frightfully inconvenient."

Mark looked him over. A post-war soldier, for certain. He smiled with pretended sympathy. "You should have been here eight months ago, when I first arrived. Hong Kong was almost at a standstill after a year of strikes, riots and wholesale desertions of employees in a bid to ruin the economy and destroy the colony we built. The *Chinks* . . ." he used the same word deliberately, "decided they had had enough of us. They found it *frightfully inconvenient* to be governed by foreign devils."

The youngster flushed, apparently unused to such plain speaking. "Yes, I heard there had been . . . er . . . something of a *fracas* out here last year."

Mark smiled again. "That's right. But that *fracas* was the warning sign of something much bigger to come. The Reds never abandon anything they have instigated. Before your tour of duty is up you might find you have more to worry about than the peculiar odour of Hong Kong's streets." A hand touched his arm, and he looked away from a face that had grown even redder to find a subaltern beside him. "Yes, Brian?"

"Excuse me, Major Rawlings, but the second-in-command would like a word with you. It's rather urgent."

Mark frowned. "Urgent?"

"That's what he said." The young officer made an apologetic face. "A direct request from Sir Kenneth through the Commanding Officer, I understand."

Puzzled, Mark finished his drink in one gulp. "A royal command, no less! Well, I'm a hopeless after-luncheon speaker, so it can't be to ask for a speech, and I never play my ukulele at parties." He gave the boy a swift smile. "It must be something military, don't you think?"

He turned to the group he was with and murmured an apology for his departure. His progress through the pressing throng of military men was slow enough to allow him to overhear the red-faced youngster ask someone, "Who the hell is *he*?" and the man reply, "One of the few who survived the whole four years of the war. He drinks too much and is more inscrutable than the bloody Chinese. Shell-shock, I suppose. It usually is. But he's a clever bastard, for all that."

The frown returned to Mark's brow. Was that how others saw him? Shell-shock? Oh no, it was more than that, and if it made him inscrutable it was because he could never bring himself to speak of it. The frown must have remained, for the second-in-command greeted him with a laugh and a friendly hand on his arm.

"Don't look so worried. This is something you'll be rather pleased about, I think."

"Sorry, I was miles away," he explained. "What's this all about, Reggie—a direct word from Sir Kenneth?"

"It concerns a bridge. A railway bridge, to be exact. Ah, I knew you'd prick up your ears. Told you so, didn't I?"

"What about the bridge?" asked Mark with immediate interest.

"It's collapsed."

"Now, wait a . . ."

"Taking a train with it," inserted the other major.

"Oh lord, that's serious. Any casualties?"

"Forty-seven, so far. The train was packed. They're still digging them out."

Mark whistled through his teeth. "How did it happen?"

"That's where you come in."

"Oh-oh! If it's a repair job you want . . ."

"Direct request to the Governor for the loan of our bridge expert. Seems someone up there knows your reputation."

"Up there?"

Humping his shoulders the major spread his hands apologetically. "It's top priority from the highest level. More of a command than a request, if you see what I mean. More than that we just don't know. You'll be leaving on a boat for Shanghai at sixteen hundred today."

"*Shanghai . . . four o'clock today!*" exclaimed Mark. "It can't be done."

"Orders!" replied the major significantly.

"But, damn it all, my things are all over at Kowloon!"

"A signal has been sent across for your boy to pack what you'll need and bring it to the jetty for you. Your professional gear will be put up by a fellow officer. Sorry, Mark, but your Chief Engineer has given the go-ahead for this." He broke into a smile. "Honour of the Corps, and all that. You might even get a knighthood for it."

Thoroughly rattled, he struck out. "Why can't this be handled by the bloody fool who built the bridge?"

"Because the 'bloody fool' was in the train when the bridge went," came the slow answer. "He's dead."

The luncheon dragged on. All Mark's thoughts were on the implications of his hasty departure. His Chinese houseboy would know instinctively what to pack by way of personal belongings, and one of his colleagues would assemble all the right gear for bridging work, but there were still things to be done. Invitations had been accepted and courtesy demanded that he inform his intended hosts of his unavoidable absence. He had promised to judge the annual Christmas swimming gala at the hospital for handicapped children. Now he would have to cry off. His financial affairs—always in a rocky state—would have to be discussed with his bank manager because he would need to have money transferred to the Shanghai branch ready for his arrival.

The minute the meal was ended he was excused the coffee-drinking period when Sir Kenneth would contrive to speak to all those present. His short conversation with the visitor before luncheon had left Mark with no clear idea of what had happened up in Shanghai except that there was an unusual urgency about the situation. If he had been gratified by Sir Kenneth's flattering comments on a reputation that had made Mark's name respected among men of his own profession, he was nevertheless annoyed at the peremptory manner in which he was being treated. As an army officer he was obliged to obey orders: a civilian engineer would have demanded more time and information before taking on a contract.

But bridges had never failed to capture his imagination and, beneath it all, Mark felt a certain excitement as he wrote a note to the headmaster of the school holding the swimming gala, and another to a fellow officer asking him to contact his expectant hosts and explain the situation. He left the barracks with three-quarters of an hour in which to see his bank manager and get aboard the ship. But Hong Kong was not geared to haste. To get down from the barracks Mark had to take a sedan chair to the nearest station of the Peak tramway, then a rickshaw from the foot of the Peak to the premises of the Hong Kong-Shanghai bank.

The rain had stopped but the greyness of the afternoon highlighted the squalor and dinginess that the brilliant sun normally threw into shadow. The streets were jammed with sombrely-clad Chinese who hawked and spat with scant regard for others or the state of their streets. Most faces looked lined and weary—even the young ones—and too many frames were skeletal. They moved along in moody silence, oppressed by the weather and the burden of living another day, another week. The rebellion designed to crush the British rule of Hong Kong had hit the rebels a hundred times harder than their victims. They had found that trying to live without their masters was worse than living with them.

Mark had no time to ponder great issues: time was racing past and the ship would not wait for him. His sharp order to the rickshaw boy to hurry was not born of British imperiousness, but necessity. It was touch and go whether he would reach the jetty on time. From the bank to the docks he was literally watching the seconds tick past, and he arrived to find the gangplank being removed altogether. Uncomfortable in his parade uniform and irritated by the whole sequence of the day, he waved and shouted at Ah Wu, his boy who was standing beside three cases, telling him to stop the seamen.

Violent gesticulations, rapid Chinese words, and a short sturdy body standing firmly on the foot of the gangplank did the trick, and Mark jumped from his rickshaw, paid the runner, and shouted to Ah Wu to get the luggage aboard. There was a great deal of noise accompanying the departure of a big ship, but the Chinese boy heard him and began scurrying aboard with Mark's things, still shouting and gesticulating at the seamen to indicate his master's arrival.

Pushing his way through the throng of those waving goodbye Mark cursed under his breath as he saw the gangplank was now held by just two burly sailors, who looked set to lower it to the jetty before he could scramble aboard. Running fast up the swaying wooden way Mark had to take the last few feet at a jump, much to the smug delight of the grinning seafarers who had scant respect for the military. His momentum took him headlong toward a stanchion on deck but, swerving instinctively, he collided with a small figure coming around it and his foot crunched something soft. The girl gave a yell, grabbing the stanchion for support as she held her foot from the ground in pain.

"I'm terribly sorry," he panted, steadying himself with difficulty. "It was entirely my fault. Have I hurt you?"

She was still moaning as she clung to the cream-coloured pillar. "I'll say! I may never walk again," came her theatrical declaration.

Mark cursed the circumstances that had put him in this predicament. She was clearly going to be awkward over it. All he could see was a pale-blue cloche hat which obscured her face as she studied her foot, and he set out to extricate himself as fast as possible.

Addressing the hat he said, "Allow me to help you to a seat. Then I'll fetch someone to assist you."

Taking her arm in a manner that gave her no alternative he led her, limping exaggeratedly, to a barred seat along the bulkhead, where she sank down and began unbuckling a pale kid shoe that now bore the muddy imprint of his army boot. Watching her he realised that he could see beige silk stocking right up to her thighs where the pleated wool skirt in soft caramel shade fell across her legs. They were well worth revealing—long, slim and beautiful—and he could not take his gaze from the point where they finally disappeared beneath her skirt.

She looked up at him then, reading his thoughts without a doubt. "It might be of more help if you were to massage my toes for me," she said in mocking tones. "You are a very big man, and my foot is most devastatingly crushed, sweetie."

He recognised what she was then. In Hong Kong he had been vaguely aware of the new breed of wealthy emancipated women who flouted all the conventions and drew public attention to themselves by using shock tactics. He had never been this close to one before, and he had never seen a skirt quite as short as the one she was wearing. Dragging his gaze reluctantly from those legs, he studied the rest of her more closely. The cloche hat cupped a very young face with large blue eyes made startling by heavy black outlining. The girl's skin was golden from summer sunshine that was no longer considered fatal to feminine skins, and her mouth was painted an astonishing scarlet shaped in a bow that suggested a surprised 'oh'.

The overall effect made Mark want to laugh, more than anything, but the day had been a bastard, and he longed to get to his cabin where he could change from his uniform and relax with a drink. This young girl must be in the charge of some adult, so he determined on delivering her into those hands right away.

She held her leg provocatively higher and wiggled her toes at him. "Aren't you going to massage my foot, then?"

"No. This is a very public place."

"*This* is where you jumped on it."

He decided firmness was the only answer. "I think you should go to your cabin, and I'll arrange for the ship's doctor to have a look at your foot. Is your mother on deck?"

"My *mother*!" she cried. "No, she is not; she's in Shanghai."

The disdain in her voice advertised her society upbringing even more than the diamond clip that fastened the cockade of dyed feathers to the brim of her hat.

"Well, you can't be travelling alone," he reasoned, pressing on.

"Whyever not!" Her black-rimmed eyes filled with scorn. "Don't tell me you are one of those old-fashioned men who believe women are completely helpless."

He was getting nowhere with her and it was beginning to irritate him. "What I think is of no consequence. I'll go and arrange with the purser for a stewardess to assist you to your cabin, then fetch the doctor. Naturally, I will settle any expense that might be incurred." He began to turn away.

"Just a minute," she called in an imperious manner, forcing him to turn back again. "What about this shoe? It's quite ruined, and I had the pair made especially to go with this costume."

The pale-blue shoe dangled from her finger as she challenged him to deal with another problem. Mark lost any desire to laugh at her. She was being a damn nuisance, and the suspicion that she was vastly enjoying every moment of the encounter did not improve his temper. Passengers in the vicinity were growing very interested in the scene, and he felt extremely annoyed that a silly young creature should be getting all the attention she so plainly sought—and at his expense.

Aware that others were watching closely, he said in a low tone, "My boy, Ah Wu, is very good with leather. If you'll let him have the shoe, I guarantee he'll restore it to its original state, Miss . . . ?"

"My friends call me Sandy."

He did not take up the invitation. It was unlikely he would ever become one of her friends. "I'll see the purser," he repeated, preparing to move off. "Once again, I apologise for my carelessness."

"Oh, don't apologise," she cooed. "It was your impressive last-minute embarkation that drew me to the rail. Do you make a habit of performing hair-raising stunts? It was absolutely terrif!"

Ignoring that and doggedly pursuing his conventional winding-up speech, Mark said, "I trust your foot will suffer no lasting damage."

She smiled, ruining the effect of the scarlet bow. "You'll be able to see for yourself, Major. We shall be spending the next three days at sea together, won't we?"

Not at your age, we won't, he thought, giving a brief nod and turning away toward the purser's office. But her voice floated after him, deliberately loud in the offshore stillness.

"My cabin number is A44, darling."

He turned and caught the shocked glances of nearby passengers who had translated her words just the way she had hoped. He opened his mouth to speak, but she added in a bubbling undertone, "Your boy will want to know where to collect my shoe, sweetie." Then she closed one eye in a deliberate wink.

Mark could not analyse the feeling that ruled him all the while he arranged for someone to tend the girl he had left on deck, then ascertained the number of his own cabin. He thanked God he would be living nowhere near A44 for the next few days. Striding along the uneven deck closely followed by Ah Wu he grew very angry. 'Bright Young Things' they were dubbed—young men and girls with too much money and no sense of purpose or responsibility. Off with the old and on with the new, was their rallying call. Fun and pleasure; forget the grimness of war. Yet none of them was old enough to have taken part in it, or appeared to care what it had all been for.

Whilst Ah Wu unpacked, Mark went through the equipment put in a bag for him by a colleague. The task took his mind from contemplation of a pale-blue shoe, exciting long legs, and an overemancipated girl, allowing him to concentrate on things professional instead. Ever since he could remember he had wanted to build bridges. As a boy he had drawn them by the hundred and spent his free time studying those in the vicinity of his home. At seventeen-and-a-half he had been a senior pupil at a good private school, all set for an engineering career. War had come, and he had been filled with the same patriotic fervour as his friends, seeing glory and adventure in taking up arms. His parents, who had scrimped and saved to give him an education they could not afford for his two sisters, had never understood or forgiven him for volunteering. Even a commission in the Royal Engineers had not consoled them, despite the fact that he would have been conscripted eventually. The rift with his family had never healed, but his working-class background had imbued him with strong moral standards and the awareness of the responsibilities of an only son. When his father had been killed early in the war, those responsibilities had descended on the eighteen-year-old Mark and remained there, like a financial millstone around his neck.

He reflected briefly on the conversation with his bank manager that afternoon and sighed heavily. Life in Hong Kong involved him in more expenses than in England, and his bank balance was as much a constant worry to his banker as to himself. The allowance he made to his mother each month made a large hole in his pay, and some new expense always prevented his accumulating enough to feel really secure. Then, in a to-hell-with-it-all mood, he rang for the steward and ordered a bottle of brandy. The war had taught him to rely on spirits to remain sane, and the habit could not now be easily abandoned. He knew he drank far too heavily but, since it was the only thing he did to excess, had no intention of trying to stop. It still kept him sane.

With a couple of stiff drinks inside him he stripped off his uniform, had a shower, wrapped a bathrobe around his body and settled in the chair, bottle beside him, to think about what lay ahead. A wrecked train mixed up with a broken bridge would complicate things no end, and since the poor blighter who had built it had died in the accident—poetic justice, if you like!—it would mean questioning umpteen other people before he could make even a guess at the likeliest cause. With an arm up beneath his head, and his bare feet resting on the other chair Mark sipped his brandy and wondered once again why everyone was in such a blazing hurry to get him up to Shanghai, yet appeared to have no details of the affair.

Getting nowhere with that line of thought he moved on to the flattering fact of his being asked to go. Sir Kenneth had spoken of his 'name being respected in engineering circles', but it still surprised Mark that an army man had been selected when there must be many men of talent in China during this present period of expansion. Also, there was the slumbering threat of conflict which surely demanded that military strength should be maintained. The Nationalist revolutionary leader Chiang Kai-Shek had an army designed to liberate the Chinese people from the yoke of subjection, and it was anyone's guess whether he would march against the white man along with the tyrannical warlords. If he did, Mark's services as a fighting officer would be more valued than his work for the Chinese railways.

He poured himself another drink while he considered the facts. Of course, he had become something of a specialist in railway bridges, although he had never yet had to deal with one that had simply collapsed under a train. During the war he had blown them up, set fire to them, shot them apart, sunk them, and mined them. He had thrown pontoon bridges across rivers and taken them up again; had helped to drop a wooden trestle construction over a narrow chasm so that vehicles could cross. But it was not until the war was over that he had *built* his first bridge. Oh God, that first bridge!

The level of the bottle grew lower as it always did when he embarked on memories of Russia, and his thoughts travelled no further than that period seven years ago. Time and brandy had dulled the pain of all that had been lost during that year of 1919, but it was still strong enough to blot out all awareness of the present as he sat lost in remembrances of those who had gone beyond recall.

When Ah Wu returned to lay out his clothes for dinner Mark realised he was sitting in a dark cabin and was three-quarters drunk. Since his constitution was well used to it he knew a hearty meal would go a long way toward sobering him up, so he made his way to the restaurant as soon as he was ready. The Chinese boy, wreathed in smiles over the thanks of his master for the excellent way he had packed the cases, hastened to gain further favour by assuring Mark as he prepared to leave the cabin that "Missy's shoe had been returned to her and was now looking like the face of the moon".

"Missy's shoe?" repeated Mark groggily.

"Missy A44."

It all came back to him then. "Oh, good . . . let's hope that is the end of the matter," he muttered to himself and went out, blaming the rolling of the ship for his unsteadiness.

The restaurant contained only a sprinkling of people, mostly elderly. Dancing did not commence until ten, so the younger passengers would not appear yet. It suited Mark. He was shown to a table which he shared with three pasteboard cards telling him that Mr Jeffries, Professor Meisten, and Dr Peabody were late diners. In his present mood he was glad of the fact.

After dinner he went into the lounge to down several cups of black coffee, then sat on, oblivious of the comings and goings, reading a newspaper. He grew suddenly alert when he saw some reference to the disaster at the bridge, but it turned out to be no more than a factual report on when, where and how. There was no clue as to why. But the article at least told him it was a steel girder bridge over a canal some way up from Shanghai and in the middle of nowhere. *His* bridges always were, he reflected resignedly. Then he read the article again feeling that it was extremely restrained for a major disaster as far as loss of life was concerned. One enigmatic sentence even hinted that there had been an earlier mishap at the spot, but it was glossed over in a manner that suggested it should not be regarded seriously.

Mark frowned, a sudden uneasiness flowing over him. The feeling that there was more to the affair than he had been told grew stronger. Now he had time to reflect on the events of the day he realised he had been swamped with flattery by Sir Kenneth, which had denied him the opportunity to question the man—or anyone else—about the nature of the disaster. He had been rushed onto the ship with luggage packed by others, although he had spoken on the telephone to his Commanding

Officer before he left. Colonel Maine had sounded hearty and encouraging, but knew no more about the job than anyone else, it had seemed. Lowering the newspaper thoughtfully Mark realised the honour and glory side of the affair had been highly emphasised. Had it been an attempt to hide something unpleasant? His uneasiness increased. Just what was he getting into up there in Shanghai?

At that point his attention was partially taken by a steward nodding in his direction, then smiling at a girl in a yellow evening-dress. She smiled back at the man and walked across.

"Hallo," she greeted gaily.

There was no one else near him, so Mark struggled to his feet wondering what it was all about. "Good evening. Er . . . can I assist you in some way?"

"You look different out of uniform," she continued. "That peaked cap gave you a definite air of authority that dare not be flouted. You're much more approachable now. Thank you for the shoe. Your boy worked wonders; it looks as it did before you jumped on it."

It was then he realised he was not as sober as he thought. Her eyes seemed bluer and more softly accented than before, her skin a warmer shade of gold beneath the lights. The yellow dress was of silk embroidered with vivid scarlet, green and gold thread, two-tiered with gold fringing at hip length that shimmered as she moved. It revealed her sun-kissed arms, and a great deal of her body through the scooped neckline. The hem was well above her knees, and the whole effect was causing a sensation amongst those in the lounge.

Only vaguely aware that everyone was staring in his direction Mark's gaze was riveted on the girl's hair which had been completely hidden by the cloche hat during their earlier encounter. It was fashionably bobbed and waved, but a glorious gleaming auburn that made everything about her glow with life.

"How is the foot?" he asked with automatic formality.

She smiled. "The sawbones worked miracles. *He* seemed very willing to massage my toes." Her glance flicked over him. "A man of your size lands very heavily, you know."

"Yes, I realised that at the time. I apologise again, and I'm glad there was no lasting damage." It was a good bowing-out line, he thought, and expected her to go.

But this girl did as she pleased. "I suppose I ought to know you. I know most people of importance."

It took him unawares. "Importance . . . me? Good lord, no."

"But they held up the ship for you. Aren't you off to Shanghai on vital military affairs?"

"Not at all," he said, feeling trapped between the chair and the coffee table. "I'm just obeying orders from above."

The pencilled eyebrows rose in delicate surprise. "I didn't realise you were a chaplain, Major."

He stared at her for a moment, in incomprehension. Then he saw her eyes were sparkling with merriment, and a smile touched his own lips as awareness filled him.

"The orders came from a slightly less exalted level than *that*."

Music was starting in the ballroom now. He could hear the jump rhythm of a dance tune that was attracting a flow of young passengers from the restaurant through the lounge. There would be no more peace in his secluded corner. He prepared to leave, stepping round the low table.

"No doubt you intend to dance the night away now the doctor has worked miracles on your toes, so if you'll excuse me. . . ." He was beside her now, clear of the table.

"Don't you dance?" she asked tilting her face provocatively up to his.

"Not when I can avoid it." It was as final as the nod he gave before turning away. But he bumped full tilt into someone directly behind him and had to grip her arms to steady her. This girl was no older than the one called Sandy, dark haired with a startlingly white skin. She gazed up at him with heavily-lashed green eyes as she stood melting in his hold.

"I beg your pardon," he murmured automatically, then released her quickly because there was a young man behind her who did not look too happy.

"Come on, Sandy, we've been waiting for you. There won't be room to move in there before long," he said fiercely, his gaze on Mark the whole time.

"Then we'll *make* room," came the cool reply. An arm was slipped through Mark's, and there was a gurgle of laughter in her voice as she said, "You really shouldn't be travelling alone, Major. All you do is bump into people."

The other girl's mouth formed an O. "Is *this* the Valentino type who jumped on you, Sandy?" Her eyelashes fluttered madly. "You can crush *my* toes any time you like, darling."

"Are you two going to dance or not?" demanded their angry escort.

"We *three* are going to dance," said the red-haired girl in a manner that suggested it was all settled. "Come along," she said to Mark. "It's the least you can do after the way you have treated us both."

His other arm was taken by the friend who vamped him with her eyes. "Do you tango divinely?"

"I can manage the waltz," he said as they began to drag him toward the ballroom. He was being shanghaied, he knew, but the entire day had been impossible and it seemed easier to go along with them than create even more amused interest from those nearby. He did not doubt the pair were capable of *anything*.

The ballroom certainly was crowded, but the trio appeared to wield some kind of influence because a steward had a table reserved for them with champagne already cooling in a bucket. The dance floor was full of couples jerking their way through a ragtime tune while a plump man in tails, his black hair as smooth and shining as if it had been painted on his head, sang hectic lines that all seemed to end with "boh doh de-oh". The atmosphere was heavy with French perfume and smoke from Turkish cigarettes.

It made Mark's head thicker and, under the circumstances, it was probably foolish of him to order a brandy from the steward after declining champagne on the grounds that he had never acquired a taste for it.

"Aren't you divinely antediluvian!" cried the dark-haired girl. "I couldn't *live* without champagne."

Mark kept his comments on such a thoughtless statement to himself as the girl was introduced as Dot Armitage, and the young man as her brother, Lion.

"Lion?" queried Mark.

"Lionel . . . but no one uses *that*," was the scathing explanation. "I'm in banking."

"Lion had to make a business trip to Hong Kong so we decided to join him," said his sister in artificial tones. "Shanghai is *miserable* at this time of the year, and shopping on the island is very diverting. We spent absolutely *fortunes*, didn't we, Sandy? My *mama* disapproved, poor dear, and has taken herself off to her cabin with a headache, thankful we have now left temptation behind."

"No doubt she is also antediluvian," said Mark. "Only not divinely so, like me."

Dot looked at him for a moment, then laughed in immoderate delight. "You do say the most delicious things."

"If you are set on dancing, Sandy, there is a waltz just starting . . . and there might not be another until much later in the evening," put in Lionel with undisguised pointedness.

Mark was in accord with him. He stood and took the girl in his arms in the manner he used toward colonels' wives and daughters at military functions. He began chatting in much the same manner.

"Your young man is very put out over my presence this evening," he said to the top of the girl's glowing head. "Was that your intention?"

The blue eyes were indignant as she looked up at him. "I should say not. Lion is a sweetie, but much too intense about everything."

"Perhaps you shouldn't bait him, in that case."

The singer was announcing to everyone that "I'll be loving you —*always*" and they were dancing very near the orchestra, so she said nothing until they had shuffled into a quieter area of the ballroom.

"I'm baiting no one. Do you really have no idea of the glamour it gives a girl's reputation to be seen with an older man?"

He was highly amused. At thirty he had never thought of himself as 'an older man'. "They might just think I'm your father," he suggested meekly.

The bright head shook gently. "You're holding me too close."

He held her even closer, just to make sure. "What does it do to an older man's reputation to be seen with you?" he asked next, feeling his tongue was running away with him.

"Oh, I'm the perfect cover for your secret mission."

"My *what*?"

She had lovely teeth when she smiled, and her mouth lost its artificial pout. "It's quite obvious you are on a vital military mission. Why else would they have held the ship while you made that perfectly divine dash up the gangplank?"

Lost in thoughts of how pliantly she moved against him, he murmured, "Very well. If you must know, the Chinese secret societies are all after me. They'll extract the vital information by means of terrible torture if they ever lay hands on me."

His levity plainly annoyed her, and she snapped, "You don't dance very well, you know."

"I did warn you."

She bristled for a moment. "I suppose you are one of those brawny sporting men—all cricket and water polo?"

"Something like that." He said no more while they glided past the band again, then asked, "Why did you tell me you were travelling alone?"

Her lovely eyes widened. "I didn't. You imagined I was, and it would have spoilt the fun to tell the truth . . . but I'd do so if I wished," she added defiantly.

"I'm sure you would." Her perfume and golden skin was beginning to affect him as much as the brandy. "It might be a little dangerous, you know, with hair that colour. You shouldn't let people call you 'Sandy'. It's a much nicer shade than that."

She looked up at him and laughed softly. "It's short for Alexandra . . . which is too frightfully stuffed shirt for words, isn't it?"

"No. I like it."

She laughed at him again. "You can't be as old as *that*, surely! Or do all those sporting activities keep you looking overyouthful?"

"How long are your activities going to keep you looking youthful?" he countered with sudden feeling.

It did not please her to be outmanoeuvred. She frowned. "You sound like my father."

"I'm not that antediluvian, divinely so, or otherwise."

Changing moods with lightning speed she snuggled closer in his arms and rested her head against his shoulder so that her bright hair tickled his chin.

"I know you're not . . . but I do think you are just the teeniest bit drunk."

He nodded. "You'd never have got me into this ballroom otherwise."

She pressed even closer. "Oh yes I would!"

He felt it was as well the music ended then, and they were able to return to the table. But the dance had lasted too long for Lionel Armitage who was looking like a storm cloud. Silly young fool, thought Mark, with a strange twinge for a very young subaltern who had once felt that way over a girl. But it soon vanished. This aggressive young banker was twenty-two or three, and that same subaltern had become an old man by that age. The slight exhilaration brought on by the dance died leaving Mark with a familiar hollow sadness. Escape from it was never permanent, he had discovered. He remained standing, feeling it would be possible to leave within a few moments, but another young man arrived at the table and introductions were made.

"How do you do, sir," said the new arrival, evidently feeling Mark was of an age to command formality from him. "Having a spot of leave in Shanghai, are you?"

Feeling his ego was suffering too many ups and downs that evening, he was tempted to invent a secret mission, after all. But he merely said, "No, it's duty, I'm afraid."

"Suppressing the natives, I suppose," sneered Lionel, with surprising vindictiveness.

Mark lowered his glass in the act of finishing his drink. "A bit out of date, aren't you?"

"Isn't that what you and your kind are here for?"

"Not as I understand it." At that stage he was still casual. Jealousy made young men behave irrationally. He should know.

"What did you do at Shameen Island?" It was a gauntlet Mark could not ignore, so he sat down in order to avoid curiosity from others in what threatened to be a tricky situation.

"I wasn't there at Shameen," he began reasonably, "but I heard there was an unfortunate need to put down Chinese rioters who were attacking foreign property guarded by our troops."

"*You heard*," said Lionel in a scathing manner. "That's what we all heard. But the truth is, it was simply another case of foreigners refusing to give back territory annexed for Western expansion. When the Chinese demanded occupation of it they were mown down by army rifles. Don't you call that suppression of the natives?"

"No, I call it defence against unbridled mob violence. That is never the right way of doing things. People get hurt."

"Sometimes it's the only way, when successive representations have failed to do the trick. People get hurt, I agree, but it is worth the loss in order to be free."

Mark looked at the young banker in expensive evening clothes, whose youthful face showed no signs of suffering and disillusionment, and he thought of all those youthful Russian faces that had been etched with the agony of their country. Anger raced through him.

"You sit in a bank all day juggling with people's wealth and look out on the world with eyes that have seen nothing yet. You are talking of *revolution*. Kill a few thousands, destroy a culture, devastate and pillage the land until it is barren. That is what revolution brings. You have no idea what you are advocating."

Lionel looked at him with contempt. "I have lived all my life in China. Men like you come for a few months and pride yourselves on knowing what is best for the natives. You do it everywhere you go—whether they are Chinese, Indians, Zulus or Irishmen. Soldiers make no friends amongst the populace. The only friends they have are guns." His mouth twisted. "Men like you are all the same. Because you have been through a war you think the world owes you respect, gratitude, and a slavish adherence to your opinions."

"No, you are wrong," put in Mark wearily, having heard that line far too often from youngsters like Armitage. "All we ask is that you never start another one."

"Revolution isn't war, it's an expression of national freedom," snapped the youngster. "I know what is seething beneath the surface of this country. When the time comes, the people will rise and take what is rightly theirs."

"Then God help them all, if they do," was Mark's only comment. "I have seen it happen, and national freedom is the last thing that is won. The very last thing."

The subject had been ill-timed, too soon after the dark thoughts in his cabin not so long before. He tossed back his brandy and poured himself another very quickly. The group around the table had become silent, baffled by the alien mood. They only understood gaiety. No one seemed equipped to break it, until Lionel got to his feet and seized his partner's hand.

"Come on, Sandy, let's get back to the land of the living. 'Grandad' is determined to play Russian roulette with the brandy bottle, and he's already half under the table."

Next minute, the couple were deep in the athletics of the Charleston, apparently having forgotten everything but the determination to 'have fun'.

Dot touched Mark's arm apologetically. "Lion is always like that. We take no notice of it. He's . . . he's a *socialist*, you know. Against the class system."

"So was my father—a very ardent one," said the man who was being condemned because of his rank. "He was a sergeant during the war—killed in France during the first year."

"Oh . . . well, that's what we fought the war for, wasn't it? Freedom for the ordinary people," said Dot with no idea what she was talking about.

It was not worth answering. Mark gazed at the pair on the dance floor while the tension inside him slowly died leaving depression. The girl had been right. He was too old for this company. They danced well and with complete abandon, so much so that others began to fall back from the vicinity of their kicking feet and expressive arm movements. Mark tossed back the last of his drink as he watched the long slim legs of the girl in absent appreciation. There had been another girl in another place, no older than this one—a girl with sweetness and understanding in eyes that had seen a world's suffering. The girl in the yellow dress that he watched now was a child, in comparison—a careless, selfish child of the twenties.

Right now she was oblivious of everything but her partner and her own twisting body as they grew wilder and wilder. Couples began leaving the floor to watch what was turning into an exhibition by the pair. Some of the older passengers were put out at being obliged to abandon their own stately pleasure because it was now impossible to dance with comfort on the tiny floor.

The band-leader, caught in the enthusiasm of skill and rhythm, prolonged the tune, urging his orchestra into a reprise which caught some of the wildness of the two dancers. Lionel's slim elegance was perfectly suited to the movements. His face grew flushed, but not a strand of his sleekly-oiled blond hair fell out of place as he swung his partner around with practised ease.

The jerky beat drummed in Mark's head as he followed their movements. The girl's face was glowing with life and a strange kind of elation: when she put back her head the arch of her throat put an ache in Mark's—an ache for something long ago. As she spun, the skirt of her short dress flared out to reveal the tops of her thighs, and the golden fringe shimmered around the silk stockings.

The band seemed to be so mesmerised it could not bring the tune to an end. The younger element started to clap and stamp their feet by way of encouragement to the dancers. Lionel began to lift his partner and swing her right over, revealing beige lace-trimmed panties and a pair of emerald green garters each time she turned. The watching passengers began to murmur amongst themselves, the older ones with shocked disapproval, the younger with awed excitement, sensing a daring disregard for society and convention. Caught up in their own recklessness, the couple sought new diversions and jumped onto a table to continue their dance. Those sitting around it had a total view of the girl's legs and heaven knew what else as they gazed up at her twirling figure. Awe began to turn into disgust. The mood in the entire room underwent a change. Amused curiosity hardened into embarrassment. When the dancers began to jump from table to table, sending glasses flying as they went, embarrassment was replaced by uproar. They had gone too far even for the most modern minds.

Mark got to his feet wishing he had never allowed himself to be dragged into the group.

Dot looked up at him with shining eyes. "Aren't they dee-*vine*!"

"She's . . . she's . . . out of this crazy world!" cried the young man beside him, practically lathering at the mouth. "Only Sandy could do a thing like that!"

They did not see Mark leave. He was not the only one who felt the evening had suddenly turned sour, and they expressed that feeling in strong words to each other as they streamed from the elegant ballroom. "*Scandalous*" . . . "quite without shame" . . . "completely wild and unmanageable" . . . "no sense of modesty" . . . "will undoubtedly come to a bad end."

All these comments Mark heard as he made his way to his cabin with the rhythm still pounding in his head. But one conversation caught his attention more than any other.

"It's the same wherever that girl goes. Last week she caused a sensation in Hong Kong by turning up at Government House in satin evening pyjamas—at a *ball*, my dear. It upset a great many people."

"Who *is* she?"

"Alexandra Mostyn—Garrard and Alice Mostyn's daughter."

"Do I know them, darling?"

"If you don't you really should do something about cultivating them. Most frightfully rich, my dear. Of course, it's very tragic about her—such a *nice* woman. He is something to do with railways, but a gentleman, for all that."

Mark continued on his way to his cabin, head still pounding. It really was the only end to this impossible day, he supposed. Garrard Mostyn was the man he was going to Shanghai to meet.

CHAPTER TWO

The ship had docked. There was the usual pandemonium of disembarkation, but no one lingered on the upper decks on a cold raw day that had an icy wind blowing in from the sea. Those privileged to go aboard and greet influential people gathered in the vicinity of the purser's office while young cabin-boys roamed the ship with their two-toned dulcimers, paging the passengers.

Mark expected to be met, but by whom he was not sure. His departure had been so hasty there had been no time for such details, although the circumstances of his journey demanded that he be put in possession of the facts by someone from this end as soon as possible. He decided to wear uniform, partly because he felt he would be more recognisable to someone looking for an army man, and partly because the only overcoat he had was his military one. It was already apparent to him that clothes that were suitable for December in Hong Kong were nowhere near warm enough for weather as bitterly cold as he encountered that morning.

It came as a surprise to hear his name being paged almost immediately after docking. Leaving Ah Wu to supervise the luggage he made his way through chattering crowds of excitable passengers who were hindering the work of the cabin staff by crowding the narrow gangways. The lad pointed to a tall plump young man near the companionway. Mark gave him a tip, then walked across to introduce himself. The stranger saw him coming and advanced, a self-conscious smile on his face.

"Major Rawlings? Welcome to Shanghai. My name is James Clitheroe."

Mark shook his hand firmly, but the other's grip seemed slack. "Thanks for meeting me. I left Hong Kong in such a hurry there was no time for a briefing on the best place to stay, and so on." He smiled. "I must say this is much better than standing around on the jetty waiting for someone to claim me. How did you manage to get aboard?"

James Clitheroe's eyes goggled at him. "I work for Garrard Mostyn."

Feeling that the statement should mean more to him than it did,

Mark tested his theory. "Mostyn pulls a lot of weight in Shanghai, does he?"

The eyes goggled even more. "I take it this is your first visit."

"I've only been in the Far East for eight months, all of them spent in Hong Kong." He shivered in the blast of wind whistling down the companionway from the upper deck. "It's a hell of a lot colder here."

"That's not the only difference, as you'll soon discover. Shanghai is a completely international city run by a group of men who are wealthy, influential, and in positions of power that are unique. It cannot in any way be compared with a small island colony governed by the Crown, in which the British residents are protected by their own police and an army garrison. In Shanghai we have to live by our wits. It's a constant chess game between them and us." He grew strangely elated. "They're clever, you know, far more so than most people realise . . . but when they come up against men like Mr Mostyn each move in the game becomes more of a risk, more deadly."

This outburst did nothing to boost Mark's enthusiasm for the mysterious job ahead of him. Judging 'they' to refer to the Chinese, he could sense that there was going to be nothing straightforward in the rebuilding of the bridge. He also sensed that Clitheroe resented him, for some reason. The indifferent handshake, the disparagement of the English colony, the edge of superiority when speaking of his own city all suggested that the young businessman held army engineers in small respect. It was an attitude he had encountered often, but in this man he found it irritating.

Wasting no more time he said, "If you'll tell me where I'll be staying I'll leave a message for my boy and we can get going. The crush is getting worse, and we won't be able to hear ourselves speak in a minute."

Given the address of a hotel, Mark left a message with the purser and fought his way back to Clitheroe. They climbed the companionway in silence, crossed the deck, and were about to walk down the gangplank when the civilian pulled up short. In some surprise Mark saw that he had flushed a deep pink, and followed the direction of his gaze. A small knot of people were disagreeing loudly with each other while two coolies stood by in detached patience. At the edge of the group was a long-legged girl in a brown coat lavishly trimmed with fur and a hat in an ochre shade that hid most of her face. She spotted them and approached with candid curiosity.

"Jimmy! What on earth are you doing here?"

"Hallo, Miss Mostyn. I heard you were arriving on this ship," came the awed response. "Did you have a good voyage?"

"Hardly a riot," she declared in bored tones. "But we did *oodles* of shopping in Hong Kong and livened up the staid old things at Government House." Her overemphasised eyes rolled in Mark's direction as she asked again, "What *are* you doing here, Jimmy?"

"Someone had to meet Major Rawlings." He made it sound like a tiresome chore.

"Why you?" she asked, not realising the connection Mark had with her father.

"There wasn't anyone else, and Mr Mostyn asked me if I would mind obliging him, just this once." It suggested that he did not normally undertake such lowly tasks as meeting army majors and conducting them to hotels.

The curiosity in her eyes deepened as she turned to Mark for the first time and asked, "Why didn't you tell me you knew Father? I'll allow the past three days have passed like a dream, but it was very naughty of you to tease me by keeping such a thing secret, darling."

The coy note in her voice, together with the endearment, suggested they had spent the entire voyage locked in each other's arms, when, in fact, they had not spoken to each other after that first night. The infatuated young man beside Mark was evidently intended to believe what she had hinted at, and he bridled, betraying himself.

"The Major is up here to do a job for your father, that's all," said Clitheroe quickly, dispelling any suggestion that Mark might be of equal standing to Mostyn.

The girl's scarlet mouth pursed. "A job for Father? I thought you were a soldier, sweetie . . . putting down the natives," she added slightly maliciously.

Mark looked her straight in the eye. "I also put things up. I'm an engineer. Your father wants me to rebuild a bridge that collapsed under a train. The man who put it up died in the disaster."

She pouted even more. "How beastly you are! Why didn't you tell me this before?"

"I thought you were more interested in creating a disaster of your own."

She smiled, much too sweetly, while her eyes flashed with temper. "So you are just a common builder. So much for your secret mission, darling!"

"Ah well, reality catches up with us all eventually—even you, Miss Mostyn." With a brief nod of goodbye Mark stepped onto the gangplank. It was too cold to stand around talking nonsense with silly creatures of society, and what little he could see of Shanghai recommended a quick journey through it to the warmth and comfort of a hotel where he could relax and have a drink. He had a feeling he would need several prior to hearing the facts about the bridge.

The interchange with Alexandra Mostyn had not improved matters. Garrard Mostyn's employee did what he had to do with even worse grace than before, and Mark let him alone to sulk. A car was waiting on the jetty, but it soon became apparent to the new arrival that it would have been quicker to walk. All along the Bund, where the big offices of commerce and banking houses stood side by side, much as they did in Hong Kong, it was fairly easy for the driver to thread between the trams and cars on the wide thoroughfare, but once they turned into the side streets they ran into frequent jams of rickshaws, wheelbarrows, produce carts and coolies carrying laden baskets dangling from poles across their shoulders. Everything slowed to pedestrian pace, and the only advantage of the car was that it kept the passengers warm while they waited.

During one prolonged hold-up Clitheroe launched into a lecture on the city of Shanghai, pointing out with tutor-like care that there were three main areas: the International Settlement founded by the British and soon joined by the Americans and other foreign residents, the French Concession housing those nationals of France and associated colonies, and the Chinese City.

"The government and control of Shanghai is an extremely complex arrangement," he went on, "which in the hands of the wrong men would be disastrous."

"I do know the general history of the place," put in Mark cutting short the lesson. "Before we go overseas we are encouraged to find out anything we don't already know about the area. You pointed out that there was no military garrison here, as in Hong Kong, but the defence of the city by our armies in the past has contributed to the growth of the port and the importance it now holds, I think you will have to agree. Western presence here was bought with soldiers' lives, Mr Clitheroe. It was a battle of wits right from the start, but it needed a show of strength to win it." He was jerked forward as the car began to move off. "It might be necessary again before long. If the Nationalists ever get this far north with their revolutionary army your wealthy influential gentlemen who govern the city might be glad of a few extra rifles to back up the Shanghai Volunteer Corps."

Clitheroe looked at him in astonishment. "What do you know about the SVC?"

Feeling he had scored his maximum points, Mark relented a little and smiled. "Army engineers do more than build bridges. Are you a member?"

"Of course." It was said with pompous indignation. "I was on duty all through last summer when the student riots were at their height. It was a very dangerous time."

"So I understand. We army boys were very impressed down in Hong Kong. It's not every man who is prepared to act as an emergency soldier with the risk of being killed."

When the other man gave him a suspicious look, he went on, "I mean it. There's something rather grand about men being prepared to stand and defend their own little corner of the Empire—especially these days."

"Well . . . we do our best," mumbled Clitheroe, embarrassed by open praise.

Since the car had stopped once more Mark seized that moment as the opportune time to broach the subject uppermost in his mind.

"Before I see Mostyn perhaps you could fill me in on a few details about the bridge disaster? No one in Hong Kong seemed to know much, except that the matter was urgent. I did see a short account in a newspaper on the ship, but it didn't tell me a lot. In fact, it left me with the impression that the whole affair was being deliberately glossed over. That surely can't be right."

Clitheroe became even more embarrassed and twisted on the leather car-seat to study the cause of the hold-up in the road. "I can't tell you anything. I'm not an engineer, you know."

"But you do work for Garrard Mostyn?"

"I'm his assistant."

"And he is a member of the Railways Corporation?"

"He wants to see you at three-thirty this afternoon. I'm sure he'll be able to tell you all you need to know."

Mark could see he would get nowhere and relapsed into silence, pondering on the strange usage of the word *need* instead of *want*. It only added to the feeling that something odd hung over this whole affair. But his mind was alert enough to catch what his companion said to the driver when he asked him to pull up outside a large colonial-style hotel.

"You called him Ivan," he said with a quick lift of his heart. "Is he Russian?"

"Yes—White Russian, of course. There are thousands of them in Shanghai: refugees from the Civil War following the Revolution. Most of the men have taken up arms again—some with the Shanghai Volunteer Corps, others with the armies of various Chinese warlords."

"You mean, they have become mercenaries?"

Clitheroe nodded. "What else can they do? You'll find them as chauffeurs, doormen, private bodyguards, strong-arm men at the nightclubs, even chefs in the more cosmopolitan hotels. There is even a balalaika orchestra in the restaurant I frequent. They are excellent musicians, the Russians."

"I know." Memories were rushing back and filling Mark's mind with all kinds of impossible hopes and longings. "What about the women —are there many of them in Shanghai? Refugees from the war, I mean," he asked with ill-concealed eagerness.

Clitheroe looked at him strangely. "Why do you ask?"

Mark was away on his private path of never-ending hope. "What do they do? Is it possible to seek them out? I mean, is there any special area where they congregate?"

The other man smiled self-consciously. "Well, yes there is. Orientals are not your style, I take it. There are some very good White Russian girls who will do anything you like for the price of a meal—and I do mean *anything*. I can give you some addresses, if you like."

As Clitheroe's meaning broke into Mark's attempt to catch at any straw that might banish his nightmares, the crude reality of the words only echoed them. He stared at the other man, seeing instead a face from the past that broke him apart every time he thought of her. Unable to trust himself to speak, he got out of the car without a backward glance, and walked into the hotel leaving Clitheroe to think what he liked.

"Are you all right, sir?" asked the receptionist, as Mark stood leaning on the counter trying to steady himself.

"Yes . . . yes, thank you. Major Rawlings. A room has been booked for me, I believe."

The room turned out to be an entire suite, but Mark was still shaken and spent the first minute or two at the small bar. The brandy warmed and relaxed him so that he began to look around in some surprise. As an officer he was expected to use first-class accommodation, although he economised where he could, but he had been placed in a suite more suited to the taipans who abounded in the Far East. He fervently hoped this was at the expense of Shanghai Railways and not his own pocket. His finances were in a desperate enough state as it was.

As he wandered through sitting room, then bedroom with adjoining bathroom he puzzled over it. He was an engineer called in to rebuild a bridge. For some weeks he would be sleeping at the site in the usual rough conditions. He was used to that, but this set of rooms with French furniture, Chinese rugs, and Japanese paintings on the walls was more in keeping with a visitor of some influence who would wish to entertain rich, cultured guests for business reasons. Fires were alight in both rooms, the bar was well stocked. and there was a ladies' boudoir leading off the bedroom. Provision for *everything*, he thought cynically, and felt a swift stab of pain once more at the thought of White Russian girls being forced to prostitute themselves in order to stay alive. At the first opportunity he would seek them out, hoping against hope for the impossible . . . for a reprieve from despair.

Several brandies later he was calm enough to concentrate on the reason for his presence in Shanghai. De luxe accommodation for an engineer was verging on the ridiculous: it smacked of . . . he could not find the precise word, and the nearest he could get was 'bribery'. Surely that was too fanciful. He had allowed the peculiar circumstances surrounding this job to suggest all manner of things that could not be true. Yet, from all he had heard, Garrard Mostyn was a man to be reckoned with. He had never heard the name in engineering circles, so it must have been as a financier that the man had made his mark. Men who lived only to make money could be incomprehensible to outsiders.

The receptionist had said that any rickshaw would get him to the building which housed Garrard Mostyn's office within fifteen minutes, but Mark had not been sitting in it for long before he realised the lightweight suit he had found adequate in Hong Kong was nowhere near thick enough to keep out the Shanghai temperatures. Before he set out for the bridge he would have to buy himself a coat—probably one of the padded cotton ones worn by the Chinese. It would suit his purpose very well. When in the city he would have to wear uniform or freeze. He could not afford to buy a civilian overcoat he would not use again until he returned to England.

It was in a chilled and uncomfortable state that he paid the rickshaw boy and mounted the steps two at a time to enter the impressive colonial-style building. It was warmer inside, but he still shivered as he studied the information-board to discover his destination lay on the first floor.

The building had been designed to cope with the very hot humid summers, and was mostly of stone and marble with wide cloistered verandahs now closed off by a series of shuttered doors, which dimmed the interior of the corridors. His heavy footsteps rang on the bare floor and echoed in the surrounding silence. He supposed work was going on as usual: he had seen no one since he had entered the building. It smelt musty and unused, but such places always did in coldness that followed humidity.

Walking into the room exactly on three-thirty, Mark found an elderly man in a dark suit at a desk unmarked by anything as vulgar as 'RECEPTION' but which was, in fact, just that. He was given a surprised stare, as if the man had expected him to knock for permission to enter.

Mark nodded at him. "Good afternoon. Mr Mostyn is expecting me."

With deliberate dignity the man rose, pulling his jacket into creaseless perfection. "What name shall I say, sir?" he asked in abstract tones.

Good God, thought Mark, a 'gentleman's gentleman' in Shanghai, of all places!

"Major Rawlings. Royal Engineers," he said.

It brought a movement to the man's lips that could have been a smile. "My son is in the Engineers, sir. Second-Lieutenant Gatesby. Perhaps you know him?"

Mark shook his head. "No, sorry."

The smile died. "I'll inform Mr Mostyn that you are here."

It was all a ridiculous bureaucratic pantomime. Mostyn had set the time of the meeting himself, yet the receptionist was pretending he knew nothing of it. When he returned it was to tell Mark that Mr Mostyn would see him as soon as he was free, which suggested the visitor was receiving a favour by being admitted that afternoon. Used to such vanities by colonels, visiting generals, and various military boards, Mark sat down with a newspaper, knowing it would be seven or thirteen minutes before he was called. It was always one or the other, depending on the nature of the coming interview. Exactly seven minutes later the buzzer on the desk rang and the ageing employee rose to usher Mark into the inner office.

"Major Rawlings of the Royal Engineers, sir," he announced in ringing tones, and Mark walked into a large office nicely warmed by a fire that sprang in a stone fireplace.

He had seen it all before—expensive carpet, enormous oak desk, bookcases holding matched sets, black marble knights on the mantelpiece, photographs in silver frames on the desk. The plain walls were covered with framed enlargements of steam engines and rolling stock, together with several paintings of the embryo Shanghai back in the previous century. From the high ceiling hung two large fans, motionless now, of course.

Mark walked across, hand outstretched. "How do you do, Mr Mostyn? Thank you for sending your assistant to meet me from the ship."

Garrard Mostyn was tall and slender with silvering blond hair, and pale eyes that summed up his visitor immediately.

"Major Rawlings." He shook Mark's hand firmly, then gave a calculated lightning smile. "You . . . you're rather younger than I expected. I was told you were a *senior* major."

"So I am. Promotion was quick during the war."

"Ah . . . yes. Seen a little action, have you?"

"A little," agreed Mark, dismissing four years of indescribable hell and horror in what he had found to be the best approach toward those who had never known it and did not wish to be told.

"Sit down, sit down," came the hearty invitation. "One gets into the habit of never standing when one can sit. In summer it gets devilish hot, you know. Very exhausting."

Mark sank into the chair on the other side of the desk and found himself gazing at a photograph of a pretty woman, and a girl of around fifteen. Alexandra Mostyn had certainly changed in four years!

"My wife and daughter," said Mostyn. "It was taken some time ago." He sat in his elegant swivel chair. "My daughter came up on the same ship as you, as it happens."

"I know. We . . . bumped into each other on board."

"Really? She said nothing of it at luncheon today."

Mark smiled. "There's no reason why she should remember me. It was just a passing incident."

"Mmm, but you remembered it, Major." It was said with suspicion, and Mark guessed all was not well between father and erring daughter.

"Miss Mostyn is very attractive," he said, having no wish to play telltale. "It would be a dullard of a man who did not remember her even after a very brief encounter."

Mostyn smiled absently. "You are a bachelor, Major?"

"Yes, I am." Feeling that enough time had been wasted in small talk and anxious to get on to the subject that was so intriguing, Mark said, "I caught that ship by the skin of my teeth, so there was no time for me to hear the whole story of the disaster from Sir Kenneth. You are acquainted with him, I take it, sir?"

"Indirectly, yes. That is why I was able to avail myself of your professional services at such short notice. I apologise for the haste with which you were summoned, but it is a matter of the utmost urgency."

"Yes. I read a somewhat guarded newspaper account on the voyage up. A steel girder bridge over a wide canal, I understand, and on a vital branch line."

Mostyn looked at him shrewdly. "Nothing can move out of Shanghai on that line until the bridge is rebuilt."

Mark frowned. "I understand the need to reopen the line at the earliest opportunity, but until I see the extent of the damage I can't give you any idea of a date. I take it the wreckage is already being cleared from the track, but as the waterway is also much used that will have to be cleared of all obstacles. I shall need to find out availability of materials, the numbers of coolies at my disposal, and the length of the bridge before I can even hazard a guess at a completion date." He gave the man a straight look. "I understand how vital to Shanghai the railway is, and give my word I'll get the work done and the line open as quickly as is humanly possible."

There was a prolonged pause during which Mostyn's face was covered with conflicting expressions, none of which was encouraging. Finally he leant forward with his arms along his expensive desk.

"Major Rawlings, you were, indeed, brought up here in ignorance. You . . . ah . . . have not been called in to rebuild the bridge. We can find an engineer to do that."

"I am an engineer," said Mark through stiff lips.

"I meant a *civilian* engineer. This is not in any way a military railway."

"Then what the hell have I been sent here for?" he demanded, thoughts of a de luxe apartment, a restrained newspaper report, and James Clitheroe's attitude all swirling around in his head as he felt Alexandra Mostyn's eyes watching him from the photograph.

"I think we can best discuss that over tea, don't you?" came the voice reminiscent of a governess jollying her charges up to the nursery where they will not annoy the adults. He pressed the buzzer on his desk—a prearranged signal, no doubt—then stood up to warm his back at the fireplace while he treated Mark to another of his pseudo-smiles.

"Sir Kenneth should have made the position clear to you, of course, but the time element is so vital . . . and you must be used to obeying orders at a moment's notice without time for a full briefing."

"In time of war, yes. But on peacetime engineering assignments I am usually given all the facts first. I was told that a request had been made to the Governor of Hong Kong to send me up here on loan because your engineer was killed in the disaster. When the reason is a collapsed bridge, and I am known to have a great deal of experience in bridging, it naturally suggests I am expected to rebuild it. You have just now said nothing can move out of Shanghai until it is."

"A new bridge will certainly be built . . . with all speed," came the smooth reply. "As I said, each day that bridge is down merchandise is piling up in Shanghai. Trade is suffering and huge sums of money are being lost." He rubbed the seat of his pinstripe trousers to disperse the heat from the fire. "What you certainly will not appreciate is the unique and delicate situation existing in Shanghai. The city should in no way be compared with Hong Kong—a British possession ruled by . . ."

"Yes. Clitheroe was at great pains to impress that fact upon me," put in Mark tonelessly, realising that somewhere along the line his pride and professional reputation had taken a knock. So much for all the flattery!

"Clitheroe is perfectly aware of the situation. Only those who are resident here can be fully cognisant with the . . . shall we say . . . *difficulties* which should be avoided whenever possible."

A diversion was created by a white-coated boy entering with a tea-tray, and conversation lapsed while he poured tea into two cups and handed it to both men with a small bow. Mark did not want the tea. He felt like walking out there and then. But he drank it to prevent himself from letting fly with words. He had a quick temper, but had learnt to control it over the years. Until he had heard the full story concerning this extraordinary business he would try to take it calmly.

"We are not at liberty to do exactly as we would wish, Major," continued Mostyn after sipping his tea with relish. "Notwithstanding the fact that all our plans result in benefit for the Chinese they have protested, argued, boycotted, or downright *fought* every project put forward by any of the foreign powers. They are a people ruled by suspicion, ignorance, greed and inbred adherence to ancient tradition." He sipped again rather noisily from his cup. "This city is a monument to perseverance and patience on the part of the men from the Western world."

"What has this to do with the railway bridge?" asked Mark feeling the history lesson could wait.

Mostyn looked annoyed. "A great deal. A very great deal. Are you aware that the Chinese regarded steam engines as 'devil machines' and refused a railway system of any kind for many years? We finally achieved our goal against great odds, but trains are still regarded with suspicion by many, and by others as instruments of the devil which offend the spirits and dragons that roam the interior of China. Such people find excuses to blame misfortune, poor crops, epidemics, and any kind of reverses on the smoking monster that roars across the country." He put his cup and saucer precariously on the corner of the desk and bent toward Mark to emphasise his next words. "The first track ever to be laid was torn up again by Chinese officials because a coolie had wandered onto the line and been run over by an engine. The man was probably doped to the eyebrows with opium. In 1877 the speed of any engine was such that people could move off the track with time to spare if its approach was heard. But they used the incident to suit their determination to thwart us. Now, fifty years later, they will do the same."

"Are you telling me the line over the collapsed bridge is about to be torn up by the Chinese?" Mark asked incredulously.

Mostyn apparently felt it did not merit a reply. He walked across to the tray and poured himself some more tea, offering the pot in Mark's direction.

"Not for me, but I'd appreciate it if you would tell me what part I *am* expected to play in this drama."

Again the lightning smile that was slightly patronising. "This isn't a military operation, Major, that is all cut and dried." Bringing his tea back to the desk he sat in his chair and leant back at ease. "I have been attempting to clarify the delicate relationship we have with the Chinese in this city, as simply as possible and in a way you would understand."

Mark gritted his teeth and read himself a lecture on the advisability of holding on to his anger. "You have succeeded. Please go on."

"Although the collapse itself was not all that serious, carriages on each side of the bridge were derailed and were so crowded panic ensued, killing more than was actually attributed to the failure of the bridge."

"How many died?"

"We are still not certain."

"Good God,.the accident took place four days ago!"

Mostyn cleared his throat. "You are not familiar with the terrain, Major. Most of that area is flat marshland scored by waterways. The track had to be embanked along the whole length. The derailed carriages plunged down into the marsh."

It painted a nasty picture in Mark's mind, but still he commented, "I would have thought four days adequate to recover bodies."

"Under normal circumstances, yes."

It was just the opening he needed. "It has been apparent to me from the start that there is something abnormal about this affair. Perhaps it is time you brought it into the open."

The other man was intensely annoyed. His thick lips pressed together as he cast Mark a withering look. "There is nothing *abnormal* about it. We have here a delicate and extremely trying situation, that is all. Because of the unnecessarily high loss of life, the Chinese authorities are demanding extortionate compensation from us and insisting that we are entirely to blame for the accident. In addition, they have resurrected an old argument we had with them when the line was first laid, and claim we disregarded the dangers they pointed out to us at that time. If we handle this with anything but the most intelligent of approaches it could turn into a major confrontation. With anti-foreign feeling running as high as it is at the present moment, we must take all steps to bring this to a hasty and satisfying conclusion."

Still uncertain as to what his role was to be, and disliking the man very heartily, Mark could not resist saying, "Satisfying to whom?"

It was the wrong approach. "Major Rawlings, you are trained to obey orders without questioning them," came the biting reply. "The Chinese have agreed to abide by the decision of an independent investigator. Because you have some knowledge of bridging, you have been appointed."

To the man who had a list of fine engineering achievements to his name it was something of an insult to refer to 'some knowledge of bridging' but Mark sensed a worse insult was about to follow.

"The Chinese are charging us with professional negligence and intent to harm the people of this country by ignoring their warnings when the bridge was built. Harry Deane, the engineer who built the bridge, died in that train, so cannot defend his reputation. It is your job to do it for him. There is no doubt whatever in our minds that the fault lies with the Chinese contractor engaged to supply materials and labour to construct the bridge." He got to his feet to walk round and look down on Mark. "The Chinese contractor, Major, is the wiliest, most devious and blackest villain on this earth. He will swear to anything. He will show you one sample of materials then use an inferior brand behind your back. He will nod and promise you the earth, knowing very well he cannot possibly comply with your demands. He will rob you left, right, and centre, withdraw his labour as it suits him, and dig up some ancient legend or superstition to account for his failure to comply with the contract. Civilian engineering is not in the least as simple as your kind, Major Rawlings. You can issue your orders confident that the men under your command are bound by military law and the desire for promotion. Those two are guarantees that the job will be done to your satisfaction."

Everything clicked into place then, and Mark's anger could no longer be held back. He had been rushed up to Shanghai at great personal inconvenience because as an investigator, he had that great advantage of being 'bound by military law and the desire for promotion'. All Sir Kenneth's words about his professional reputation had been so much flattery. And the de luxe hotel suite? Bribery had not been the wrong word to think of in connection with it—a softening-up touch for a man who should be impressed by such treatment. Did Mostyn and his friends truly believe they had in their hands a man—a war veteran —who was afraid for his future in the army to the extent that he would do just as they instructed? No wonder Mostyn had been taken aback when faced with a young man. He had plainly expected an ageing major who would leap at any chance to gain a last vestige of recognition for his services. He got to his feet and faced his companion.

"As you have already pointed out, Mr Mostyn, I have some knowledge of bridging. Whether it is military or civilian, British or native built, a bridge only collapses because someone has made a mistake," he began with tight anger deepening his voice. "When people are killed because of it, it becomes a criminal mistake. Now, I may be a soldier trained to obey without question, but I know that when a battle is lost it is the general who is blamed, no matter what an individual captain may have done wrong . . . and when it comes to bridges, the ultimate responsibility lies with the engineer. The man is no longer alive to defend himself, but if he died because of his own carelessness it will show in my report. If you wish me to act as an independent investigator you must bear in mind that that is what I shall be."

Mostyn was thrown, he noticed with savage pleasure, but men of that calibre recover very quickly, and Mark was caught unawares by his next move.

"One of our directors is a great personal friend of the Governor of Hong Kong, which is why you were made available so quickly. I understand your Commanding Officer is exceedingly gratified at a member of his own staff being asked to act on such a vital issue. It adds distinction to the Corps, as a whole, and is bound to do your career a bit of good." He flashed the smile on and off again. "You have had some problems in the past, I understand. Some kind of trouble in Russia over expenditure of government funds, wasn't it?"

Mark stared at him with hostility. "My God, you have friends in the right places, haven't you?"

"It is the formula for success. You could do the same by handling this right." He perched on the corner of the desk, completely at ease. "All that is necessary is that you should go out to the bridge and take a look at the wreckage. Since Harry Deane is dead it is a little pointless laying the blame at his door as the man who is *ultimately* responsible, don't you think? And since Chung-Li, the Chinese contractor, has mysteriously vanished from Shanghai, the result of your investigation is a foregone conclusion. All we want is a document to counter the claim for compensation for negligence. That, together with the losses being sustained by the closure of the line, would be crippling to the company —not to mention the blow it would deal to our standing with the Chinese. We have persuaded them to agree to stand by your findings as an investigator who has no connection with the company, and you must at least be seen to be doing your job." He put an encouraging hand on Mark's arm. "There's no need to stay out there too long. I think you could combine work with a spot of pleasure. Shanghai in winter might be cold, but its amenities are the same all year round. Clitheroe can take you to some clubs . . . or wherever your tastes as a bachelor lie." He patted the arm in benevolent style. "Might even be able to arrange invitations to a few Christmas parties while you are here. Shanghai society is very lavishly hospitable."

"I don't think you understood me, Mr Mostyn." Mark was almost choking with anger by this time. "The truth will have to be told. *People have died.* Of course the Chinese want compensation if we are responsible.

The pale eyes narrowed. "You are out of your depth, Major. The Chinese authorities don't give a damn for the deaths of those people on the train. Life is cheap in China. Coolies are not even worth two a penny. If fifty people die at one blow it is simply fifty less mouths to feed. No, man, this is a political and racial matter, nothing more. It is one more attempt to bleed us dry and expose us to further humiliating restrictions. They cannot be allowed to get away with it just when the population of China is ripe for revolution against oppression and the 'foreign devils'. You must see that."

"I am aware of the very highly-charged political scene in this country at the moment," Mark said, with determination, "but if trouble comes I shall, as a soldier, be expected to play my part to the utmost. However, my only other role in life is as an engineer. I am not, and never have been, a politician or diplomat. That I leave to people like you. What you are asking me to do, as an engineer, is search out the fault in a bridge that caused a tragic accident. My every inclination is to refuse the commission, but I am bound by the need to obey orders from my superior officer so I am forced to accept it. That being the case, I shall do the job to the best of my ability. I cannot put my name to a falsified report. That would do neither my career, nor the Corps as a whole, any good at all. I wonder you and your friends in the right places did not see that, sir."

He was, indeed, out of his depth, because he thought that was the end of the matter. But before he knew it he was being propelled toward the door, and Mostyn was talking fast.

"Unfortunately, I have a very important meeting with the Shanghai Municipal Council in fifteen minutes, but let us continue our discussion this evening, over dinner. My wife and daughter will be delighted to entertain you. I'll send a car for you at eight." He opened the door. "Accommodation at the hotel all right, is it? Anything you want, just send for it. Don't worry about the bill; you're our guest while you're in Shanghai. See you this evening, then."

Out in the corridor Mark stared at the closing door, furious and marvelling at the innocence of the very wealthy.

★

Alexandra was surprised when her mother told her they were entertaining a Major Rawlings and both her parents would be glad if she would arrange to stay at home for the evening. She was surprised because the man she had met on the boat was not the kind of person her father normally invited to dinner. That there were no other guests invited with him was understandable, but why her father had found it suddenly necessary to entertain some obscure man from Hong Kong who repaired bridges, she could not imagine. Nor why she had received a summons to help entertain him, for a summons it was when phrased in that manner.

She had been obliged to cancel her plans to go with the Armitages to hear a jazz band from America play on one of the ocean liners that lay up the river at anchor. It was not too much of a wrench. She had heard jazz bands before and they were all much the same. Besides which, Lionel had been something of a nuisance on board after his quarrel with Mark Rawlings, and she did not feel like another evening of jealous passion interspersed with socialist doctrines. Both were equally melodramatic. So she wrote a note to Dot explaining, with some impish delight, that the foot-crushing major they had met on the ship from Hong Kong had turned out to be someone of *devastating* importance whom her father was entertaining that evening, and she could not avoid joining the party since their guest had particularly asked to meet her again. After the boy had gone out with the letter, she wished she had not yielded to impulse. It was a little childish to tell lies simply to tease Lionel. But it was too late, and she shrugged it off. What did it matter?

As she dressed that evening she thought about Mark Rawlings again. He was refreshingly quaint. He had pre-war manners and a lack of sophistication that smacked of marching feet and banners held aloft. Of course, he also had a virile physical attraction that cried out to be exploited. She smiled. The evening might be quite amusing, really.

It did not start out that way. Her father was already downstairs, immaculate in his dinner jacket, when she descended. He began their usual opening skirmish with a demand as to why she was not dressed for dinner.

"I am, Father," she said sweetly. "This is the latest thing in evening pyjamas. They cost you a fortune down in Hong Kong."

"Evening pyjamas! Good God, what will women wear next?" His face took on the deep flush that usually accompanied a discussion on his daughter, or anything connected with her. "I particularly wished you to dine with us tonight. Is it too much to ask you to wear something feminine, something a little more . . . *alluring*?" he demanded. "You can look very attractive when you wear normal clothes."

"Don't you mean 'old-fashioned' clothes?"

"If a charming full-length gown is old-fashioned then, yes, I do mean that," was his retort. "You speak all that nonsense about emancipation, Alexandra, and ally yourself with silly creatures like Dorothy Armitage, yet you all daub yourselves with cosmetics that turn you into clowns and go around in outfits that defeminise you to the point of ridicule. Equality of the sexes, you preach, yet a bigger demonstration of lack of intelligence I have never witnessed."

"We have been into all that before, Father," she said heavily. "I thought there was no more that could be said on the subject. Mother is the epitome of old-world femininity, yet you have never credited her with an atom of intelligence."

"I think you forget to whom you are speaking," he told her with cold anger.

"And so, dear *Papa*, do you," she flung back. "When will you accept that I am not a Victorian miss? You know very well there is only one reason why I stay here so that we can repeat these fruitless quarrels."

"Because you are too used to the luxury my wealth provides to attempt to live without it." He smiled with bitter triumph. "So much for your emancipation, my dear. It is simply a puffball of words that disintegrates when put to the test."

It still hurt no matter how many times he said it. She turned away so that he would not see the fragility of her sophisticated veneer, and made for the door. But he stopped her with words that brought some surprise.

"As you said, these repetitive quarrels are fruitless, Alexandra. It was not my intention to level criticism, and it might be that our guest this evening does not share my views on ladies' fashions. I am sorry if you were obliged to cancel your own plans for this."

She turned. Apologies? He must want a very big favour from her, for some reason. "*Mother* asked me to stay at home this evening."

He came across wearing a fond look. He could turn on the charm when he wished. "You didn't say you had met Major Rawlings on the voyage up from Hong Kong."

Wariness crept over her. What had the wretched man said about her? "I met a great number of people on the ship."

"Of course. But he appears to have remembered you, in particular."

"He does?" It sounded quite nonchalant, she was glad to hear.

"I suspect he admired you from afar."

She relaxed. "He's a little old for that, isn't he?"

"My dear Alexandra, you seem to think everyone over twenty-five has one foot in the grave. He is thirty and a bachelor. Younger than I had foreseen," he added reflectively.

Alexandra's curiosity was aroused. "You seem to know a lot about him. Why *is* he coming to dinner? He can't be important or we'd have half Shanghai society here to meet him." Her father had reached her now, and she saw the look of calculation on his face. "*Is* he important?"

"Mmm . . . well, more important than I had bargained for, shall I say? It is all rather tiresome and unnecessary: he is digging in his heels over trivialities when vital issues are at stake." His pale eyes glittered at her. "The situation between us and the Chinese has never been more explosive, and this mulish young man threatens to blow it sky-high."

"How?" She did not really expect an intelligent answer.

"Just accept my word for it, Alexandra. It is a high-level matter of some delicacy."

"Which I would never understand," she commented drily. "You still haven't told me why we have to entertain the man to dinner."

He put his hand behind her shoulder and led her back toward the fire. The gesture implied a closeness they had never experienced.

"Major Rawlings has lowly origins and has 'blotted his copybook' in the past. The two circumstances together make him vulnerable to pressures of a certain nature. He has a reputation for pugnacity, but he is governed by strict military law—something a civilian engineer does not experience. He will *have* to do as he is told in the end, but I would much rather he did it from the start." They halted before the fireplace and he smiled down at her with that supreme self-confidence that had put him where he was in the world of finance. "I have met men of his type before. They unfailingly succumb to flattery and attention from people of influence and breeding. It boosts their ego beyond the need to assert themselves in other ways. It undermines their hostility, and fills them with pathetic eagerness to live up to the standing you have suggested they possess." He pouted in self-satisfied amusement. "A susceptible bachelor would be putty in the hands of a young woman of your class, my dear. Do you see now why I had hoped you would wear something a little more, shall we say, *intriguing*?"

For a moment she felt like striking that well-formed disdainful face, but she would not give him the satisfaction of reciprocating. Instead she fell back on the only refuge she knew would protect her.

"Had I known what you had in mind, I would have done so," she cooed. "Why didn't you tell me at the outset that, purely as a business move, you wanted me to rape our guest?"

It worked. Garrard Mostyn, man of influence, smooth negotiator of business deals, charmer of susceptible women, did not know how to handle a girl who spoke to him on modern equivalent terms. His face paled with fury.

"You have not only grown decadent, Alexandra, but disgustingly vulgar. How dare you speak to me in that manner?"

"Because it is the truth. Well, isn't it?" she cried with all her hatred of him churning up her stomach. "Ever since I can remember I have been obliged to dress up and perform on your behalf. It began with satin bows, frilly dresses, and instructions to 'smile and sit on the nice gentleman's knee'. It progressed to tighter fitting dresses and pinches on my cheek and bottom by 'the nice gentlemen'. Oh, don't look at me like that! You know damn well they have taken advantage of your subtle business methods by stepping over the line with me. That I tolerate as much as I do is not for your sake. It's fortunate that you had a daughter instead of a son to take over from Mother. You can't make *her* do it any longer. Even for the sake of business, your guests draw the line at trying anything with a woman in a wheelchair."

He moved toward her, but she stepped back quickly. "The truth hurts, Father. That is what you are always telling me."

At that precise moment the boy appeared at the doorway to announce the arrival of their guest for the evening, and Alexandra, with no time in which to compose herself, fixed a bright smile on her face as he came down the four shallow steps into the room.

He was dressed in a high-collared, dark-blue, military tunic and close-fitting trousers strapped beneath his shoes. The uniform suited his athletic looks and made him seem taller than she had remembered. He presented a picture of implacable solid strength that made Garrard Mostyn appear elegant and assured beside him.

Her father led him across to her, and she began rather theatrically, "So Fate has dictated that we should meet again. How are you, Mark?"

"Rather cold, I'm afraid. I made a detour on the way here and discovered nights in Shanghai can be bitter."

"We must endeavour to warm you up," she said with meaning, as she studied him anew, noting that his close-cropped, dark curly hair made no allowance for the current slicked styles for men. His face, deeply tanned by the Hong Kong sun, nevertheless showed a sprinkling of freckles that gave a youthful softness to the austere military air he adopted, and suggested a vulnerability lurking beneath the implacable exterior. Then she realised that he was angry—stiff with anger, in fact. His lips were tightly clamped, his rich brown eyes burned darkly, and he was holding himself in rigid control. He had an attractive voice that betrayed nothing of what her father had called 'lowly origins', but his words were clipped, lacking any rise and fall of vocal melody as he gave brief replies to her father's small talk.

Her own anger increased. Just who did he think he was? An obscure major, who had blotted his copybook and now dared to stand up to Garrard Mostyn, was presented to her with instructions to ravish him, and he had the effrontery to arrive like a Christian martyr in the lions' den! Just who was *he* to be filled with anger over her father? One meeting, that was all he had had, whereas she had to live day-by-day with one of the most powerful and ruthless men in Shanghai. This man Rawlings could not know the meaning of anger!

Only at that point did she realise his attitude was extended to her, also, for he was responding to anything she said with only the barest civilities in cool tones. His dismissive manner put the remaining fuel on her fire of retaliation. Her father saw her merely as a female to soften up a difficult male, and Mark Rawlings was doing his utmost to show he did not believe she could influence *anyone*. She would show them both how wrong they were before the evening was out.

"My wife, Major, is an invalid," her father was saying in tones that suggested he was struggling against overwhelming odds. "I fear it takes her some while to prepare for dinner." He gave Alexandra a brave smile. "My dear, be so good as to entertain Major Rawlings while I slip up to see if your mother is ready to be brought down."

Although he had done it so often, she had never grown immune to his callous exploitation of her mother's tragic illness. It hurt her deeply and increased her bitter anger against men who saw women only in terms of their usefulness to the male sex.

In such a mood she turned to their guest when her father had gone. "Have I succeeded in warming you up, Mark?" she asked, eyes wide and innocent.

"Isn't that your object with every man you meet?"

"Of course," she purred. "It is usually delightfully easy. You put up very little resistance on the ship, sweetie . . . or have you forgotten?"

He considered her for a moment, the dancing flames putting shadows across his face. "That was before you provided the floor show."

She tried to hold on to her temper by keeping up the pose of sophistication. "You disapproved? How sad!"

"I think you have hardly lived long enough to know what true sadness is, Miss Mostyn."

"Oh, how noble and upright that sounds," she countered hotly, at his attempt to put her in the place he thought women should be. "But that is what you are, isn't it? Defender of king and country . . . fight to the last man for the jolly old traditions. Is that why you are in uniform tonight—to remind me?"

He appeared to be controlling his own anger with an effort. "No, I am sorry to tell you it is not for your benefit, but your father's. It should remind *him* that I am a serving officer. It will save me from the insult of being offered a bribe, and him from the embarrassment of discovering he is not able to buy a man ruled by military law. I knew very well why I had been invited here. He tried every other means but financial inducement this afternoon."

She began to laugh, partly to relieve the tension and partly because he had played right into her hands, giving her the perfect opportunity for a *coup de grâce*. But it was brittle laughter.

"My dear Mark, you have much too simple an outlook on life. My father possesses every refinement of subtlety in the book. He would never be so crude as to wave a wad of notes in your face." She laughed again. "*I'm* the bribe, darling. I have orders to seduce you."

His expression took on a mixture of disbelief and disgust. "Don't you think you've gone far enough already? You are not in the least amusing."

"How disastrous for the plan if I were," she flashed back. "My father sees you as a susceptible bachelor who admired me from afar on the ship. He has given me orders to break down your 'mulishness' as only a woman can. Although I have made the terrible mistake of not wearing a dress full of allure, which a man of your type would find irresistible, I know enough of the male sex to overcome that initial setback, I assure you. There is to be nothing *amusing* about this evening, sweetie, unless you make a habit of laughing whilst succumbing to the inevitable loss of your honour." Carried away by anger and the way he was looking at her, she moved closer and spoke in sultry undertones. "I think I am expected to make a start whilst he is upstairs."

To her complete stupefaction he pushed past her and made for the door, leaving all manner of thoughts swirling in her head as she faced the consequences of his leaving the house. Her father would be more angry than she had ever known; there would be a humiliating scene, accusations, distress for herself and her mother. On top of that, there was the incredible evidence of her lack of ability to win over any man she wished. How dare this army officer with humble origins walk out on her in such a way!

He was halfway across the room when she cried involuntarily, "*Coward!*"

It halted him, but his expression was unnerving when he turned to face her. "There is also a word for girls like you."

It hurt her, deeply and shockingly, as she had never been hurt before. For some inexplicable reason this one man's contempt pierced the armour of emancipation to strike the vulnerable girl inside. She stood fighting the unfamiliar pain of sexual rejection, as she heard the distant sound of doors opening and shutting, heralding the arrival of her invalid mother. Then, pulling her pride around her like a cloak, she said to the houseboy hovering in the bead-curtained archway, "We are ready for cocktails, Lai-Hi. Serve them immediately . . . and a brandy for Major Rawlings."

The visitor hesitated too long. Escape was denied him by the approach of her father pushing the invalid chair with a semblance of compassion.

"Make that a double brandy," he told the servant harshly. "This is the kind of evening I am going to need it."

CHAPTER THREE

By the time they went in to dinner they were all behaving like a normal family entertaining a relaxed and welcome guest. The miracle had been worked by Alice Mostyn. Still a very striking woman despite the trials of her illness, she derived a very sincere pleasure from the company of interesting people who were invited to dinner by her husband, for whatever reason. The restrictive life she was now forced to lead was only enlivened by social encounters, and the natural charm her husband had found invaluable to his own interests overcame any awkwardness guests might feel at her plight.

Alexandra always felt ashamed when she saw how her mother coped with what her life had become, but it also sustained her hatred of the man who had been the cause, and strengthened her determination not to go under herself. Garrard Mostyn's arrogance looked no further than his wealth as the reason for his daughter's remaining under the parental roof: it never occurred to him that there might be a bond of love between his wife and daughter strong enough to keep her there.

But that evening Alexandra was full of other emotions, and watched in some abstraction as Mark Rawlings gradually warmed to her mother's gentle gaiety. Normally it would have pleased her to see such natural rapport between a stranger and his invalid hostess, but all she could think was that her mother was only eight years older than their guest and very much more of his generation than she was.

Alice Mostyn was beautiful in the old style—golden hair drawn back in a shining chignon, sweet mouth barely touched with lipstick, and lovely violet eyes. She was gentle and compassionate, yet had the capacity to be lively, witty and entertaining whilst retaining the submissive quality demanded by men with old-fashioned ideas. That had been her one mistake. Reared by Victorian parents Alice Mostyn had never doubted that she should be obedient and dutiful to her husband, so she had hardly realised her home and very existence had been devoted to his ambition. Pressure had followed pressure. She had entertained people she heartily disliked, given tea parties for obnoxious gossiping women married to those Garrard found useful, and flirted to order with lecherous associates who needed subtler persuasion than her husband could give. It had all been done in a mistaken sense of wifely duty, until truth had dawned too late. The effort such a life had cost her gentle personality, plus a climate of extremes which took toll of her constitution, had so weakened her she had succumbed to the illness that had left her paralysed from the waist down. Now she suffered the enlightenment her situation brought, and found her only escape from it in the company of others. Whether her eyes had been opened enough to realise her husband now exploited her in a different, even crueller way, Alexandra was not sure. She, herself, saw through him and bore her mother's hurt deep inside.

Alice Mostyn was vitally alive tonight as she chatted, and Mark Rawlings melted slowly beneath the glow of her warmth, as most men did. The visitor revealed that he hailed from Devon, from a small market town of which Alexandra had never heard but which was apparently only a few miles from the village where her mother had been reared. Memories flowed fast and eager between the pair as the soup was followed by turbot. No one broke into the conversation. Garrard was delighted over the fortuitous coincidence, and Alexandra was too preoccupied with her unhappiness. She fervently wished she had gone to hear the jazz band after all. Everyone there would have been gay and bent on enjoyment. The evening stretched interminably ahead, with disaster inevitable at the end of it when she was certain to be left alone with the man whose hostility had left her raw and vulnerable. The young men of her own set would have been awed by her behaviour; he had reacted with something approaching violence. The encounter left her silent and disturbed as conversation flowed over her.

"I left Devon just before I was eighteen," he was saying to her mother, "with only a brief visit since then."

"Your family moved away?"

"No, my mother and sisters still live in the old house. I was in France and Belgium for several years, which broke my association with the area."

Alice Mostyn gave an understanding smile. "You went through the entire war? You are one of the blessed, Major. Was it as terrible as reports said?"

"Yes, I'm afraid it was."

"It hardly touched us here," she went on with perfect poise. "Apart from expelling the Germans and Austro-Hungarians from the British clubs, and the loss of most of our young men who felt they were needed elsewhere, life out here changed very little. Of course, during the final stages of the war we had a few violent disturbances between the local people and the Japanese. But I regret to admit that the world upheaval enabled a few of us to make a great deal of money whilst remaining in comparative safety."

He smiled, an instinctive response to such gentle frankness. "It would have been even more terrible if no good had come from it at all."

Alexandra paid half-hearted attention to what they were saying. War, war! Why would they keep dragging up the past, these people? If he really had been through hell in France there was all the more reason why he should forget it and enjoy himself—have fun! But her full attention was taken next minute because it became obvious her father had decided it was time to make his move, and the results took her by surprise. Suddenly, the evening was full of interest.

"And whilst we were here trying to maintain Britain's trading strength, you went straight from one war to another, Major," said Garrard smoothly, and when he received no reply went on, "You were in Russia in 1919 fighting with the Whites, I understand."

"I was . . . I saw some service in Russia, yes." The words were strangely wary, hesitant.

Alexandra was struck by the complete change that had come over a man who had been talking in such a relaxed manner only a moment before. Her curiosity deepened when her father gave his pouting smile and probed further.

"Rather more than that, Major, from what I have been told. A heroic dash to freedom disguised as peasants, a race against oncoming winter, and a single-handed action at a bridge that saved your troops and nearly cost you your life. Is it not true that you were awarded a DSO to go with the MC gained on the Somme?"

With a swift glance at his hostess the visitor confined himself to saying, "I can't imagine where you heard such details."

"These things get around in influential circles," came the smooth reply, "and citations for bravery are made public. Don't be so coyly modest, Major."

Alexandra found her interest in the man grow. Before dinner she had been told he had 'blotted his copybook'. This present conversation was plainly the flattery her father used as a prelude to his demands, but it hinted at something quite remarkable about a man she had dismissed as refreshingly quaint and unsophisticated. Was there more to him than she had imagined? If so, it was supremely clear he did not wish to discuss it.

"Perhaps Major Rawlings prefers not to revive his memories of such a terrible period in his life, Garrard," put in Alice with observant diplomacy. "It was such a tragic affair and one that is still having repercussions. Each time I see those poor Russian refugees I feel so sorry for them. It must be dreadful to be exiled, and dispossessed of everything. Many of them were once people of great consequence."

"Wasn't there a Tsarist colonel's family with your party, Major? Aristocrats, I heard, who had been marked down by the Bolsheviks as targets for revenge, and whom you took to safety beneath the noses of the Reds."

Mark Rawlings was visibly resistant now. Only a man like her father could have pursued his subject so ruthlessly, thought Alexandra, feeling a reluctant admiration for his methods. She hoped the tussle would be prolonged. It livened up the evening and gave her great satisfaction to see her two antagonists face each other.

"Your informant was remarkably knowledgeable. You plainly know all there is to know of the incident," said the Major harshly, then turned to his hostess in an attempt to change the subject. "This is delicious duck, Mrs Mostyn. It is still a mystery to me how the Chinese manage to fillet it completely yet present the bird on the table as if still whole."

"It is certainly a unique culinary skill, Major, especially when one considers that the vast majority of Chinese people exist on rice alone, and too little of that."

"They'll have no rice at all if they persist in their present revolutionary frame of mind, my dear," her husband told her, firmly taking back the conversational lead. "Anyone who has followed the rise of Communism in Russia can see that it has only been achieved through the ruthless murder of thousands of helpless people, and the driving out of all those with wealth, influence, education and a love of culture. They have destroyed all the fine estates, despoiled the land, and plunged a knife into the civilised heart of their country. Would you not agree with me, Major?"

With a set face the visitor replied, "Anyone who is not a Bolshevik must agree with you."

"I see you still refer to them as Bolsheviks. A result of your personal experience of them, I take it. Has it not made you particularly violently anti-Red? To be forced to watch highborn women humiliated at the hands of peasant soldiers, knowing any attempt by you to help them would betray your identity and put an end to your hopes of seizing control of the train that was your only means of escape, must have been a terrible ordeal for any man—particularly one with your notions of gallantry. Then, to run the gauntlet of a barbarous rabble with two wanted women hidden beneath tarpaulins in one of the trucks behind your old steam engine, must have left you with very strong feelings."

Alexandra stared at Mark across the table in amazement. Could this reserved, gentle man with an air of naïveté and a scattering of boyish freckles on his face in truth have done what her father had just described? Excitement flared in her, dispelling the earlier sensation of rejection by him.

"You crossed Russia on a train, smuggling two aristocratic women to safety beneath the noses of the Reds!" she cried. "How tremendously exciting."

He looked back at her with obvious dislike. "*Exciting!* If you had any notion whatever of having to fight for one's life, you would know it was anything but exciting. Revolution is depravity. When brother fights brother, neighbours destroy each other out of fear, and men and women are forced to become traitors in order to save a loved one, it is beyond human endurance. At the end of it all they have destroyed their land and heritage, and nothing will ever be the same again. The scars go too deep," he ended with vibrant emphasis.

No one spoke for a moment, then Garrard picked up his expensive crystal glass, studied the colour of the wine against the lights, and said smoothly, "That is exactly what will happen here in China if the Western powers ever leave." He took a sip, then continued, "It is absolutely essential that we retain our financial and political standing in China. Every possible step should be taken in that direction . . . even if it means shedding a personal scruple or two. What is one man's petty pride against the fate of a nation?"

For a long time Mark Rawlings stared at his host across the table, and Alexandra sensed that the verbal seduction of the army officer had reached its climax. Would he succumb? Half of her longed for him to do so, yet she was glimpsing a surprising person beneath his formality that the other half of her longed to champion, to join in battle against her father.

"The Communist threat won't be allayed by a report on a bridge, Mr Mostyn, neither will the might of Britain fall."

Her father looked extremely annoyed. Alexandra now realised what he had meant by saying their guest was being "mulish". She wondered about the importance of what he was refusing to do for a man who usually got his own way, and decided to join the fun.

"I was speaking to some people attached to the Soviet Embassy last week and they seemed to feel that agitation in Shanghai was doing the Chinese no good at all. In fact, they agreed with me that this city and the Chinese economy in general would collapse without foreign money."

The two men turned to look at her in mild astonishment, and she smiled at them with the smugness of knowing she had put a hefty spanner in the works.

"People from the Soviet Embassy," repeated her father. "However did that come about?"

"Lionel Armitage knows them. They play tennis together, or some such thing. He mixes with all kinds of people. He's very sociable."

"He wasn't the night I met him," put in the Major quickly.

"Ah, he was jealous."

"Oh no, he wasn't. He linked my rank with the class system he pretends to despise. His sister told me he was a socialist, but if ever I saw an embryo Bolshevik there was one. They could turn him into an active comrade in an instant." He turned to Garrard. "It's the Lionel Armitages you should worry about, not a man's professional integrity."

"Shall we have coffee in the sitting room?" suggested Alice with perfect timing, and the ball stayed in her husband's court.

Conversation was carefully light and ran on to the best place for the visitor to buy a padded coat to wear whilst out at the bridge. Alice, with a fine understanding of the haste with which he had had to set out, offered the loan of two thick rugs to keep out the bitter night temperatures and promised to ask her grocer to put up such supplies as would be needed on the Yangtze delta marsh in midwinter.

"Poor man," she said sympathetically. "It's the very worst time of the year to work out there."

"In the summer there's malaria, cholera, and marsh fever," put in Alexandra provocatively. "You'll have to console yourself with that thought on Christmas Day, Major."

"Oh Garrard, you surely will not expect him to work over Christmas," exclaimed her mother.

"Certainly not. The job will be well finished by then."

"Not necessarily," came the deliberate answer. "It all depends on how quickly I find the cause of the collapse."

"I thought we had settled that issue," came the grating comment. "I cannot believe you have not understood all I have been saying this evening, Major."

The visitor still sat at ease, but there was anger in his voice now that the issue had been brought out into the open.

"I understood perfectly well. You have somehow found out a great deal about me and my past record, and hoped to use my well-known hatred for the Reds in order to persuade me to see things your way. But you are forgetting one thing, Mr Mostyn. I am a soldier as well as an engineer. In engineering matters I consider only the ethics of that profession. If my country or any of its nationals in China are threatened by Reds, or anyone else, I shall be among the first called to defend them. Those are the demands of the other half of my everyday life. I can be a fighting soldier or an engineer—or both at the same time—but please don't try to involve me in diplomatic or mercantile plots. If the revolutionaries have to be subdued I shall have to do it face to face with guns while you shelter behind barricades, so I think you should not ask me to abandon my principles in your cause, also."

Alexandra had never seen her father so nonplussed and it gave her a rush of delight. Nothing would dispel her certainty that Mark Rawlings would eventually fall, but she knew her father well enough to see he was temporarily beaten.

"I sincerely hope that is not your final decision," he said through tight lips.

"If you would prefer to select another investigator I will happily stand down," was the unconcerned reply.

Garrard's hand slapped down on the arm of his chair in anger. "There is no time. Money and prestige are being lost hourly all the time that bridge stays down."

The military man made a gesture of neutrality. "Look, your guess at the cause of the weakness in the bridge is most probably correct, in which case I shall submit a full report placing the blame squarely where it belongs—with the Chinese contractor."

"But how long will it take, doing it your way?"

"Until I find indisputable proof. Who can say how long it will take?"

"Huh, you haven't been to the site yet. We'll see how long your noble sentiments survive out there in the freezing marshland, Major. I guarantee you'll find the evidence very quickly indeed, and return hotfoot to the comfort of your hotel suite."

The officer took in the implications of that remark, and turned to his hostess as he got to his feet. "Forgive me, Mrs Mostyn, but I think it would be better if I left now."

Her distress was evident. "No, please, it is so early and you've had no time to make other friends in Shanghai. Life will be very bleak once you get out to the railway. Won't you stay a little longer?" She looked up with a pleading smile. "You can't desert a fellow Devonian halfway through the evening."

Although her mother never used her disability as a means of blackmail, Alexandra realised she presented a picture that evening few men could resist. In a heavy silk dinner-gown of Parma violet scattered with palest green sprays of blossoms she looked particularly tragic in the heavy invalid chair that kept her a prisoner. It would take a hard heart to refuse her, and Mark Rawlings apparently did not have one, although he took a long time over his surrender.

"I'll stay on condition that you forgive me my bad manners in speaking on professional matters far too long and too exclusively."

She smiled delightedly. "Nonsense, Major. Garrard likes to combine business with pleasure in the comfort of his own home. I am glad he does. I was most interested in all you had to say, and feel immeasurably more secure now I know you are prepared to stand and defend me against the Reds should they attack."

He recognised the gentle teasing and smiled back his capitulation. "I daresay I should be only one of many rushing to your defence if the need should arise, Mrs Mostyn."

She was further delighted by him. "Now I insist that you stay, if you are going to indulge in such charming nonsense. Come and sit beside me for a while, and perhaps my daughter will play for us. Do you care for music? Yes, surely you must."

He studied Alexandra broodingly. "My taste is very conservative, I'm afraid."

Bedevilled by the urge to play the hottest ragtime and jazz tunes she knew, Alexandra crossed to the piano and raised the lid, knowing she was forced to resist the temptation. Her mother loved Chopin and Brahms, with the occasional romantic ballad, and she had a strong feeling their guest would echo that taste. Yet, as she played the familiar melodies, the rawness of nerves which had marred the earlier part of the evening was slowly soothed by the beauty of the classics. Denied by her father the true outlet for her artistic talent, she tended to interpret music with haunting sensitivity, which was why she played ragtime by choice. There was something defiant in the bouncy rhythm that suppressed her yearning for self-expression.

That evening, however, it was suddenly there in full. The Chopin was sadly nostalgic; the Brahms brought a peaceful atmosphere that had been absent so far. Glancing up across the room from beneath the open lid of the grand piano, Alexandra saw her mother sitting in relaxed contentment beside their guest. The dancing firelight played on her bright hair, and the diamonds at her throat. It also caught the polished buttons of the Major's dark-blue tunic as he leant forward to catch her words. In a flash, Alexandra could see how different life could have been for her mother with another man—how full it could still be if love were offered her, or had ever been offered her. A lump rose in her throat. They were both trapped by an unfeeling ambitious man—victims of womanhood.

Mark Rawlings was smiling and nodding gently, engrossed in her mother's conversation. He had a particularly attractive smile that suddenly touched Alexandra in a novel way. Thirty and still a bachelor.

Why? He was as rigidly, arrogantly masculine as her father, and yet . . . ! The mood of her evening shifted into one of subtle revelation as he glanced her way, his smile fading as he met her gaze. He was strong, there was no doubt of that, but was that strength tempered by some quality to which her father was a complete stranger? She looked back at the keyboard and her own fingers, long and scarlet tipped. Useless hands that should be creating the vivid pictures that were in her mind, putting on canvas all that was locked away inside her.

She played on, filled with visions of a snowy landscape and figures in uniform fleeing for their lives—visions inspired by all she had heard that evening—proud, beautiful women being reviled by crude peasantry; gentle, high-born creatures crouching beneath the weight of tarpaulins as a train rushed through the snow-swept night toward freedom. Filled with painful emotion she realised she was playing Tchaikovsky now without being aware of the subtle compulsion to do so. In a daze she knew there would be no rest until the drama had been recorded by her with sweeping strokes of her brush. The haunting quality of the music had awoken the slumbering inspiration born an hour or so ago, when she had been resistant to it. Having merely dabbled with subjects before, she now knew this was the inspiration all artists dreamed of finding. It possessed her completely.

A voice broke into her reverie, sending away the white vastness of Siberia in a flash. Looking around sharply she found her father on his feet by the invalid chair.

"My dear, it is plain you are beginning to tire. I am sure Major Rawlings will understand if you retire to your room now. We both know what the consequences will be if you overdo things."

Alice Mostyn's radiance belied her husband's words, but she was well trained and recognised his message. With dutiful obedience she hid her disappointment with a smile.

"I tend to forget how time is passing when I am listening to music, Major." She held out her hand. "It has been so wonderful to talk to someone who has seen my beloved Devon so recently."

He stood up. "I'm glad. But, you know, I have spent so much time in foreign countries since I joined the army, I have forgotten what it was like to be in an English home. Tonight, in the middle of China, I have been reminded of it. Thank you for making me so welcome." He took her hand in both of his for a moment. "Goodnight."

"Goodnight, Major. I do hope the bridge doesn't cause you too many problems."

Her husband went round behind her. "I will just take my wife up to her room and hand her over to her nurse," he said, then looked toward the piano. "Alexandra, give our guest another brandy, will you?"

With that he swung the wheelchair round and began pushing it across the polished floor. Alexandra recognised her cue. It no longer made her angry, and since she had impetuously already enlightened their guest on her proposed role for the evening, it did not matter if he guessed why they had been left alone. For once, her sympathy for her mother was overshadowed by her eagerness to probe this stranger's enigmatic personality further.

She went across the room to take his glass. He held it out without a word, and she took it to the decanter, poured a generous measure, then walked back to where he stood. He watched her all the way.

With the glass back in his hand he said, "I apologise for what I said to you this evening. I arrived here very angry indeed."

It took her unawares. She had almost forgotten that scene: she was a different girl now.

"I was very angry, too."

The flame-light gleamed on the gold insignia decorating the high hooked collar and put bronze lights on the dark curly hair. She thought of this same man taking people to safety across the snowy landscape that now hung with tantalising half-clarity in her mind; thought of him risking his life to save a group of Russians in his charge.

"Are you going to do whatever it is my father wants you to do?"

"No."

"He usually wins in the end."

He took a pull at the brandy. "Not this time."

She moved back to the piano, strangely breathless. "The seduction plans are pointless, then?"

He followed her and stood in the curve of the Steinway as she took her seat at the keyboard. "You didn't wear the 'alluring' dress," he said with gentle pointedness.

Her breathlessness grew worse. "Would it have made any difference?"

"That's something we shall never know." He looked pensively into his glass, then back at her abruptly. "Why do you adopt that silly pose designed to shock people?"

"I . . . I . . ." For once she had run out of quick repartee. "I think you have had too much to drink."

"Probably. I usually do." He swirled the brandy around in the glass. "You won't beat your father that way, you know. Cool determination is the only answer. You are showing all the signs of panic and doing yourself no good at all."

"You have been here one day and think you understand him?" she cried in quick defence. "Just wait! I have had nineteen years of experience to reflect on."

"I see," he said after a moment. "It just seems to me that while you are vamping men and showing your lace underwear to the world, the real you might be missing something worthwhile."

It so reflected her own longings connected with what had been said that evening, she found herself on the brink of confiding in him. But he was already turning away: the moment was evading her. Inspired she began to play, a melody that echoed softly in that large room to fill it with haunting Slavic sadness.

It worked. He stopped, then slowly turned back to look at her with such naked pain on his face, her fingers faltered over the notes.

"What is that tune?" he asked with an effort.

"Something they play in the cafés in Shanghai. It's Russian."

"I know . . . I've heard it before."

"When you were on that railway in Russia?" Her hands stilled. "Tell me about it, Mark."

At first, she thought he had not even heard, so still was he. "It was . . . a long time ago. A very long time ago—and it's all over now." He tossed back the brandy remaining in the glass, then put it on the table. "I think I should go. One more brandy will be one too many, and your father will be wasting his time if he intends returning to his original theme."

There was nothing she could do to stop him this time. But more than ever she wanted to know what lay in his past, for in that lay her promise for the future, she felt certain.

The muddy water of the canal bore pieces of wreckage upon its bronze surface several miles before they reached the bridge. Splinters of wood, scraps of cloth, fragments of basketwork all floated past the boat as it chugged through the mist-laden noon.

Mark shivered, as much with the feeling of tragedy around the corner as with the cold. There was an eerie silence all over the endless flat marshland that made the noise of the outboard motor almost blasphemous. There could have been only himself, Ah Wu, and the little man at the helm left in the world. Then it was there ahead of them, materialising through the mist as the boatman cut the engine. In the sudden quiet Mark felt his scalp prickle and grow icy. It was an appalling sight.

The whole of the two centre sections of the bridge had gone: the sections each side of them had been twisted and tilted by the sudden wrench, and hung over the water with precarious impermanence.

All that he saw with the eye of an engineer, but it was the rest that shocked him as an observer. The canal was completely dammed by the remains of shattered coachwork impaled on steel girders, great iron wheels twisted and broken from their axles, jagged panes of glass, seating splintered and crushed yet still fixed to panels of wood by sturdy brackets, doors concertinaed and wrenched from their hinges. Over it all hung a kind of bunting: pieces of rag that had once been clothing, torn and bloodstained coats of padded cotton, lengths of blue stuff used by the Chinese to hold bundles of possessions, fur caps, basket coolie-hats, fragments of flowered china, rice bowls, pictures of ancestors, dirty and unrecognisable now, shoes of all kinds, a child's doll without a head.

Sickened and shivering Mark looked away to the high embankment on each side designed to keep the railway above flood level. There was much the same story. Carriages had been forced from the tracks and hung down the steep sides covered in the same grisly evidence of overcrowding and panic that had caused so many casualties. Through the greyness he could see the breakdown trains on the line each side of the canal, but there was no sign of activity in any direction.

He switched his gaze to the little fleet of sampans tied together along the canal bank, and frowned. They appeared deserted. Where was everybody? Why had the work stopped? In the middle of an angry confusion of thoughts he pulled himself up. His job was merely to inspect the wreckage and discover the cause of the collapse. He was there as an impartial investigator, nothing more. The clearing and rebuilding of the bridge was none of his concern. He remembered all too clearly Mostyn telling him an engineer would be called in to do that. But as he looked around at the scene Mark knew he would give anything to be that engineer.

As soon as the boat had been tied up he jumped ashore and scrambled up the steep embankment on the Shanghai side of the canal to where the breakdown train stood neglected. There was no sign of movement anywhere. The wreckage was being cleared, there was evidence of that in the big open containers attached to the train. But the chaos in the canal itself had naturally been left until he should arrive. It was five days now since the tragedy, long enough to have picked up everything that lay scattered on each side of the embankments. Baffled and uneasy he walked back to the boat, hunching his shoulders into the padded coat that had a fur collar turned up around his ears.

"Ah Wu!" he called as he approached. "You ask where man takee go. Whyfore man no wanchee work canal-side."

The little plump boy turned to the boatman and questioned him, gesticulating toward the train. But the boatman shook his head unimpressed by the urgency of his two companions. He either did not know or would not tell, that much was plain without translation. Mark was slowly learning Mandarin, but it would be of little use to him except with the written word. It seemed to him nearly everyone spoke a language particularly his own. Indeed, Ah Wu was having difficulty in conversing with a man from another district. Mark left them shouting at each other to walk closer to the tragic barrier stretching across the water.

It was going to be a long tricky business. Before he could inspect the bridge all the wreckage of the train would have to be removed, but in doing that the steel girders would almost certainly shift and resettle. Vital pieces of evidence might fall to the bottom of the canal to join those already there, and more time would have to be spent in getting them all up. He had brought diving equipment with him, but he knew what the average canal collected over the years, and in China that amount was sure to be doubled. His heart sank. In such weather and temperatures the less time he need spend under water the better. At first glance the prospect was a gloomy one. At best, he would find signs of metal fatigue or substandard workmanship somewhere along the structure hanging above the canal; at worst, he would spend interminable hours in a diving suit searching for a bolt that had sheared and fallen into the muck-strewn silt at the bottom of the canal.

He metaphorically took off his hat to Garrard Mostyn. The temptation to make a show of investigating the accident then getting back to the comfort of a Shanghai hotel to write a fictional report was very strong. After all, who would ever find the real cause? . . . and whatever the truth, it would not bring back those who had died. The canal as well as the railway was an important link with inland towns. The sooner this site was cleared and work begun on reconstruction . . . He broke off. That was not his job. His wide experience in bridge building was merely to be used to scavenge in the wreckage for a hint of the cause. Then, a 'civilian engineer' would take over. His attitude hardened. Oh no, he would find the real reason for the tragedy if he was forced to stay for a month, or more.

Turning away his attention was caught by a movement up on the embankment. A man was standing where it had been deserted before —a thin figure of uncertain age staring down with eyes that were blank with semi-intelligence. Mark swallowed the little dart of apprehension his sudden appearance had created, and set off toward him, calling Ah Wu to follow.

The man's face was ochre, lined and ingrained with dirt. His wide cheekbones stuck out beneath the sagging skin to give his features a triangular appearance, but as Mark drew nearer he saw it was malnutrition and not age that had taken its toll. He wore no warm padded coat, but several layers of tattered cotton coats over voluminous trousers tied around his thin waist with a piece of cord. His footwear consisted of pieces of sacking wrapped around and tied in position beneath the ankle. He stared impassively as Mark approached and tried a few halting expressions in Mandarin.

Ah Wu arrived and, being of sharp intelligence, repeated the questions with which his master had asked him to quiz the boatman. An arm went up like a signal blade pointing away into the mist, and a weary high-pitched voice began to recite in monotones. It went on for a long time. Mark understood no word of it and was soon frustrated.

Finally, Ah Wu turned to him, a dramatic contrast with the other, in good warm clothes and full of lively expression.

"Man say go chop-chop Shanghai-side, Lu-Seng. Foreign devil-head man go all along, no b'long likee Chinee."

"Lu-Seng—is that a village?"

Ah Wu nodded and pointed. "Here b'long Shanghai-side."

"Everyone has gone there—the Englishman and the coolies?"

The boy nodded again. "Makee plenty bad Chinee."

It did not make much sense, even then. For some reason, the whole work force including Hamish Corcoran, the Scottish supervising engineer, had gone to a village on the Shanghai side of the canal, where there was plainly some trouble amongst the inhabitants. Reminding himself again that it was no business of his Mark was nevertheless annoyed that work of great urgency, to say nothing of valuable equipment, had been abandoned to the charge of one shaky dim-witted Chinese, who had plainly been asleep on the job. He was also annoyed that Corcoran saw fit to ignore his arrival so blatantly. He might be only the independent investigator, but he was surely entitled to a little professional courtesy.

His first instinct was to go to Lu-Seng himself to discover what was going on, but he had to bow to commonsense. The village might be some distance away, there was mist over the marshes and he did not know the terrain. His military training told him no man should move under such conditions unless it was essential.

Swallowing his annoyance he set about doing what he could toward getting started. It was not much without coolie labour on hand. So while Ah Wu cooked a hot substantial meal he checked his equipment, then set in position the four big inspection lamps that would illuminate the site as well as possible with their great curved reflectors. As he did so he smiled to himself. Mostyn had told him to order anything he wanted whilst in Shanghai and charge it to the businessman's account, so he had acquired the best equipment he could lay his hands on and fitted himself out with a Russian-style padded coat with fur collar and matching cap, several thick pullovers, and long woollen underwear—all of which were essential for a man straight from the warmth of Hong Kong. He knew it was not that Mostyn had had in mind when he made the offer, but like all engineers Mark knew that comfort and high-grade equipment produced efficient and skilful work in the shortest possible time.

He sited the oil lamps on their tripods, then returned to his boat to eat some lunch. The cabin was cramped and warmed only by the feeble stove on which Ah Wu had cooked the meal. Mark kept his coat on as he ate. The little covered area was barely long enough for him to stretch out full-length when he wanted to sleep, and it smelt of fish, rotten vegetables, and joss sticks. There were one or two other odours Mark chose not to recognise since he had to live in it whilst he was at the bridge. He was used to strange accommodation. In Canada he had used a logger's cabin, in Africa a thatched hut, in France a hole in the ground, and in Russia. . . . No, he would not think of Russia. Instead, he thought of Alexandra Mostyn who had played a tune to revive so many agonising memories.

Hearing that melody again on an evening which had brought the past too close had been more than he could take. Before going to the Mostyn home he had toured the quarter of Shanghai he had been told many White Russians frequented, questioning, probing, pleading, all the while knowing in his heart it would be the same as always. They were all suspicious, afraid. No one ever admitted being there; no one ever knew anything of her. After seven years why could he not accept that the chapter was irrevocably closed? Why was he haunted by the unknown? If she was alive it was better that they did not meet; if she was dead it was better that he did not learn the details of her death. What perverse facet of his character persisted in hoping against hope? What kind of masochistic stubbornness led him to torment himself by chasing every outlandish possibility? What depth of emotion could chain a man to a memory for so long, giving him no peace? The answers eternally eluded him.

Arriving chilled and bereft at the house which was a monument to affluence and success, the Mostyn girl's crude sexual challenge had seemed the final unacceptable insult to all he valued. Only the arrival of Alice Mostyn had prevented him from leaving, and her quality of gentle intelligence had banished the violence surging through him due to her daughter's insensitive approach to life. Only when the girl had betrayed something near to sincerity in her interpretation of music had he suspected there might be more to her than she chose to reveal. It was that which had finally driven him away. To no one, least of all Alexandra Mostyn, could he ever speak of that time in Russia. Returning to question those who had emerged with the night hours in the bars and brothels, he had finally reached his hotel to banish clear thought in the habitual manner with brandy, seeing her lovely tear-washed face in the nightmares that had followed. He saw it again now as he sat lost in introspection, until brought back to awareness by a voice hailing him from the bank.

"Halloo! Halloo!"

He looked up to see a short sturdy man in his mid-forties stepping aboard without ceremony. The boat began to rock as the visitor dipped his head beneath the bulkhead to enter.

"So, ye arrived through the murk well enough! I regret I wasna here to greet ye, but there was a wee ha'porth of trouble I couldna ignore."

Used to military formality it would have been easy to take offence at the brusque greeting, but Mark had worked with civilians often enough to know what to expect. He did not attempt to get up. In that low cabin it was safer to remain seated.

"Mr Corcoran?"

"Hamish'll do," was the brisk reply.

"Can I offer you something to eat?"

"Nae . . . but I'll tak a drop of whatever ye have." He came further in and lowered himself onto one of the suitcases standing near. It gave an ominous crack.

"There's a wooden crate over here," hinted Mark as he poured a measure of brandy.

"Och, this'll do." Corcoran took the glass and held it high. "Here's good health to ye, and to all the wee bairns ye father." Tossing back the liquid he added, "It's nae as good as whisky, but it warms a man up and I won't be saying nae to another. I need it after the deeds of this morning."

"At the village?" As he tipped the bottle over the glass Mark decided to assess the man a little before broaching the subject of the bridge.

"Aye." The brandy vanished down Corcoran's throat. "I've been in China twenty-five years and seen no change in the plaguey devils from then until now." His bushy eyebrows rose. "A major is it? Ye're awful young for that."

"What happened at the village?" Mark pushed away his plate. The man had brought a strong smell of sweat to add to the odorous closeness of the cabin, and he wanted to get to work in the open as soon as possible.

"I brought some of the villains to book. Ye've seen the unholy mess outside?" He nodded at the tiny cabin window. "Scrambling like ants they came, looting and killing." The eyebrows rose again. "Oh aye, some of the victims trapped in the carriages were finished off with a quick snap of the neck, all for the sake of a bundle or basket of meagre goods. The minute I saw what was going on I posted guards, d'ye see, but all their yellow hides are equally treacherous. What did I do but catch them letting their own kinsfolk through to snatch at what they could lay their hands on. Old Kwai-Wok at the village pretended to know nothing about it, but he's a canny old rascal and there was naught I could do but make an example of the culprits. He knows he'll not be safe frae me if he doesna toe the line. I took the rest of them there to watch, as a warning."

"A warning?"

Corcoran nodded. "Aye, they'll mebbe behave theirselves for a bit now. Kwai-Wok had four of his men garrotted. The twa women were put against a wall and stoned." He gave a grin. "There's also twa of his laddies in the cangue. It'll keep them out of mischief a wee while, and we can get on with our work."

Mark stared at him with a prickling sensation rising in his scalp. "You watched them being garrotted . . . and women stoned? It's barbaric!"

The Scotsman looked back shrewdly. "As I said before, ye're awful young. This is China, laddie, not the playing fields of Eton. I tak it ye've not seen much of the world. Those yellow scum'll carve up anyone in sight for a bowl of rice, and their women'll stab ye in the back even as they lie beneath ye, given half a chance. Barbaric, ye said. Aye, and that's what they'll always be. Cunning, thieving, murderous, filthy bastards, that's what they are. Once let them get away with anything and ye'll nae do a thing with them. Barbaric? I make sure they practise it on each other and not me, laddie. If ye'll tak a wee tip, ye'll do the same."

A strong dislike of the man had overtaken Mark. He had completely misread the remark about barbarism which had referred to the watching of such atrocities more than the perpetrating of them. That Corcoran was also treating him as a nincompoop of the officer class who had never been beyond the quad of his public school until now, did not trouble him that much. Many people did, but they soon found their mistake. He was more worried about the morale and attitude of the coolies.

"I have to get my work-force from that village, Corcoran."

"Nae need to fret." He smiled broadly. "There'll be nae trouble now. I've never seen a more tractable clan than the devils squatting outside on their hunches. They know they'll get nae rice for twa days, and then only if they've earned it."

Mark had had enough. He got to his feet, remembering just in time to bend his head free of the low roof.

"Men can't work if they're not fed."

"Chinks can, laddie."

"I have brought rice with me as payment for the men who work for me. Each man will get it right from the start," he told the other in tones meant to indicate that it was final.

The Scotsman looked unperturbed. "As ye will, but ye'll soon discover it's different from yon soldiers. There'll be nae 'yes, sir; no, sir' from these. They only respect the man who kicks the hardest."

Mark picked up his fur cap from the table. "I think you've been in China too long, Corcoran. There's a revolution afoot to save the coolie from kicks. Don't tell me you haven't heard of it."

Corcoran rose, too. "Och, yon Chiang Kai-Shek and his Kuomintang, ye mean? He'll nae get far, laddie."

"He already has Hankow, and his army is growing as it moves northward."

"Aye, with what results? His troops are kicking the coolies now. It'll never change, laddie, tak my word. The history of China shows a constant succession of invaders, none of which last long. This Kuomintang'll go the way of the others when the next upstart comes along . . . and the coolie was born to be kicked."

Mark knew it was pointless to argue with a man as dogmatic as Corcoran, but he could not let the remark pass.

"The Kuomintang is different from all other conquering armies. It is Communist-backed—Soviet Russians, in fact. I wouldn't dismiss *them* too lightly, if I were you."

Corcoran shook his head. "It'll nae last. The Chinks and Ruskies are long-standing enemies. Yon Chiang Kai-Shek'll be a fool if he can nae see what the Ruskies are up to. It'll be China for the Russians, not for the Chinese, as they're so fond of preaching. Besides, we wouldna let it happen. We've too firm a foot on Chinese soil. I know the Soviets kicked us out of Russia in 1919, but we'd nae right to be there. This is different."

As one of those who had been 'kicked out of Russia in 1919' Mark said bitterly, "This is different, all right. In Russia we were trying to save a nation; here, we would be trying to save the lifestyle of men like Garrard Mostyn, that's all."

He received another shrewd look from the Scotsman. "The China trade is worth a king's ransom to Britain. Would ye nae call it also saving a nation—your own, this time?"

Suddenly weary of the subject, Mark put on the cap and made for the door. "I'd like to take a start on saving a bridge first."

Corcoran followed him out onto the deck." I tak it ye put up yon lights."

"Yes." He stepped onto the mist-shrouded bank. "There's a hell of a lot of debris to be cleared before I can begin to look at the bridge. With those lamps we can work after dark."

"They'll nae do it, laddie."

Mark stopped and turned to him, conscious of a row of silent coolies watching him from the top of the embankment. "What do you mean?"

"Yon lamps—nae one of these coolies'll work if ye light them up. They're a superstitious clan. The slightest thing and they down tools."

"Isn't that where you kick them?" Mark asked sarcastically.

Corcoran smiled. "Now, now, there's nae need for that. The Chinks are more in fear of dragons than any man's boot, as I know to my cost. They claim this is a place of bad *fung shui*—it's known as the Bridge of a Hundred Dragons. Yon lights will upset the spirits, and the village will suffer the consequences. They'll nae work, I tell ye."

"I thought this job was urgent." It was said with some heat, the oppression of the mist-laden marsh playing on his nerves.

"Aye, that it is. The sooner ye tak a wee look at that mess and get back to Mostyn with a report, the happier we'll all be. It'll tak ye nae more than a day or two to make it look convincing, then ye'll be out of it back to the pleasures of Shanghai."

"No," said Mark gritting his teeth. "From the look of that wreckage it could well take me several weeks before I get down to the truth . . . and I'm not leaving until I do."

Hamish Corcoran gave him a long thoughtful look. "I thought ye military laddies built bridges with planks on little boats."

"Oh no," he returned trying to remain unruffled. "We military laddies often do much more than that, as you'll soon discover."

CHAPTER FOUR

For three days they concentrated on clearing the wreckage from the canal. Corcoran was proved right. The coolies would not go near the lamps and all work stopped when darkness fell. On the first night Mark stubbornly continued alone, thinking his example would serve to show the Chinese there was nothing to fear. But he was dealing with people whose superstitions dominated all they did: he needed a work-force and had to bow to their ethnic demands. Once the shattered carriages had been cleared he could work alone by the lights on his inspection, dragons or not.

Although he did not like Hamish Corcoran Mark had to admit that he was knowledgeable and dedicated, giving him every assistance if he asked for it. The Scot was tough, hard-drinking, careless of manners, and very shrewd. Expatriates of his kind fell into two categories. They either turned native—adopted local customs, dress, beliefs, and a wife of the country—or they resisted to the point of unreasonable excess. Corcoran was the latter. Intensely and volubly true to a land he had left as a youth and never seen since, his every word and action showed his contemptuous hatred of those amongst whom he had chosen to work. He treated the coolies abominably, flung insults at them in his thick brogue, and refused to have them anywhere near his boat. His servant was a Portuguese from Macao who not only handled the boat but cooked and washed for his master. In fact, the lad's devotion was so intense Mark wondered if there was a stronger bond between the pair, until the Scot's endless and ribald stories told over a drink proved conclusively that he had a strong, if somewhat vicious, interest in women.

Yet even Corcoran's overbearing contempt stopped short of attempting to force his workers into defying the dragons and spirits of which they lived in fear. He also had a healthy respect for their hatred of 'foreign devil-heads' for he kept a guard dog on his boat which was let loose at night. A great gruesome mongrel, it detested all Chinese but acted like a slobbering lap dog toward any European. The Portuguese fed it on fish and vegetables, and it had a dish of rice wine at dusk every evening. It smelt vile and had a nasty temper during the night hours, but Mark aroused slavish admiration in the beast that was comforting, if unpleasant.

Apart from the coolies who worked like automatons throughout the day, there was one other character out on that marsh who made quite a strong impression on Mark right from the start. Hong was the Chinese foreman employed by the railway. His home was in Shanghai and he was a Christian, educated in an Anglo-Chinese school. By comparison with the coolies he was well off: by European standards he was scraping a living. His wife was amah to an English family in Shanghai; his four children were being looked after by his sister-in-law along with her three. His elder brother had worked as a clerk with Jardines, then gone to England as a cabin boy on one of the liners. There, he had educated himself to a high degree before returning recently to take up his rightful place as head of the family.

All this Mark heard in those first three days. He put it down to the fact that Hong had found a confidant, at last. The coolies were beneath his social standing; the Scotsman too belligerent. It never occurred to him that Hong might recognise in him another man out on his own at that bridge. Hong, taller than the average Chinese and neat in his padded coat, woollen breeches and high boots, brought from Lu-Seng village a group of sullen men and women and somehow persuaded them to work for Mark despite their obvious reluctance to do so. Thankful for his interpretive qualities Mark also made use of his intelligent approach to the work by explaining what he was attempting to do once the wreckage was cleared. Hong was profoundly impressed.

"It was said to me, Major, that you would be here just one or two days. It was said you would soon see that Chung-Li was at fault, then go."

"Chung-Li?" Mark looked up from the sketch he was making of the angle of the girders as they lay at present. Once they shifted they would tell a different story.

"The Chinese contractor—a very bad man."

He grinned. "So you have him as the villain, too—before he has been proved guilty."

Hong looked shocked. "Oh, no. Because a man is bad within himself his work must not be blamed. Mr Corcoran is even more bad, but it is plain he is most clever with the railway."

They both looked across to where the Scotsman was driving his coolies to further effort beside the breakdown trains. An uncompromising figure in thick plaid coat and woollen hat, he strutted up and down blaspheming at the top of his voice. Mark had seen sergeants doing much the same thing to a row of sappers, but there was a subtle difference. Army sergeants had an accepted vocabulary that was recited whenever they wanted to ginger things up a bit; this man Corcoran really meant every word he said.

Unwilling to be disloyal or undermine the Scot's authority Mark said, "I don't think he's as bad as he makes out."

Hong nodded. "Oh, yes, he is bad. I have known him for a very long time now. He makes Lu-Seng afraid."

"What, the whole village? How?"

"He makes them afraid," reiterated the Chinaman with an authority he plainly felt needed no further explanation.

Mark dropped the subject. Corcoran extended his treatment of the coolies to Hong, who was a man of some countenance amongst his countrymen. Although he thought it deplorable and completely unwarranted, Mark had his own problems and decided not to get involved with something he would leave the minute his job was done.

It was not easy to refrain from involvement. Although it was bitterly cold even when the weak sun shone, although living on a canal was damp, smelly, and uncomfortable, although he had for company a force of sullen Chinese, a curious but unlikeable Scotsman, an educated Christian Chinese who spoke in riddles, and an ugly hound with halitosis, Mark had to fight against the fascination of the bridge he was not allowed to reconstruct. Never before had he studied a bridge that had been destroyed then walked away from it. To his professional mind it was untidy, to his personal sense of fulfilment it was a severe setback, to his pride it was a bodyblow. To blot out all those things and to ease something that had been revived by the Mostyn family at dinner that night, he worked relentlessly. When he could escape Corcoran's company he turned in early; when he could not he drank far too much.

On the evening of the third day the Scot walked aboard just as Mark was rolling himself into his blankets.

"Taking a wee nap, were ye? It's a great pity when I feel in the need of company."

He squinted up from his makeshift bed. "Why not head for the nightspots of Lu-Seng? I've heard they've to be seen to be believed."

The comment brought an astonishing change over his visitor. The harsh face flushed dark red. "I'll tell ye straight, laddie. I underestimated ye."

"A lot of people do."

The Scot gave him a long hard look. "Aye, mebbe, but there's some things ye'll do well to leave alone."

"Such as?" He was still laconic, unwilling to spend half another night listening to the man's somewhat obscene humour.

"Interfering in a man's private life. It's something I'll nae tolerate, d'ye hear?"

"In that case you won't interfere in mine, will you? I'm ready for sleep." Sensing that Corcoran had already been at the whisky bottle his next remark was something of a risk. "Don't rock the boat as you leave."

Turning over in the narrow bunk Mark was relieved to hear the man begin to laugh. He had half expected to be pulled upright and punched on the jaw. The laughter went on for some time until the boat moved gently on the water as Corcoran left.

"Aye, laddie, ye'll do. Ye've more spunk in ye than all the Chinks put together."

It was not until the following day that he thought back on the incident and realised it was his mention of Lu-Seng that had sparked off the man's aggression. Put together with Hong's remark that the whole village was afraid of Corcoran it suggested a mystery, but there was too much work to be done and no time for things that would not concern him for long. Once the wreckage had been cleared he began his painstaking study of the bridge itself—a bridge that was half underwater now. He clambered over the steel structure searching for metal stress or signs of a buckled girder. He measured the girders and plates with a gauge and checked with the required specifications. He examined bolts and splices. He studied the blue prints. He tested the supports. His assistant in all this was Hong, willingly lent by Corcoran. The Chinese took an awed and avid interest in all that was done. He had a small steady hand, infinite patience, and a flattering faith in the engineering skill of the man with whom he worked. The pleasure he felt at being trusted with such work showed in the glow of life that appeared on his round friendly face.

However, the work took time, and a week dragged past without any success. Many times Mark thought of how much simpler it would be to do as Mostyn had suggested. The monotony of the days, the isolation of that spot swept by bitter winds, and the looming prospect of having to go underwater before long settled on him heavily. He told himself it would not be so bad if he had the prospect of rebuilding the bridge as a reward. He was stubbornly sticking to a principle that had earned him little thanks in the past, when he could be away and on a boat to Hong Kong whenever he wished—on a boat to Hong Kong with the blessing of everyone and a bright mark on his service record. Yet, every time he thought of Mostyn's well-bred sneer and that absurd girl saying "*I'm* the bribe, darling", he knew he would stick it out.

It was only that thought which sustained his resolution once he began his search underwater. The canal was not deep, but he needed to be completely submerged as he worked and it was something he never liked. The diving suit reminded him too vividly of walking around during gas attacks in the trenches, and he had often had to come up prematurely in the past, because panic took hold of him. That great helmet clamped over his head, the need to suck in air, and the noise of the water unnaturally loud in his ears produced a nervous reaction he could not always control. Water itself held no fears for him—he was an outstanding swimmer—but trapped in a diving suit he felt threatened.

It was after his third fruitless descent to the canal bed that he came closest to giving in. Warmed by a hot drink and his complete set of pullovers, he squatted on the bank sifting through the evidence he had brought up from the bottom, pointing out various features to Hong. In the middle of it he realised it had gone very quiet and looked up. The cranes were still; the track deserted. The coolies had all stopped work and lined up above him to stare in morose fascination. Corcoran was standing beside them with his arms folded, grinning broadly.

"What's that all about?" he asked Hong. "It's not a coolie strike, is it?"

"No, Major." The man looked uncomfortable. "Mr Corcoran is doing it to frighten them."

"To *what*?"

"They . . . they think you are a devil spirit."

Mark laughed uncomfortably. "Good God . . . why?"

Hong's black eyes were troubled. He plainly felt it would be bad mannered to say what was the truth, yet he had been asked a direct question by someone of higher consequence than himself and was obliged to answer.

"The diving suit allows you to walk about under the water. They do not understand it and say you must be protected by a powerful devil—and the hundred dragons."

A bell rang in Mark's memory. Corcoran had said this was known as the Bridge of a Hundred Dragons. He gave a quick glance at the coolies, then got to his feet and faced Hong.

"I think it is time you told me about these dragons. What is behind it all?"

The man looked even more uncomfortable, but the greater demand on his consequence won, in the end. "It is a story told by the people of the village."

"All right. Tell it to me, then."

Hong spread his hands apologetically, as if it would ease his bad manners at having to recount something that would undoubtedly be seen as an insult by the Englishman.

"They are not Christians, sir. They believe many things that their ancestors have passed down to them. They say that many years ago this plain was dry as bones and no crops would grow here. The people were starving and under great sorrow due to the greed of their lord, who took everything within his own palace walls and left them nothing. One day a great warrior came from a land far away and made his camp on this plain, but when he asked for sustenance and water for his soldiers the villagers told him of the barrenness and advised him to camp in a better place.

"The warrior was a wise man and, seeing how the people suffered, promised to make the land fertile and rich if the lord would give him his three beautiful daughters as wives. The wicked lord, seeing the chance to take even more riches into his palace, agreed and asked the warrior to do as he promised. Whereupon the warrior took up his great sword and cut gashes in the earth so that the sea flowed in. The land grew fertile and the crops flourished. Soon, there was food for everyone, and the villagers grew rich. When the time came for the warrior to leave he asked for the three daughters to be made ready for their long journey. An escort of one hundred soldiers on white horses was sent to the palace by the eager bridegroom. The procession set off, and camp was made that night just here." He waved a hand at the broken bridge, then seemed unwilling to go on.

"Where do the dragons come in?" asked Mark impatiently. All this fantasy seemed to be getting nowhere.

"Apologies, Major. It was necessary to tell the earlier part of the story. The people of Lu-Seng tell that the three daughters made tea of the finest kind for all the hundred soldiers to show their joy at being given in marriage to so great a warrior. But the tea contained poison. The lord was pleased to have the sea flowing through his land to give him riches, but a warrior was regarded as very lowly in his eyes, and great was his rage at being asked to give his daughters to such a man. The three given by him were beautiful young men dressed in finery, who rose up from the palanquin and killed the warrior as he slept. After the deed was done, they returned to the lord with the hundred white horses, and laughed as the warrior's army fled from a land where three women were stronger than a hundred soldiers and their great leader.

"But the spirit of the warrior roamed the plain, and the sea grew bigger and rushed through the cuts he had made in the land until the flood swept everything away—all except the hundred white horses who became dragons and flew above the level of the water. They also roam the plain and when they are angry the sea pours in once more and ruins the crops."

Mark knew the Chinese loved legends, lived by them quite often, and it was true the Yangtze flooded from time to time, covering the plain. It was easy to see how the story evolved, but he still did not understand the connection with his diving suit.

"What has all this to do with the work I am doing here, Hong?"

The Chinaman grinned broadly, often a sign of acute embarrassment at having to say something which he felt was impolite.

"They expect that you will die, Major. They see you disappear beneath the water, then you are back and walking about. It must be a devil-suit you wear, they say, and are afraid it will make the dragons angry again. Already, the hundred dragons have pushed down the bridge to stop the devil-machine from crossing this place of bad *fung shui*. They have killed the white man who built the bridge . . . and there was the other time."

Mark began to feel unnaturally cold. "What other time?"

"When the bridge was being built."

Some vague memory of the newspaper report on the catastrophe returned to him. Had there not been an enigmatic reference to an earlier tragedy at the bridge?

"You had better tell me all you know, Hong."

He nodded. "Yes, Major. There was another white man who came up with Mr Deane once. . . ."

"The engineer who built the bridge?"

"That is correct. They were standing out there over the water." He twisted to point at the centre of the canal where the bridge hung shattered. "They were talking about the construction when suddenly the other man stepped back and fell into the water, hitting his head on one of the boats tied up at the bank. He did not come up from the canal again until they brought up his body."

"Good God!"

Grinning broadly again in apologetic manner, Hong went on, "The *fung shui* man advised that the bridge should not be built here where the warrior was murdered, but the railway officials ignored him. Now the dragons are angered, and the people are afraid until the beasts rest again." He tittered to cover his obvious uneasiness. "It is only what these simple villagers believe, Major."

"Go on," prompted Mark, seeing that the man was not immune to such beliefs despite his Christianity. He had the blood of his ancestors in his veins, and superstition was a powerful element.

"They are saying that three must die to avenge the three youths who dressed as the brides and killed the warrior. Two have already gone . . . but you do not die in the water, Major. They say the Devil protects you and defies the hundred dragons."

Feeling ridiculously uneasy Mark tried to laugh it off. "Why should they feel *I* have to die? The villains in the story were Chinese youths, not adult Englishmen."

The Chinese wagged his head in superior understanding of the situation. "It was an Englishman who built the bridge and angered the slumbering dragons. Now they have been reminded of how the warrior died, and will take vengeance from your countrymen."

He laughed self-consciously. "So they twist their story to suit the circumstances, eh? You'd better explain to them how the diving suit works, then they can relax."

"Ah, Major, they no longer trust me," was the sad reply. "Because I work the pump that keeps you alive beneath the water they say I am hand in hand with the Devil." He shrugged fatalistically. "They are simple country people, Major. They are suspicious of anything or anyone they do not understand. You disturb their peace. In Lu-Seng they are offering gifts they cannot afford to their gods for protection until the hundred dragons sleep again."

Silence fell between them. Mark swung his gaze from Hong's face to the tangled wreck of the bridge, on to the malevolent stares of the coolies, and finally to Corcoran who stood in gleeful satisfaction at their fear. Cold depression ate slowly into him.

"So they won't feel safe until a third Englishman has died at this bridge, is that it?"

The eerie isolation of that Chinese marshland made his words easily acceptable. He thought of those hours he must spend underwater when he had no control over what happened at the surface. He thought of his lifeline operated by Ah Wu and Hong—two Chinese! He thought of all those coolies working for Corcoran. If they really wanted a third victim to satisfy their dragons, would one sadistic Scot and a tethered dog be able to prevent them?

"Please try not to upset your father today, dear. He is very worried over the situation in Hankow."

"Then he will scarcely notice me," said Alexandra reasonably. "When business problems occupy his mind he has no time for anything else."

Alice Mostyn turned from the window to move her chair across the room. "It is not business, this time. It is that dreadful man Chiang

Kai-Shek who is advancing further than anyone thought. It would be disastrous if he came as far north as Shanghai."

Alexandra crossed one leg over the other and studied the new shoes she wore. She was not certain the tangerine shade looked right with the pale misty blue of the shantung costume she had chosen to wear.

"Mother, it would be disastrous to *Father* if he came this far north. That is why he is worried. He does not give a fig for China except inasmuch as it affects business."

Alice stopped her chair in front of her daughter and gave her a reproachful look. "You should allow everyone at least one saving grace. Have you ever considered the responsibilities that weigh on your father's shoulders? He and men like him have brought Britain a great deal of prosperity which was vital to the nation after the excessive cost of the War."

Alexandra smiled gently and took her mother's hands. "How loyal you are! But I cannot believe Father has his nation in the forefront of his mind. Prosperity for Britain is a noble disguising epithet for prosperity for Garrard Mostyn. Admit it, Mother, saving grace or not Father would not live the knife-edge life he does were he not making a fortune by it."

Alice sighed and surrendered. "It is as well he does, judging by your tastes. He is extremely generous to you."

She got to her feet, filled with the new restlessness that had plagued her since that dinner a week ago. "It takes only a few seconds to write a cheque. That dismisses his obligation to me for a whole month . . . until the next cheque has to be signed. His parental love flows with the ink for as long as it takes to write my name and the amount."

"Alexandra!"

She turned and put her hand on her mother's shoulder. "It's true, although you never like to hear me say it. Don't let's spoil a lovely sunny day by talking about something that has no solution." She smiled fondly. "I really came in to ask your opinion on this costume Kah made for me—a subject we shall enjoy much more, don't you agree?"

Alice smiled a little sadly. "You always avoid upsetting me with such adroitness."

"Well, of course. We women must band together against masculine arrogance and show them our strength."

It was said lightly enough, but her mother frowned. "You sound so . . . militant . . . when you say things like that, dear."

"Good," responded Alexandra firmly. "Now, about this costume."

Alice gave up and studied the stylish draped jacket, and skirt with contrasting godets. "The colour is perfect for you, and the jacket is very elegant. But that skirt, Alexandra!"

She laughed gaily. "That skirt dear *Mama* is just what you would have adored to have worn at my age instead of those long trailing lengths of muslin wrapped around you."

"Well, I daresay the freedom is quite delightful but, you know, dear, those long trailing lengths of muslin hid a multitude of sins." She laughed attractively. "On one occasion when there was a chill wind I wore a pair of long flannel drawers that were my mother's to a luncheon aboard the flagship of a visiting naval squadron. Those long skirts were also the saving of many a young girl admired for her figure. You have very beautiful legs, Alexandra, but some of today's beauties are betrayed by skirts that show 'skinny pins.'" She laughed again. "We had a maidservant when I was a girl who was always bemoaning her 'skinny pins'. I have never forgotten the expression." Giving her daughter an appraising look she put her head on one side. "According to the journals you look the height of fashion, and really most attractive. But I don't understand you, dear. I thought your creed was to put an end to the inequality of the sexes, but I fear any young man you meet today will think of you in terms quite opposite. You look an extremely desirable young woman, I must say."

Alexandra sat down again quickly and took her mother's hands again. "That is the whole point, don't you see? We no longer sit smiling beneath lacy parasols gazing with adulation at men who are doing things we can do every bit as easily. Today we challenge them. They can't resist our fine feathers, but they soon discover we can peck. If they want us they must accept our minds along with our bodies."

Alice sighed. "I still find such frankness disturbing . . . but I suppose each generation must make its mark, and I daresay we were equally headstrong in a quieter way. But, Alexandra, my dear, don't allow yourself to be hurt in the course of your challenge to the male sex. Human nature has a way of stepping in despite all one's determination."

She knew what her mother meant and answered at once with great conviction. "I won't get hurt. No man will ever rule me. He will have to accept me on my terms or not at all." She looked at her watch. "I must fly. Lion is picking me up in ten minutes. We'll probably come back with Dot to tea."

"Oh, good," said her mother. "Dot is such a delightfully silly girl I am always amused by her, and Lionel is always dressed in such startling clothes it quite takes my mind off his very earnest theorising."

"Mother, they are my closest friends," protested Alexandra laughing.

"So you have always said, dear, but I am certain you share my opinion of them, all the same."

"Not at all . . . but I'm glad they amuse you. Goodbye, dear. We'll see you later this afternoon."

She kissed her mother and went down to the large hallway where Lai-Hi helped her on with her black coat. As she pulled on the black-felt cloche hat with tangerine feather fastened by a diamante clip, she blew herself a kiss in the mirror.

"Oh no, dear girl, no man will ever rule *you* to the extent of driving you into an invalid chair."

With that thought strong in her mind she treated Lionel's bombastic suggestion of daring-do in his expensive car with complete indifference. The roadster was new, the pride of his heart, and designed to give its owner an enviable edge to any aspiring rival in romance, but Alexandra hid her interest beneath a languid boredom.

She had not seen him since the postponement of the evening engagement when Mark Rawlings had dined at her home. If Lionel was jealous he hid it beneath his enthusiasm for his car, and Alexandra had time to reflect on her mother's words. Her companion was dressed in a tweed plus-four suit with a vivid yellow pullover and matching handkerchief in his breast pocket. To keep his blond hair immaculate he wore a leather helmet reminiscent of those used by wartime fliers, and a long leather overcoat kept out the cold experienced by those riding in cars with fold-back hoods. A heroic image for a man with smooth good looks, but as he prattled on and on Alexandra had a sudden memory of a dark-haired man with freckles who had apparently been a true hero, yet refused to speak about it.

"Lion, darling," she broke in. "I'm sure she's too divine for words, so why not leave it that way? Who are these people we are lunching with today? Tell all!"

Annoyed but diverted he said, "Americans that Dot and I met on that liner last week—the night you let me down for that puffed-up fool of the military system."

"Papa's orders," she snapped. "I had to obey."

He cast her a fierce glance as the car turned into the Bund. "Oh yeah?"

She was not a bit amused. "That American gangster idiom does nothing for you, sweetie. You look far too much like a puffed-up fool of the class system."

He stepped on the accelerator and raced the car along the wide

Bund, careless of rickshaws and wheelbarrows in his flash of anger.

"Why are you always so damned provocative, Sandy? A fellow never knows where he is with you."

"Then I'm achieving my object." Her hand went to her hat. "There's a draught in this car that is ruining my plume."

Furious at her criticism of his car he put his foot down harder than ever, heading for the heart of the Settlement at breakneck speed. Alexandra clung to her seat as the grand buildings of the waterfront gave way to smaller, densely-packed dwellings in the Nanking Road. Other motorists were sounding their horns in protest and pulling to the safety of the kerb as they passed. It seemed a miracle that they avoided the rickshaws as they flashed by, and she wondered how long it would be before they were stopped and arrested by the Sikh police. There appeared to be an unusual number in evidence that morning.

The roads had narrowed further. Normally such recklessness would have thrilled her, but for some inexplicable reason she found no joy in it and Lionel's behaviour grated on her. On the point of telling him so she was forced to cling to the sides of her seat as he made a tight skidding turn around a corner. Then she was shrieking at him to stop, sick with panic. He pulled frantically at the brake: the car twisted and skidded toward a solid mass of people stretched across the street. Alexandra was thrown forward over the dashboard, knocking her hat across her face. She heard a mixture of alarming sounds that set her heart racing, then the car came to a standstill in a cloud of steam.

Cautiously she sat up, pulling her hat off and dropping it on the seat beside her as she breathed with relief.

"By jove, I'd forgotten about them," murmured Lionel.

Looking at him she realised he had gone white around the corners of his mouth. "Forgotten what?"

Following the direction of his gaze, she saw a confusion of coolies and wheelbarrows where men had tried to run from the path of the car and merely fallen over each other in their panic. Her heart was still racing, and her legs felt weak. She realised they could have ploughed through that crowd.

"Whatever are they doing there?" she asked in brittle tones.

"Striking. The levy on wheelbarrows has gone up again and they can't afford to pay it."

Still shocked she said angrily, "Striking? If they stop work they won't have any money at all!"

"Exactly," replied Lionel in similar fashion. "They are prepared to starve rather than bow to imperial demands. If *that* doesn't show where their loyalties lie nothing ever will."

"Oh, for heaven's sake, this is hardly the time to throw your ridiculous socialist theories at me," she cried. "The point is *they* shouldn't be blocking the street, and *you* shouldn't have been driving so fast."

He rounded on her. "Oh, that's just dandy coming from *you*."

Alexandra had had enough. She seized the handle of her door with the intention of walking off away from him, but her attention was taken by movement ahead. For a moment or two she stared in disbelief. The whole scene had turned ugly. The coolies were moving slowly toward the car waving their arms angrily. Some were brandishing sticks and chunks of rock. There was no doubting their intention.

"Lion, they're going to mob us," she whispered appalled. "Back out quickly!"

But he had recognised the danger and was already struggling to get the engine started. "The bally thing has stalled and the front wheels are wrenched too far round," he panted. "It'll take some manoeuvring to back out."

It was then she felt a surge of real fear. It was the first time she had actually come face to face with the anti-foreign violence that had been prevalent in Shanghai for some months, and she was shaken by a curious thrilling apprehension that made her feel intensely aware of everything around her. She had lived all her life in Shanghai, but never had the narrow Chinese-style streets or their inhabitants appeared threatening, as they did now. Her nerves jumped as the advance guard of the mob swarmed toward the bonnet of the car and began beating the metal with their sticks. They were shouting, gesticulating, and crowding in as those in the rear jostled against their fellows. The noise of the thrashing sticks reverberated throughout the interior of the car, menacing and determined. Her throat grew dry. Surely they would do no worse than that? Yet as she looked at the sea of faces around her there was a hatred written on those lined features that shook her.

"Lion, *please* get this thing started," she began, but her words were drowned by the roar of the engine.

Her companion gave a shout of triumph and began pulling levers as he tugged the wheel round. "That's made them back off a bit. Hold tight, Sandy. I'm going to try to bring her round and we might shoot off suddenly."

The coolies had backed off somewhat, but when she risked a quick glance over her shoulder Alexandra saw the main reason for the partial retreat. Streaming around the corner was an entire detachment of Sikh police which began to fan out all around the car in defensive protection. A sergeant poked his head through the window with advice to Lionel on the best route to take to avoid further trouble. Students were on the march again in support of the wheelbarrow men, he said, and rioting had now begun in the Nanking Road through which they had just passed. He advised the pair to get home as soon as possible and remain there for the remainder of the day. Violent clashes were expected to grow. The Shanghai Volunteer Force had been put on full alert.

No sooner had he finished speaking than stones began to fly as the policemen charged the coolies now sheltering behind their wheelbarrows. With all her senses alert Alexandra recorded the savage notes in voices surrounding her, the look of fear and hatred in dark, dark eyes, the jerky defiance of men whose movements were governed by recklessness. Her memory filed away the sound of stones clattering on the pavement, glass windows shattering, grunts and yells as men faced each other in violence. As the car slowly eased round and backed she was conscious of faces peering from the minute window apertures in the first floors of tiny, dark shop premises, of the absence of dogs and children who had fled their normal playground in the streets and, lastly, of another crowd of Chinese pressing toward them down a side street, waving red flags and chanting in unison.

The car was moving away from it toward safety, yet she felt the apprehension of pursuit and escape. The yearning she had felt all week grew within her breast and, as Lionel turned the car into an empty street, the visions now cut off from her view began to merge with her mind visions of a snowscape and the relentless pursuit of women born to wealth. All at once, her body grew weak with excitement and the yearning within her swelled to unbearable proportions. So *this* was the heart-clutch of fear and danger; *this* was emotion at its most expressive! How well she would now be able to interpret it with brush and colours, how well she could express such emotion on faces and in movements.

She heard Lionel's voice, but nothing of what he said. All she wanted was to hold on to that feeling, that acute awareness of life in the balance, and all the way to her home her thoughts hung in an elusive opaque mixture of snowy wastes and crowding odorous buildings peopled by coolies. The visual kaleidoscope was so nearly within her grasp, it needed but one more experience, one more moment of emotional revelation to complete it. In a flash, she knew without doubt that the only man who could give her the final answer was out on the Yangtze plain working on a railway bridge. It seemed unlikely she would be given the opportunity to unlock his soul in order to release her own.

On their safe return to the house they encountered James Clitheroe in the hall, standing at the foot of the stairs talking to his employer. Both men turned as the pair entered.

"You did the best thing to return," said Garrard briskly. "It looks like turning into something of a nasty day. There has already been rioting in the Nanking Road."

Alexandra looked only at her father. "We were caught in it. The wheelbarrow men surrounded us brandishing sticks and great pieces of stone. The car had stalled and we couldn't get away. They were banging the bodywork and shaking their fists at us. I have never been the recipient of such active animosity before."

Garrard turned to Clitheroe with a nod. "There you are, James. Evidence of attacks on foreign residents. I think you should mobilise at once."

Alexandra continued to stare at her father, a burning, protesting sensation rising with every minute, but it was James Clitheroe who turned to her in some anxiety, trying to ignore the presence of Lionel beside her.

"Are you all right, Miss Mostyn? They didn't hurt you?"

"Not in the slightest," she replied with brittle bravado. "I found it all just too exciting for words. There was I, the helpless victim of maddened Chinamen, about to be dragged off to a fate worse than death, when a detachment of police rushed to my rescue and defended my honour to a man. It was the most *divine* adventure."

To her satisfaction she saw her father's lips tighten angrily and knew he had been moved by *some* emotion. But Clitheroe looked acutely nonplussed by her response, and she felt suddenly very sorry for the young man who was obliged to go out into the violence she had just left. The echo of her fear was still with her, causing her to smile warmly at him.

"You look very impressive in your uniform, Jimmy. Dressed as a soldier and armed with a revolver you'd make any wilting damsel feel safe."

His plump face turned pink, and she realised he thought she was making fun of him. Thinking suddenly of firelight shining on the buttons of a dark-blue military tunic she impulsively put her hand upon his sleeve.

"I was frightened out there, to be honest, Jimmy. I hope you'll be all right."

His feelings were much too plainly revealed in his eyes. Her conscience smote her. Having always treated his dog-like adoration like a mistress keeping her pet in its proper place, she wondered momentarily if he had been hurt by it. Then she caught her father's steely, aloof glance and dismissed the thought. Jimmy should have more strength of character than to languish after a girl he knew he could never have. He deserved to be hurt.

Any lingering sympathy vanished when the young man in the uniform of the Shanghai Volunteer Corps gave a showy military salute in farewell. It was so reminiscent of a musical comedy, so overmeticulously executed, so foreign to a man she had known as a sober clerk for years, an irrepressible laugh burst from her.

"Oh, Jimmy, this isn't the Western Front you know! It's just a few striking wheelbarrow coolies with sticks."

Clitheroe departed with unusual speed, and her father said coldly, "Do you never take *anything* seriously, Alexandra?"

She rounded on him in instant anger. "Yes, I take myself seriously—especially when my life is in danger as it was just over an hour ago."

His lip curled. "Danger? You said yourself they were only a few striking wheelbarrow men."

"It *was* dangerous, sir," said Lionel breaking his own long silence. "This time someone will have to take note of them because they have the support of the students and the workers' unions."

"The support of the Communists, you mean."

Lionel bristled. "Someone has to protect their interests."

"*We* protect their interests—the Shanghai Municipal Council."

"With a minority of Chinese members? The Council is overwhelmingly full of influential foreigners."

Garrard began to walk away from him into the drawing room. "This is an international city, Armitage. Naturally, it must be governed by an international body."

"An international city *on Chinese soil*."

Lionel must have been more shaken by their experience than Alexandra thought or he would never have argued so stubbornly with her father. She took off her coat and hat, handed them to Lai-Hi, then followed the two men down the shallow steps into the large room where a fire danced despite the brilliant sunshine. Garrard was lighting a cigar, and when he had sucked and puffed sufficiently to make smoking possible, he took the Havana from his mouth and fixed Lionel with his cold stare.

"Your father was a member of the Council until he had that tragic boating accident. He was a prominent man in Shanghai, much loved and respected by the Chinese. Through him much of the white slaving was stopped and he worked tirelessly on schemes for cleaning up the brothels and ending child prostitution." He waved his cigar at the young man. "Yes, you are about to tell me he made a fortune out of China. I will not deny it . . . but you are only too happy to take advantage of the fact and adopt the same style of living he enjoyed. Your sentiments sound very noble, but are synonymous with the thinking of the new generation. You can't have it both ways, Armitage. If you preach championship of the coolie you must get completely into his skin. All you are is a wealthy young political fool who thinks in idealistic terms. From the extreme comfort of your position you chant 'China for the Chinese' but have no concept of what that would involve."

Provoked into a flood of political fervour, Lionel furiously defended himself. "I know it would involve a complete revolution before it could be achieved, and that would rid China of the grasping landowners and warlords who have bled the common people dry for centuries. It would mean freedom from oppression, a chance for the Chinese people to advance their own abilities and talents for the good of the populace, and give them the right every race should have to govern itself."

Garrard drew on his cigar with slow unconcern. "*Idealistic balderdash*," was his comment after blowing a cloud of smoke. "My dear fellow, if it was as simple as that the whole world would be paradise. As I said, before preaching ideals one has first to get inside the Chinaman's skin. He is simple, governed by superstitious paganisms, and so used to oppression he would not understand freedom of choice if given it. I will grant that there is now in China a nucleus of civilised, Western-educated men who are awake to China's vulnerability and national weakness. Aided, partially financed, and fiercely spurred on by Soviet Russians they aim to 'liberate' the Chinese people—by which they mean they intend to overrun the entire country with an army of untrained, uneducated zealots who are quite prepared to slaughter thousands of their countrymen along with any foreigners who get in their way, in order to make China a better place to live in."

"It succeeded in Russia," snapped Lionel, as white around the mouth as he had been in the trapped car.

"The revolution succeeded, yes. But is the country a better place? One sees thousands of 'Whites' down in Shanghai who are prepared to live by their wits and without a country rather than accept what their masters dictate. Russia has merely exchanged one form of oppression for another."

Lionel flung down the motoring helmet in anger. "I will not accept that. The country's wealth has been fairly distributed, the great houses given over to accommodate those who formerly lived in hovels, and each man given a status. The nation is ruled by a government rather than a tyrant."

"An elected government? I suggest the Russian people have no more choice now than they had before."

"They are no longer starving in the cities or slaving for the aristocrats in the country estates. The land has been given to the people."

"Who have no idea how to husband it."

"They can be taught."

Garrard tapped the ash from his cigar, very calm in contrast to the youngster. "Therein lies the crux of the matter. Revolution imposes instant changes. Those at its head have been training for months, often years, for their new roles as rulers. But the masses, the simple citizens, are forced into instant situations they cannot handle. They can be taught, as you said, *but it takes time*. In Russia it is too late. The dread deed is done. The people agonised for freedom, but they go on agonising. Who knows when or if they will ever recover? Here in China it has not yet happened. There *is* time for the people to be taught . . . and that is what we are doing."

"By holding monopolies on all public services, and a working majority on all committees or boards of directors? They will never learn that way."

"Neither will they if we listen to Chiang Kai-Shek and sail away home. Western men may control this city, but Western money controls the Chinese economy. Withdraw that and you will have a situation even worse than in Russia."

Lionel was so carried away he leant forward in challenging fervour. "Will men like you *ever* sail away home?"

"Will you ever exchange your desk at the bank for a coolie's wheelbarrow?" snapped Garrard. "You can discuss with me the long-term policy for China when you are no longer wet behind the ears, Armitage. Until then, I advise you to keep your adolescent ideas to yourself, or your countrymen might wonder about your loyalties. By God, I believe Rawlings was right when he said you were ripe for Bolshevik recruitment."

Alexandra had been listening to it all in silence, but the references to Russia, and the evidence that her father was prepared to agree with Mark Rawlings on anything at all were too much to resist.

"I can't see what Chiang Kai-Shek's little army has to do with the wheelbarrow strike, or the revolution in Russia."

Her father turned in astonishment, as if he had forgotten she was present. "I don't suppose you can, Alexandra. I am surprised you have even heard of Chiang Kai-Shek. You are usually far too busy making a spectacle of yourself in Shanghai society—mainly in the company of Armitage himself." He turned back to Lionel. "You should practise what you preach, my dear fellow. Is it any wonder the Chinese have fears for their future when they see how the new generation of foreign residents behaves?"

With that crushing question he threw the stub of his cigar into the fire and went out. Alexandra shrugged resignedly, but Lionel, less used to such treatment, was shattered. In his household he was the only male. His mother and Dot tended to look up to him and respect his opinions. With no father or brothers to argue his authority he liked to believe himself infallible. Alexandra never questioned his pronouncements. She found them boring or amusing, according to her mood. Now, quite suddenly, she wanted to know the facts; wanted to know so much that had become important to her since meeting the man who had been part of it all.

"Don't be upset, sweetie," she murmured. "He speaks like that so often there is no longer any personal venom in his remarks." She patted the sofa. "Come and sit beside me. There's so much I want to ask you."

He stood defiantly. "I think I'll go home."

"Oh, don't be silly, Lion! He says things like that to me daily."

"You're a girl. It's different."

That comment was like a red rag to a bull, but she was well versed in methods more subtle than anger—methods which brought the results she aimed for where men were concerned.

"Of course it's different, sweetie. That's why you have to tell me what all this is about revolution. You are such an authority on politics, and I don't understand them in the least. For instance, Mark Rawlings apparently made a madly heroic dash across Russia with a trainload of troops and a Tsarist colonel's family. Father says he was decorated for outstanding bravery when he reached England. Mark wouldn't talk about it, naturally, but I'm just *dying* to know why they should have been hunted like animals. The Reds actually vowed to murder every one of them, because they didn't agree with the revolutionary dictates. Surely you wouldn't advocate something similar in China, if that were true. I mean, you *are* English, darling, aren't you?"

The strategy worked even better than she had hoped. Lionel snatched up his helmet in a passion.

"I suppose it was not enough that I got you safely back here this morning. Their policy is to kill all foreigners, you know. It was only because *I* was there that they didn't smash into the car and finish you off. They know me and know I support them. I'm one of the few Englishmen they trust." He walked away to the foot of the steps, then turned to accuse her. "I suppose it would be entirely different if I wore a uniform covered in insignia. I saw how you vamped that fellow

Clitheroe just now. Well, if that's what you want, go off with your imperialist medal-covered major with one foot in the grave. But the time for men like him is coming to an end. The foreign-devil soldiers will be the first to die. I hope you are prepared to go down with him, because I won't rescue you again."

It was all too melodramatic for her and she began to laugh. "Oh, Lion, you really are too amusing for words."

He gripped the helmet hard. "The time is not far off when you won't find life at all amusing. I feel sorry for you, Sandy."

He went out leaving her suddenly disquieted. He had never been quite so passionate before, neither had her father bothered to take him seriously until this morning. An embryo Bolshevik, Mark had said. Surely that could not be true? She had believed Lionel adopted his political views to suit fashion. He could not seriously ally himself with something that not only opposed his own nation but advocated such terrible tyranny over helpless people, could he? Yet Mark had spoken to her mother of defending her against the Reds and, more seriously to her father, of facing them with guns while civilians hid behind barricades in Shanghai. Revolution! Not here in China where she had lived all her life! Not here, where they were outnumbered by their own servants who had always appeared so happy! Not in Shanghai with its confidence and prosperity!

The fear of that pressing angry crowd began to return, however, and she was no longer certain of those things she had always taken for granted. Her father had just said that instant change was disastrous. Her own life appeared to have undergone just that since an evening a week ago, and she was finding it difficult to handle. She prayed it would not become disastrous before long.

CHAPTER FIVE

The riots continued sporadically for several days in Shanghai. The wheelbarrow strike was used by students, political agitators and Russian Communist agents in the city as an excuse for large-scale disruption in the factories and godowns. Mobs rushed through the streets shouting anti-foreign slogans, waving a mixture of Nationalist banners and the red flag of Communism (most being unsure of the difference, if any, between the two creeds) and calling upon all Chinese to rally behind the Kuomintang army led by their great liberator Chiang Kai-Shek, which had already triumphantly marched from Canton to Hankow sweeping everything before it.

The foreign powers in Shanghai grew deeply worried. Not that the Nationalist/Communist army was invincible—indeed, its advance had been made almost without bloodshed due to the warlords' armies fleeing without firing a shot. But where Sun Yat-Sen had failed ten years earlier Chiang Kai-Shek was arousing fanatical national fervour in people who saw, at last, a glimmer of hope in the darkness of their oppressed lives. Aside from his own army of men with mixed ideals, beliefs and aims, the Chinese leader was stirring the ordinary coolie to express his feelings violently. Workers and merchants in the cities were listening to Soviet agents who preached the overthrow of those presently in power; villagers were listening to tales filtering from the south and resisting the ways they had been forced to follow for centuries. The women were proving most militant, driving their menfolk to answer the call, arranging demonstrations, and showing themselves to be ready to take up arms against any of their own people, aside from the hated 'foreign devils', who opposed them.

The taking of Hankow was a blow that alarmed those in Shanghai. It was far too close for comfort. Canton, way down in the south, had always been violently anti-foreign, so the fall of that trading port had merely been a case of history repeating itself. Shanghai was entirely different. Throughout the history of East-West wars it had stood open to all and grown the more prosperous because of it. The newly-occupied city of Hankow was on the Yangtze, the great waterway that led straight to the international port and the open sea. If the Kuomintang advanced up the river, there was no foreign fleet to stop them. There was not even a regular army garrison in Shanghai.

In the Mostyn household the tension was all too apparent. Garrard was hardly ever at home. Those hours he did not spend in his office were devoted to discussions at clubs and the various business premises of other prominent members of the International Settlement and the French Concession. The result of these meetings was a doubling in strength of the Shanghai Volunteer Corps, and an earnest request to foreign military sources for detachments of regular troops to be sent to the port on stand-by.

For the moment, the crisis in China took precedence over the railway bridge disaster on the few occasions Garrard shared with his wife and daughter, and Alexandra thought it boded well for Mark, who might be let off her father's hook, after all. She could not banish him from her thoughts during those days that followed her experience with the angry wheelbarrow-men. He seemed to be wholly intertwined with her new-found interest in the political situation and her artistic yearning for fulfilment through his hinted experience of violence. He had spoken of his own inevitable role as a soldier should there be conflict in China, and the rumours of an emergency force gathering to the defence of Shanghai left her with the hope that he might have to form a member of it and return to the city. It would be her only opportunity to wrest from him details of that which presently held her fascinated.

Yet her chance to see him again came in an unexpected way. Descending the stairs one morning a week after the rioting she found James Clitheroe waiting to accompany her father to a meeting.

"Good morning, Miss Mostyn," he said with some awkwardness after her teasing at their last meeting. "Your father asked me to come in and wait while he collected his notes."

"Hallo, Jimmy," she said quietly. "Duty done and no wounds, I see."

He swallowed. "There might be worse yet." It was said with a suggestion of suffering to come, and she smiled with unusual gentleness.

"So everyone says. But with people like you to defend us there is really nothing to worry about, is there?"

Unsure of her he mumbled something about defences having to be built around foreign concessions and troops being sent to protect Western residents and their property.

It touched a chord in her memory. "Major Rawlings spoke of barricades around Shanghai. I didn't take him seriously then," she said thoughtfully. "I wonder how this will affect him out there at the bridge. Which duty comes first—the bridge or our safety?"

Clitheroe puffed himself up with self-confidence. "I shouldn't think it will affect *him* in any way. He goes back to Hong Kong in two days' time."

Her pulse quickened. "Two days? How do you know?"

"He came in from the bridge last night. I understand he intends to write his report and deliver it to Mr Mostyn's office this afternoon at three. My own secretary booked a berth for him on a ship for Hong Kong leaving on Monday." He snatched a glance at his watch. The passing of time was plainly worrying him. "A pudding-headed kind of fellow, I should say. Who, in his right mind, would choose to stop out there on a freezing marsh when he could have made a quick inspection then come back here where there's a bit of life?"

"Perhaps he resents being told how to do his own job."

"Then what is he doing in the army? He's supposed to obey orders."

"Is that why my father chose him?" she asked quietly.

He adopted a superior attitude—the kind Alexandra resented so much. "I really couldn't say why he was chosen. Mr Mostyn does not care to discuss confidential matters except with his most immediate staff."

"I'm his immediate family, sweetie," she said bitingly. "I don't think you'd be letting down the side by telling me."

He flushed. "Miss Mostyn, I didn't mean . . ."

"Didn't mean what?" she demanded, not allowing him to get away with a half-finished sentence.

Wallowing in the mire of embarrassment he made matters worse for himself. "I mean, of course you are his daughter . . . but this is *business*, not social. You wouldn't understand his reasons."

"Is your understanding so superior to mine that you do?" she asked icily. "I have known my father much longer than you have, Jimmy, and where Mark Rawlings is concerned I suggest his reasons are inexplicable. He has found a man he cannot buy, for once, and the usual procedures have had to be abandoned. No doubt, Father will eventually triumph, but I back Major Rawlings all the way and for as long as he can hold out. The only one with a pudding head is you, darling, if you pretend my father has the whip hand in this situation. No wonder the poor man is being rushed back to Hong Kong on Monday. Have you been given the task of delivering him gagged and bound to the ship?"

The suggestion that he was no more than her father's errand boy completed Clitheroe's humiliation, but he was saved from answering by the arrival of Garrard Mostyn who muttered an emotionless greeting to his daughter and hurried the young assistant away to the waiting car.

Despite all the daring things she had done in the past, Alexandra was ridiculously nervous as she walked into the building at five past three that afternoon and made her way up to the first floor. One could never be certain that this man would react according to plan. With him her bold approach did not always work, and he must not slip through her fingers when the meeting meant so much to her.

The corridor was icy as she walked up and down, tensed for the sound of a door opening. She prayed no one who knew her would come along before her quarry appeared. She shivered in the fur-trimmed costume of dark-green wool and thought gloomily that 'sex-appeal' was something of which he had never heard. Being the kind of man to appreciate her mother's brand of feminine attraction, she might just as well have worn an unflattering tweed coat for warmth for all the good her new costume and close-fitting fur hat would do her.

Time passed, and she began to fear he had not come as planned. She did not want to go to the outer office to enquire because old Gatesby was an inquisitive devil who would give her away completely. Twice she was on the brink of giving up, then called herself faint-hearted. When the door finally did open along the corridor all her nerves jumped in expectation. She did not immediately recognise him for he wore a padded jacket and twill breeches, but the thick curly hair and the manner in which he strode away told her all she wanted to know. She set off in pursuit. Several yards from him she undid the clasp of her handbag, then dropped it onto the floor so that the contents spilled everywhere.

"*Damn!*" she cried loudly, stepping hard on a small mirror. "It's broken. That's seven years' bad luck."

Quickly squatting beside the bag and keeping her head down she prayed hard that he was gentleman enough for her purpose. The toes of two highly-polished boots appeared beside her lipstick and powder compact.

"How careless of you, Miss Mostyn."

She looked up, eyes big with surprise. "*Mark!* Whatever are you doing here? I thought you were out on the Yangtze plain." It was just as she had rehearsed, but she spoilt it all by asking involuntarily, "How did you know it was me?"

He was not smiling. "You are the only girl I know who uses language like that . . . and who wears such short skirts."

She got up slowly, heartbeat quickening. Had his eyes always been such an arresting dark brown? "You've been with my father?"

"Yes."

"He's made you angry again."

"Not really. What are you doing here in such an unlikely place?"

Her rehearsed words had long since flown, so she improvised badly. "Oh . . . er . . . talking to James Clitheroe. He has an office two doors beyond my father's."

"Yes, I know." He seemed about to say more, then changed his mind. He looked on the point of leaving.

"It's very cold today," she said desperately. "I was just going for some tea. Will you come with me?"

It gave her some satisfaction to know he was nonplussed, and she took a gamble by adding, "It will do wonders for my reputation to be seen with an older man."

He gave her a long look. "You are your father's daughter, right enough. Determination in every inch."

"That isn't an answer."

"I . . . I'm hardly dressed for a tea-dance."

"I'm not wearing my 'alluring' dress, either."

He fought the smile for a moment or two, then it broke through to touch her unexpectedly and painfully. "You'll come to a sticky end one of these days, if you persist in going around inviting men to tea."

She smiled back, hardly knowing what was happening to her, and decidedly light-headed. "It's the risk that is so exciting."

When she began walking away along the corridor he halted her.

"I think we should pick up those things you threw all over the floor, don't you? They appear to have served their purpose."

She spun round with a question on her lips, but he was already bending down to gather up the feminine trifles with fingers unused to handling them.

"I met Clitheroe on my way in to see your father," he went on. "He was off to the French Concession and did not expect to be back this afternoon."

In silence she held out her handbag while he put all her paraphernalia inside, then stood up to kick the broken pieces of glass to the side of the corridor. Still in silence they left the building and turned into the Nanking Road. Alexandra was now feeling far too warm in the flattering dark-green costume.

When they reached the elegant hotel, Mark stopped at the entrance and faced her. "I'm quite willing to have tea with you, alluring dress or not, but these are my working clothes and are bound to raise a few eyebrows in a place like *that*. It might be better to make it some other time."

"What other time?" she asked too quickly. "You go back to Hong Kong on Monday."

"So you know about that, too!"

Taking refuge in habit she grabbed his arm and pulled him toward the revolving doors. "Sweetie, you'll be a sensation in there. With me as your companion you can get away with anything, I promise."

He protested no more, even when the head waiter resolutely looked in the other direction as they entered the palm-dotted tea-rooms.

"Luigi!" called Alexandra imperiously, and the man turned with a resigned smile of welcome. "Miss Mostyn, apologies. I did not see you." His thin, superior, middle-European face reflected the look of a man forced to serve those of whom he disapproved, yet who were too influential to ignore. "Your *usual* table?" he asked in a tone that suggested she might prefer to hide her escort away behind the potted plants.

"Of course, the usual table," she told him. "I have given you tips large enough to have *bought* it by now."

With that she swept between the tables with such panache all eyes were drawn to her and, inevitably, to the tall man in breeches and pullover following behind her. She was delighted. It restored the command over herself she had been in danger of losing so short a time ago.

When they were seated and had given the order to the boy, Mark leant toward her and said in a low voice, "I warned you how it would be. There are four matrons behind you busily gathering their belongings prior to leaving."

She leant forward too, liking the excuse to be close to him. "They'd do that if I had come in alone." She smiled. "You're not worried, are you?"

"So long as you are not planning to dance the Charleston on the table tops."

It caught her painfully unawares and uncertain of him. Something told her he was perfectly serious. "I don't think you'd make as good a partner as Lionel Armitage," she said sharply.

He frowned. "It's my advanced age, I suppose."

Her rehearsed script had gone from her head. All she could think was that he had become very important to her, and unless she handled this meeting right he would go out of her life before giving her all she needed.

"You look tired," she said, noting the strain on his face.

He nodded and leant back in his chair. "It's not easy to sleep in a small boat built for the Chinese who are a lot shorter than I am. It was too cold to sleep much anyway. The canal iced over nearly every night."

The small string orchestra appeared through a curtain at the back of a large rectangular alcove, and made much of settling into their chairs and tuning up.

Above the noise Alexandra said, "You withstood it for two weeks. That's twelve days longer than my father expected."

"So he told me this afternoon."

"Did you provide the answer he wanted, after all?"

He shrugged. "I found the truth. It wasn't exactly the answer he wanted. He was pretty cut up about it when he saw my report."

The thought delighted her. "Did you fall to fisticuffs?"

"What?" he asked, startled out of his memories of the meeting, apparently.

She made punching motions in the air with her fists. "Blows! You are the athletic type, you once told me."

He gave a faint smile. "Swimming is more my style. I certainly wouldn't box with men as influential as your father, Miss Mostyn."

"But you box with words, no matter how influential he might be," she reminded him. "And don't you think it's time you stopped this 'Miss Mostyn' business?"

"I refuse to call you 'Sandy'," he said at once.

"Alexandra is out of the question, from you. Only my parents call me by my full name."

Conversation was halted by the arrival of the tea-wagon which was left beside Alexandra, the plates of sandwiches and cakes being placed on the table between them.

"How about 'Alex', then?" he asked as she began to pour the tea.

"Oh . . . *yes*." She looked up to meet his glance and knew she would never want anyone else to use that name. "I like that very much," she said softly.

The orchestra began on a selection from *Showboat* and the conversational level of those taking tea rose accordingly. In that high-ceilinged room cooled in the summer by fans, heated now by fires in two large open hearths, sat the high society of Shanghai, gossiping and passing the afternoon in the accepted genteel manner that kept at bay all noisome dragons. In that elegant tea-room it was possible for patrons to imagine themselves in London, Harrogate, Bath, Paris, Lyons, Vienna, Budapest, Berlin or New York—whichever city their inner selves hugged close. For an hour or so over cucumber sandwiches, buttered toast and petit fours, noisy, smelly, incomprehensible, wild, beautiful but alien China was forgotten. To step through those doors into the fern-softened austereness of Western civilisation was a safety valve. It was not half a world away; just a step through double doors on any afternoon of the week. It was comforting, especially to those whose age told them they would never see home again.

As Alexandra ate sandwiches with unusual lack of appetite she was well aware of all the eyes turned in her direction, and the confidential whispering over teacups. Mark seemed quite unconcerned about it now, although he did look very out of place in a room filled with tea-gowns and tailored suits. She personally found him visually exciting. The casual clothes emphasised his athletic build and gave her a glimpse of the engineer as opposed to the soldier. Despite the disapproval of the older element, he was easily the most interesting-looking man in the room.

The well-known atmosphere of the place helped her to recover her composure, and she felt it was time to broach the subject for which she had planned the meeting.

"I had an adventure last Saturday," she began.

He raised his eyebrows. "And they still let you in places like this?"

It did not amuse her at that stage. Could he not see she was perfectly serious? "My life is not entirely devoted to scandal, Mark. We ran into a mob of coolies."

"We?"

"Lionel."

"The budding Bolshevik—he must have been in his element. Where did this happen?"

"On the edge of the Settlement. We were going to lunch with some Americans and almost ran into the coolies who were blocking the street. They were wheelbarrow men who were striking because the levy has gone up again."

"Mmmm, well the things are a bit outmoded, aren't they?"

The Shanghai resident was immediately up in arms. "They might be by your railway standards, but the wheelbarrows are a feature of this city. Before the advent of the rickshaw they were the only means of transport. Even now, the poorer Chinese depend on them. Higher levies for the owners mean higher charges for the passengers, and they can't afford to pay."

He held up his hands defensively. "Sorry! Had I known you were such a student of Chinese internal affairs I would never have attempted to denigrate your whimsical wheelbarrows."

Her temper began to rise. "Don't humour me, Mark."

He took in her expression and pursed his lips. "Perhaps we should try another subject—something more suited to afternoon tea, and a little less sensitive to you."

"How about Russia in 1919?" she challenged.

He grew still, his eyes darkening. "I thought I had already said all I had to say on that subject to you."

"You said nothing. For some reason you refuse to tell me."

"I wasn't aware that there was any reason why you should expect to be told."

He had grown resistant, almost hostile. It was all going wrong, yet she seemed powerless to say the words that would make him understand. Her own stubborn personality brought up her hostility to match his, fighting what she saw as his attempt to dismiss her as inconsequential.

"A citation for bravery, a dramatic train journey across hostile wilds, a Tsarist colonel's family saved from mob murder at the risk of your own life—everyone else knows what you did," she cried. "Why should you withhold the facts from me in this ridiculous fashion?"

He put down his napkin angrily. "You begin to sound too much like your father. My private life is not for hire, Miss Mostyn, only my engineering skill . . . and I'm certain *you* are not interested in that."

The unmistakable suggestion of patronising disapproval put the torch to her explosive mood. Such treatment from men usually brought shock tactics from her. To this one man in particular was added the desire to hurt him, cut into his armour and expose the soft flesh beneath to her searching eyes.

Offering him the plate of cakes, she asked in clear ringing tones, "Could it be that the Tsarist women were saved from murder, but not from a 'fate worse than death'? In the absence of the Colonel did you perhaps console them too well? Is that why you refuse to speak about Russia?"

If a gun had been fired in that staid tea-room he could not have been more stunned. With the orchestra between items, those near their table heard her words quite clearly and reacted typically. The entire room seemed to be waiting with bated breath for his answer as he sat staring at her with the same look on his face that he had worn on his arrival at her home for dinner.

"I had no idea you sank to this kind of thing for amusement," he said slowly under his breath.

"I'm . . . I'm not laughing," she managed, appalled by the total success of her intent to hurt him.

"I am certainly not staying until you do. My abrupt departure will hardly be a surprise to anyone here: it must happen to you very frequently." He stood up and flung some notes onto the table. "That should cover everything. I'm too much of a gentleman to let you pay for your own entertainment."

"Mark . . . I'm sorry," she whispered.

"*Sorry!* That's just another word to someone like you."

He was off across the room, the subject of every titillated glance. Unexpectedly out of her depth in a situation that had run away from her, Alexandra snatched up her bag and followed. She caught up with him on the pavement, forced into a hopping walk in order to keep pace with his long angry strides. He ignored her, but it was as if he was so distant he was unaware of anything surrounding him in that Chinese street. For the first time in her life she found herself caring deeply for a man she hardly knew. Never had she regretted her instinctive behaviour more. The young men of her set were either too shallow, too bent on creating a new and better world, or too self-absorbed to earn her admiration. She did not respect her father, or his earnest assistant, but this hurt and angry man beside her had suddenly prised open the shell of protective emancipation to expose her to an emotion she did not yet understand.

What she had done was hit out because she felt Mark treated her with disdain; as a social butterfly with gaudy wings and little intelligence. Yet, had she ever given him reason to believe she was anything more? With this particular man respect had to be earned. It was useless taking him by the collar and attempting to shake it from him. In that tea-room she had merely humiliated them both and dispelled what little rapport there had been between them. She preached equality, but he had shown her it was not gained by shouting as loudly as the rest. It came from within. Garrard Mostyn was socially powerful, financially superior, yet Mark Rawlings with 'lowly origins' had matched him with quiet determination and integrity. There was no doubt in her mind who had emerged the better man.

They were nearing his hotel now. Once he went inside she would have lost all hope of reaching him. All at once, it seemed more important to be part of his future than to draw out his mysterious past, but it would take something drastic to halt him now. Searching wildly for a solution, she decided sincerity might do it.

"You're right, Mark," she began rather breathlessly due to the rate of their progress. "Lots of men have walked out on me . . . but I have never come after them like this. I admit to being all the things you say I am, but if you go back to Hong Kong without giving me the chance to make amends I'll never learn the meaning of the word sorry."

At first, he appeared not to have heard, then he slowed his pace until he stopped to face her. His expression was still frightening in its bleakness.

"Is this a further means of amusing yourself?"

She swallowed her hurt. "None of it was meant for amusement, please believe that."

"But you engineered the meeting outside your father's office."

"Because I wanted your help. I appear to have made a mess of the whole thing."

"You appear to be making a mess of your entire life . . . and that of anyone you meet," he retorted coldly.

Perhaps she deserved it, but it hurt very deeply. "From anyone else that remark would have left me untouched," she admitted, shivering in the thin costume as a gust of cold wind raced through the street. "From you it is particularly wounding."

For a moment or two he stood regarding her uncertainly then, as she shivered again, he sighed and took her arm. "You'd better come inside to finish this conversation before you freeze to death in that inadequate costume. However, I warn you, if . . ." He thought better of finishing the sentence and led her into the foyer, which was warm and practically deserted. Waving away the white-coated boy who approached, he headed for a corner well away from the desk and entrance, and discreetly screened by potted plants.

It did not help Alexandra to realise why he had chosen such a distant corner-seat, and the knowledge that he did not yet believe one word she had said told her it was going to be uphill all the way. His impatience was patently obvious but, now she had been given another chance, she refused to allow him to rush her through something she sensed would have to be handled carefully. Sinking onto the velvet banquette she took out her cigarettes, inserted one in the long jade holder, and lit it. The action steadied her and gave her time to think. It also forced Mark to abandon his suggestion of imminent departure, and sit down on the opposite seat.

"Jimmy told me you were going back to Hong Kong on Monday," she confessed, "so I came to Father's office today because I had to talk to you."

"About what?" It was sharp and suspicious.

Drawing on the cigarette she blew out the smoke slowly. He was still extremely prickly, and she would get nowhere until his distrust had been removed.

"Father had his own unscrupulous campaign at dinner that night, Mark. It was very evident you had no wish to talk about that time in Russia, and only a man like him would have pushed you as he did.

However, it *was* brought into the open, and I have thought of little else since that evening. No . . . please listen," she added hastily as he made to get to his feet. "I won't question you about it. I merely want to explain why I tried to do so. It might help you to understand and forgive me for what happened just now."

It took him by surprise, that much was plain, but she did not miss the lingering air of scepticism in his expression. Doggedly she went on without allowing him to comment.

"You are the first person I have come across with the courage to stand up to Father. I was deeply impressed, and I worked out the reason for it. Your profession means more to you than social acceptance. Whatever may have happened to you in the past, you do still have a purpose in life. I have none."

"Whose fault is that?"

Realising that he was still restless, even bored, and all set to bring the encounter to a close, she retorted, "The fault is my father's." Letting that hang in the air while she drew once more on the cigarette, she saw that he was still sceptical. "I want, more than anything, to be an artist. I have talent," she added quickly seeing the dismissive look in his eyes. "I have a great deal of talent, Mark. Ask any connoisseur. I also have a great deal of money and every day of the week empty and yawning in front of me. There is nothing to stop my becoming as dedicated to art as you are to engineering, but it does not suit my father to have a Bohemian daughter. Garrard Mostyn's child does not wear smocks covered in paint, live in a garret, and mingle with a set of amoral loafers who thumb their noses at the world and demand huge sums of money for gaudy travesties of human life. *His* words," she explained through the sudden thickness in her throat.

Her companion frowned as he threw an arm along the back of the velvet seat and shifted position restlessly. "You defy him over everything else. Why not this?"

She gave a bitter smile. "There is an excellent art school in the French Concession, but one of its principals is a friend of my father so my application was turned down. I have quite a few good canvases at home, but no gallery in Shanghai will dare to exhibit them."

"So you exhibit your underwear instead."

It took her breath away, and she asked in despair, "You really have no time for me at all, have you?"

"I get very angry when I see youth being wasted. So many of my friends had no chance to do anything with theirs."

Silence fell, and she crushed out the cigarette with shaking fingers. Why had she imagined he would listen and sympathise after the way she had behaved? He did not walk off as she half expected, however.

"If it means so much to you, and you really have the talent you profess to have, why don't you simply go off and become an artist?" he asked. "There are other cities where he has no influence, surely."

She shook her head, looking at the pile of the carpet. "It's not that simple. If I left home he would sever all contact."

"Ah, *now* I understand."

Her head shot up as colour flooded her face. "*Oh no, you don't!* You don't understand any more than he does. It has nothing to do with money. The only thing that stops me from leaving—has stopped me all along—is that it would break my mother's heart. I'd go tomorrow, I'd work to earn money for canvases and paints, I'd make for London and paint until I dropped," she told him hotly, "but I won't let him do any more to her. You saw her in that chair. He drove her to it. Each time he puts on that air of a successful man bravely enduring the yoke of an invalid wife, each time he exploits her helplessness to gain sympathy, I hate him more. If I allowed him to drive me away, he would never let me see her again. I couldn't bear that, and it would break her completely to know I was alone and penniless." She faced him frankly. "Mother has old-fashioned ideas about women . . . as you have."

He studied her flushed face for quite a while, then put a hand to signal the hovering boy. "I think it might be a good idea to have a drink, after all." Ordering tea without consulting her, and a brandy for himself, he turned his attention back to her. "Things *are* different for women, however much you might fight the fact. My parents sacrificed a great deal to send me to a private school which would give me a good start in my engineering career. Yet I walked into a recruiting office and joined the army without even consulting them when I was still under eighteen. It seemed the right thing to do, and I went ahead without soul-searching. It probably broke my mother's heart, but everyone else saw it as my patriotic duty. However, had I been a *daughter*, I would have been condemned for deserting her after all she had done for me."

Not certain what he was really saying, Alexandra pointed out that his mother was not an invalid in a chair.

"I would have done exactly the same," he replied. "Men traditionally do what they feel they must, whatever the circumstances. Women cling to the home—have done since time immemorial."

He took the glass from a proffered tray and sipped his brandy as the boy arranged the tea things on the low table before Alexandra. She poured tea she did not really want whilst trying to sort out her thoughts. Was he telling her to forget her ambitions and tamely accept her female role in life? She had expected more understanding and sympathy from him, despite his old-fashioned notions on women. Perhaps she had hoped he would see an ally in his defiance of her father. The hope had been in vain, it seemed.

"I don't yet understand why you contrived a meeting with me in such a manner; why you thought I could help you," he said then. "I know nothing whatever of art."

"You know a great deal about emotion, though," she countered, hardly able to believe he had given her the exact opening she needed to broach the forbidden subject once more. "When you spoke so guardedly about Russia that evening I saw it revived feelings too strong to deny, but which you could not share. Father only created a brief word-picture, yet it lit a glow of inspiration inside me. I have talent so I paint, but nothing has ever filled me with such desire to express myself on canvas. All I have, at present, is a flat picture. It needs emotion to make it come alive and gain reality. *You* are the only person who can describe those emotions: what it felt like to flee for your life across that wild barbarous terrain, the fear, exhaustion, and sense of dedication toward those whose safety lay in your hands alone. Mark, I arranged this meeting today so that I could ask you for the missing link between my father's bald account and an experience so profound you cannot forget it, even now."

As he gazed at her across the few feet between them she realised, with a shock, that artistic fulfilment was no longer important against the longing now coursing through her. Then she identified the expression on his face as he got slowly to his feet, and it hurt her more than any words he had said that afternoon. He seemed to have difficulty in speaking at all, at first, then brought out his first sentence in a voice that shook.

"What happened in Russia in 1919 was not . . .. is not a subject for a *painting*." He almost spat the word at her in his anger. "My God, you have absolutely no understanding of life apart from the artificial cavortings that pass for social intercourse. Small wonder you only paint *flat* pictures. You'll never be an artist until you have *suffered*, Miss Mostyn . . . and dancing on tables or smoking cigarettes in imitation of men is no substitute, believe me."

He walked away from her for the second time that day, but she made no attempt to follow him now. Shaken she lit another cigarette, then crushed it in the ashtray immediately. Like her father, Mark Rawlings would never accept that she was anything more than a useless, shallow creature dependent on the wealth and security surrounding her, but, whereas she could not reach her father emotionally, she had aroused astonishing depths of feeling in Mark in a way she had never done with any other man. Someone on that life-or-death journey across Russia had touched him deeply—so deeply he had not recovered after seven years. Knowing it must have been a woman could not exactly be called suffering, but it was painfully near to it.

Monday morning dawned fine and bright, so Mark decided to walk to the bank. He had nothing else to fill the day until the boat sailed at five p.m. and he would spend too much time at the bar if he stayed in the hotel. Still fighting the urge to go once more to the White Russian quarter for further fruitless enquiries, he strolled along lost in thought. The first sight that met his eyes was one of Shanghai's famous wheelbarrows, two passengers sitting with their legs dangling while the old coolie pushed them along on the great front wheel of his hired vehicle. It brought an involuntary memory of the Mostyn girl's heated defence of them, and he frowned. It was impossible to fathom her. A mixture of boy and woman. Slim and flat as any youth, her daring, her defiance of rules and restraint, her cigarette smoking were all synonymous with boys testing life and finding their feet. Yet she was vividly feminine when she used her attractions the right way. Even he was not proof against them.

He had reflected on their last meeting when enough time had passed to enable him to think dispassionately, and admitted he was puzzled. Her loyalty to her mother had impressed him, along with her suggestion that Mostyn had been the root cause of his wife's condition. If her words had been sincere it suggested the girl might lead a lonely and unhappy life in that house, trapped there by her misguided attempt to compensate her mother for her limited life. Did she not realise nothing would compensate for a loveless marriage and life in a chair? He could not believe a woman like Alice Mostyn would wish her daughter to abandon all chance of happiness simply to stay at her side. So what was the truth about that family? He thought the parents easy enough to place—Garrard was ambitious and ruthless; Alice gentle, charming, but foolishly weak. It was their daughter who defied catagorising. Was she a mere social butterfly with the faults of both parents, or did she hide a deeper personality beneath defiance because she was afraid of being hurt?

He walked on along the street still frowning. Perhaps he should have been more tolerant, but it had been her heedless probing into his past that had made him so angry, her exposure to public ears of things locked away inside his soul. When she had revealed to him that what she wanted was to *paint* his experience, something inside him had exploded.

Suppose he had asked for details of her mother's illness because he wished to write a song about it? How would she have reacted? Mostyn had painted a word-picture of adventure, excitement and glory . . . and she had been inspired.

Those months in Russia had changed his life. He had gone out to a wild and enormous country of which he had known very little, from the simple need to avoid the England for which he had fought and sacrificed his youth. He had been unable to find the spirit he thought it should hold, found it impossible to communicate with or understand those who had stayed at home during those terrible four years. But his play for time had rebounded on him. That Slavic summer had been full of fear, exhaustion, horror, desperation, love, and immense inner pain. There had been achievement and destruction, close friendship and terrible loss, and at the end he had been left deeply scarred—emotionally as well as physically.

Lost in memories of those days, the whole thing seemed to come alive again when the air was rent by a fusillade of shots right beside him. Heart pumping his hand went instinctively for his revolver as he spun round to face his enemy. But he wore no gun; there was no enemy. He stood stock-still in that bustling street, recovering from something that had lived with him throughout his youth. The 'shots' had been nothing more than firecrackers let off by Chinese builders at the completion of yet another cigarette factory. 'Joss' had been good during the construction work, and thanks must be expressed, but the firecrackers were also to ward off any roaming evil spirits who thought to make a home in the new building.

He sighed heavily. Eight months in Hong Kong should have familiarised him with the rattling bangs of the Chinese firecracker. His nerves were too jumpy. Since he had arrived in Shanghai there had been too many reminders of the past—of conflict, of a Russian wilderness, of his first bridge. Those fourteen days on the Yangtze marsh had been strenuous, nerve-racking and uncomfortable. The underwater work had made him tense; the talk of that old legend of a warrior and the hundred dragons had stayed in the back of his mind until he left. The villagers of Lu-Seng wanted a third Englishman to die at that bridge. Well, it would not now be him. At five p.m. he would be on a ship bound for Hong Kong. Suddenly, he was immensely glad. Hamish Corcoran was an uneasy colleague, the coolies were hostile and withdrawn. As for the high-powered calculating world of the Mostyns, he had no affinity with or understanding of it. He walked on away from the cigarette factory with the prospect of Hong Kong's mild climate already warming him.

Once at the bank it should have been a simple matter of closing his temporary account and arranging for the balance to be returned to the Hong Kong branch, and it started out that way. But whilst looking through the several forms and letters clipped together with the card bearing Mark's name, the clerk came upon something that led him to excuse himself and go off to an inner office. Then he returned and asked Mark to go with him to see one of the junior under-managers who would like a word with him.

Mystified he went, but pulled up short at the door to the office when he read the name stencilled upon the glass in gold letters: 'MR LIONEL SUMMERFORD ARMITAGE'. Inside, at the desk, sat the youngster who had behaved so immaturely on the ship from Hong Kong, his hair smoothly oiled back, his face still unmarked by experience.

"Come in, Major Rawlings," invited the well-bred voice. "Take a seat, please." He nodded at the clerk. "That will be all."

For a junior under-manager the office was impressive. Plain walls, marble floor covered in oriental rugs, carved desk with out-turned legs, chairs of polished wood with rattan seats and backs; a telephone, nameboard and jade cigarette-box with matching lighter on the desk.

Armitage pushed these toward him. "Smoke?" he asked, playing the executive to perfection.

"No, thanks. I take it this is not merely to renew a shipboard acquaintance."

"Hardly. Besides, these are my business premises."

His tone was impertinent, but Mark resisted the temptation to put the boy down until he knew what the meeting was about. He did not wait long.

"Your account is considerably overdrawn, Major. The sum you arranged to transfer from Hong Kong was nowhere near adequate to cover your expenses. We were obliged to call upon your main account, only to find the amount to your credit disastrously small. The manager of the Hong Kong branch regrets he is unable to meet your debts. This raises the serious question of the loan we have been obliged to make you."

Disliking the fellow intensely for other reasons, Mark could only be glad of a legitimate opportunity to deflate the youngster with a quick stab of a financial pin.

"You've made a serious mistake, Armitage," he said with confidence. "I transferred enough funds to cover a prolonged stay in Shanghai. As it happens, it lasted only two weeks, and apart from a small bill for drinks and afternoon tea in a hotel, I have spent nothing."

The pale eyebrows went up. "Really?" With maddening slowness he opened a file on his desk and took out a sheaf of flimsy accounts, placing them before Mark as if dealing cards, and reciting the details of each as he did so.

"Hire of one diving suit, air pump, and auxiliary emergency breathing-apparatus . . . hire of four construction lamps . . . hire of four tripods for said lamps . . . hire of cabin motor-launch for one week and four days . . . account for food supplies for one week and four days." He smiled triumphantly. "The total comes to almost exactly double the sum you have on deposit in the Hong Kong branch of this bank."

Something began to burn inside Mark's chest, and he lost all inclination to take the sprig down a peg or two. Looming at the back of his mind was a possibility he was unwilling to accept.

"I'm not sure what this is all about, but I gave those people instructions to send their accounts to Garrard Mostyn. He told me to order whatever I needed to do the job."

"Just so," said the banker in accepted style. "It appears that in Mr Mostyn's opinion the job he gave you did not require the services of a diver, and should have taken no longer than three days. That being the case, he has settled all expenses to that order . . . leaving all costs incurred over and above that as your personal expenditure." He tapped the papers. "These accounts were settled by us five days ago in the confidence that you had enough in your main account to meet them." He leant back to regard Mark with infinite relish. "I fear, Major, that you are in debt to us for seven hundred and fifty pounds."

The smooth voice ran on outlining the details of various means of repayment, warning him of the interest that would be charged on the loan and which would accumulate the longer it remained effective. He went on to speak of the need to notify the army authorities of such a large overdraft, but Mark sat through the stages of shocked anger hearing Alexandra Mostyn's voice saying "*My father usually wins in the end*!"

Then, in the middle of a long speech on extended loans by the young banker, he got to his feet and silenced him.

"You are wasting your breath, Armitage. I'm not letting Mostyn get away with this."

The smug smile appeared again. "He seems to have already done so. Of course, I don't know all the jolly ins and outs of your arrangement with him, but no one tangles with men like Mr Mostyn unless he knows well what he is doing." He got to his feet as the smile faded. "I told you on the ship that you army fellows think you know bally all. I have no love for people like Mostyn who think they own a part of China, but they have, at least, put their lives and money into the country. You contribute nothing, but will be the first to put down the Chinaman's attempt to get what he deserves . . . and I will make certain we get back from you every penny you owe."

"I gave the Chinaman what he deserved, Armitage—the truth. For that Mostyn is trying to make me pay. I tell you now, no one tangles with *me* unless he knows what he is doing. Just keep that in mind. It might save you from doing something even more foolish one day."

He left the office in a raging temper. Throughout the short walk back to his hotel he thought of those fourteen days out at the bridge and how hard he had worked in the worst possible conditions. Then he thought of his report that had placed the blame equally between the Chinese contractor, who had plainly supplied substandard rivets, and the British engineer, who had been killed because of his own failure to inspect the centre section which contained the faulty rivets. Over twenty witnesses had testified to the fact that Harry Deane had neglected to check every box of materials sent by the contractor, and had also been absent on business of his own during the vital construction of the centre span, leaving Corcoran in charge. All would have been well except that Corcoran had fallen ill with marsh fever and was out of action during that period. Hong, unaware that an inspection had never been made by either senior engineer, had instructed his coolies to place the span in position, and Harry Deane returned to connect the whole thing—also in ignorance of or careless to the lack of a thorough check of the workmanship.

All this had only been discovered when Mark had recovered from the canal bed some of the rivets that told the whole story without a shred of doubt. He had also recovered several bloated corpses that had been pinned beneath the sunken bridge, so when Mostyn had said blightingly that he thought the army man had taken his work to ridiculous extremes, Mark had retaliated with some heat. Being shut into a weighted diving suit was bad enough, without coming face to face with disintegrating bodies in a murky underworld of water. The suggestion that he was being unnecessarily zealous for the hell of it had touched him on the raw.

Striding into his hotel that morning Mark told himself Mostyn might not have liked the report one jot, but he would like their next interview even less. Along with the key to his suite the receptionist handed him a letter, but he did not open it until he got upstairs. It was surprising in view of his planned afternoon departure: a request that he should call at Mostyn's office immediately on a vital matter.

Marching over to the cocktail cabinet he poured himself a stiff brandy. "I was on my way to you, Mostyn," he said under his breath, "and the matter I have to discuss is more vital than any you might have."

The 'gentleman's gentleman' treated Mark with the same abstract civility as before, reserving that air of bestowing a favour on an unexpected visitor as he went through the ritual of informing his employer of the arrival of Major Rawlings, Royal Engineers.

"Tell him there is no need for the prescribed seven-minute wait," said Mark savagely, "because I shall just walk in."

The man looked pained, as if not used to dealing with ruffians, and went into the inner office. He returned immediately, holding the door open for the visitor to enter. Garrard Mostyn was sitting behind his desk which seemed unusually laden with documents. He waved a hand at the chair opposite him and told Mark to sit down.

Ignoring it he stood looking down at him in anger and contempt. "I never took you for a man of much honour, but I thought you had *some* principles. I thought you also might appreciate the fact that I am a man as dedicated to his profession as you are to yours. But you are a bastard through and through, Mostyn."

"And you are a very bad loser," came the lazy voice. "I have far more at stake than you, Major. No man walks over me with heavy army boots and gets away with it."

"I played the game with all my cards on the table."

The pouting smile touched Mostyn's mouth as he got to his feet. "You played the game like a bull in a china shop. That is no match for finesse."

The photograph of Alexandra gazed up at him from the desk. *I'm the bribe, darling!* "Finesse? You might be full of it, Mostyn, but those you employ are not. Although you have chosen not to recognise it I do have something of a reputation in engineering circles. If a story like this got out it would spread like wildfire. A bribe to hush up the cause of a fatal accident, a young daughter offered on the altar of personal chagrin, a Scottish site-engineer who drinks on the job and has a peculiar attitude to coolies, and an army engineer being hired then made to pay for his own equipment. All this, to shield the shortcomings of a man, fortunately now dead, who was persuaded by you to build a bridge on a spot that defied the prejudice of the local Chinese." He walked a few steps around the desk. "You spoke to me on the last occasion I was in this office of the unique and touchy situation in Shanghai between East and West. If this is the way you handle things, I understand why."

"Professional blackmail, Major? I think you are a little out of your depth. You might have some little consequence in engineering circles, but I have a name and reputation that is known worldwide. I also have powerful friends in most places, as you have already discovered. Who is likely to believe your word against mine—or dare to believe it? You were asked to do this job because you were a convenient nobody obliged to do as he was told. My story would sound more plausible than yours. The job in question was something that would take any competent man two days—three, at the most. At the end of that time, when you still had not found the answer, you panicked and ordered all kinds of elaborate and unnecessary equipment. Even then, it took you two weeks to discover a simple matter of substandard rivets." He smiled once more. "As for Corcoran drinking on the job, I understand he had an excellent match in you. Your heavy drinking is noted by your superiors, Major . . . and your penchant for spending public money without authorisation is written in your service record, I understand."

Clenching his fists Mark said, "You understand a great deal more than you should, Mostyn. I'd like to know how you came by information that a man has a right to expect to be kept confidential—not from my colonel, I am certain. That money in Russia, in case you were not told the full story, was used to buy people's lives in time of war. This is entirely different. You indicated to me quite openly that I could order anything I wanted and charge it to your organisation. I used that offer to hire equipment instead of drinking and whoring in Shanghai. That last would have cost you as much."

"Far better that you should have done *that*, instead of taking on an opponent you could not possibly handle."

Mark knew then that he was beaten. He had a fleeting memory of telling Alexandra the only way to deal with her father was with cool determination. This time he had come up against a man just as coolly determined, and with every advantage on his side. For some moments he stood there, lost in counting all the consequences of a debt he could not pay. The monthly contribution he made to his mother had to be maintained, his mess bill could hardly be cut any finer, and his membership of the Institute of Engineers must not be allowed to lapse. Socially he was already practically a monk. To cease all off-duty activities would lead to even heavier drinking which would increase his mess bill. It was a damned vicious circle!

He looked up at Mostyn and asked huskily, "Did you realise when you did this that it could completely break me?"

"Did you, when you decided to cross me?"

"I'll never be able to pay off that debt."

Completely untouched by the admission, Mostyn pressed the buzzer on his desk and moved to stand before the fire.

"Now that you have finished your somewhat bourgeois outburst we can broach the reason for which I asked you to come here. But I think we'll have some tea. Very cooling beverage when tempers run high, I always find. At board meetings I always arrange for it to be served at an appropriate time."

"This is not one of them," Mark told him with heaviness in his voice, "and I am not interested in why you asked me here. The job I came to do is done to my satisfaction, and I shall be on a boat in five hours, thankful that I no longer have to deal with people like you."

"Your berth on that boat has been cancelled." With that enigmatic statement, the financier turned his attention to the tea-tray and the boy who was preparing to serve the visitor. "Sugar?" he asked.

Still reeling from the impact of that morning, all other thoughts in his head were blocked by the roundabout of disaster suggested by his inability to write off his overdraft. Unlike many of his fellow officers he did not own a car or a polo pony which he could sell. The sports trophies he had won were mostly on loan for the period of honour during which he held them. There was his gold watch awarded for swimming prowess, and two small silver medals, but they would fetch very little because they were engraved with his name. What, in God's name, was he going to do?

Mostyn put down on the corner of the desk the cup and saucer he had been holding out to his visitor, took a long drink from his own, then began.

"At our first meeting I told you the relations between Chinese and Europeans were at a most critical stage. Now, with the fall of Hankow, and Chiang Kai-Shek taking his government up to that city, the slightest piece of mishandling would put this port and all its vested interests in great danger. It is our hope that, should the Kuomintang advance as far as this, the Chinese in Shanghai would stand with us in resisting capture. To that end, it is necessary for a certain amount of prudent concession on our behalf. In other words, the Chinese element that combines with us to govern Shanghai must be kept sweet. That is why we have had to agree to their demand, on this occasion."

He emptied his cup and stood looking at the bottom of it as if the leaves were divining his future. "They were extremely impressed with your report. It allowed them to claim compensation in some degree from us, and saved 'face' by dividing the blame equally between the two races. They liked that. An Englishman of outstanding honesty, they felt," he added dryly.

Honesty that has never got him very far, thought Mark in bitter defeat.

"So they have written back in great praise of our findings, and stipulate that they give the go-ahead for the rebuilding of the bridge on condition that *you* are Engineer-in-Chief of the project. We have no option but to comply with their request, however much we feel they are making a grave mistake."

It was what Mark thought he had been sent to do; it was what he had dearly wanted when he had first sighted the scene of the disaster. It was a challenge, a chance to improve his considerable reputation for achieving success in difficult situations, but it had come too late. He intended to be on that boat at five p.m. and shake the dust of Shanghai from his boots.

"They are not making a grave mistake," he said coldly. "I'm very good. However, this time I'm going to do what you want and turn down the offer. That should let you off the hook very nicely."

Mostyn frowned. "Of course it won't, man. You can't turn it down."

There was surprising urgency in his tone: a complete reversal of attitude. All at once, Mark saw a faint light in the dark tunnel of bankruptcy. The burden that had descended so heavily on him began to lift again. Relief raced through him. He had Mostyn over a barrel. He was not beaten, at all.

Taking up the cup of tea he sipped it, relishing his moment. "All right, I'll build that bridge for you on condition that you settle all those bills you passed to my account."

Mostyn looked at him shrewdly for a moment, then smiled as he crossed to pour himself another cup of tea. "No, Major, you'll build that bridge because you've been ordered to. Your Commanding Officer will be sending written confirmation of the military directive in a day or so. He is delighted with the honour this reflects on the Corps as a whole. It appears the army sets great store by your ability. I trust you will not let them down."

CHAPTER SIX

It was the first time in his career that Mark found no delight in working on a bridge. There were too many aspects of uneasiness, hostility and duress which overrode his normal professional pride in his work. During that next week he toiled unceasingly on organising the final clearance of the site, the removal of all parts remaining of the bridge that he could not use, and the reopening of the canal to limited traffic. He measured and calculated, drew plans of his proposed new bridge, made lists of materials he would need. He went back and forth from bridge to Shanghai sounding out contractors to find the man who would supply all he needed in the shortest possible time, and to inspect the available materials.

To this end he had asked for, and been given, a small working engine which covered the distance between the two points in three hours instead of the six needed by a boat on the canal. He had also demanded a *written* authorisation from Mostyn to order anything he needed or personally felt was necessary to the speediest rebuilding of the bridge, at the expense of the railway authorities. He would not be caught a second time.

Throughout that week he was numbed by the cold, oppressed by the watching hostile coolies, irritated by Corcoran but, above all else, completely demoralised by the dragging weight of that debt he could not possibly pay. He had always been hard up, but this he could not survive. It would mean leaving the army—officers and gentlemen were expected to be solvent, at least. As a civilian engineer he could probably command a higher salary, but Britain had still not recovered from the crippling cost of the war. Jobs were scarce and hotly contested. At home there had just been a general strike and industrial unrest. It was not the best time to change careers, especially when he was doing very well in his present one. Yet, despite continuous brain-searching and pages of figures, he could not come up with a solution that produced seven hundred and fifty pounds spare cash. The Bridge of a Hundred Dragons might be the last bridge he built.

So deep was his worry over his future, so bitter was his hatred of the man who was prepared to ruin him merely for the sake of personal triumph, that the most serious problem of all, now looming ever larger, almost became lost beneath the others during those days leading up to Christmas. It was not that Mark was unaware of the situation. Along with his written orders to remain in Shanghai to put his professional services at the disposal of the British administrators, came brief advice on the present position of the Nationalist army, the speed of its advance, and the contingency plans should the International Settlement and all its foreign residents in Shanghai be put at risk. The orders indicated that Mark should be prepared to return to the city at a moment's notice to take up arms in defence of the Settlement area, and his whereabouts had been notified to the Shanghai Volunteer Corps until such time as any other military force might arrive at the port.

The inclusion of such matter told Mark that the Kuomintang was being taken very seriously indeed, and he thought fleetingly of that large densely-populated city without a garrison such as was maintained in Hong Kong. Yet he could not imagine the international elements allowing it to be lost: the nucleus of China's trade would be lost with it. The Western world was not at war with the Nationalists, but should there be a threat of attack on foreigners a show of united strength would be warranted and sufficient, he believed. Shots were not likely to be exchanged. Although the Soviet advisors to the Nationalist army would be delighted to run the other foreigners off Chinese soil leaving the way clear for Russian dominance, Chiang Kai-Shek himself had expressed his wish for foreign trade to continue. He was no fool. His country was not economically sound enough to stand on its own yet. But the barbarity of Chinese soldiers was well known, and if they should get out of hand anything could happen.

Mark thrust that problem to the back of his mind. The Kuomintang was a long way off: he intended to build his bridge and be away long before troops could draw near Shanghai. But he was faced with a blow that made nonsense of his hopes just as he was about to start the reconstruction. The night had been exceptionally cold and he had slept very little. Plagued by worry over his future he had lain rolled in blankets, listening to the squeak and groan of the boat's hull as ice forming on the canal gripped the wood tighter and tighter. By first light he was chilled, morose and heavy-headed. Breakfast of bacon and tinned sausages warmed but did not cheer him, and he shrugged into his padded coat before walking out onto the bank feeling none of his usual elation at starting a new bridge. Then he pulled up short. The site was deserted.

In the strange mauve light of early morning the mobile cranes and his little engine stood upon the embankment stark against the skyline, silent and isolated. The nightwatchmen were nowhere to be seen; there was no squatting team of coolies waiting for instructions. The narrow, barren dyke leading from Lu-Seng through the rice paddies was empty. There was no labour force coming from the village, and the regular coolies under Corcoran had vanished during the night.

It took a while for Mark to assess what had happened, then he strode toward Corcoran's boat hailing him in a loud voice. The Scot was just emerging dressed in his thick plaid coat, looking refreshed and full of health. But his expression soon changed when he was told the news.

"The coolies have gone—every last one of them . . . and no one has come in from the village. What's going on?"

"Treacherous little bastards!" exploded Corcoran. "Look, they've taken twa of yon small craft. That means they've gone frae good, laddie."

"In God's name, why? What happened yesterday?" demanded Mark furious and frustrated. "This damned business has taken far longer than it should already. I wanted this finished well within a month so that I could get back to my unit in Hong Kong. I have other duties, you know."

The Scot hardly listened. He was off to the next boat roaring, "Hong, ye son of a whore, where are ye? Get out here, at once, or I'll put a curse on your ancestors that'll deliver their bones to the devils."

Hong came wiping his spectacles before fitting the loops of the frames around his ears. He seemed to have been waiting for the summons because he was immaculately dressed for work, as usual. But he remained on the bank silent and impassive as the Scotsman reached him. Mark followed quickly.

"Ye know where yon coolies are to, ye yellow dog, so don't give me a pack of Oriental lies. Ye'll never get work again, if I can help it, letting them go with never a word to me, damn ye." With that, he struck the man across the face with the back of his hand.

Mark seized him by the shoulder. "That's not necessary, Corcoran. Give the man a chance to speak." His voice was husky in the raw morning air, echoing his feelings more than the Scot's violence.

Corcoran rounded on him. "Leave this to me, laddie. I know these sneaky curs better than I know my own wee toe. He knew yesterday they were going, I tell ye. The canny bastard stayed close and said nae a word about it. Ye'll nae get at the truth bar beating it out of him."

Suddenly, Mark's temper could stand no more, and he began to shout as loudly as the other man. "What you know about these people is little more than the wee toe of your foot tells you. You've been in China too long, *laddie*. I'm in charge of this project, and if my men have walked out it is up to me to discover why. And I'll do it *my* way."

He turned back to Hong who was looking blank and unconcerned—a sure sign that he did know all about it. Angered that Corcoran was probably correct, Mark hardly lowered his tone when he questioned the man.

"Did you know they were going, Hong?"

"They were not going yesterday," was the evasive reply.

"No, they were going last night. Did you know *that*?"

"I was asleep last night."

Mark gritted his teeth in the face of true Chinese skill in avoiding telling the truth without actually telling lies. This could go on for hours. He tried a more direct line.

"Where have they gone?"

Dark eyes blinked behind the spectacles. "Where the boats have gone."

"Dammit man, *why* have they gone?" he cried losing patience. "They were working well enough until yesterday."

"Work is now finished."

"Finished? It hasn't started yet."

Hong waved his hand at the cleared canal and surrounding embankments. "Work all finished."

Running his hand through his hair in exasperation Mark said, "That bridge is only half finished. They knew we were going to start reconstruction—and there's work for another three to four weeks yet. What made them walk off now?"

Hong rubbed the cheek where Corcoran had hit him. "They want more money."

This sudden reversal of his attitude of knowing nothing about it, plus a willingness to divulge their reasons did not deceive Mark. He knew enough now of the Chinese character. Hong was telling a deliberate lie rather than tell an unpleasant truth. The coolies had been paid the accepted rate, and none had been near Shanghai to hear the existing propaganda by unions who urged wage demands backed by strikes. Whatever the reason for the desertion it was something far removed from money. Mark also knew enough to realise the Chinese foreman would never provide him with a clue all the time Corcoran was standing there. Having been accused by the man of being in on the desertion plans and allowing it to happen, he would lose 'face' to admit it. Corcoran would play merry hell over the fact; Mark just wanted the truth so he would know how best to act.

Taking Hong back to his own boat where they were alone, he

continued the questioning with as much patience as he could muster. It took him another fifteen minutes before something of the truth began to emerge. His heart sank. Not all his experience in engineering or the handling of men equipped him to deal with this. He thought about it for some minutes, then reluctantly went out to Corcoran who had returned to the comparative warmth of his boat. Stepping past the slobbering attentions of the great mongrel, he dipped his head to enter the cabin.

Corcoran looked up unsmiling. "It's taken ye twenty minutes to my five."

Mark ignored the taunt. "We appear to be in serious trouble. They won't build the new bridge. They say the *fung shui* is bad."

"They said that the first time."

"I know, but fifty-eight people died or were injured in that crash. Nothing on earth will persuade them to build another bridge in that same spot, so Hong told me. I think we have got to believe him." He sighed with heaviness of spirit. "What the hell do we do now?"

A malicious smile spread slowly over the Scot's face. "Ye're in charge of this project, laddie. It's up to ye to sort it out *your* way."

Christmas Eve in Shanghai. The hotel had provided the usual Christian accessories to the festival and arranged a dance for those who were not invited to private houses. There was a tall tree in the vestibule. Candles and coloured ribbons made it gay, whilst gilded ornaments, spun-glass baubles and artificial frosting brought from England provided the garish decoration deplored by Continentals but loved by the British and Chinese.

In the ballroom the Oriental flavour had triumphed. Strings of beautiful paper lanterns festooned the large hall whilst banks of flowers vied with brilliantly painted models of peacocks and birds of paradise at every alcove and corner. Tables were romantically illuminated by candles shielded by Chinese table-screens of translucent discs, painted with long-tailed exotic birds that glowed in the light of the flame. Drinks were flowing, an army of boys glided expertly through the moving crowd, and the orchestra pleased all ages with its mixture of sentiment and modern rhythm. Yet there was an air of forced gaiety amongst the white foreigners. It was as if they knew it would never be quite the same again.

Mark was used to foreign Christmases. Since the age of seventeen he had spent more of them abroad than at home. He was used to the sentiment, the exaggerated merrymaking, the way expatriates clung together with their differences forgotten in order to allay homesickness. Even so, he did not join them. As they danced and made merry he sat at the bar steadily drinking at Garrard Mostyn's expense. He had nothing to celebrate: only the prospect of going back out to that marsh on Boxing Day. After four days of kicking his heels in Shanghai whilst various contractors attempted to raise a force of coolies, he had received a written directive signed by Mostyn saying that he had been informed by the Chinese members of his organisation that the bridge must be re-sited. A *fung shui* man had been consulted, and the only favourable spot was fifty-five yards west of the old bridge.

The message had gone on to say that the organisation was aware that a short distance of track would have to be re-laid under this circumstance, but that coolies would now be instantly available and work on the new bridge should commence on December 26th. It was businesslike and told Mark all he needed to know, but he could detect the anger and chagrin Mostyn and his colleagues must have felt at this implacable Oriental manoeuvre. As Corcoran had said, the Chinese were more afraid of dragons than the toe of a boot, and not all the white man's wealth, expertise and learning could overcome it.

The news had deepened his depression. Re-siting the bridge meant two, possibly three, more weeks of work out there on that wind-whipped marsh. It also meant the coolies had the upper hand now. They could invent dragons galore at any given moment, and he would have to comply with their wishes. They claimed there were a hundred of the beasts roaming that water-logged plain with a haunted warrior. If they took them one by one they could make that bridge last six months or more. Such was his frame of mind as he gazed morosely through the archway leading into the ballroom on that most festive of occasions.

"Have you drunk enough yet to stop you from walking away?" asked a soft voice, and he turned to find Alexandra Mostyn climbing onto the high stool beside him, a cigarette in a ridiculously long holder in her hand.

She was the most vivid creature there. Her dress of shimmering silver georgette over apple-green silk was embroidered with bugle beads and cut in handkerchief points around the hem. A waist-length rope of jade beads, beautifully matched in size and colour, was echoed in the long drops set in silver clips hanging from her ears. Around her glowing auburn waves was a green satin bandeau sporting a silvered plume held in place by a diamanté clip. Mark thought she looked absurd, but undeniably beautiful. One glance at her legs as she crossed one over the other banished the word 'absurd' from his mind and left only the other.

"Why aren't you at home tonight?" he asked for lack of a better opening line.

"To wait for Santa Claus?" She gave him a dazzling smile. "Why did you turn down my mother's invitation?"

"Because your father would be there."

"And because I would be there?"

He nodded. "That, too."

"Well, there's much more fun here, anyway."

"Yes."

She drew on her cigarette, then held the jade holder aside while she gracefully blew smoke into the air. "Why aren't you joining in?"

He tried not to stare at her legs. "I don't dance very well. You told me that yourself."

"So I did. In that case, will you buy me a cocktail?"

He felt uncertain. She clashed with his mood—her vivid dress, her youth, her pert challenge. Yet he was reluctant to turn her away and go back to being alone.

"Not here," he said eventually, disliking the sight of a woman sitting at a bar. "I'll find a table where it is quiet."

She put out her hand to touch his arm as he made to move. "Don't worry, Mark, I won't do anything shocking."

He saw something in her expression that took him aback, then decided he should ease up on the drinks before he imagined something even more ridiculous. Nevertheless, he led her to a secluded corner, feeling those hundred dragons moving further away by the minute.

"I'm sorry about your bridge," she said when they were seated. "Will it mean a lot of extra work?"

He did not want to discuss it. "Is that what you came here to ask me?"

She shook her head, setting the earrings wobbling. "I had a feeling you would be sitting here alone and took a chance that you would prefer even my company to none at all on Christmas Eve."

While the boy brought and arranged the drinks he studied her wistful expression that contrasted with her glad rags. Christmas Eve was a time of romance and gaiety for the young unmarried set. Why had she chosen to spend it with him, especially after their last parting?

"Lionel's loss is my gain," he said lightly. "Or did he accompany you here?"

A strange shadow flitted over her face. "He is attending a political meeting. Not my idea of suitable entertainment for the festive season."

"And I am?"

"I didn't come to find entertainment, Mark, but I hoped you'd let me stay for a little while."

He was growing more confused. Did he want her to stay for more than a little while? "I thought you always did as you wished, regardless."

"Not with you—not this time."

Her eyes were deeply blue and full of a concern that he had never seen in them before. Feeling the preliminary sparring had gone on long enough he asked, "Why did you really come here?"

"Because you refused to come to me," she answered with disarming frankness. "I very much wanted to see you again."

His immediate suspicion that she was playing some kind of game at his expense quickly faded. "If it's about your career as an artist," he began, but she stopped him as she crushed out the cigarette.

"No, it's not about my career . . . it's about yours."

"Mine!" he exclaimed wondering where on earth the evening was heading. "You've come here to talk about my career!"

She leaned toward him holding the stem of the cocktail glass with both hands. "It means everything to you, doesn't it?"

"It means a great deal," he temporised, wondering if he really was as drunk as he felt. Her nearness was affecting his concentration.

"I have seven hundred and fifty pounds in my handbag for you."

"You . . . *what*?" he exclaimed, feeling as if he had been hit by shell-blast. "What in hell's name are you talking about?"

For a brief mad moment hope leapt in his breast. Had Mostyn given in, after all? No, he would hardly send his daughter on Christmas Eve with a wad of banknotes in her handbag. Or would he? *I'm the bribe, darling.*

"What is this all about?" he demanded fiercely. "You are surely not referring to a matter that is strictly between your father and myself . . . at least, I *thought* it was."

"And Lionel Armitage," she added quickly. "He's jealous of you, Mark, but prefers to call it 'contempt'. He's also very silly, at times. His mother and Dot encourage it. At a party last night he told me what Father had done to you. I suppose he hoped to show both you and Father in a bad light, but it just lowered my opinion of him." She put her hand on the bag as it lay on the table. "Of course, I could have just transferred the money from my account into yours, but I thought you would prefer it this way. Knowing how you must be feeling I came at the first opportunity, although the bank won't be open again until after you have left for the bridge."

He tried to marshal his thoughts. The situation was too bizarre even for anger. "Are you telling me that that fool Armitage discussed . . ." He was lost for words. The evening had become an Oriental fantasy—a Chinese Christmas, a bridge that had to be moved to please some dragons, a young girl showing far too much of her body telling him she had banknotes in her evening purse amounting to a sum that was about to break him.

Completely out of his depth he said, "You're not seriously offering to lend me seven hundred and fifty pounds!" Yet, knowing this girl, he acknowledged that she probably was.

"That *is* the sum, isn't it?"

He tried again to bring some kind of sanity back to the evening. "I couldn't possibly borrow money from you."

"Don't be silly," she said with impatience. "I don't want it back."

It took longer than usual for the implication to reach him, bemused as he was by the heavy atmosphere, the music drifting from the next room, and her shimmering low-cut dress. But suddenly he *was* angry, in the way of an older brother toward a young girl who has got herself into a scrape.

"You really are the limit! Don't you realise how dangerous it is to flit around Shanghai at night with a huge sum of money in a ridiculous silk purse dangling from your wrist? They'd cut your throat for a tenth that amount."

"Nonsense," she replied calmly. "Whoever would suspect that I had it? It was the only way of getting it to you."

"Well, you can take it back the same way as soon as possible."

She looked astonished. "Don't you need it any longer?"

Exasperated, still feeling he had wandered into Bedlam, he tried to get some sense into her. "Alex, the whole idea is absurd. I couldn't possibly take money from a girl."

Her eyes flashed. "Would you take it if I were a man?"

"You're not a man."

Her fingers tightened around the glass. "Mark, if *you* were exceedingly wealthy and *I* was about to be ruined for a sum of money you wouldn't even miss, wouldn't you give it to me?"

"Perhaps," he said cautiously. "But that would be entirely different."

"Why?" she demanded loudly enough to cause several heads to turn.

He lowered his own voice, in consequence. "It is perfectly acceptable for a man to give money to a woman."

Her glass thumped on the table as she flared up. "Ooh, that is just the kind of attitude I deplore! If one person has too much and another not enough, isn't the solution pure commonsense? Will you seriously endanger your career, worry yourself sick for months on end, and try to live on nothing rather than accept help from me merely because I am female? *Will you*?" she cried, in the throes of temper.

Attempting to quieten her with movements of his hands he leant nearer. "Help I will always accept from anyone . . . but you are talking about giving me a very large sum of money. You must see that it is quite out of the question."

"I suppose you would prefer to blow your brains out in the good old masculine tradition," she said scathingly with no attempt to keep her words at conversational level.

Afraid that she might do something reckless, touched by what she was misguidedly trying to do, angry that she should have been told of his circumstances by that young prig, Mark decided to end the subject in the only possible way. Getting to his feet and seizing her hand, he said, "They're playing a waltz. It might be the last one for an hour or two."

She went without a word and silence fell between them as they glided around the floor once or twice. Gradually, her slender body relaxed in his arms although she remained silent. When he judged the moment was right, out there surrounded by couples drifting lovingly to the music, he drew her closer so that he spoke against her ear.

"See how right this is, Alex? If you began to guide *me* around the floor, the whole concept would be wrong . . . and I would look a fool." He took her a few steps further. "It's not a case of stiff-necked ingratitude, you know. The only *true* way of removing that debt is for your father to pay what he rightly owes me. It is not only a question of the money. Can you understand that?"

After a while she nodded against his shoulder. "I suppose so. But this is *his* money, of course."

He held her closer. "Then I suggest you spend it on furthering your own career—the one he won't allow you to follow."

She looked up anxiously. "But what are you going to do?"

Suddenly full of confidence he smiled. "I'm going to move a bridge fifty-five yards to please some dragons first. I'll worry about my future after that."

With her quietly contented in his arms as they circled the floor, he began to relax. Why worry about tomorrow when tonight was proving so enjoyable? At the end of the dance a buffet supper was produced, and he felt it advisable to eat something to counteract the strong effect his drinking was having on him that night. A glow of warmth was starting to spread right through him, and he felt more light-hearted than he had for years. The hotel brandy must be top quality at festive occasions. It had not done this to him before.

They piled food onto their plates and took them off to their secluded table, where Mark discovered he was ravenous. As they ate they talked about other Christmases, and Alexandra asked him about English celebrations. He found himself telling her of his childhood in a red-brick terrace house, when he and his sisters had given the pudding a lucky stir before his mother put it in a basin with a cloth tied around it. He told how his father had always played the trick of slipping a shilling onto his plate as he ate his portion, setting the children fruitlessly searching for one rather than the silver threepenny pieces his mother had always scattered in the mixture. He spoke of pasting coloured strips of paper in long links to make garlands, and painting fir cones with silver and gold. He went on to describe how his father had given a magic-lantern show on that last Christmas before the war, and all those children in the street who had come to watch had been sent home with a balloon and a stick of liquorice. He stopped in his catalogue of memories realising he had been speaking of things he had put behind him with his lost youth. For a short time they had become vivid again.

"I have never done any of those things," said the girl opposite him with surprising wistfulness.

Remembering who she was, he said, "I suppose not. My family had very little money."

"But a great deal of fun. You must miss them all at a time like this."

The warmth began to leave him. "My father was killed early in the war. It changed my mother completely, and she never forgave me for volunteering as I did. My younger sister is now the talk of the neighbourhood, I understand, and the older one still grieves for a young airman who was blown up over Flanders. The war altered everything."

She put down a canapé and wiped her fingers on her napkin. "You went right through it—all four years?"

He nodded. "I was one of the lucky ones who lived."

"Then why don't you?"

"I . . . I don't understand."

She stretched out her hand until their fingers were touching. "You're all locked up inside. You wear those terrible years as some kind of impossible penance for those who didn't survive. They wouldn't want you to do that. Whatever it is that makes you so unhappy is not going to be lessened by devoting your whole life to it."

He looked at her thinking how lovely she was in the candlelight, how youthful and vivid with expectation, how untouched by the anguish and tragedy he had witnessed at her age.

"You don't understand," he said bleakly.

"No one who was not there can understand. Don't blame us for that," she pleaded threading her fingers through his until their hands were tightly linked.

He tried hard to adjust to another facet of someone who was getting beneath his guard far too easily, murmuring, "I don't *blame* you, Alex . . . not exactly. I just find your attitude to life so incomprehensible."

"So *you* are the one who doesn't understand!"

Her smile was a slow warm message of something he had suspected at the start of their meeting, which he no longer wished to misread or divert. This girl had sparked off a response in him at their very first encounter, but it had been purely physical, at that stage. Intriguing hints of something deeper during subsequent meetings had always been banished by her extravagant behaviour, yet it was suddenly there in full force. There was no defence against it when he was artificially relaxed by spirits, desperately lonely in the midst of group revelling, and aroused by sexual desires ignored for some years. The girl he saw tonight wielded as much power over him as her father, but in a manner so irresistible he capitulated willingly.

"I think I have had far too much to drink, because I can think of no further argument," he confessed with an answering smile.

"Thank heaven for that! Now we can start getting to know each other. Tell me what you've been doing since the war," she invited.

He was not so artificially relaxed that he did not immediately recognise what she was after. "I have been following my profession," he replied firmly. "You already know a great deal about me. I think it's time you followed up that accusation of a few minutes ago by giving me some facts that will help me to understand you. Sandy, Alexandra, Alex—which girl is the real one? You change guises with bewildering speed."

She was still holding his hand across the table, and he made no attempt to break contact despite the fact that it was having a headier effect on him than the brandy.

"I don't think there was a real girl until you created her," she said with startling honesty. "Maybe there was once a tiny tot with all the normal little-girl dreams of handsome princes and happiness ever after." She gave him a swift upward glance. "Do you believe in that, Mark?"

He shook his head. "Handsome princes have a habit of being assassinated by political madmen, and happiness ever after is a ridiculously naive concept."

"I could make you happy . . . possibly for ever after."

It was slipped in so skilfully beneath his guard he was totally unprepared for the bitter-sweet stab of pain. He riposted immediately.

"You can't even make yourself happy."

"I thought you were prepared to try to understand," she cried softly. "You haven't budged an inch in the right direction yet."

"Sorry." Knowing too well which direction he would like to take, he smothered the treacherous impulses and invited her to go on. "So your childhood was the kind that allowed you the standard fantasies small girls have." He squeezed her hand slightly. "I have two younger sisters, remember, so I'm a connoisseur on princes and all that goes with them." He smiled to soften his next words. "I can't help feeling, however, that little Alex Mostyn's princes would have to toe the line more than the average royal gents."

The low lights put dancing fire on her hair as she shook her head. "Believe it or not, they followed the standard pattern—and that meant they respected my point of view and recognised that I had wishes of my own which had to be taken into consideration." All at once, she seemed desperately serious as she leaned further toward him to appeal with voice and eyes. "Mark, I was always glad for them to go off and fight my battles for me. I had no desire to don armour and go to war myself . . . until I discovered that real-life knights are sadly disappointing. They fight their own battles, not mine. That's not all," she added bitterly. "Instead of returning to lay their honour at the lady's feet, they're either so lost in self-congratulation they ignore her, or they expect her to deliver the *coup de grâce* to their adversaries at the sacrifice of her own honour."

It was all a little too metaphorical and fanciful for his state of inebriation, besides expressing a female point of view his very sex hampered understanding of to the extent she wished. He sensed her deep sincerity, however, and frowned.

"Why continue to sacrifice it with your own behaviour? While I sympathise with your disillusionment, I can't understand how you hope to redress the balance by creating one scandal after another. No prince is ever going to respect you if you shock everyone in sight," he concluded, not entirely sure what he was saying with all the royal similes flying between them.

"Is that why *you* don't?"

Suffering another thrust for which he had been ill-prepared, he was silent for a moment or two while he recognised what was happening between them. It was dangerous, badly timed, and doomed to failure yet he knew it was too late to prevent it.

"I'm no prince," he said finally.

"But you're the type to lay your honour at a lady's feet," she accused with a soft sigh. "I think you did so in Russia, and it is still there. Pick it up, Mark. There might be another girl who will try very hard to deserve it, some day."

He was still assessing the implications of those words when a roll on the drums, followed by a cymbal crash heralded the announcement that it was five minutes before midnight and a waltz would carry them into Christmas Day. Drawn to his feet by the girl who appeared to have taken on yet another guise, he held her in his arms enjoying the perfume teasing his nostrils, the soft tendrils of hair against his throat, and the gentle curves beneath his hand despite the disguise of the straight dress. He had fallen beneath her spell that evening, and desire swept through him, along with a sense of happiness he had forgotten he could experience. Could it last, this time? Could a wild, spectacular, vividly individualistic girl who longed for understanding and love make happy-ever-after a reality? Holding her closer he let himself believe it while the moment lasted. The dream was better than the nightmares he had to drown with brandy.

The tune ended; the chimes of the clock announced the turn of the day. Couples were bidding each other '*Joyeux Noël*', '*Herzliche Weinachten*', and a host of other national greetings. Alexandra looked up at him with lights in her eyes that could have been caused by tears.

"I know there's an accepted way of doing this, also, but I can't risk missing it," she whispered, as her arms circled his neck to draw his head down to hers. On tiptoe she touched her mouth lingeringly against his. "Merry Christmas, darling."

Something he had once glimpsed and lost caught him up and overtook him as he gazed down at her, and recognised youth and hope. Then he pulled her hard against him and began kissing her with all the ferocity of his need for what she promised. At some time during that passionate embrace the hundred dragons slipped quietly away leaving him at peace.

When he reluctantly released her he discovered they were alone on the dance floor, the subject of eager and amused scrutiny from all those back at their tables. Alexandra began to laugh softly at his dismayed expression.

"My, my, sweetie, think what *that* has just done to my reputation."

With his mind full of far more drastic things he would like to do to her reputation, he led her from the floor, murmuring, "You should never have worn that alluring dress. It was bound to bring about something like this—especially with an older man."

Out on the marshy plain it rained for an entire week. Visibility was obscured by sheets of grey misty wetness that brought up the level of the canal and turned all the dykes into mud. When daylight came it brought no more than leaden skies and a greyish pall that lasted until it grew dark again. The wind that usually raced across that great flat area had died, and there was nothing to disperse the low threatening storm clouds.

After two days it was no longer possible to be dry. Working in the open, even in the waterproof coats, for a whole day meant that they became soaked to the skin with no means of drying their clothes. Mark had several sets of clothing with him, but they were all uncomfortably damp in no time at all. Ah Wu did his best to hang lines across the tiny cabin of the boat where the slight warmth from the cooking stove set the clothes steaming, but the cabin became unbearable to sleep in and all the clothes became impregnated with stale cooking smells. He told the Chinese boy not to bother except to do what he could with the flat iron.

The coolies had no such luxuries. They just huddled on the barge-like boats in which they slept and cooked their rice, squatting in sheltered places and protected only by the great circular basket hats and pieces of rattan matting which they clutched around their shoulders. Whilst the two white men cursed and swore to relieve their feelings the coolies remained impassive, doing what they had to do with the resigned acceptance of experience.

There was no trouble from them now the bridge was to be moved. Most of the old work-team had returned, plus half a dozen new ones, and the men from the village of Lu-Seng appeared on that first morning as if there had never been a break in their labours. Mark was tempted to tell them to get lost, but Corcoran had hired them—he also paid them—so presumably he was the man to fire them, if necessary. They still performed their tasks with a sullenness that was uncomfortable, and Mark felt their eyes on him whenever he was anywhere near the canal. However, he just smiled somewhat grimly to himself, and murmured under his breath, "Oh no, lads, I'm not going to miss my footing just to satisfy your bloody dragons."

But despite the rain work went ahead very well in the week between Christmas and New Year. Leaving the broken bridge as it stood, Mark organised the lifting and re-laying of track in a new layout that would lead to the site fifty-five yards along the bank. It was a more involved job than usual because the track had to be embanked along the whole length. Digging and escarping in such weather was hard and dangerous work due to the danger of landslips, but the coolies trotted back and forth with their double baskets of earth on poles across their shoulders, heedless of the downpour and steady on their feet. Mark wondered if white navvies would have worked with such uncomplaining rhythm.

The new site posed him a few small problems. The canal being slightly wider just there necessitated a readjustment to the length of each span, and all the calculations he had done the previous week had to be abandoned. But he did all his paperwork and sketching after darkness fell, because he felt a strange compulsion to show the coolies that he could survive the conditions every bit as well as they.

The job was hard and demanding, the weather appalling. The boat grew more uncomfortable daily. He had no really congenial company, and at no time did the Chinese relax their morbid scrutiny of his movements. Yet he felt a new sense of peace and contentment that softened the hard edges of those days. Despite the heavy physical strain, mentally he felt rested and went about the task of building his bridge with some of his usual enthusiasm surprisingly returning. It no longer loomed as a *bête noire*. He put the legend of the warrior and the hundred dragons in proper perspective, and treated the hostility of the labour-force as an unavoidable eccentricity, nothing more.

His future he put where it belonged, concentrating all his thoughts on the job. Even when the train bringing up a consignment of steel girders also brought a packet containing his written orders and some mail forwarded fom Hong Kong which told him his sister had become pregnant then been deserted by a commercial traveller, he refused to worry about it. The letter from his mother was full of woe, telling him of the hardship and unemployment in England, how difficult it was to make ends meet, and how much they depended on the money he allocated to them each month.

> After all, son, it's only right that you should help out after all your dad and me sacrificed for you when you were a lad. I'm getting on now and with no man in the house have to do all the heavy chores, which don't help my bad back. Nora can't do it, poor dear, not in her condition, and I don't know what we shall do when the brat is born. I'd be glad if you could see your way to sending us a little more. It's not as if you had a wife and children to support, and officers are well paid. Your dad was only a sergeant and managed to keep us all and pay the rent and coal. Lucky you, don't need coal out there in that lovely sunshine. The price has gone up again and it's raining cats and dogs here today. . . .

He put the letter aside feeling immeasurably sorry for the little bastard his sister was carrying—his own niece or nephew—but unwilling to dwell on what his mother had said. One thing at a time. He had a bridge to build first.

So he worked. By day he trudged up and down in the mud giving orders and advice, inspecting, checking, measuring. By night he sat in the foul-smelling cabin doing calculations and drawings by lamplight, afterwards rolling himself into damp rugs to sleep soundly. His intake of brandy dropped; his hours of sleep increased.

He knew the cause of his new contentment and, although he recognised the pitfalls, allowed his thoughts to dwell on those two days with Alexandra. Adamant that she would not let him spend Christmas Day all alone, she had deserted her parents and their guests to go to his hotel for tea, after which they had been driven in her father's car to a service in the Anglican church, then on to a quiet restaurant for dinner. They had quarrelled briefly when Mark realised the bill was to be charged to Alexandra's standing account, but she had threatened to force him into agreeing, and he had not dared risk her challenge. When she had finally left him that evening their farewells had been long and lingering, testing him to the limit of a control weakened by sexual abstinence.

In his saner moments he told himself there was an age gap of eleven years, and she was simply diverted by his maturity whilst temporarily out of step with young Armitage. He also told himself he was sailing deep waters. He was due to return to Hong Kong next month, he was deeply in debt, almost certain to be out of work before long, and the last man in the world Garrard Mostyn would allow his daughter to love. For her sake it would be best if they did not meet up when he returned to Shanghai. For his sake? He shunned answering that question the same way he avoided trying to find a solution to his inevitable bankruptcy. He had a bridge to build first.

Despite his saner moments, it was thoughts of a golden, vivacious girl that restored his confidence and optimism; it was recollection of those two days with her that pumped the blood so vigorously through his veins and touched his last waking moment each night. The delight and happiness of a girl who had taken his past by the scruff of the neck and shaken it was with him in all he did now, and he could have faced several hundred dragons without a qualm.

Hamish Corcoran departed down the line to spend Hogmanay in Shanghai. He had remained at the site during Christmas while Mark had been away, so it was only fair that the Scot should take his break at the time so dearly loved by his race. He took the small engine, charged with the task of bringing up several loads of shingle for ballasting when he returned two days later. Mark watched him depart with mixed feelings. Not a particularly likeable man, he nevertheless proved dependable, hard-working and skilful on the job. Apart from his handling of the Chinese, which Mark felt powerless to stop although he deplored it, some kind of rapport had grown between the two white men which was far from friendship but possible to live with. He was now officially in command over the Scot, but the man acknowledged it in his own bluff way without rancour or sarcasm, even though he continued in his assumption that his chief engineer was a novice to the ways of the world.

Never having used command to unreasonable lengths, Mark made a habit of keeping his subordinates fully informed and occupied. Neither was he averse to asking for advice from them if he needed it, and this applied particularly to Corcoran. He knew the capabilities of his coolies, if not their characteristics, and was invaluable on advising on the way they would best tackle a certain job. So when he departed for Shanghai, Mark knew he would miss his professional help, if not his company. But mostly he envied the man his visit to a city that housed Alexandra Mostyn.

In the event, Corcoran's departure brought no problems. The atmosphere at the work site seemed to ease, in fact, and on Hong the Scot's absence had a magical effect. Despite the deluge of rain his face was wreathed in a perpetual smile and he worked with a will that transferred itself to the others.

Late on New Year's Eve the rain stopped, leaving a curious bronze light over the plain that allowed the first glimpse of the distant hills for over a week. The sign promised a brighter start to the coming year, and the breeze that sprang up allowed clothes to be dried on lines strung along the decks of the boats. As Hong was the only other Christian present, Mark invited him into his cabin for a drink to the new year of 1927 and all it might contain for them both, but it arrived whilst he was soundly asleep with no maudlin thoughts of other faces, other such occasions.

In brilliant, invigorating sunshine the first day of January passed in hard work. Mark went to sleep that night telling himself that when Corcoran returned the following morning with a hangover, he would be astonished at the progress that had been made in his absence. Still with that thought he ate a hearty breakfast, determined to be well on the job by the time the train arrived shortly. The sunshine and sense of well-being made him light-hearted, and he pushed away his empty plate with a smile at Ah Wu.

"You b'long plenty good cook, Ah Wu. You number one boy China-side."

The little round-faced man laughed with delight, responding to his master's good humour, of late. "My savee man plenty work, b'long plenty baconegg. Sun come all along my plenty wash."

He laughed. "Laundry day, is it? Good. I'm down to my last pair of dry socks, and yours are too small for me."

The boy went into paroxysms of giggles, looking at his own tiny feet in comparison with his master's socks, and finding it tickled his child-like sense of humour. Grinning at his boy's pleasure, Mark shrugged into the padded coat before leaving the boat and heading toward the railhead where the bridge had been started. The mud was beginning to form a crust, he noted with satisfaction. It made movement easier and negotiation of the bank less hazardous when going down to the boats. Corcoran would be pleased. He had nearly gone into the canal one night—although only he knew what he had been doing out in the dark and pelting rain.

As he passed, Mark looked idly at the Scotman's boat, then pulled up sharply, hardly believing what he saw. The deck was a terrible mess and, although he had had no affection for the great mongrel, such savagery made him sick to the stomach. He approached reluctantly, his thoughts full of what could have happened. Wolves? Not in China, surely. Tigers? Not in this part of the country. Jackals, wild dogs?

Reaching the deck he looked at the remains of the beast still chained to the iron ring on the bulkhead. Why had he not been let loose at dusk, as usual? Whatever had fallen on him had given the beast no chance, for the brown body was ripped apart so that it was hardly recognisable in the pool of blood and fur. Then he saw something that had the back of his neck prickling with the import of the sight. No animals' work, this! The carcass had been beheaded, and the bloody mask was perched on a barrel, staring glassy-eyed at him.

Turning slowly away he moved along the deck toward the cabin, knowing he must go in yet holding back as he reached the door. Then he took a deep breath and turned the handle, dipping his head beneath the low lintel to enter.

The interior smelt much as his own cabin, with the addition of pipe smoke. It had been ransacked with the idea of making as much mess as possible. All Corcoran's clothing and equipment had been thrown about the small space, together with the pots and pans, and foodstuffs. Mark stepped through it, careful not to tread on anything. Then he saw what he had dreaded. The young Portuguese cook-cum-boatman who had practically idolised his master lay beside his small stove, his olive features twisted in the anguish of death. He had been garrotted—a popular method of killing with the Chinese. He had seen hundreds of bodies in wartime, some in the most appalling state of death, yet this still affected him badly. In the midst of peace and the normality of his work, the sight of this young lad with a thin cord around his throat, a simple length of fine bamboo twisted into it to apply pressure to snap the windpipe, conjured up a feeling of menace once more. The dragons began returning one by one.

"Oh God, however am I going to tell him this?" he breathed, turning away from the sight.

But he was saved that dreadful duty. As he left the cabin Corcoran was already striding down the bank, staring with shocked eyes at the gore on deck. Mark made no attempt to stop him from going inside the cabin, or warning him first. Like himself, Corcoran must surely have guessed the boy was also dead, and he was blunted enough by life to take the sight that would meet him. But Mark had reckoned without the depth of affection between the Scot and a lad he had treated with almost paternal interest, and as he stood trying to recover from all the discovery implied, he heard Corcoran swearing and crashing about the disordered cabin.

Next minute, the man was outside, striding away with tears streaming down his cheeks and the light of madness in his eyes. "They'll pay for this, yon bloody murderers," he swore. "They'll pay as they've never paid before, and when I'm through there'll nae be a man of them who'll hold up his head again."

He was off up the bank and away along the dyke that led to the village before Mark realised his intention.

"Wait, man, you can't be sure who did this," he cried. The words went unheeded, and he said no more as he realised not one of the men from Lu-Seng had appeared for work. In addition, the other coolies were watching Corcoran's departure with a mixture of fear and hatred.

"Oh, hell and damnation!" cried Alexandra in exasperation after three hours of struggling against defeat. Flinging down her brush she moved moodily across to the cluttered table, took up her cigarettes and lit one, before going to gaze from her window which gave a view of the busy waterway of the Yangtze. Somewhere miles along that waterway a bridge was being built. If only she could get into a little boat and find the right tributary that would lead her to it.

Just what were Mark's feelings for her? Had those two days at Christmas meant as much to him as she hoped—as much as they had meant to her? There was little doubt she had bridged the gulf between them, to a certain extent, glimpsing the person beneath the tense, haunted man afraid to allow anyone to draw near. Yet he had celebrated Christmas with alarming quantities of brandy, which might have done more to relax him than her charms and, although he had spoken freely of his past, the facts she longed to hear still remained elusive. Russia held his secret still.

Despite his maturity he had a surprisingly reticent manner with women, as if he were unused to their intimate company. Yet, compared with the kisses of her young society friends, his had been hard, deliberate, and infinitely exciting. Was it possible that since the woman in Russia there had been none who had meant anything to him? If so, it suggested a devotion so deep he might never recover. She would have preferred the prospect of a long string of mistresses. There might be jealousy of a host of promiscuous women, but one true unforgettable love could totally defeat her.

Restless she moved back to study the canvas that had been occupying her for most of the day. *What happened in Russia in 1919 is not a subject for a painting*. His scathing admonition still seared her, and every canvas she had attempted since then had reached a certain stage then died on her. In the corner were two flat, lifeless snowscapes, empty of figures, abandoned in the face of his hostility. The one on the easel was intended to be an interpretation of her confrontation with the wheelbarrow men, but those narrow Oriental streets with secret eyes watching from tiny upstairs windows were beginning to fill with tall bearded men in Russian uniforms.

Her shoulders drooped resignedly. The truth was, she had seen that experience through an echo of the mystery of his, and now she could not divorce one from the other. Neither could she begin on any other subject with success. At her feet was a half-finished sunset over bamboos, on the bench lay a pair of small canvases showing a pagoda in the rosy glow of morning then in the pale wash of moonlight, entitled *Gold and Silver*. Yet, in the first, the elegant pagoda looked to be on fire from within, and the moonlight of the other gave the tall building with its upflaring roofs an atmosphere of cold menace. Danger and threat —the two crept into everything she painted now. She had told Mark he should forget the past, yet she had become a new, avid student of it.

Lighting another cigarette she went to gaze dreamily from the window once more. Her life seemed to be inextricably bound up with the man she had first thought to be quaintly old-fashioned, who had now shown her a strength as great as her father's, but one which had been tempered by suffering. To her searching spirit it was an irresistible combination. As she watched the great junks with their brown sails, the busy sampans zigzagging their way across the river, and the merchant ships of all nations of the world navigating the yellow-coloured river that served the port of Shanghai, she realised Mark had drawn from her a confession she would have made to no other person—even her mother. This Oriental city had been the only home she had known. Like Mark, her childhood had been happy with a close family unit. It had differed from his in that she had always been surrounded by good things, and had been cared for by an amah rather than her own mother, as all her friends had been. In her infancy her parents had spent a great deal of time with her: playing games and reading to her, or taking her on outings. Those distant memories had them as happy, laughing people who held hands and kissed each other as frequently as they had kissed her. Only gradually had she realised how things were changing. The playtimes had grown infrequent, then stopped altogether as her parents spent more and more time entertaining visitors who were guests rather than friends. Her father had started going away for days at a time, then returning to shut himself in his study from where he only seemed to emerge when the groups of cigar-smoking men and sharp-voiced women came to dine.

Alexandra still remembered that day when she had tired of waiting for her adored father to pay her some attention and had entered his study, intending to beg him to see a picture she had drawn of Lai-Hi. At first, he had simply brushed her impatiently away, but when she had determinedly pursued her request, adding a childlike tug on his arm to gain his attention, he had rounded on her so violently she had fallen and cut her lip. He had picked her up full of concern, of course, but had rung for her amah and handed her over to the Chinese with instructions to keep her away when he was so very busy. That incident had marked what Alexandra later learned had been Garrard Mostyn's promotion to a position in Shanghai society any young ambitious colonist would have envied. From then on, he had gone higher and higher in the social and professional scale to his present position of power.

The climb had cost him his family life. His gentle pretty wife had been unable to stand the strain of her new position, and her health had deteriorated as her husband's dedication to his career had increased. As for the little girl who had once thought her father the most marvellous man in the world, in the way of most baby daughters, a new role was in the offing. Her large blue eyes and winning smile had softened hard-headed businessmen who were treated to a performance of her latest recitation or shown her most promising drawings. There had been pats on the head and indulgent laughter at her childish prattle. She had been only too willing to engage in the little entertainments, believing she was winning back the father she had once known. Not until the big blue eyes and winning smile had been augmented by a swelling figure, and the pats on the head had become pats on the arm or even the bottom, had she realised the truth.

The incredible hurt of knowing she was being heartlessly used by her father in the most unforgivable way, had put protest of such a violent nature within her it had never died. Yet, to her immense shame, she could not finally give up hope that he still cared something for her as his own child. Try as she might, she could not deny that the underlying reason for her crazy stunts and exaggerated behaviour was to earn *some* kind of feeling from him. That much she had confessed to Mark, although she was uncertain whether he saw through the balderdash about handsome princes and jousting knights to divine what she had really been trying to explain.

With a deep sigh she acknowledged that she was faced with a second challenge. Having given him an impression of a social butterfly from the start, what must she do to win the love of this man? There was so little time; they were so far apart. What chance did she have of doing something which would earn his respect, make him look upon her as a worthy successor to a Russian woman who must have been quite wonderful to hold him for seven years?

For several days after he had returned to the bridge she had searched for a means of forcing her father to pay the bills liable to break Mark, determined the debt would be written off before he left Shanghai. Knowing it would only alienate him if she went ahead with her plan to give him the sum, she also knew any scheme would have to be brilliant to defeat a man like Garrard Mostyn. The solution had been presented to her by, of all people, Lionel Armitage.

Unable to stay away from her for long, the young banker had called several times in the hope of repairing the strained relationship between them, and something he had said on the subject of the growing unrest provided the inspiration she needed. Knowing all along that any kind of social misbehaviour would do no more than earn her father's contempt, she saw a chance of blackmail and seized it eagerly. Lionel had proved ridiculously gullible, and Alexandra told herself he was getting just reward for his bombastic treatment of Mark. Flattering the young banker with all the skill she possessed, she had told him her interest in his political views had been aroused by what he had said to her father after their encounter with the wheelbarrow men, and she was avid to learn more.

Lionel drank in every word, and she had had to endure several long earnest lectures on the evils of capitalism, imperialism and any other social structure which oppressed the people. Controlling the urge to ask why he continued his own privileged mode of existence, Alexandra had finally achieved her goal. Full of triumph she had accompanied him to her first political meeting marvelling at how simple it had been to make him dance to her tune. It was only when the final deed had been done that she realised his easy capitulation had been governed by his knowledge of how it would increase his own standing. So it proved. His political associates were volubly delighted that he had recruited the daughter of one of the most powerful financiers in the mercantile nucleus of Shanghai—a supporter of foreign intervention in China and an ardent opponent of Socialism/Communism.

Alexandra had been welcomed with open arms, but it did not take her long to realise there was no need to repeat all her lies. These people knew her for a wealthy socialite who had the entrée everywhere and was always in the public eye or the columns of the newspapers. Just to be *seen* to support them would do wonders for their cause and put a great crack across the fabric of the established imperialistic monopoly of China's most important port. Garrard Mostyn's standing in the eyes of his Western colleagues would be shaken, his home viewed as an unsuitable venue in which to hold serious discussions, and his dedication to the international ownership of Shanghai suspected. With Mostyn's authority in question at such a time, who knew where it might lead?

No time had been lost in spreading the news over the city—a casual word over the teacups, a comment at the bar of a well-known hotel, a pithy observation in the dimness of the nightclubs on Bubbling-Well Road. It was also discussed over ricebowls, chop suey, and sharks'-fin soup. Not least of all, it was considered in great detail over borsch, shashlyk, and vodka.

Alexandra had not dreamed of such success for her plan. The expected outcome would surely come quickly. In the meantime, she had dutifully played her part by accompanying Lionel wherever he wished to take her and agreeing with everything his friends said. But she was not so lost to her own plans that she did not receive a few surprises. Lionel had always openly preached socialism, but amongst the supporters of the self-styled Yellow Creek Political Fellowship were several people she had known as pillars of the international establishment who must have been there for reasons more serious than her own. There were also two men in grey suits who always stayed unobtrusively in the background and whom she had once overheard speaking to each other in Russian. *Reds*, she thought to herself in her new awareness of things—the people who had hounded Mark and his party of aristocrats across the snow. They looked quite ordinary.

But, all in all, she found herself forced to agree with her father, for once. What Lionel and his friends advocated was too perfect ever to work. They might have found the ideal answer for a land peopled by robots or trained dogs, but they made no allowance for human needs and frailties, and they always brushed aside the question of what must first happen before their Nirvana reached the people. Some of the men and women of the Fellowship had had experience in missions or charity homes dotted about the interior of China; others had been involved in investigating conditions in factories and businesses run by Europeans. One or two were permanently occupied in fighting vice—a hopeless task in the wickedest city in the Orient. All these were serious, dedicated people who would probably devote their lives toward improving the lot of the coolie.

Those like Lionel earned her derision, however. It was they who made the most impassioned speeches, they who attended every single meeting, yet who, without exception, did nothing to help the Chinese save write cheques. Like herself they were wealthy and privileged, yet not one appeared to realise he was tolerated only for his financial contributions. It had taken Alexandra just one meeting to see it, but she was not a political reactionary for lack of something better to do, as they were. Neither was she wooed by the men in grey suits as Lionel very plainly was. As an experience she found it interesting and somewhat surprising, but she longed for an end to her role.

Whilst she waited impatiently, she had set about trying to solve her other giant problem. Success eluded her this time, increasing her frustration. Hours spent in her father's library and deliberate questioning of those with personal experience or knowledge of the war and its aftermath in Russia had given her detailed knowledge of the 1917 Revolution, its causes, its wholesale slaughter—including the Tsar and his family—and subsequent Communist domination. She had also learnt the facts of the White Russian struggle, aided by the British, Americans, and other European nations until their cause was seen to be hopeless, and how the Tsarist troops and civilians were brutally tortured or killed when overrun and captured. Gradually Alexandra became caught up in a drama that had happened whilst she had been a heedless schoolgirl, but all her reading and probing by questions did not reveal what she really sought. Her father knew about that train, a Tsarist colonel's family, and events that had earned a Royal Engineer officer a medal for valour, yet he was the one person she could not ask. From what source had *he* learned the facts? Where could she turn for information that would shed light on a story which remained tantalisingly out of reach? Until she knew what—or *whom*—she was fighting, Mark could not be won. Once he finished the bridge he would return to Hong Kong. Time was so precious, and too much was being wasted while she chased the identity of a ghost woman. The conviction that knowing her adversary would be halfway to victory haunted her, increasing her restlessness and hampering artistic inspiration.

She was once more staring moodily at a ruined canvas that afternoon when her maid entered to say 'Master' wished to see her at once. Alexandra's mood underwent a swift reversal as excitement rushed through her. Not only was it rare in these days of political tension for her to be summoned in this manner, it was very unusual for her father to return home so early. Could the moment she had been awaiting have come? If so, she must handle it with extreme finesse. Even with all the aces in her hand she must not forget she was gambling with an expert, who might have a card up his sleeve. Taking off her painting smock, she wrapped a vivid blue draped coatee over her velvet lounging trousers and went downstairs filled with the fire of battle.

He was in the sitting room, cup of tea in hand, drumming on the lid of the piano with agitated fingers, but she was shocked at the sign of age on his face when he swung round at her entry. For once, he did not appear to notice what she wore.

"Have you taken leave of your senses?" he cried immediately. "Do you have any notion what you are doing? Can a child of mine *really* be so unintelligent? Over these past two years I have suffered the indignity of your outrageous behaviour being reported to me by men of consequence and authority. To some extent they uneasily turned a blind eye to 'youthful high spirits' but this is totally unacceptable. I have just had one of the most unpleasant and humiliating luncheons of my life."

She went across to the tea-tray and poured some into a wafer-thin cup for herself, then returned with it to sit on a footstool.

"If it was because I tangoed with Mrs Bellamy's nephew at her sedate tea-dance, I can't think why she ran to you with the tale. *I* didn't ask Nigel to take down the moose head from the wall and start a bullfight just because I wore a dress with a red cape . . . although it really was the most *divine* fun, until he crashed into one of the tables and knocked the choux pastries into his aunt's lap. It really wasn't *my* fault at all."

Her father put down his tea and walked toward her, fists clenched. "Alexandra, if you continue to talk such inane nonsense I think I shall strike you. I have long suspected that your excesses are committed with intent to hurt me, for you display a very sharp intelligence, at times. But now you have gone beyond all bounds of reason. You will cease this political charade immediately."

"I find it stimulating," she responded lightly, enjoying every moment. "It's by far the most serious way I have passed my time. I had not realised how decadent we are as a family." She waved a hand at the huge room. "All this for three people when families of fourteen or more are living in a room no bigger than our scullery."

Her father's face twisted. "You don't give a damn for that! Luxury is a way of life to you, and you'd be lost without it. Otherwise you'd go off and attempt your silly daubing in some damp garret. No, my dear, money is your god. You'll stop this dangerous association or I'll stop your allowance."

She gave a brittle laugh. "Oh no, you wouldn't care for Garrard Mostyn's daughter to look a pauper. I'd wear last year's fashions and start going to the moneylenders in the Chinese quarter. How would *that* affect your dignity?"

He stared at her with utter dislike. "If I thought you really believed in all that socialist pipe dream I might even have some respect for you, some hope that there was more in your head than a selfish desire to demonstrate your misguided ideas on female equality. Has it really not dawned on you yet that women have powers of persuasion that do not require aggression?"

"Yes, dear Father, that dawned on me at a very early age when you demanded that I start using them on your influential guests," she pointed out cuttingly. "I prefer aggression. It discourages the pats on the cheeks and avuncular cuddles, yet gets results."

"This time it won't—it most certainly won't," he raged. "I am not certain how far into this commitment you have gone, but you are playing with fire, Alexandra. Political devotees have very little sense of humour where their cause is concerned. You have chosen a dangerous board on which to play this game of chess . . . and you have chosen an opponent who *will* not lose. Have I made myself clear?"

"Yes, Father." She leaned across to the carved ivory cigarette box, took one out and fitted it into the long holder. She made much of lighting the cigarette and blowing a cloud of smoke. The action always gave her great confidence when matching her wits with men, and it seemed to unnerve them in some way. "But I have not yet heard you suggest a move that would ensure you victory."

He controlled himself with difficulty, she noted with grim satisfaction.

"I do not intend to discuss the subject further. You will either dissociate yourself with that group or catch the next sailing for England. If you will not realise the consequences this could have on my reputation and, indirectly, upon your mother, for God's sake think of the effect on the situation presently existing in Shanghai. In the coming days it is essential for us to present a united front against this Communist threat. I have devoted a lifetime to this city, and a great many people look to me at such times. When they see my daughter rush to the enemy camp their confidence is shaken. If it appears that I am unable to convince my own child of the right values they doubt the sincerity of mine. The enemy would use that small crack in confidence to the full. Dear heaven, do you not realise there are Soviet Russians advising the Yellow Creek Political Fellowship?"

"Oh, yes," she assured him calmly. "I have spoken to them."

She thought he really was going to strike her then. For a moment or two he stood above her in the throes of an emotion so strong it took her aback. Then he turned away and went to stand hunch-shouldered at the fireplace to stare at the flames.

"A lifetime of endeavour and *you* betray us!" he said in muffled tones. "I'll instruct Clitheroe to book a passage for you on the next ship for England. You can stay with your Aunt Freda or go and live in Chelsea with the arty set you admire so much—*anything* so long as you leave Shanghai at the earliest opportunity."

She rose and went across to stand beside him. "That's a poor kind of victory, isn't it? It will hardly restore confidence in your strength if it appears you must send me away to solve the problem. The only way this game can be brought to a conclusion entirely satisfactory to you would be for you to show me the error of my ways and woo me back to the fold." She took a draw on the cigarette then held the long holder away as she adopted an elegant pose of languid nonchalance. "Good is seen to triumph . . . and the wicked Reds gnash their teeth."

He cast her a sideways glance that was full of bitterness. "You think it is that easy?"

She shrugged. "It's easier than anything else you've suggested. It'll be a nine-day wonder in these days of unrest."

He turned, and once again she was taken aback by the emotion etched on his face.

"I told you you would go too far one day. I pray to God my fears are never realised. You are not nearly as independent as you care to imagine, and when life catches up with you that fact will be brought home to you with a vengeance." He gave a long deep sigh. "What is your price to renounce your assumed interest in these people's aims? I suppose it is my public blessing on this Bohemian nonsense."

She stood shaken by the evidence that her lifelong hope was within her grasp. It meant tuition by the most distinguished artists, a career which would make her wonderfully independent, the continuance of her allowance while she pursued her studies and, greatest of all, freedom to visit her mother whenever she wished . . . all because Garrard Mostyn would make a showing of public approval for what she longed to do. For a moment she stood irresolute, torn in opposite directions, until she acknowledged that Mark had become more important to her than a career as an artist.

"No, Father," she heard herself say. "All I want is for you to deposit seven hundred and fifty pounds in Mark Rawlings' account at the bank."

He looked thunderstruck. "I don't understand. What is all this about, Alexandra? How is it that you know of the affair? It is a matter between the man and myself." Then his lip curled. "By God, he didn't come whimpering to you for help!"

"Lionel prattled about it at Christmas," she snapped. "Mark wouldn't ask me for anything."

"*Mark?* That sounds a little too familiar."

She tapped the ash from her cigarette with a crimson-tipped finger. "You wanted me to seduce him, if you remember."

His mouth tightened. "I will not tolerate an association between you and that man."

"You don't have to. Just pay him what you owe."

"There is no kind of serious interest in Rawlings on your part?"

"You should know by now that men never interest me seriously," she told him, avoiding the trap.

"Then why this?"

"Because it is bad for *my* reputation when boys like Lionel go around disclosing your ruthless activities. I have no wish for the whole of Shanghai to know that my father is prepared to deliberately break a man's fine career out of pique, and for the cost of a sum equal to that with which he buys his daughter's allegiance each month." She crushed out the cigarette with shaking fingers. "It's a very small price to pay for getting you out of this frightful jam, isn't it?"

CHAPTER SEVEN

The studio was silent except for the ticking of the clock. The little maidservant had entered twice during the morning to bank up the fire, but Alexandra worked on without halting. It had been a long time since she had felt so fired with inspiration and so committed to working. For two days now she had been on the canvas, and it was already possible to see the quality of this particular subject.

The success of her confrontation with her father had restored her artistic confidence. The very fact that he had been prepared to let her follow her chosen path somehow made fulfilment possible where it had never been before. It also removed the heavy weight of his invincibility. With the right weapons he could be beaten. Cool determination, Mark had said, and that was what she had used.

Strangely enough it had also been Mark who had inspired this present work. Abandoning her fruitless attempts to capture his past experience, she had turned to his present one. He had told her of the legend, and how the local villagers called his bridge the Bridge of a Hundred Dragons. That was what she was creating. From that ancient legend had come visions of the past—an ornate, wooden, zigzag bridge that defied devils to cross it, watched over by a giant warrior and his escort of ghostly dragons.

Even after so short a time on it the vague suggestion of that marshy plain evoked a feeling of menacing isolation, while the Oriental pattern of the bridge symbolised the pagan elements of people governed by a fear of devils. Alexandra was honest about her worth as an artist and, at last, she could see signs of the talent she knew she possessed. All at once, everything seemed possible, everything seemed within her grasp. She had never been so happy before.

It was late in the afternoon when Alice Mostyn came to her daughter's studio and asked tentatively if she was interrupting. Tiring and hungry Alexandra put down her brush and stretched.

"No, dear, come in and give me your opinion," she invited with a smile. "I say that with perfect confidence, because this is the best thing I have ever done."

With the usual pang she watched her mother manoeuvre the heavy chair, but resisted the instinct to help her. Only when Alice had reached the easel and turned her chair into position did Alexandra put her arm lightly across the invalid's shoulders.

"Well?"

Her mother considered the embryo painting intelligently, then nodded. "I think I agree with you. But I shall wait until it is completed before giving a final judgement."

Alexandra smiled. "You won't change your opinion, I guarantee."

Alice smiled back, still studying the canvas. "So sure? Then it will be your greatest work, so far. The colours are so . . . so *mysterious*. Almost ghostly."

"That's just it," cried Alexandra delightedly. "When I put the figures in you'll see why. It depicts a legend that is tied up with Mark's bridge. He told me the story of why he was obliged to move it."

"Mark? Is that Major Rawlings who came to dinner with us?" A small frown creased her mother's brow. "You've seen him since?"

"Yes, several times." She sat back on her high stool and confessed. "I spent Christmas Eve and most of the following day with him, not at the Armitages', as I pretended."

The frown deepened. "Alexandra, you are not becoming involved in anything, are you?"

"Yes," she admitted happily. "And I hope to become even more involved."

"Oh dear, whatever do you mean by that?"

She laughed at her mother's expression. "I am not about to have an *affaire passionée* with him. Mark isn't that kind of man. He'd insist on making an honest woman of me."

Suddenly, Alice was upset. "That kind of remark is so immodest! Wear your short skirts and smoke your dreadful cigarettes, if you must, but leave open discussion of such things to men and fast women. You are a fresh young girl of nineteen. Please, don't become vulgar in your search for emancipation. Youth and innocence go so quickly. Try to preserve something of their charm while you can."

Unprepared for such a reaction, Alexandra was touched by the sadness in her mother's face. "It's only talk, dear," she said in soft reassurance. "It's the smart thing to say, and doesn't mean anything."

"It means that you are forgoing something very precious—femininity. You might think my generation were namby-pamby creatures in long dresses and tight corsets, but in France and Belgium many hundreds were nursing soldiers and driving ambulances. In England they worked in factories in place of the men. Strength of character is shown by achievement, not flat bosoms and unbecoming language. A woman's frailty is very often her greatest strength."

Dumbfounded Alexandra remained silent. Criticism from her father was commonplace, but this was different. It upset her.

"Major Rawlings is some years older than you and a man with considerable experience of life, Alexandra. What part is he playing in this association, may I ask?"

"A rather static one, at present. *I* am pursuing *him* . . . but I think I'm making him happier," she said with honesty. "That great experience of life you mentioned has brought him nothing but sadness."

"Pursuing him?" cried Alice. "My dear girl, whatever are you thinking of?"

"I'm thinking of marrying him when he gets round to asking me."

It was Alice's turn to be dumbfounded. *"Marrying him!"*

"You liked him, I could tell."

"My liking him does not make him a suitable husband for you."

"I'm in love with him, Mother."

"Dear heaven, have you taken leave of your senses, child? A mature man with a past tragedy in his life, and you are pursuing him because you imagine you are in love! All this will bring you is heartache," came the fervent verdict. "If he is as gentle as I suspect, he will be kind in his rejection of you, but you will still be hurt." She moved her chair over to the warmth of the fire, and silence fell as she gazed into the flames lost in thought while Alexandra tried to come to terms with the unexpected lack of the support for which she had hoped. When the invalid turned back to face her daughter there were tears on her lashes. "You know nothing of men, my dear—I cannot call those callow creatures with whom you mix *men*—so therefore you know nothing of women. There is no greater pain on earth than rejection by someone to whom you have given your deepest devotion. I have personal experience of it."

It was a terrible moment for Alexandra. Throughout her mother's painful illness she had never seen her cry, had never seen her without outward dignity. Now, she had been forced to surrender it because of her own need for sympathy. Going to her quickly Alexandra put her arms around the slender figure, close to tears herself.

"I think it is that same pain that Mark has suffered. Is it so wrong of me to want to ease it?" Putting up a hand she wiped her mother's cheek. "I *am* a woman, dear, despite the flat bosom and unbecoming language, and you are the only person I can talk to about him. Please don't be sad or angry. He has become a part of my life I can't let go."

Alice sighed as she searched the young face before her. "You will have to, nevertheless. Your father would never agree to such a marriage, even if your Mark should want it."

"I have defied Father before. I'll do so again."

"Not this time. An army man has to obey the rules or surrender his career. What's more, I can't believe this particular one would subject you to any kind of gossip."

Alexandra had not thought of that, and remembered Mark's old-fashioned approach to life. "I can wait until I come of age."

"At nineteen and in the throes of first love, two years can seem an eternity." Her mother took one of her hands, squeezing it tightly. "I said you know nothing of adult men and women. You see him now as a mature and exciting contrast to silly young men like Lionel Armitage, and there is no doubt he is an exceedingly attractive man in both looks and manner. However, as you freely admit, he is playing a static role in your relationship. That is probably for one of three possible reasons. Firstly, he may have no serious interest in you. Secondly, he may accept that your youth and social status make any kind of liaison with him out of the question. Thirdly, he is a man who has achieved a great deal at a young age. Due to his war experience he has gained military rank quickly, and it would appear he has a considerable reputation as an engineer. It can't have escaped your notice that he is jealous of both—to the extent that he even stood his ground in the face of all your father's persuasion and arguments that evening. That proves he has personal ambition to a strong degree." She sighed. "Even if he were madly attached to you, my dear, two years can bring many changes to a man of that type. In addition, as an army officer, he would very likely travel the world and meet any number of other women whilst you are here waiting."

"You're wrong about that, Mother. His devotion runs deep. I have proof of it."

The fair head shook gently. "Even the deepest devotion can fade during pursuit of great goals. It happens so slowly one is not aware of it until it is too late. Alexandra, a man chasing success and acclaim needs no more than a foil for his ambition in his wife. You are worth a great deal more than that."

Dismayed by this open declaration of something so personal, Alexandra sank back on her heels. "What are you saying I must do?"

"Stop this pursuit at once, before you hurt yourself so badly you will find it difficult to recover."

Dinner that evening was a strained affair. Since his daughter's ultimatum regarding the money owed to Mark, Garrard had not spoken to her, confining his few terse remarks at the dinner table to his wife. That particular evening Alice was also uncommunicative, which meant that heavy silence hung in the dining room broken only by the distant chattering of the cook-boy and his assistant when Lai-Hi opened the door leading to the kitchen at the back of the house.

Alexandra was still affected by her mother's reception to her confidence earlier in the day. She had hoped for an ally and found none. It was not only the hopeless picture her mother had painted, it was what she had said about the women of her own generation; the women at war who had shown their strength by courage. Had it been one of those who had won Mark's devotion and not yet lost it? Had she been a woman of compassion and gentle femininity? If so, what chance was there of his ever growing to love a modern emancipated idler? Once again, her longing to know what had happened to him in Russia burned within her. She was prepared to fight for him tooth and claw, yet unless she knew her opponent her campaign was pointless. Only he could tell her the truth, and that he steadfastly refused to do.

When Lai-Hi approached her whilst they were drinking their coffee in the sitting room she was still far away in such thoughts. Mr Armitage was awaiting her in the hall, he informed her, and she had to search her mind rather hastily. Lionel! Had she arranged to go out with him that evening? She did not think so. Although in no mood to face him, she could not pretend to be out since Lai-Hi had already told him the truth. All the same, she went out to the hall with the firm intention of pleading a headache and getting rid of him at the first opportunity.

When she saw how he was dressed she knew she had been right in thinking they had no previous arrangements for the evening. Instead of formal clothes he wore a tweed plus-four suit and leather motoring-coat. Goggles and a helmet dangled from his hand. She thought how silly he looked. A motor drive through Shanghai was hardly to be compared with the Red Baron on a mission.

"Lion, whatever are you doing out this way?" she asked in feigned astonishment.

His face looked as yellow as the smooth hair in the shaded lights of the hall. "It's the project meeting tonight. Sandy, you can't have forgotten!"

"Project meeting?" she echoed, her mind still full of Mark and his secret love in Russia.

"To decide on whether we shall support the demand of the steamer crews for a hundred percent rise. If they strike, which they will, we must provide financial assistance."

She stared at him for a moment while her thoughts adjusted to the new direction. "Oh Lion, just another dip into your pocket. Do you call that political involvement?"

He bridled. "Most definitely. Without money to back them no political party could survive. They'll expect a fat cheque from you, too."

"I can't come. We have guests," she lied.

"You must come," he told her sharply. "You've known about this date for over two weeks. It's the most important meeting we've had since October. Every member has got to attend."

His tone annoyed her. "*Got* to attend? My dear Lion, this is a voluntary organisation, not a military one."

"It's a *militant* one. That is the whole purpose of it—to force its aims through." He stepped closer. "What's the matter with you? I accepted your excuses for not attending the last two weekly meetings but, guests or no guests, you'll come tonight. They won't accept your absence."

Irritated and moody she took strong exception to his attitude. "What are you going to do, sweetie, carry me out bodily? They'll accept my absence tonight . . . and forevermore," she told him with sharp anger. "I resign my membership."

He appeared to turn even yellower. "You can't! You can't do that!"

"Watch me! Their brand of earnestness is too exhausting for words."

His hand shot out and seized her wrist with furious strength. "This is no time to stage one of your reckless stunts, Sandy. These people have no patience with levity when such issues are at stake."

"Such issues at stake?" she cried, shaking her hand free in a rage. "I don't give a damn about the steamer crews. They are lucky to have work at all when so many are starving and dropping dead all over the streets." Really worked up by now she spoke her mind in no uncertain terms. "If you truly wanted to help the people you'd go and scatter a handful of notes down in the Chinese quarter where the limbless and diseased sit and beg, you'd go down there with a spade and clear some of the corpses lying about waiting for someone to bury them, you'd carry buckets of night soil away from the hovels where it spreads dysentery and fever. It would be more creditable than joining a roomful of hotheads breathing fire and revolution, and patting each other on the back to show what splendid fellows they are." She took a deep breath. "If you want the truth, sweetie, I found them all completely nauseating and their ideals absurd. For a while it was a delicious joke, but now it has stopped being funny . . . and so have you, Lion."

She turned and began walking away, then was shocked when he seized her arm and swung her round to face him. His features were like a mask now, pale eyes gleaming with some kind of frenzy.

"You damned fool, they'll never let you give it up. I recruited you, and you're a member. You can't play your stupid games with this. They won't stand for it."

He was behaving as she had never seen him before, almost beside himself with agitation. Struggling in his fierce hold she cried, "Stop being so melodramatic. Let me go—unless you want me to shout for Lai-Hi." Escaping his grasping hands she took several steps back, out of breath. "You're either tipsy or you need to grow up. Go to your damned earnest meeting and pretend you are going to improve the world, but I am not coming nor will I ever be coming again. I am free to do as I wish. No ridiculous little band of blind idealists can dictate to me . . . or to anyone else. You must be crazy to think they can."

He stooped to pick up his helmet and goggles that had dropped during the struggle, and she saw that his hand shook as he straightened up.

"They all knew you were an empty-headed little bitch, but it didn't matter so long as you were seen to be supporting us. You were the most valuable fish they had caught, and I got all the credit for it. You are going to be very sorry about this. I'll see to that . . . and so will they. You don't know the half of what you are doing tonight."

He left, but for some minutes after the door closed behind him she was held in the grips of an inexplicable fear.

The first week of January brought a grave revelation in that land of perpetual conflict, one more shock to those Western men and women who still, after several centuries of experience, naively believed that pledges and treaties would be honoured by the Chinese.

Despite assurances by Chiang Kai-Shek that all foreign residents and property would be respected, despite the avowal of the Nationalists that their quarrel was not with the Western merchants, despite the fact that the long-standing residential settlements of the international trading nations made no show of armed resistance to the advancing army, the British Concession at Hankow, inviolate under a negotiated treaty, was occupied under threat of massacre of the white women and children. With a crazed mob flowing into the area, whipped up to killing point by agitators of uncertain affiliation, the British families fled from heavy clubs, stones and firebrands to the waterfront, where they crowded onto steamers bound for the safety of the Shanghai Settlement.

But would they find safety there? The action at Hankow cast doubts on the intentions of the Kuomintang army steadily and relentlessly gobbling up China. When other steamers appeared along the Yangtze full of foreign residents forced from their homes or businesses in other towns, it seemed to point to dedicated persecution of the white races and removed hopes that the Hankow affair might have been an isolated attack.

The attitude of expatriates in China hardened. This was unprovoked aggression, and it appeared to be escalating. Was there to be a repetition of the Boxer massacres? Already, missionaries who had loved and worked amongst the people of the interior of China were appearing on the dusty roadways that led to the Yangtze, with tales of violence and repudiation of all they had taught during a lifetime devoted to salvation.

Fear began to grow that even Shanghai would not be protected by those treaties so hard won by past merchants and the lives of soldiers. Plans were drawn up for the immediate evacuation of the women and children by British and American warships should it become necessary. The menfolk would stand and defend the Concessions, if not to the death, at least until they were breathing down the barrels of Chinese guns. Demand was made and approved for an emergency force to be shipped to Shanghai, and units from nearby island garrisons, and some from England, were equipped and embarked on troopships. Meanwhile, the Shanghai Volunteer Corps recruited a great many members, and even formed a whole company of White Russians to swell the ranks.

Mark knew of all this. He had arranged with his Chinese contractor in Shanghai for newspapers to be sent up the line with every consignment of materials. The news disturbed him. It suggested that there was no question of the Kuomintang being halted yet, and the attacks on foreigners reminded him much too vividly of Russia, when the Reds had advanced inexorably northward sweeping all resistance into the sea. Such thoughts brought a return of his depression. Where would the Red menace ever stop? The emergency plans for Shanghai made him think of Alexandra's safety, and the desire to see her again grew ever stronger.

To counteract his worries he threw himself into his work as January wore on. He wanted the bridge finished as soon as possible. For that reason he had done nothing about the killing of the Portuguese and the dog. Perhaps he was simply evading unpleasantness or shunning responsibility, but he had a long list of reasons to back his decision.

Firstly, the lad had not been employed by the railway, nor by Mark himself so, strictly speaking, did not come within his sphere of responsibility. Secondly, the working association with Corcoran was for a very temporary period, which Mark felt did not justify his interference in an affair between the Scot and villagers over whom he seemed to have some kind of personal hold. Corcoran was unlikely to mend his ways on the word of an army engineer brought in for one job only, and the outcome would almost certainly worsen the relationship between the two men at a time when close co-operation was essential.

Thirdly, to make a great song and dance over the murder would lead to all work on the bridge coming to a halt while long-winded investigations were set in motion. It could not fail to worsen relations between East and West at this tense period. Mark ruefully admitted to himself that the Chinese would not give a damn about a dead Portuguese boy, and even the lad's own nationals would probably see the incident as a great nuisance when greater issues were at stake. He had been just one of those pieces of human jetsam to be found in Shanghai who commanded no real loyalty from anyone. Had he been the victim of a diplomatic incident the matter would have been different, but his death on a canal boat by persons unknown would evoke no more reaction than the tears of a hard-bitten Scot.

So Mark had put the reconstruction of the bridge before all else and left Corcoran to deal with it. What had happened at Lu-Seng that morning he did not try to guess, but the Scot had been away all day, only returning at dusk to bury the lad and the remains of the animal on the canal bank. Mark had kept his distance. He had seen men in such a condition of shock before and knew he was likely to have a spade swung blindly at him if he approached with an offer of help. Corcoran had kept to his boat for thirty-six hours, probably with the whisky bottle for company, then emerged to get on with his work, as usual. He said little other than professional comments to Mark and neither man mentioned the incident again. But Corcoran's treatment of the coolies was even more savage than before.

Whatever had occurred at Lu-Seng had ensured that the men no longer appeared for work at the bridge. Mark had no intention of going to the village to sort it out. Corcoran had hired them in the first place, so if he had sacked them all there was nothing to be done but continue with a smaller but efficient work-force. Truth to tell, it was something of a relief to be rid of them. Aside from wanting him to make a third drowned Englishman to satisfy their legendary dragons, they had been the cause of the bridge having to be re-sited. He had had enough of Lu-Seng's inhabitants. They had been more trouble than they were worth. But there were still problems. The regular coolies could be working well when a squabble would break out between two of them over something insignificant and the whole force would start going at it hammer and tongs, shouting and shaking their fists at each other. After the third of these outbursts Mark lost his patience, and turned to Hong who was doing nothing to get them back on the job.

"What's the trouble this time?" he demanded. "We're working

short-handed and I can't have these constant fights . . . and don't tell me they want more money, Hong. This job is falling behind, and I'm in no mood for an Oriental roundabout before we reach the real reason."

But the foreman was, for once, very willing to explain. "They argue about the Kuomintang, Major. Many say that the soldiers will take every man's savings, his women, even his rice bowl. Others say these soldiers are different from the others. They say these men are their true brothers marching to unite China under just rule." He waved his hand toward the haggling crowd beside the breakdown train. "These men are from both North and South, Major. They are very different. They are long-standing enemies."

"That's all I need," exclaimed Mark in disgust. "Go and tell them to hold their political meeting after dark. This section must be finished by the end of the week whether they are enemies or not."

Hong shook his head regretfully. "I am sorry, Major, but it must be settled now. It is our way, when there is discord, to examine every statement for its truth to discover if a man is justified in what he has said. To stop without giving an opportunity for this would make one man lose 'face'. He will have disputed what his opponent said without showing that he had reason for what he did. It would mean he could not continue to work with the others."

Mark closed his eyes and counted to ten, but he still felt the same at the end of it. "In God's name how do you people ever get anything done?" he exclaimed.

Hong looked offended. "I have no wish to be discourteous, Major, but you only have to read the history of China for your answer."

"Yes," he retorted half to himself. "Behead a few hundred as incentive to work. Perhaps that's what I should start doing." He looked at his watch. "It'll be dark within two hours and that pair of girders must be made secure by then. If we should have a wild night they could slip loose and fall into the canal. Get the two ringleaders of that argument and let them stand up on the track shouting at each other until they are hoarse, but I want the rest back at work within five minutes."

"It cannot be done, Major. I could not intervene in such a case."

"*Intervene!*" cried Mark. "You are their foreman. It is your job to tell them what to do."

"Only when they are working," Hong pointed out with Chinese logic.

Mark tried to remain calm and reasonable. He took several deep breaths, told himself he must respect the ways of the local people . . . then exploded.

"Don't attempt to break up their quarrel, then. Just go over there and tell them that when the Kuomintang soldiers get up this far there'll be no work for anyone, so they had better earn what money they can now, while there is still time."

Hong was quiet for a moment, then looked away at the first span of the bridge standing with sharply jutting spars reaching out into space.

"I cannot tell them that, Major. The Kuomintang will bring work to everyone—work, prosperity and a strong future for China."

Nonplussed Mark said, "You surely don't believe that, Hong?"

The round face was full of earnest expression as the man turned back to state his case. "At Christmas I spoke to my brother in Shanghai. I have told you that he returned not long ago from England. He has spoken with men of great wisdom in your country, Major, and it has now become clear to him that this is the great will of the people of China. It will bring an end to such terrible things as we have now. There will be peace and plenty for us all. The great warlords and rich merchants will be brought to their knees."

"To be beheaded, no doubt," concluded Mark. "Hong, you are an educated man compared with these squabbling coolies. You have seen the reports in the papers. Kuomintang soldiers are killing, raping and looting just like the soldiers of the warlords. The people of the southern cities they have 'liberated' are being robbed and abused yet again. There is no peace and plenty in their wake."

"It will come," was the obstinate answer.

"No, it will never come," said Mark with sudden heat. "I have seen it happen in Russia. It brings nothing but misery."

"My brother left to join the Kuomintang army at Christmas. He would not go with men of dishonour."

"I see." It seemed fruitless to go on, but he could not help saying, "Those same honourable men have attacked British people—women and children—who are protected by treaties."

"It was not the Kuomintang."

As Mark looked at that impassive bespectacled face he realised the understanding between them was a myth. He had believed there was some kind of warmth, some level of respect between them as men of different backgrounds that stood apart from racial considerations. But Hong was, after all, a man of his country. The Christian faith, the good English, and the Western clothes had blinded him to the fact that Hong had an Eastern mind. Suddenly weary, feeling weighed down by the incomprehensible ways of the Chinese, and seeing the bridge as a monster that kept him out in that wild lonely place, he had a sudden longing to see Alexandra. Her youth and gaiety, her zest for living, her absurd yet irresistible attraction was just what he needed to help him forget dragons, the macabre killing of the Portuguese and the dog, and the fact that his own bank account was overdrawn by seven hundred and fifty pounds, which he could never recover. For once, he wanted to forget responsibility, command and all commonsense, and the best place to do that was by her side. At that moment, her attitude toward life was immensely appealing.

The longing for her remained for the next four or five days as he drove himself hard in an effort to advance construction toward the day he could return to Shanghai. The time came earlier than he had foreseen, and certainly not in the way he wanted. The coolies were working as hard as coolies could work—whether on advice from Hong or not Mark could not be sure—and the supports for the central span were ready to be driven in. The weather had been bright and favourable, and all seemed to be going well until the expected load of gusset plates and rations failed to turn up as scheduled. All day Mark listened for the approach of the train then, when it did not come, waited with impatience all through the next day.

When Hong questioned a passing boatman on the canal he was told that the railway had been sabotaged by Nationalist sympathisers, and a night train from Nanking had been derailed because a length of track had been removed. But as their line branched off before reaching Nanking Mark could not believe his supply train would be affected by it. When a third day passed without its arrival he was forced to go to Shanghai to investigate.

As he had supposed, the line was open all the way and they made good time on the little engine, arriving at Shanghai yard just after mid-morning. It was good to see civilisation again even if there were Oriental touches with brown-sailed junks at some of the jetties, and rickshaws, along with the famed wheelbarrows, thronging the streets. There in the International Settlement one hundred dragons and a ghostly warrior took on a proper perspective, and the sight of that garrotted boy and a severed dog's head began to fade from his memory.

There were several letters awaiting him at his hotel, but he left them where they were. Two were from home and one from the bank: he was in no mood for either. After a hot bath and an excellent luncheon in what was, for him, comparative luxury, he took a rickshaw to the offices of the Chinese contractor all set to do battle. But he was foiled.

A nervous fast-talking clerk was engaged in showing an American exporter over the deserted set of three offices. When Mark asked the whereabouts of Mr Sun, a tale of woe poured from the lips of a man plainly caught in a dilemma. His employer had gone, he said. His business interests were wide and varied, and Mr Sun had heard what had happened to men of his exalted position in Hankow, and other places. When Kuomintang soldiers took the city, his money and possessions would be taken from him, his wife and daughters thrown to the soldiers for sport, and his ancestors denigrated. All that for working hard for his country! But because he had entertained the Northern generals and supplied them with the normal requirements of life that any merchant would innocently sell to a customer, he was now in danger. As they advanced, the Nationalists had beheaded anyone suspected of allegiance to the warlords: there were rows of bloody heads strung along the main street of every city they had conquered. A time of terror and death was coming to Shanghai. There were many evil people in the port but one of these who had, by curious chance, become acquainted with Mr Sun had warned him that retribution would be swift and terrible when the Kuomintang reached the gates of the city. Mr Sun had taken his family to safety. It was not known where.

It said much for Mark's 'Orientalisation' that he left without a word, even though Sun had been paid in advance for a whole consignment of steel, and rice for the coolies. He devoted his energies, instead, toward the more rewarding task of finding another contractor who would *not* be paid in advance. The whole afternoon had passed before he had doubtful success. The rice was easy enough to obtain, and he arranged for two weeks' supplies to be shipped up by barge immediately. The steel plates were more difficult. The size, gauge, and quality had to be just right and one man, rather too glib for Mark's liking, assured him he could have a batch of the very thing required by ten o'clock the following morning. He left with a promise to return at ten the next day to inspect the goods. But he did not count on it. He was learning very quickly the Chinese habit of never admitting to failure. In the morning the man would probably tell a long tale of how he had been lied to by the steel manufacturer, and Mark would have to start all over again.

It was dark when he returned to his hotel. The evening stretched ahead of him, a lonely prospect in that city of sin and pleasure. In the Chinese quarter outside the Settlement boundaries, every manner of exotic or vicious indulgence could be found—opium dens, brothels, nightclubs peopled by homosexuals, live performances of perversions by male and female participants, *kinder*-brothels with child prostitutes, gambling casinos, cockfights, dog-fights, bear-baiting, nude sectarian rituals, or just plain drinking hells. The only one that might remotely interest him was the last, but he preferred to drink in decent surroundings with civilised people . . . and he had had enough of Chinese fantasies for the moment.

There was only one thing he longed for yet, after four weeks of thinking about her, he had come down to earth now he was back in Shanghai. It would be madness to see Alexandra again. He was a man with no money and an uncertain future. He also had a lead on her of eleven years. At the moment she was attracted to someone she saw as a fellow victim of her father, a lame dog with a mysterious past. In her world such a man would prove diverting, but diversions were quickly replaced. When he went back to Hong Kong she would not find it difficult to amuse herself elsewhere, but he . . . ?

Reluctant to finish that conclusion he nevertheless acknowledged that another meeting with her would worsen the situation where he was concerned. Those two days at Christmas had put back into his life something he had thought gone forever. For seven years he had lived with memories that could not be banished. Only twice had he tried to do so. Both those nights had been desperate, unhappy experiences. Yet Alexandra, the glowing wand of youth, had aroused him from the moment he had jumped on her foot. Aroused him to a wide mixture of feelings, admittedly, but his period of emotional hibernation had been concluded by her springtime lure and he was in danger of succumbing completely.

So he dressed for dinner and ate it in solitary style, resigned to the sensible course of an early night in a comfortable bed. After an hour at the bar chatting to men like himself who were just passing time, he went upstairs, hung a 'DO NOT DISTURB' notice on his door and undressed, ignoring the rebellious voice within that told him he was behaving like a maiden aunt at a wedding reception. To drown that voice he had another drink or two, which left him muzzy enough to open his letters and read them as he sat in bed. His mother was still bemoaning her lot. To strengthen her arguments his sister Nora had put pen to paper for the first time in years with a long tale of woe, self-pity and the wickedness of men. It was so reminiscent of Victorian melodrama he tossed it aside with an inebriated grin.

"Since I am one of the rapacious beasts, my dear Nora, hasn't it occurred to you that I might have several bastards of my own to support?" he muttered thickly. "Anyway, I haven't any more money to give you. I haven't got any money at all—which solves that problem very nicely."

In that mood of bravado he opened the envelope from the bank. He had to read it twice, then he was still not certain he was seeing aright. If only he were a little more sober! Five minutes later he was out of bed and stumbling joyously across to the telephone. He was solvent, his future was extremely bright, he felt eleven years younger . . . and he wanted to kiss that girl until she begged for mercy.

Miss Mostyn was out, the houseboy told him, and he hurled a shoe across the room in disappointed frustration. The best he could do was write a note saying he wanted to see her at the first opportunity, asking her to telephone before ten in the morning. The note having been despatched by messenger, there was nothing else to do but go back to bed with another drink and wonder happily how on earth she had managed to do it. Wild relief at his debt being settled combined with thoughts of what it would be like if she were there with him at that moment and, drunk with brandy and desire, he succumbed to physical exhaustion and fell asleep.

He was awoken to a continuation of his dreams. Alexandra was sitting on the side of his bed shaking him gently. But he remained slumbrous only a few seconds before he was wide awake to the fact that this was no dream girl.

"Good God, how did you get in? Are you mad?" he cried, sitting up swiftly.

She put a finger to her lips, her eyes brilliant with laughter. "Shhh, it's only six o'clock. Do you want to wake the entire hotel?"

"*Six o'clock!* You must get out of my door . . . my room . . . at once." He was still in the throes of waking and stumbled over his words. "It will be all over Shanghai by morning. Think what *that* will do for your reputation."

She was smiling as she stood up and put her hand lightly across his mouth to silence him. "If you continue to shout like that it *will* be all over Shanghai. Don't be angry with me, darling. I sneaked in without anyone seeing me."

His heart was racing as he got out of bed. "Alex, this is complete folly, coming to my room in the early hours! Of all the crackbrained things you have done, this is the most dangerous."

"Why? No one has seen me, so far . . . and I know I am perfectly safe in a bedroom with you."

"Oh no, you're not," he said swiftly.

Next minute he was pulling her hard against him, kissing her again and again instead of giving her the thrashing she really deserved. But it was dangerous. The urge to take her over to the bed was getting much worse and, half-naked as he was, his need was getting out of hand.

"Alex," he murmured, coming up for air, "unless you leave at once all your ideas about my old-fashioned chivalry are going to be grossly contradicted."

Suddenly, she was arching back, her palms against his bare chest, her eyes glowing with desire as she looked up at him. "So you do want me?"

"*Want* you?" he breathed, feeling as if he had been hurled against a brick wall. "I've wanted nothing else since Christmas, you crazy beautiful creature."

The need to be sensible no longer seemed to matter. Her open fur-trimmed jacket fell to the ground as his hands moved from her breasts to her shoulders, where a row of tiny buttons fastened her silk blouse, and his mouth greedily travelled the line of her neck downward from her right ear. The caressing touch of her hands on his back, moving up and down his spine with the lightest of teasing, set him edging her toward the rumpled bed where he had spent a night of frustration. She was sighing, moaning, and arching her body against his to heighten her pleasure in all he did, and there was only one thought then in his mind.

The moment was shattered by a shrilling sound that appeared to be right beside his ear. It was loud and went on and on, giving him no peace. He put back his head and closed his eyes in an attempt to steady himself, then sat her gently on the edge of his bed and picked up the telephone receiver.

"Yes?" It was hollow and immensely tired.

"Your early morning call, Major Rawlings. It is now six-thirty."

He said nothing, just stood with the receiver in his hand, trying to cope with interrupted passion and a returning sense of responsibility. There was a click on the other end as the receptionist disconnected the line, but Mark stayed as he was, his back to the girl on the bed. Thank God for his request for an early call!

"I want you to know I'm not in the habit of doing this," said a shaken voice from behind him.

"I have never thought you were," he replied, still with his back to her.

"I read your message, and was so delighted that you were back in Shanghai I didn't want to waste a minute of it. I was afraid you'd be going straight back to that beastly bridge." There was a short pause. "I love you, Mark."

In control of himself now, he turned to her. "Love demands honour, trust and respect. This isn't the way for you, Alex. You have seen that I'm every bit as human as the next man, and these kind of games can be dangerous."

She looked at him mutinously, her blouse falling open. "Not if you love me in return."

He was suddenly angry with her, and with his thwarted passion. "Have you no sense of responsibility, to yourself or anyone else? All these larks you kick up simply cause raised eyebrows and a lot of unpleasant gossip for your mother to hear. A girl can survive certain things on the excuse of extreme youth, but the game we were about to play is far more serious. You must have been aware of the risks to yourself of unplanned passion."

She stood up slowly, her eyes reflecting unsatisfied desire and the pain of sudden rejection. "Are you sure you're not really thinking of the risks to your career?"

"No . . . but they do enter into it," he admitted. "A scandalous involvement with the underage daughter of a man like Garrard Mostyn could finish me as far as the army is concerned. All else apart, Alex, this kind of thing should wait until a man has the legal right to take a woman."

A smile began touching her lips already swelling from his kisses. "Then you'll have to obtain it as soon as possible."

Sensing that the danger had not yet passed, he ran his hand through his tousled hair and snapped, "I'm very hard up, and far too old for you. What's more, your father would never agree."

She moved closer, saying softly, "Nonsense! I can deal with him, and I have enough money for us both. As to your age, what you were doing just now was definitely . . ."

He seized her shoulders, turned her around, and marched her toward the door, grabbing up her jacket as he went. "Go downstairs and wait for me to dress. We'll have breakfast together and talk sense instead of nonsense. There are a few things I need to say to you, my girl."

She turned, leaning back against the door, gazing up at him with the full force of her undeniable love. "There's only one thing I want to hear you say, darling. You are going to tell me you love me to distraction." Standing on tiptoe she kissed him unrestrainedly full on the mouth. "You *are*, Mark, aren't you?"

Feeling desire returning he thrust her from the room before they got back to the stage they had reached before the telephone call. He dressed swiftly, trying to think straight. He had damn near lost his head and taken a rich society girl to bed, and he was about to have breakfast with her while they discussed a future they could not possibly have. It was utter madness, but it was like being reborn. With Alex all obstacles seemed surmountable; the impossible presented no problems. The pain of the past flew to be replaced by the happiness of today.

Mark spent the next two days trying to get a batch of plates to his precise requirements. As he had feared, that first promise of instant acquisition had been Oriental optimism on behalf of the contractor, and he had no intention of repeating the folly of listening to it. So he went round the Shanghai godowns and warehouses himself, asking about stocks from various suppliers. When he tracked down what he wanted he would then engage a contractor to buy them and ship them to the bridge, otherwise he could wait weeks for mythical consignments to appear.

Those two days had an air of unreality about them. He was torn between opposing wishes: to get back to the job and get it out of his system, and to stay as long as possible with Alexandra in Shanghai. She had transformed his life literally overnight. From the moment she left him he longed for the next meeting with her. When he was with her the world was full of hope and firm promises but, after so long in emotional limbo, he was finding it increasingly difficult to resist her frank sexual challenge. Emancipation, or not, her naïve belief in love conquering all smacked of old-fashioned femininity of the sweetest kind. It was an unexpected facet of her that delighted yet frustrated him. Even so, it was only the knowledge that he would be courting complete disaster that stopped him from trying to possess her.

In consequence, his love was heightened by overwhelming physical desire, and he hammered his brains for the way in which he could make her his wife as quickly as possible. In his most frustrated moments he could see no answer except to wait two interminable years. Even then Mostyn would undoubtedly do all he could to hinder such a marriage. But Alexandra, as desperate as he, boosted his spirits with her confidence. She was certain she could persuade her father to let her pursue an artistic career. He would be glad to send her away from Shanghai now, she told Mark, then she could go to Hong Kong to be near him. After that, she would go to England or wherever else he might be posted.

He felt her idea turned her into a kind of camp follower, but she would not listen, so full of plans was she. With danger presently threatening all her father held dear, she was convinced his dislike of Mark would be swamped by greater considerations. After a few months he most probably would not try to stop them from marrying, she said.

When he sat with her, watching the soft glow of love in her eyes and letting his gaze wander over the bright hair, and golden complexion of her face and her throat, he believed everything she said, but once alone he told himself he had no intention of dangling on Garrard Mostyn's string. The first step was to finish the bridge that was proving such a problem, then get back to Hong Kong to consider his future. To marry before Alexandra was twenty-one would risk a certain amount of scandal, but it would be far less if he was no longer in the army. He would have to weigh up his chances of employment with a civilian engineering company, or as a freelance. The fact that he would never be able to give his wife all the advantages to which she was accustomed did not weigh with him at all. Alexandra had known that from the very start, and he had lived long enough now to dispense with noble ideals and seize happiness when it was offered. He had lost it once: he had no intention of letting it slip through his fingers again. She was determined and resilient. If it meant following him from country to country, living in foreign towns while he built his bridges, having no permanent home, she would take it in her stride. With that knowledge and with consuming love driving him, he was prepared to take any step that would allow them their happiness.

When he returned to his hotel that night, after another hopeless quest for steel plates, he was again torn between frustration at the delay on the bridge and delightful anticipation of a further meeting with the girl he loved. He took his key from the receptionist who told him there was a lady in the salon awaiting his return. She had been there about half an hour taking tea. He smiled as he tossed up the key and caught it again. She was as eager as he; as greedy for every moment together. How he loved her honesty! No blushing simpering flirt, his girl, but a sweet reckless creature who gave her love unconditionally. He strode eagerly to the salon with its velvet-covered banquettes and turned into the quietness it afforded. The only occupant looked up at his approach and rose.

"Mark! *C'est vrai!*"

The lights dipped and swung, the crimson velvet blurred, the air grew icy cold. Seven years fell away in a moment. Faces swam around him—passionate Slavic faces—and he heard their voices as they worked and sang. He heard the desolate howl of wolves; the rattle of rifles in the still air. The elegant salon vanished: all he could see was a bridge and an old steam-engine as he took it across that great span of wooden sections, praying it would not be the end of their journey when they reached the other side.

Then he could evade it no longer, and surrender was agonising. Her voice came to him from the past as if she said the words there and then: *I told them you were my husband, but you play your part too well. I shall never forget, never again love like this*. He saw the grave beauty of her face as they had parted, saw the pain in green eyes that had witnessed the death of a nation and the loss of a love that could not be, saw the dark hair wound around her head—an aristocrat forced to live as a peasant. He remembered every word she had ever said to him, everything she had ever done when he was present. He remembered her courage, her despair, her fear and her tremendous compassion. He remembered her undying love for him . . . he remembered her being led away as he stood silently between two fellow officers.

Shaken, sick at heart, torn apart by that past tragedy once more, he stared at the tall striking woman who seemed as lost in that other time as he. Then, a small figure appeared from behind her skirt to gaze up at him, and Mark knew he was looking at his own son.

CHAPTER EIGHT

For the first time in seven years Mark sat with a bottle of brandy beside him and did not touch it. He was full of a pain that could not, must not be subjugated. Since that terrible day he had watched the shores of Russia growing more and more distant, he had been running from it. Tonight, he faced it fairly and squarely knowing he must run no longer.

You are young and have a future beyond this. Live it, my dearest. He had held her words as a talisman against the anguish and loneliness of those first years without her. Apart from the drinking he had shown little outward sign of what they had done to him, those months in Russia, and all he had achieved had been for her. He had built his future with determination and single-mindedness. He had worked, studied, endured, until his name was respected in engineering circles and his professional skill in demand. He had gone on living because she had said he must, but those years of not knowing her fate had cost him dear. Now they had all dropped away, and he was back in a time the world preferred to forget with cocktails, ragtime and the mad desire for *fun* at all costs. As he sat staring into the fire he saw it all again as if looking at a movie at the cinema—himself standing alone on a railway track in Russia, which was how it had all begun:

He was very young—not yet twenty-three—but he had been through four interminable years of war which had made him an old man in experience. Even so, he knew little of women; even less of Russians. By volunteering for Russia immediately on his return from the trenches of France he was being paid an additional allowance but, as the extra went to his mother and sisters, he was personally just as hard up as he had ever been. As head of a small detachment of Royal Engineers he was responsible for a length of railway track to the east of a White Russian base where the Red advance was being resisted.

The fire shifted and settled into a new pattern, yet Mark, lost to all else, continued to stare down the years into that scene playing out before him. During that summer when darkness hardly touched the night sky resistance to the Red forces was fierce, and Mark struggled to find inner peace on a lonely stretch of line crossing spectacular terrain. For a while he did, then the Bolshevik troops overran the base, barbarously killing all Russians, military or otherwise. A large number of British, French and Czechoslovakian troops were allowed to board a train bound for Vladivostok on the written guarantee that they would leave Russia on the first available ship when they reached the eastern port. On its journey the train stopped to pick up any foreign troops who managed to reach the railway, and Mark had climbed into one of the trucks with mixed feelings. The vast wilderness of the land had, in some part, provided the tranquillity for which he yearned, yet there was a sense of fighting a doomed cause by then which made him thankful not to be in at the death. Halfway to its destination the train was blown up, flying apart in a spectacular example of ignorance of explosive power by peasant-soldiers. From the appalling carnage a young British captain had crawled, bleeding and almost senseless, but alive.

Mark then saw a succession of flash pictures like a movie being run too quickly through the projector, until they slowed to show him a large house on a country estate, and a man near to death lying there gazing up at a face more exciting and full of emotion than he had ever encountered.

"Oh, dear God," he breathed as he put his head in his hands, unable to look at the flames in the hearth any longer. "*Katya!*"

The pictures continued to come, defying his closed lids. There was no way of stopping the whole story unfolding before him now. The injured Mark had somehow crawled five miles to the country estate of a Tsarist family, where Colonel Alexei Pavlovich Drozdov had left his youthful wife, his sister and two young brothers for safety while he was fighting in the north. There, Mark was tended by the two highborn girls while his life hung in the balance, until one of the servants returned from market with the news that Bolshevik troops were sweeping toward the area, drinking and raping as they advanced, and shooting anyone in a uniform on sight.

Dressed as peasants they left within half an hour, Mark propped up in an old cart, looking every bit the simpleton he was meant to be. For two weeks they travelled, making detours around areas where the Reds had been seen, posing as a young married couple with brothers and an unmarried sister. Mark grew stronger and took command, seeing that their best chance was still the railway. At a country junction they met up with a small group of White troops who had been separated from their main force and lost heart. Persuading them to push east with him Mark gained valuable help for his plan to steal an engine when the chance occurred.

In that hotel room in Shanghai he then relived those desperate days—the fear, the stealth, the burden of responsibility, and the love for another man's wife that he could not control. He recalled the fearful waiting while Red troops caroused in the village where they were hiding; the anguish of being forced to watch two dignified aristocratic women being stripped to their underclothes by drunken troops before being seized by a peasant-officer, who decided they were too good for the rank and file. Mark would never know if he would have broken cover and betrayed them all to prevent rape, because fighting had begun in the surrounding forest, drawing the troops away in a panic. The train was then left unguarded, and Mark took it to begin an incredible journey to freedom. The days and nights passed. They stole food when they were starving; they suffered from thirst and the heat. Then, there was one bridge between them and the retreating White forces, and it was heavily guarded by the enemy. For an entire day Mark clung to the timbers beneath that bridge, waiting for nightfall. When it came, he crept to the log huts the Bolsheviks used for their supplies and stole explosives to blow the bridge once they had crossed. While he placed them, the group he now led disposed of the guards. Taking the train across naturally alerted the enemy, so when he ran back to light the fuses they were tumbling from the huts in confusion. With the match in his hand he was shot in the leg and fell; but the fuses were lit and the tiny flames began travelling through the night toward the bridge. Struggling to his feet he staggered as far from the spot as possible to divert attention from those little snaking lights, then was attacked again, sustaining several severe knife wounds. He would have been killed had not the bridge then blown almost as spectacularly as the train on which he had first travelled. Rescued by the men who had become his friends as well as his followers, he was again nursed back to health by the two women.

Unable to prevent them Mark found tears standing on his cheeks as he recalled the end of that journey no one could believe they had made. He saw so clearly the White Russians, savage, suffering, knowing their cause was lost, refusing to give horses to the women. They took the young boys into their ranks as child-soldiers, but in the midst of massacre and mayhem two women counted for nothing where they were concerned. Only by buying their lives with the promise of money from the British at Vladivostok did Mark persuade the ragged Tsarists to take them safely to the free port. His own people had, at first, refused to pay. Then, a harassed senior officer who had heard of their incredible trek across Russia honoured Mark's promise.

He parted the following day from those with whom he had shared every emotion known to man. The war had hardened him to loss and farewells, but nothing had prepared him for the killing pain of severing himself from a girl who had been his wife in every sense during those months when the past twenty-three years of his life had been forgotten, and the future years counted for nothing.

The tears now ran unchecked as he thought of the fears, the desperate enquiries, the searching letters, the pestering of anyone who had knowledge of Russia or records of those final days before the Red stain had covered the whole of that wild, beautiful land. He thought of his recent questioning in Shanghai for any news of the Drozdov family, knowing in his heart it was a vain hope. Yet, those suspicious exiles who closed ranks against strangers who asked too many questions, had given him the answer he had sought for almost eight years. Katya was dead.

The anguish grew too great and he sat racked by sobs as the fire died to a faint ruby glow that no longer highlighted the luxurious furnishings surrounding him. For seven years he had coped with the hideous uncertainty of her fate, always living in the hope of finding her again. Had she been captured, pegged out on the ground, and submitted to bestial rape by a whole company of soldiers before dying? Had they paraded her through a village and performed humiliating degradations to show their contempt of aristocrats? Had she been tortured before dying slowly? Finally, he knew the truth.

Colonel Alexei Drozdov had killed a commissar of great importance: a man almost worshipped by the more fanatical revolutionaries. For that, he and his entire family had been listed by the Cheka—the Bolshevik secret police—as Tsarists to be exterminated. The Colonel had been killed in battle, but his family had been hunted down. The adolescent boys had been betrayed by a turncoat peasant in the group that had taken them all to Vladivostok, but the women had moved into the eastern seaboard home of family friends by then.

It was there that Katya had given birth to Mark's son just before the final resistance of all those fighting the followers of Lenin. Katerina Drozdova had been betrayed by a servant, and slain whilst out trying to obtain food for her child. Her husband's sister had gone into hiding with the boy, and eventually escaped her homeland on a refugee ship heading for China. She had married a fellow refugee in return for a room in the café he opened in Shanghai. When the man had died from cholera, she took over ownership and was there, living in relative comfort compared with many of her compatriots, when she heard that an Englishman was haunting White Russian strongholds asking for information about the Drozdov family. Filled with the fear that there was something sinister behind this interest, that her enemies were using the name of a man who had gone from her life as abruptly as he had entered it, she had lain low until there was a chance to check the facts. Enquiries at his hotel had yielded the information that Major Rawlings of the Royal Engineers was a tall gentleman with dark curling hair, who was engaged in building a bridge near Lu-Seng. His first name was, indeed, Mark and his date of birth indicated that he was thirty years old. Hardly believing he could truly be in Shanghai, of all places, she had waited for him to return from the interior.

The sound of falling coals eventually brought Mark back from the regions in which his mind had roamed, and he dragged himself to his feet. After building up the fire he stood looking at the infant flames trying to stay alive, flickering through the dense smoke caused by the shovelful of coal from the hod. Turning away abruptly he poured himself a brandy, yet the spirit remained untouched as he twisted the glass slowly in his hands and thought about the boy of six-and-a-half years in the boudoir which was part of this expensive suite of rooms. A sturdy, well-built child with dark curly hair and deep brown eyes; a boy with a scattering of freckles across his cheeks and a square jaw that suggested obstinacy. Could anyone doubt paternity? Like the flames, that boy was struggling to establish a future. A child of love, he had been told his father was a very brave soldier whose duty had taken him away to the other side of the world. He believed the woman he called '*Maman*' was his mother, and had called her café-husband 'Oncle'. Now, there was no male influence in his life with Marie Roskova, at a time when he most needed it.

Mark took a pull at the brandy, but he was hardly aware of what he was doing. It had been a shattering experience to be confronted with a miniature replica of himself: a child Katya must have known she was carrying when they had parted. There was nothing in his looks to mark the boy as hers, yet he was a poignant continuation of all she had been, all Mark had lost. Michael Roskov, formerly Drozdov, legally Rawlings, had been created by him in Katya, nurtured inside her body, and given birth through her pain. Dear God, after all these years, she had returned to him in their child. Yet the boy had bowed very formally, saying in precise English, "How do you do, sir. I am pleased to make your acquaintance."

A door opened and closed, then Marie was beside him at the fireplace, tall, fair, looking older than her twenty-seven years.

"He will settle to sleep while we talk," she said.

"I'd like to see him again," Mark heard himself say.

She hesitated a moment. "As you wish, but it is late and he is very tired."

He opened the cream-painted door and walked softly into the adjoining room where Marie had been washing the child and coaxing him to rest in the silk-covered bed. Low lighting threw a pale glow over the pillow making the dark shiny curls contrast sharply with the linen. Long dark lashes lay against the boy's cheeks, and his mouth looked petal soft. For a moment Mark closed his eyes in pain and, when he opened them again, searched desperately for an echo of her in that face so like his own. The boy's eyelids flickered, then opened. For a second or two the dark eyes gazed at him.

"Have you come to tuck me in, sir?" asked the sleepy voice.

"Er . . . yes," he managed through a tight throat.

The smile widened in satisfaction. "I was hoping you might."

Stepping near Mark bent and made a clumsy play at smoothing the sheets, marvelling at how small the boy's figure looked in the double bed.

"How's that?" he asked gruffly.

Michael wriggled. "*Très bon*," was his verdict in the language he mostly used. Then he reverted to English. "*Maman* says you are building a big bridge. Can I see it?"

"I'll show you a drawing of it, if you like."

"Can't I see the real one?"

"I'm afraid not. It's a long way from here on a dangerous marsh. I couldn't take you out there."

"Because I'm too small?"

Seeing only Katya, grieving because she did not know this child of their love, he shook his head and replied with difficulty. "No one is allowed out there."

"You are."

Caught out by childish reasoning of which he had no experience Mark extemporised. "Ah . . . I'm building it . . . so I have to be there."

"*Oui, naturellement.*" Michael regarded him sleepily. "You must be a very important man, sir. Do you know the Emperor?"

"There is no emperor now."

"I suppose they killed him, like the Tsar." He yawned. "I think I'll build a bridge when I'm a man."

"Perhaps you'll build something even better—like a great cathedral."

"*Mark!*" said a voice in admonition from the doorway, and he turned quickly, experiencing another sharp pang at the sight of a girl from his past and all she symbolised. Because of it he did not realise what he was saying when he turned in farewell to the boy.

"*Spokoinoi nochi*," he said softly.

The brown eyes widened briefly. "You speak Russian? Of course, you were there once, *Maman* said."

"Go to sleep now," he whispered.

"*Spokoinoi nochi*," came the blurred voice from the edge of the slumber.

Marie closed the bedroom door behind him as he walked out like a man in a trance.

"He has no idea who I am—my own son!"

"Not yet."

He turned on her. "What you did was very cruel. For his sake, if not mine, you should have warned me first. Brought face to face like that I could have said or done *anything*."

She smiled. "You said and did all the right things, as I knew you would."

"*Knew!*" he cried with anger. "What do you know of me, Marie? Seven years have passed, and I'm not the same man I was then. My God, how do you think I felt: to walk in and see you again after . . . after . . . ?" He turned away to grip the mantelpiece. "How do you think I felt when he bowed and called me 'sir'? You should have warned me first."

Her hand fell on his arm. "Forgive me. I perhaps underestimated what this might do to you. Seven years is a long time, as you said, and memories sometimes fade."

"Have yours?" he asked harshly.

"No, Mark," she replied in heavy tones. "Has it occurred to you how *I* felt when we met? Two survivors, we are, with the same memories locked inside us."

"You have turned the key and released them." It was almost an accusation as he turned back to her.

"Was that not what you wished for when you asked for news of the Drozdov family?"

"Why didn't she tell me? How could she let me go, knowing . . . knowing . . ."

"What could you have done? You were under military orders, and she was my brother's wife."

"Everyone would know the child could not possibly be his."

"*He* never knew, that was the important thing. Alexei was killed soon after the British left Russia." She drew herself up and he saw again the dignity of her aristocratic origins that he had forgotten through the years. "They have all gone, Mark. I am the only Drozdov; the sole survivor of a proud family. Michael is the son of a woman who was also a member of a proud family. He is half Russian; he has boyar blood in him, and boyar pride. I have ensured that he speaks the language of his father's people, as well as French. I have also taught him the native language of his country, along with its history and culture. I have told him of our struggle against the people, and how we shall one day return from exile. I have told him he is *my* child." She put her hand out to grip his tightly. "I love him as my own, Mark. He is the only good thing to come from that dark terror. He is the living spirit of those who were lost. If you still care, you will aid my bid to make him worthy of them." She paused for a moment before asking, "Do you still care, Mark?"

He felt a hundred years old as he looked down at her. "Till the end of my days I shall care. You knew that when you came here today."

The following morning early, Mark made his way along the hotel corridors from the inexpensive room on the fourth floor he had occupied for what had remained of the night. They had talked well into the early hours, travelling back in time to another world peopled by those who were now no more than ghosts, and they had both been so exhausted Mark had suggested Marie and the child remain for the night in his suite. Despite the two bedrooms, he had insisted on sleeping elsewhere, for the sake of propriety. There had been little sleep, however, as he had grappled with past tragedy, present problems, and future plans. His brief spell of carefree happiness with Alexandra had caved in on him, bringing a return of the darkness which had clouded his life since 1919.

When he entered the suite he pulled up short. Marie was in one of the chairs before the fire drinking tea from a tray on the small table beside her. He was struck anew by the fine bones in a face that had developed into one of striking dignity from the adolescent roundness he remembered from the past. The woman had developed from the girl to reflect the pride verging on haughtiness so reminiscent of those old families which had been the backbone and the downfall of a great country. Marie Roskova, who still thought of herself as Drozdova, with her piled blonde hair, shrewd blue-grey eyes, and tall gracefulness, was a woman many men might find very attractive. Mark, however, recalled the streak of ruthlessness along with the urge for self-preservation which had been all too evident on several occasions during that train journey. Marie had had courage, without doubt, but it had been the selfish variety, and Mark had even found time to reflect during his troubled night on the fact that Katya had been out on the dangerous streets searching for food so soon after the birth of his son, whilst youthful Marie had remained safely indoors with the infant.

He pondered it again as she smiled and said, "I hope you do not object that I ordered tea to be brought to me here. Will you have some?"

He shook his head. "I had a quick breakfast downstairs, because I have urgent business this morning and should be on my way very soon. Please order anything you wish." He remained standing as he went on, "How is the boy?"

Getting to her feet she approached him to link her arm through his and coax him to the fire, saying teasingly, "He is the same as when you tucked him in. Children do not alter overnight, my dear."

"No . . . I meant is he still asleep?" He disengaged himself gently.

"The excitement of being in so grand a place, and the late hour tired him, naturally." She looked searchingly up into his face. "Are you proud of your son, Mark?"

It threw him. "I . . . until yesterday I didn't know of his existence. There has been no time . . . yes, yes, of course I am," he finished awkwardly. "You have done a fine job of rearing him under difficult circumstances."

"*Very* difficult circumstances, Mark," she emphasised. "As I said last night, all my efforts to trace you only brought me further humiliation. An unmarried foreign exile with a small child by the hand, who asks for the whereabouts of a British officer is treated by the military authorities with insulting contempt."

He coloured slightly. "I'm sorry. I did all I could to trace *you*."

"Me?" It was said lightly enough, but the shrewdness in her eyes told him her real feelings. "You were always chivalrous, my dear, but I knew in my heart which of us you would have saved first."

Feeling trapped by the past again, he said what was uppermost in his mind. "There is nothing of her in that child. Nothing at all. I find it difficult to believe that . . . that . . ."

"That Michael is her son? But you cannot doubt that he is yours."

"Could anyone, seeing us together?"

She shook her head. "The image of you has been with me all the while he has grown. You are quieter now, I think, and armoured against deep emotions more than you were then, but you are still the man I remember—the man to whom I owe life."

"So does Michael, poor little devil," he said with spontaneous bitterness.

Apparently shocked by his reaction she cried, "You *blame* yourself for his existence? So he was the product of an illicit love; a pretence taken too seriously! Yet he is living proof of that journey made against all odds. While he is here those who were lost will never be forgotten; while he is here I have reason to go on." She swung away in a sudden violence of feeling before twisting back to face him again. "Michael is part of us both, of our need to remember. In his veins runs the blood of my people and yours." Her voice lowered in passion. "In him is expressed her great love for you. Did it mean so little to you, you would prefer to deny him?"

"You know the extent of what it meant to me," he retorted in matching passion. "I have been tortured by it for almost eight years."

"Then never regret the existence of your son. Michael is part of that unforgettable time when they fought and suffered. He must speak for them after we have both gone."

"No . . . good God, no!" he exclaimed with force. "That boy must not be burdened with *our* past. You and I share it, and that is tragic enough. People today no longer want to know; they refuse to listen. All these years I've remained silent due to their indifference. Now we have spoken of it, relived every moment, and it has been painful but a great relief. Sometimes, reopening a wound allows it to heal. We must hope for that, not encourage the boy to keep the blood flowing after we have gone."

She had paled at his words and grown very still. "As you say, people no longer want to know. It is in the past, and they have forgotten. We in exile will never forget. If Russia is ever to be saved by a future generation, the pain and tragedy *must* live on in them."

He sighed heavily and sat down on a chair near the fire to ease the coldness taking hold of him. "Russia will never be saved, you must see that. The Bolsheviks have an unbreakable hold and are reaching out for the rest of the world. Red armies are moving steadily north over China. It's happening again here."

"It will never happen here," she replied kneeling beside his chair and sinking back on her heels to look up at him.

"It already is," he pointed out heatedly, "and this time my countrymen are making no attempt to help them fight it."

"Mine are. Already there is a unit in the Shanghai Volunteer Corps comprised of Russian ex-soldiers . . . and there is a special company formed to protect exiles from their enemies—*whoever* they might be. It is led by Gregori Petrovich Galinkov, a former officer of the premier regiment in all Russia, and a friend of my childhood. He now drives a lorry for a cement manufacturer," she informed him bitterly. "A man who was once personal bodyguard to the Tsar! Such men fight on against the Soviets. *They* will never give up; will never concede that Russia cannot be saved."

"Then they will die broken men," Mark told her sadly, "and perhaps soon, if Chiang Kai-Shek does attempt to take Shanghai." Leaning forward with his arms along his knees he said, "Marie, I gave that possibility some thought during the night, along with all else. Unfortunately, I have an urgent job on hand that will keep me up on a tributary of the Yangtze for several weeks yet, and which has already caused more problems than any bridge I have worked on so far. I'm due to chase up supplies then get back there as soon as possible. I'm under military orders to complete this as a top priority project," he added apologetically, "so I think there's only one course of action. I'll book you both a passage to Hong Kong and rooms in a small hotel. It's too risky for you here. Plans are already formed to evacuate British women and children, if necessary. The warships have no orders to take other nationals if the Reds should manage to break through our defences and rampage through the streets. You are a Drozdov, and they have threatened to kill every member of that family. They will never forget that vow, and if someone betrays the fact that you are only a Roskov by marriage your life will be in danger once more.

"It shouldn't be more than a month before I get back to Hong Kong, and we can then sort out Michael's future more thoroughly. I'm not a very wealthy man, but I'll make adequate provision for him which will free you from your responsibilities. The boy will have to be told the truth about his parentage, but I will ensure he does not suffer because of it. I was intending to leave the army, anyway, and it will be easy enough to say that a marriage took place in Russia but the papers were lost in the struggle to escape. I'll rear him as my legitimate son, and no one will be able to prove that he is not." He broke off as he realised she was looking at him strangely. "Is something wrong?"

"Is it really possible you have not understood all I have said? I did not bring him to you to hand over responsibility."

"I don't understand," he murmured, very weary and still shattered by the bizarre return of his past.

Marie got to her feet and stood looking down at him with the familiar steel in her glance. "You say no one will be able to prove he is not your legitimate son. No more will you be able to prove he is *not* mine."

Still muddled, but somewhat wary, Mark got up slowly to face her. "I'm not sure what you are trying to say. Why *did* you bring Michael to me?"

"To give him the father he needs. Gregori Petrovich has tried to fill the vacancy, but now the real father has miraculously appeared at the most vital time."

"I've said I'll take on the job just as soon as I've finished at the bridge," he reiterated sharply.

"'The job,' as you put it, holds certain conditions, my dear Mark. There is no question of Michael losing his mother to gain his father. We go together. If you want Katya's child, you must also take me."

The full impact of all she had been saying hit him then, and he cried,

"That's completely out of the question. I've just proposed marriage to a girl in Shanghai, and she's not much more than a child herself."

Marie took it with commendable calm. "Then you will have to choose between your child of love and your child-bride. You cannot have both."

The painting was clearly going to be all she hoped. It was a strange thing, thought Alexandra, that on a day when she felt depressed and restless her work should be so good. Arching backward in order to gain a more distant view of a dragon rising through a blur of mist on the marsh, she recalled Mark saying she would never be an artist until she had suffered. On a sigh she reflected that if her work could be this good because he had been absent a few days, what masterpieces she would paint if he went from her life forever. The thought increased her melancholy and she continued working on the scales of the mythical beast as she puzzled over the reason for her present unhappiness.

Mark had admitted his love for her, had vowed, albeit with reservations, that they would be together soon. He wanted her for his wife, and was prepared to wait until he could accomplish the legal tie, even if it meant enduring the two years until she came of age. As her mother had predicted, Alexandra viewed that with dismay, but knew in her heart it was probably the only way her father could be flouted without risking the loss of freedom to visit her mother when she wished. The only hope of any alternative was that Mark would make such a success of building the Bridge of a Hundred Dragons, it would bring him professional recognition amongst Shanghai men of note and make him a partner considered worthy of Garrard Mostyn's daughter. She was certain her father would quickly lose his reservations if it was expedient to do so. Yes, Mark had admitted his love for her, and it was there in his eyes, his willing smile, the gentleness of his hands, the husky tone of his voice when he spoke of his feelings. Why, then, was she filled with strange unease?

During his last visit to Shanghai he had surrendered to love that had swept all else aside. The next evening he had failed to meet her, as arranged. She had telephoned his hotel only to be told there was no answer from his room. Disappointed and very frustrated, she had continued to telephone every hour until midnight, only to be told the same thing. The following morning a note had been delivered to her home. It contained a vague reference to something unexpected which had kept him engaged for most of the night, and had gone on to explain that he was now obliged to return to the bridge immediately and would be pleased if she could meet him briefly before he left.

She put down her brush with a sigh. It was the penalty of an artistic mind to be fanciful, too sensitive to another's mood, too governed by emotion oneself. Mark had looked weary and strained, his excuse for the night before being that he had been tracking down supplies for the bridge and trying to bargain with a devious contractor. Alexandra could ally his appearance with worry and lack of sleep, but those two had not explained the fierce desperation of his kisses, or the bleak unhappiness in his eyes. The boyish gaiety she had seen two days before had vanished as if it had never existed, and she sensed he had somehow retreated to the realms in which she had first found him. There was no apparent reason for it. He had reiterated his pledge to make her his wife; he had sworn she was his only future. Yet, it had seemed to her that his past was making a last fight for survival.

Crossing to the window she leant her forehead against the cold glass and stared at the scene below. That was *her* past, that busy street in Shanghai where fortunes had been made and lost by calculating, dedicated men. Her life had been dominated by commerce and the accumulation of wealth since the day she had been born. She had never seen her mother country; could not even visualise the kind of street and home into which Mark had been born and reared. She had never been to France, where he had lived in holes in the earth for four years of tragic history which had unfolded whilst she had been learning arithmetic and poetry. She did not know what it was like for someone to celebrate his survival for one more week, one more day. She had never killed and seen others killed. Yet, strangely, it was that very lack of experience that made her certain Mark could find happiness with her, at last. He knew it, too—knew it so well he was prepared to fight a last battle to obtain it.

"Then why am I suddenly so afraid?" she whispered, her breath making darting clouds on the pane. "Why am I still so afraid of Russia . . . and why is he still afraid to tell me?"

For the hundredth time she yearned to claim that part of his life that remained a mystery. Something told her it would always be a mystery until she knew who owned the face that had haunted him all these years. What manner of woman had she been? Where was she now? What had possessed her to give him up? She sighed again. For a while she had believed he had let *her* go; now her fears had returned. There would be no permanent happiness for either of them until she knew how to bring him to terms with a past love and a new one who wished only to soften memories, not banish them altogether. In time, he would probably bring himself to speak of it, but she was young, newly in love and possessive of the prize. It was unbearable to be denied any part of him.

Her restless, moody unhappiness remained for the next three days. It inspired her artistically, but the more involved she grew in her subject, the more she longed for Mark. The Bridge of a Hundred Dragons symbolised the faraway place that laid claim to him, and she often toyed with the prospect of hiring a boat to take her down the river to him and the real bridge. Mark would be angry, of course, tell her she had behaved scandalously and given her father another opportunity to denounce her immaturity. However, it would set her mind at rest, reassure her that she had imagined that strange air of returning ghosts about him at their last meeting. It would also ease the feeling that he was in trouble, even danger, of some kind.

That last thought would not be banished. Whether at work, entertaining guests, or trying to sleep, it plagued her. Even her mother commented on her long silences and asked if she were feeling unwell.

"'A trouble shared is a trouble halved,'" she quoted to her daughter. "Even the most independent capable female needs a confidante now and again. It is not a sign of weakness, you know."

"I know, dear," Alexandra replied, but added nothing more.

Her mother probed further. "I hope you have decided to be sensible over Mark Rawlings, after all."

"Yes, I have," came her firm reply. "It would be quite ridiculous to give up the chance of tremendous happiness for us both merely because of a few material obstacles. The thing to do is work to overcome them. I'm sure you'll see how sensible that decision is."

Shaking her head gently Alice said, "Your major would have vastly different views on that, if you asked him."

"I did, and he hasn't," Alexandra confessed in a burst of truthfulness. "He wants to marry me. There's no problem over that. It's the question of timing on which we can't agree."

Greatly concerned her mother sighed. "Dear me, I thought he was a man of far greater sense. Whatever can he be thinking of?"

Alexandra did not dare answer that. Mark's lovemaking had left her in no doubt of what he was thinking of and, since she was growing more and more eager to discover what would happen when a telephone did *not* ring at the moment of surrender, the question of timing was growing crucial. However, her mother's quotation of the old maxim about halving a trouble by sharing it increased her conviction that discovering the truth about his past was the only way she could help him totally recover from it. Until she knew what ailed him, how could she provide the right remedy?

When Lai-Hi sent her little maid up with a message saying someone had telephoned from Mark's hotel asking her to go there at four that afternoon, it seemed that her opportunity had come. With a racing heart she dressed in clothes she knew would aid her cause, vowing to make it impossible for him to resist confessing everything to her. Thrilled at his unexpected presence in Shanghai she made her way to his hotel full of plans for his surrender, determined to banish those lingering ghosts with proof of a love and compassion to match any he had previously known.

Hurrying into the vestibule she scanned the occupants of the many settees there before venturing further into the salon, where afternoon tea would shortly be served to those in the discreet comfortable alcoves. He was not immediately to be seen.

"Miss Mostyn?" enquired an accented voice to her left.

She turned to see a woman who had just risen from a banquette in one of the secluded corner alcoves, and a sudden inexplicable sensation of danger swept through her. The woman was tall with upswept pale hair, and striking features. Nearing thirty she had a voluptuous figure which ignored the fashion for flat boyish lines with unqualified success, and the full-length dark-blue coat and matching toque was defiantly elegant in its outmoded style.

"Yes, I am Alexandra Mostyn," she said with instinctive coolness. "Have we met before?"

"I think you know we have not," came the equally cool reply. "It is something we both would have remembered. I am Marie Fedorovna Drozdova."

The sensation of danger increased dramatically as Alexandra realised this woman regarding her from head to toe with haughty curiosity was Russian, and undoubtedly used to luxurious surroundings despite the workaday quality of her clothes.

"Where is Mark?" she asked sharply.

"Out on the railway building a bridge, as far as I am aware."

"He is not in Shanghai?" she asked in dismay. "Then what . . . it was *you* who asked me here?"

"I thought we should have a civilised conversation together before he returned. I was a little surprised you had not approached me first, under the circumstances."

Feeling unnaturally cold in the salon, which was heated by several large fires, Alexandra said through a mouth that had stiffened to the point of almost refusing to move, "Under *what* circumstances?"

Shrewd blue eyes studied her for a moment or two while a frown slowly wrinkled the brow beneath dark-blue veiling. "Can it be . . . no, surely Mark has not kept you in ignorance? How extraordinary! He told me all about you, Miss Mostyn. I naturally thought he had fully acquainted you with the facts."

Struggling to retain something of her usual command in this bizarre situation, Alexandra said, "His time in Shanghai was limited and gossip had to be put aside. We had very important matters to discuss."

"Marriage plans, I understand."

Stunned, Alexandra could only stare at the face she felt she would remember all her life, while a sense of terrible treachery began to emerge. Mark had told this woman *everything*? It had all seemed so special, so precious.

Seeing her distress Marie Drozdova smiled and explained that it was due to the marriage plans that she had felt this meeting was essential.

"I am a very close friend of Mark's, Miss Mostyn, very close indeed. He helped me to escape from my country almost eight years ago, so I owe him my life. That forms a bond of a nature very few people can understand unless they have shared it." She half turned and said to someone inside the alcove, "Michael, come here to *Maman*, if you please. Give your greetings to Miss Mostyn, *mon petit chou*."

A small boy appeared beside the woman to bow and say a polite 'how do you do' to her. As Alexandra looked at him she felt her blood turn icy. That square freckled face told her all she had yearned for so long to know, but the truth was more terrible than she had imagined.

CHAPTER NINE

Alexandra walked back along the Bund with swift short paces, the fur trimming on the hem of her bronze chenille coat banging her thighs as it was blown by the chill wind from the waterfront. She walked blindly in the direction of her home, ignoring the rickshaws plying for hire along the road. To ride would be to sit passive, and everything within her urged action—positive physical movement.

She had left that room, that woman, Mark's son. She could not remember how she had departed, but she was certain it had been with outward dignity. In her breast there was a cold leaden weight; in her mind there was an echo of terrible humiliation. In her heart there was a cry of protest so great it deafened her to the sound of Shanghai, which was all around her. No, not again! For the second time in her life she had placed her faith, her trust and her love in the hands of a man who had seemed to be a giant full of wisdom, strength and honesty, and for the second time she had been betrayed. Mark had used her just as her father had done—as all men used women. He had condemned her fight for equality and urged her to temper it. He had exploited those weak feminine traits that were no proof against sexual attraction, and played on her artistic fascination with a past he had deliberately maintained a mystery. Oh, he had played his part to perfection, she realised now. Using an air of defiant, suppressed nobility he had won her initial interest. By refusing to speak about Russia or explain her father's veiled references to heroism and danger, he had won her admiration. The shadows of past tragedy that flitted across his face had won her compassion. By defying her father he had won her love.

She walked on, hunched into the high fur collar, as the full force of her discovery froze her bones to set her shivering uncontrollably. There was no desire to cry, just a need to hit back—not only at him but all he represented. He had no suppressed nobility in his character, and his tragic lost love had turned out to be a plump mistress with his bastard son. Judging by the age of the boy that 'desperate flight to freedom' she had imagined had been no more than a Slavic love-nest! Dear heaven, how could she have believed him when he had said with such apparent depth of feeling that sexual love should wait until a man had the legal right to take a woman? To think she had offered herself so freely; to think she had been rejected so insincerely! How could she have abandoned her aims and ideals so easily? Fool. *Fool!* How short a while ago had she blithely told her mother: "No man will ever rule me. He will have to accept me on my terms or not at all."

The bitter bile of defeat rose in her throat. At the first serious challenge she had gone under. Such weakness in any of her friends would have earned her derision. Oh God, how *could* she have let him make such a submissive, adoring idiot of her?

She reached the house and ran up the stairs to her room, slamming the door behind her as she flung off her hat and tugged at the frogging on her coat. Her greatest victory over her father had gained her nothing for herself. It had won for Mark another seven hundred and fifty pounds to pay his Russian mistress for the upkeep of his bastard. For that she had thrown away the chance to follow her chosen career and left herself open to humiliating treatment from Lionel, who had always supported her pursuit of emancipation.

Brilliantly inspired by that thought she went swiftly across to the telephone, requested the Armitage number and told Dot she would go to Bunty Frobisher's party, after all. At Dot's squeal of delight she added, "Put on your gladdest rags, sweetie. I feel like setting the town alight tonight. Shanghai will never be the same again after I'm through with it."

After a quick shower during which she punished her skin with the loofah she ransacked her wardrobe, flinging dresses all over the bed in her search for what she wanted. Her little maidservant reluctantly fetched several cocktails for her mistress, her neat exquisite features betraying her disapproval. But she gasped in awed admiration when Alexandra prepared to go out on receipt of Lai-Hi's message that a car awaited her. A last glance in the mirror put a vicious smile on Alexandra's scarlet-bow lips. As a gesture of defiance, it was all she wished for.

The vivid scarlet dress shimmering with beadwork provided a shocking, rivetting contrast with her red hair, and the foot-long black fringing at the hem parted to reveal the entire length of her silk-clad legs, plus a scarlet bejewelled garter high on her left thigh. Her back, bare to the waist, looked tantalising through the long, long black chiffon evening scarf trimmed with swansdown which dragged along the ground behind her in provocative fashion. Around her auburn marcel waves was a bandeau adorned with two huge bird-of-paradise feathers, at her ears dangled four-inch drops of pure jet which were matched by a pair of slave bangles on each upper arm. Fitting a cigarette into a long jet holder, she lit it and struck a pose, blowing smoke from her nostrils and half-closing her eyes.

"That, dear gentlemen, will show you what I think of your precious masculine traditions, your blind arrogance, your willing mistresses, and . . . and your *bastards*," she finished savagely.

Snatching up a black velvet evening purse and matching wrap, she ran down the staircase, swaying slightly from the effect of three quick cocktails on an empty stomach. From the corner of her eye she spotted her father just emerging from his study, but ignored him and went out through the door Lai-Hi held open for her into the night, which was illuminated by the great lanterns flanking the entrance to the house.

For a moment she checked. There was no Dot with a party of friends, just Lionel leaning nonchalantly against the side of his roadster. She remembered their last meeting, the things he had said to her, the aggressive way he had gripped her arms. Then she remembered why he had done so, and this added further weight to the cold lump of self-contempt in her breast. Putting up her head she walked seductively down the steps, cigarette holder held to her mouth. He watched her like a snake hypnotised by a charmer.

"Lion, darling," she drawled as she reached him, "this is too, too generous of you to take an empty-headed little bitch in your roadster."

She took a grim delight in the expression of mixed shock and admiration on his face as he tried to decide what to reply. He solved the problem by laughing in a high-pitched manner.

"I have to hand it to you, Sandy. You never do anything by halves. You look absolutely terrific." He looked her over with bright eyes. "When Dot told me you planned to set the town alight tonight, I couldn't resist it. Haven't we always been perfect partners for a spree as long as you can remember? Together we have made matrons faint with horror, monocles fall out with disbelief, and our friends burn with envy. By God, Sandy, we've shaken convention and stuffy old tradition to the foundations. Let's see if we can make them topple completely tonight, shall we?"

It was so exactly what she had in mind, so much a return to old times, that she stepped into the car and fell back into the seat to take in great gulps of the night air, which seemed especially heady.

"Heavens, how marvellous it is to *breathe* again. You have no idea, Lion." She closed her eyes momentarily. "Drive fast tonight, sweetie. I want to feel the wind rushing past me and hear the tyres scream as we take the corners."

She felt him get in and lean back in the seat beside her with a chuckle. "Sandy, old girl, I think you're a teeny bit tight."

She opened her eyes and swivelled them in his direction. "How clever you are! I intend to get *very* tight before the evening is over. It's such *fun*."

The engine started with a roar, and Lionel took the car at reckless speed down the short driveway and through the gates. It was exhilarating; it was *defiant*. She began to laugh softly at the thought of Mark's face if he could see her now—his face and that of his Russian mistress.

"There's a bottle of bubbly on the back seat," said Lionel. "Hold on to the wheel and I'll open it."

"I can't," she shouted above the noise of the engine and the din of hooters from oncoming cars.

"There's a long straight stretch ahead. All you have to do is guide it. If I can do it, you can."

Of course she could! Taking hold of the wheel as he twisted round to reach the bottle, she gazed at the illuminated city street with all its evening traffic. But it was easier than she thought. After one or two violent zigzags she got the hang of it, and most of the other drivers swerved to the side of the road to allow them to pass, which made progress easy. When the cork flew off they both laughed and, after the tricky manoeuvre of exchanging steering wheel for glasses, Lionel drove with one hand on the wheel, drinking with the other.

"Whoops!" he cried suddenly, swerving to avoid a statue in the middle of the road.

The movement flung Alexandra against the side and knocked the bandeau askew so that the feathers covered her face. It seemed hilariously funny, and she began blowing at them and giggling with helpless laughter.

"Lion, look . . . look at . . . me," she cried between giggles. "I think I'm turning . . . into a . . . *bird!*"

"Have another glass of bubbly and you'll start to fly," he suggested with hoots of laughter. "You'll arrive at the party before my roadster. *That'll* shock everyone."

Shrieking with amusement at the thought she peered through the feathers and poured more champagne for herself until the glass was full. *Have you drunk enough yet to stop you from walking away from me?* She remembered a little fool with seven hundred and fifty pounds in her bag asking that breathless question. She emptied her glass in one long draught. She would drink enough to enable her to walk away from *him* a hundred times over!

Lionel had fallen silent, so she sat up and pushed the feathers out of her eyes. "Come on, Lion, you're as dismal as the chief mourner at a wedding."

He shot her a quick glance. "You mean a funeral, old girl."

"No, I don't. I mean a wedding," she persisted, feeling strangely giddy. "I can't imagine a more mournful occasion than a woman promising some man to love, honour and *obey*."

He laughed and poured more champagne into her glass. "Let's drink to that. Down with all rules and regulations and orders. We're going to be free . . . and set the rest of the world free, too."

"Bravo, encore, and all that," she muttered. "Lion, you'll have to stop swaying about. I'm spilling this all down my dress." Drinking the rest quickly before it could slop over the rim of the glass, she realised it had grown considerably darker. Peering muzzily into the street ahead of them, she asked, "Where are we? This isn't the way to Bunty Frobisher's."

"I know." He turned to face her, one hand on the wheel as the car reduced its speed. "Sandy, I had a special reason for taking you to the party alone tonight. I was an utter beast to you the last time we met. I didn't know how to apologise—you have been so different lately. But tonight you're like your old self, and there's only one way I can show you how sorry I am for what I said."

She looked at his indistinct figure in amazement. He was actually humbling himself, admitting he had been at fault. She tried to straighten the bandeau so that the feathers no longer tickled her nose.

"I see," she said carefully, wishing he would sit still.

"You told me that if I really cared about the Chinese I'd scatter a handful of notes to the beggars in the Chinese quarter . . . so that's what I'm going to do."

"*No!*" she said, extremely impressed by such success.

"Just watch this." He opened a box on the floor beside him and took out a handful of what looked like banknotes to fling them over the side of the car into the almost complete darkness of the Chinese quarter. Then he took another handful and did the same again. Alexandra gazed at him in awe until he told her to do the same on her side of the car.

It was crazy and immensely appealing to her present mood. She had told him it was what he should do, and he was doing it before her eyes, offering the deed as atonement for hurting her. What more could she ask of him?

The slow bumpy drive through the odorous pitted tracks of the dark side of Shanghai, throwing pieces of paper left and right, became utterly bizarre. In the beam of the headlights she saw pale ragged figures crouching in the doorways of hovels; children sleeping beside the road, a brick for a pillow; small groups of squatting men, heads together, smoking opium in a communal pipe; wretched pi-dogs slinking from one pile of refuse to another in the search for food; corpses piled into a corner awaiting burial by anyone who bothered to do it.

"Lion, it's terrible," she whispered, suddenly plunged into despair and depression.

"I know. That's why I'm trying to help them." He put out a hand and turned her face to his. "You're pleased, aren't you? It's what you wanted."

"Yes . . . yes, of course I'm pleased." In fact, she felt like crying all over him, but that would be fatal now she had him thinking she was sc wise. "Is there any more bubbly?" she asked desperately.

He smiled with all his old wickedness. "There's always more bubbly, darling. Let's keep it flowing."

"Yes, let's," she agreed trying to recapture her earlier exhilaration. "Lion, let's drive on very fast."

"Righto. Hold on to your hat."

The cold rushing wind made her head spin, but the desire to laugh was returning, and they sped through the night until lights began tc sparkle in the distance and the magnum was empty. When the car finally pulled up Alexandra was not sure she wanted to go to Bunty Frobisher's party, after all. But Lionel reminded her that she was going to set the town alight, and it seemed a pity to waste the opportunity When she got out of the car her legs folded up, but Lionel held her steady and stopped her from falling.

"Ooh!" she giggled. "I think I'm a teeny weeny bit blotto." Collapsing against him she looked up muzzily into his face. "Are you blotto Lion?"

"We're all blotto, darling. Come on, let's join the fun."

It did not look in the least like Bunty Frobisher's house. There was nc forecourt and the entrance was surrounded by lurid coloured lights tha flashed on and off, but Lionel explained that Bunty had hired a hall in a hotel for the occasion, which explained the mystery. Supported by hi arm she managed to walk in, but the heat and noise made her lose al sense of balance and she fell in a heap on the floor when Lionel let go o her to speak to a man in some kind of uniform. Hands helped her up amidst much laughter, and sat her on a chair. Then someone put a glas into her hands urging her to drink up.

"It will make you feel better," said Lionel appearing before her. "It' the warmth after the outside temperature."

The drink seemed to make her steadier, so she took another whe Lionel offered it, and looked around her. The room was full of cigarett smoke which combined with the dim atmosphere to give it a myste rious, alien ambience. She did not think much of Bunty's choice o venue, but the band was thumping out a foxtrot and all the guests were having a noisy, energetic time.

"Come on, Sandy, let's show them how to really dance," said Lionel urging her to her feet. "Tonight's the night, remember?"

Yes, she remembered well enough. Alexandra Mostyn lived her life dependent on no one. She knew quite well where she was going. The world was going to be her oyster.

Once they began dancing the rhythm changed to a ragtime number she and Lionel knew well. It was exciting twisting and turning, matching her movements to his, flying like a featherweight in his hold. Her mind was empty of all but the intricacies of the dance, and when her skirt flew high, or Lionel turned her over in a cartwheel movement, she delighted in the freedom of her body. She was aware of shouts and whistles from those around her, but not in any conscious way. The coloured lights looped along the ceiling went round and round before her eyes, and Lionel's face with a puzzling fixed smile upon it went round and round with them. The music stopped, but the room went on spinning. The lights refused to stop still, and she found herself grasping him to prevent herself from falling down.

"Lion, I think . . ." but she had no chance to say more before she was dragged into a wild session of dancing again. Giddy, almost falling at every step, she tried to tell him how she felt. But he went on spinning her around and bending her over so that her dress fell back over her hips. Only when her partner turned her over and kept her upside down far too long as he cavorted around the floor displaying her legs to everyone, did she realise it was not Lionel. Wanting to escape she could not because he held her close against him, laughing with beer-tainted guffaws. The dance became menacing. Her partner began exploring her body with his hands, and his grasping fingers were on her thigh above the garter, forcing it down her leg. Men were shouting lewd encouragement, and she knew it could not be Bunty Frobisher's party.

She began to feel ill. All control over herself seemed to have gone. She could not think where she was or what was happening. Her partner was carrying her over his shoulder now. A woman walked past in a diaphanous blouse that revealed large voluptuous breasts and couples were locked together in alarming embraces. When she was lowered she slumped into the chair like a rag doll, and hands pulled off the garter with gusting mirth. Someone like Lionel was staring at her across the table. She tried to speak to him, but could not form the words.

"Set the town alight, Sandy, that's what we'll do," he said harshly.

The evening became a terrible jumble of noise, lurid colours, foreign voices. The band blasted out continuous music, setting her head spinning all the more. The long chiffon scarf had vanished, and hands kept touching her bare back. The bandeau had been pulled from her head and now rested on the greasy locks of a dark-skinned brute beside her who was trying to put her garter back on her right thigh. When she tried to get to her feet she simply fell forward across the table. If only the coloured lights would keep still she could find Lionel, who would surely take her away from this nightmare. Then other lights began flashing, white lights that started on the other side of the room and worked their way toward her. Men shouted and laughed in coarse fashion, then she was almost blinded by flashes directly ahead.

"No," she moaned turning her head away, but the great brute beside her pulled her across his lap, laughing as he slid his hand inside her dress and forced it off one shoulder just as the light flashed again.

"That'll be a ver good one to show ma shipmates," he roared. "Me with White Russian whore in Chinatown."

Alexandra told them over and over again it was a woman called Marie Drozdova who was a White Russian whore, but hands still roamed over her body as she passed out.

A week of fine weather heralded Mark's return to the bridge. The steel plates he had gone to Shanghai to buy arrived the morning after he got back, brought up the canal by a sulky Chinese in a barge that shipped water so fast its progress was sluggish and chancy. The rice supplies, also in the barge, were damp and swollen with an obnoxious smell about them. The boatman swore it was because a large ship had passed him in the Yangtze just out of Shanghai, and the wash had gone clean over his bows. But Mark knew rotting rice when he saw it and guessed the contractor had pulled a switch on consignments. Furious he had ranted and raved at the boatman, knowing there was nothing he could do about it and knowing also that the contractor would probably have fled the port by the time he got back there again. In disgust he had told the coolies to off-load the sacks. It would not be the first time they had eaten foul rice, and there were bigger problems on his mind.

With no sense of pride or achievement he assembled his bridge, driven on only by the desire to see the back of a job that had brought nothing but trouble. The Chinese were right. It *was* a place of bad *fung shui*. It was also a freezing, hostile stretch of waterlogged plain that he would be only too pleased to leave to the ghostly creatures who guarded it. They were welcome to the place.

The hundred dragons no longer haunted him: there were other things doing that. He was drinking again, very heavily. By day he attacked the job, the men working on it, the loneliness of the interminable marsh with muscle and aggression. At night he drank himself insensible. His urgent need to complete the bridge and get away to sort out his life made every day, every hour twice as long. The coolies seemed to him to do everything in slow motion and the longest possible way round. Corcoran was brooding, snappy and aggressive too, and Mark found himself constantly engaged in confrontations with the man. He made no allowance for the tragic murder of the Portuguese boy with which the Scot was trying to come to terms. He had had his own past tragedies and no one had ever made allowances for him. What Corcoran was doing about meals and laundry he did not know or care. He never went near the other man's boat, and the Scot now never visited his . . . which suited him perfectly.

Even Hong seemed set on aggravating everyone. He carried out his job as foreman with meticulous attention to detail, driving Mark to distraction with his Oriental 'stonewalling' when there were difficulties, and translating what Corcoran said with such thoroughness the coolies grew actively hostile. There was nothing Mark could actually claim as deliberate sabotage, but several steel plates were 'accidentally' knocked into the canal, a load of shingle ballast mysteriously spilled down the side of the embankment, the portable forge where rivets were heated somehow became clogged with mud. Hong's constant excuse for these 'accidents' was that the coolies were men from the North and the South, so did not work well together. When Mark raged at him pointing out that they had worked perfectly well together before, Hong explained with infuriating patience that it was the People's Revolution. The Northerners were afraid of the Kuomintang.

"Their army is away in Hankow, miles from here," Mark had told him angrily.

Hong had blinked behind his spectacles. "It is coming. My brother has sent to me that the first divisions have already left Hankow. Soon it will come, Major. The Kuomintang army will soon be here."

"Good!" Mark had exploded. "As they're so keen to glorify China, perhaps they'll help me finish this bloody bridge when they get here."

Slowly the bridge advanced across the canal during that spell of crisp, sunny weather, until they were working on the third span that linked with the other bank. It was the most awkward part, because all the supplies were on the Shanghai bank, and most of the work entailed hanging over the water all day which the coolies did not like. They were afraid of the canal, and the spirits, lurking beneath the surface, of all those who had died in the train crash. It meant Mark had to be out there the whole time with them to bolster their confidence. They knew that if the spirits pulled anyone down into the murky water it would be the

Englishman, not them. The villagers of Lu-Seng had said it would be so, so they firmly believed it. Mark, used to far more dangerous bridges, scrambled surely and fearlessly across the steel structure, taking a savage delight in the glazed eyes which always seemed to be watching him, waiting for him to fall.

All the same, hard physical activity and an uncurbed temper did not completely release him from the consequences of his last trip into Shanghai. He had no idea what he was going to do. The obstacles against marrying Alexandra had been formidable all along; now they were trebled. He still could hardly accept that he had a son, yet the boy was undeniable proof of the fact. Drunk and maudlin at night, Mark tortured himself with thoughts of Katya walking away from him knowing their child was already inside her, knowing he would never know his true father, knowing her family and friends would regard the boy as a bastard. At that point, such a word in connection with Michael made him so angry he drank all the more. He further tortured himself with vivid pictures of the gentle, courageous woman he had loved too well exposing herself to danger in the streets to go in search of food for the infant he had known nothing of. Added to that was the burden of responsibility which had fallen on him.

The boy was charming, attractive to look at, a great credit to Marie, who had reared him . . . but there was nothing of Katya in him. Mark had searched again for some sign of her when Michael had woken that morning and come into the room where Marie had issued her ultimatum, but there had been none. He longed for it; he yearned for an echo of her eyes, her smile, her beauty. The child was purely a copy of himself. Yet he was the result of a love he had been unable to surrender, until a young girl with red hair and the promise of a future had walked into the clouds around his life and dispersed them. Alexandra was very like Katya, in many ways. Apart from physical beauty, she was determined, intelligent, passionate, and with her own brand of courage. Love for Alexandra had not banished that earlier one, merely grown alongside it. In one vital factor did it differ from that other deep passion which had not let him rest. This love was full of hope: Alexandra was fully his. That Russian love had been desperate, anguished and doomed from the start.

Day after day, night after night Mark tussled with alternatives, each one as fraught with difficulties as the other. Marie wanted, in addition to the real father for Michael, a husband for herself and a passage to England where many of her countrymen had settled securely. She relied on the strength of a bond between a man and a lost love; gambled that he would forsake all else for the sake of that small living ember of a fire that had been cruelly extinguished. How shrewd she was. Having for six years been unaware of Michael's existence, Mark now could not turn away from the boy easily. Had the child resembled Katya the pull would have been stronger, far stronger. As it was, the boy laid a moral burden on him, even though he was like any other stranger of six years.

Mark knew little of small children, had never spent much time with them. Michael could be anyone's child, but for his striking resemblance to the father he had never known, and that was Marie's trump card. Although no one would ever doubt that Mark was the boy's father, he could never prove Marie was not his mother. No court would give him the right to take Michael as his son in a marriage with Alexandra—even supposing Alexandra would agree to rear another woman's child. In his more sober moments, Mark realised that to tear a young boy from the woman he believed was his mother, who had brought him up to the age of six and a half, would be incredibly cruel. Yet marriage to Marie was out of the question. Quite apart from Alexandra, there was no happiness to be found in a marriage of convenience to a woman he had never particularly liked even in Russia. Katya would want him to rear their son, but surely not at such a price! Somehow, Marie must be brought to reason, he must take responsibility for his own son, and Alexandra must be told of the boy's existence.

It was at that point in his thoughts every night that he cast aside the glass and drank straight from the bottle, until he was no longer capable of thought.

The penalty of those bright, clear days was that thick mist hung over the marsh all night, taking a long time to clear in the morning. On the last day of the week it was particularly thick when daylight came, hiding the incomplete section of the bridge by the far bank. Mark had a monumental hangover—the legacy of a week of dedicated drinking. His pulse thundered in his head like a pile-driver, his mouth was as dry as dust, his reflexes almost nonexistent. His body ached from hard work and a hard sleep across a table; his mind felt wrung out from the pounding of a hundred unanswerable questions. Telling Ah Wu he could not face 'plenty baconegg' that morning he swallowed several cups of black coffee that tasted foul, shrugged into his padded coat and stepped from the boat onto the mist-shrouded bank.

When he reached the bridge he found only Corcoran leaning moodily against the uprights.

"Where are those bloody coolies?" snapped Mark.

"Still in yon bloody boat," the Scot snapped back, straightening up with an angry look on his face. "Since ye're so keen to throw ye great weight about, use yon plank to thrash them into doing ye word." He nodded at a thin tree trunk sawn up for firewood. "Strike a few blows with that, laddie, and mebbe they'll see ye're in charge here. Start with the knees—it's the most painful."

Mark glared at him for a few moments, then turned away. "Oh, go to hell!"

But he was right. The coolies only did what they wanted to do nowadays. There was a new defiant mood about them, a resistance to him that bordered on revolt. They were restless, unsure, volatile. They were bewildered by hopes and fears, like all the Chinese waiting for the new salvation promised by the revolutionary army.

"Most of them won't be here to see it," he muttered to himself as he strode toward the coolies' barge. "They'll be dead—mown down indiscriminately by the Kuomintang. That's what they mean when they promise there'll be no more coolies."

A long frustrating argument with Hong did nothing to improve Mark's temper, and his skull felt as if it would split asunder by the time the Chinese foreman had agreed that there was nothing there in a fog that was not there when it cleared, and that the coolies knew the structure of the bridge well enough by now to go over it in any weather. Once that was agreed he changed tack completely and said the reason why they would not work was because the hundred dragons were lurking out of sight on the far bank. Knowing there was absolutely no argument he could put up against that one, Mark resorted to tactics quite foreign to him. Striding past Hong onto the barge where the coolies squatted wrapped in lengths of rattan matting, he seized a sack of rice, hauled it up until it rested on the side of the boat, and began tipping the contents into the water slowly and deliberately.

"Tell them I'll stop when they get to the bridge," he said savagely. "When this sack is empty I'll start on the next. Tell them it's a damned long walk to Shanghai, and the hundred dragons will get them well before then."

Hong was very upset. "Please, Major, try to understand."

"No, Hong," he flung back, still tipping the rice. "I'm sick of trying to understand them. It's time they understood *my* ways, for a change. I'm trying to build a bridge here. It is going to be of no future benefit to me. When it's finished I'm going back to Hong Kong. It's *their* bridge in *their* bloody 'New China'—and a fat chance it will have if this is their attitude toward creating it."

He had emptied one sack and was in the act of lifting another before the wild sing-song that flew between Hong and the coolies produced the result he wanted. But it had started the day badly and increased his depression. Corcoran's derisory hand-clapping when he regained the bridge and prepared to go across brought a vicious comment from him that he had enough Oriental adversaries to contend with without adding a boorish Celt to the list.

For an hour he drove the Chinese to work, clambering across the structure from man to man, checking, directing, swearing. They all appeared unbelievably stupid and could, or would, not understand his visual directions. Half of it he had to do himself, while his head throbbed and the cold numbed his hands. It was while he was crossing swiftly to a man on the far section who was methodically fitting plates the wrong way round that a handhold appeared nearer than it was, his boot slipped, and he fell. The canal had a fragile coating of ice floating on its surface that shattered as he hit it; then there was roaring freezing blackness all around him, until he burst through the surface again. For once, he was splashing, gasping, frantic for a hold. Normally a superb swimmer, his brain that morning would not function, his limbs were completely sluggish, his body inert and weighted down by the thick clothes he wore. The bridge loomed high above him, and clinging to it were the coolies staring down at him impassively. Not one was making any attempt to do anything to help him.

He went down again and came up spluttering, but this time his natural skill asserted itself and he struck out clumsily for the bank feeling the glass-like fragments of ice cutting into his face. The threshing of his arms made loud splashing noises in the surrounding silence, and he was aware of being the subject of intense scrutiny from above as he laboriously drew nearer the bank. Only as he dragged himself up onto the lower reaches of mud did he become aware that Hong was scrambling toward him with hand outstretched. Feeling exhausted and physically sick he ignored the Chinese as he crawled from the water, hampered by the weight of his sodden padded coat, until he knelt fighting for breath near the feet of the foreman.

"Major, are you all right? Give me your arm."

Mark lifted his head with an effort. "No, Hong. They'll say you are aiding the devils' cub." Then he struggled to his feet dripping water, and stood swaying as he looked up at the row of faces along the bridge, clearer now in the rising mist.

"They haven't got me yet," he yelled, then began to laugh loud and long, hardly knowing what he was doing. "A third Englishman they want, those dragons of yours. Well, it won't bloody well be me, however much you pray it will."

Ah Wu speedily put out dry clothes and made coffee while Mark stripped to the skin and rubbed his frozen body with a towel. He felt shaken and ill, so he laced the coffee liberally with brandy and drank vast quantities of it. His hands holding the cup shook violently. Any man could make a mistake, miss his footing, misjudge a distance . . . but if he had been on one of several bridges he had built in the past he would now be dead at the foot of a ravine, or swept away by rapids. He was growing careless, letting outside things affect his work, losing his concentration. But how could any man concentrate when his future seemed to be falling to pieces all around him? It was this damned place. He drank more medicinal brandy.

With his thick coat soaking wet he had no alternative but to pile on all the pullovers he had with him and fling a rug around his shoulders before venturing out half an hour later. He found the mist completely gone, clear blue skies, and a team of very industrious coolies working with a will.

He pulled up with a heavy sigh, shivering in the outside air. "My God, there's no rhyme or reason to their behaviour; I'm damned if there is!"

Feeling the bite of the temperature even more after his immersion in the freezing water, and groggy from the brandy-laced coffee, his ire was immediately aroused by the sight of Corcoran in the cabin of his boat, whisky bottle in hand, apparently taking it easy. Pushing away memories of the last time he had walked onto that boat, Mark strode down the bank and along the narrow deck to the door of the cabin, which he flung open without ceremony.

"When I am not on the site, you are supposed to take over," he told the man furiously.

The Scot turned, glass in hand, his face dark with anger. "Who gave ye permission to come aboard?"

"Since when have we needed permission? You've walked in uninvited on me too many bloody times." He pointed through the cabin window. "You're supposed to be out there keeping a check on what they're doing, not drowning your sorrows down here. One bridge you worked on has already collapsed under a train. I'm not having mine do the same."

Corcoran got to his feet spoiling for a fight. "Ye'll tak that back or be sorry for it!"

"Oh, grow up, man," said Mark contemptuously. "You're a good engineer going to waste. I don't know what this thing is between you and the local villagers, but they didn't kill that boy without some cause, and I'm damned if I'm going to have my bridge endangered because you can't live with it."

The Scot deliberately emptied the glass then threw it down aggressively. "I know how to hold my liquor, but I doubt ye've been sober more than an hour at a stretch since ye came back frae Shanghai. It's clear ye're half-cut this morning or ye'd never have fallen like a pregnant mountain goat off a safe plateau." He smiled derisively. "Some Russian whore rob ye of ye manhood, did she, laddie? Well, ye look nae different without it." He picked up the bottle. "Now run away and play."

High on brandy and the reaction from his fall, Mark sent the whisky bottle crashing with a wild swing of his arm.

"Don't you ever speak to me like that again," he threatened, feeling a strong urge to smash at the man's face, see the blood running over unrecognisable features, hear his cries of agony. "While you were safely out here kicking coolies around and singing 'Auld Lang Syne' with drunken patriotism, I was killing and maiming, and watching my friends being blown to pieces or blistered by gas. I was a man of your age by the time I was twenty, and I'll stand no more of your patronising insults."

"What'll ye do about it?" hissed Corcoran in his face. "This isna the bloody army, laddie, where ye can throw ye weight about. *Major*, is it? Then God help the captains!" He sneered drunkenly. "One of the boy heroes of Ypres, are ye, except that ye didna die like the rest? How did ye manage that, I wonder?" He laughed as Mark stepped nearer. "Ye'll nae hit me, laddie. Officers and gentlemen are trained not to use their fists—nor anything else, for that matter. I've watched ye practise those fancy officer manners on the Chinks like they were British Tommies, and yon yellow bastard Hong like he was a sergeant. And where has it got ye, eh? There's nae one of them lifted a hand to help ye just now. They wanted ye dead, like they want all of us."

He took an unsteady step forward and pushed Mark aggressively in the chest. "War hero, are ye? Well, that war's over, laddie, and it's time ye learnt the facts of life from men like me who've lived out here in this stinking, filthy country filled with yellow scum who smile as they run a knife through ye ribs. The war against *them* will never be over because they multiply in their thousands, and it's men like ye that are too blind to see the danger. Aye, I kick the coolies, laddie, and that's not all. I do with the Chinks what every white man should do with those who produce more of their yellow kind."

He seemed to be directing his drunken aggression against the Chinese now, and through the fuddle in Mark's brain came the return of a problem that had recently been subjugated beneath others. His own drunken aggression was now determined to bring it into the open.

"The kilted hero of Lu-Seng, are you, laddie?" he said with contemptuous mimicry. "So how is it they got on your boat and committed bloody murder?"

Lost in some strange identity, Corcoran seemed unaware of Mark any longer. His face had grown ugly and his eyes were fixed on a distant point in his own twisted mind-pictures. When he spoke it was as if to an empty cabin.

"I made them sorry for that. Aye, they grovel at my feet now. But they'll do more. I'll never rest until there's nae more of them." His eyes filled with moisture. "Filthy barbaric scum. He'd done them nae harm, poor little devil." He bowed his head and sank back to sit on the edge of the table in silence for a moment or two.

Mark stood watching him, unable to think straight or even focus properly on the other man due to mental and physical exhaustion over the events of that morning.

Then Corcoran looked up again at the far wall, an unnerving gleam in his eye. "It's the only way to stop it, d'ye see? The virgins, the younger the better. No Chink wants them after I've finished with them, little sluts. All they're fit for is beasts of burden—if they're not driven from the village." He looked blankly at Mark. "Treat them like dirt themselves, they do, but they prize their honour and won't touch them after they've been used and thrashed by a 'foreign devil'. The little whores die of starvation before they can breed a dozen more of their kind."

A terrible brand of fury was beginning to fill Mark as Corcoran's words began to make some kind of sense—a sense that was unacceptable even to a man like himself who had seen and experienced unbelievable horrors.

"In God's name why didn't they kill *you*?" he asked hoarsely.

Corcoran's head swung round with lightning speed at the sound of his voice, and recognition crept into the fanatical light in his eyes. "Kill *me*? Because their pagan evil minds are afraid of my magic, that's why, laddie. The 'foreign devils' are devious and clever. They don't understand how we defy the spirits they fear so much. Aye, they tried to stop me, at first, but I've been using my magic for years. If they protest, I put the evil light on the door of their hovels which attracts the spirits that roam about at night looking for mischief to perform. When I came here to build the first bridge, I found the people of Lu-Seng already afeared of strange lights that appear on the marshes at night. We know, laddie, that it's probably only glow-worms, will 'o the wisps, but they believe so strongly in the forces of evil they willna go near them after dark." He began to laugh bitterly. "Oh, aye, they're so afeared of yon lights they gladly give up their girl children whenever I demand them. I told ye long ago that they're more afraid of spirits than kicks, laddie, and my threat of the evil eye."

He stood up and poked his face within inches of Mark's. "For twenty-five years I've been fighting them and spoiling their young virgins. And the strange lights in the night that I conjure up? A coat of luminous paint on their doors. *Paint*, laddie, that's all it is . . . and they give their girls to me because they think I'm more powerful than their hundred bloody dragons, the stupid yellow bastards."

The sick disgust that had been gathering like a great tidal wave burst through at that point to make Mark lash out blindly in a desire to wipe the words from the man's month. Rape of simple, helpless creatures was vile and inhuman; the nightmare of such conduct had haunted him for seven years. He hit Corcoran across the mouth but, a novice pugilist, was quite unprepared for the great powerful blow to his head that knocked him off balance. Staggering backward he fell against the bulkhead, striking his temple on the corner of a shelf. Then he was aware of no more than falling into blackness.

When he came to, he was on his own bunk and the day was well advanced. Ah Wu came across as soon as he saw his master stir.

"You b'long plentee big bump, makee hurt. Much better have baconegg now."

"How did I get here?" asked Mark, pretty sure of the answer.

"Plentee coolie takee you go b'long here."

His heart sank. The morale and loyalty of the coolies was doubtful enough without the two white bosses indulging in a drunken punch-up. What little respect he still commanded from them must surely have vanished now.

"You much better have baconegg now," persisted Ah Wu, and Mark agreed to eat breakfast as soon as his boy could prepare it. Forcing himself to clear his plate in an effort to counteract the terrible emptiness in his stomach, he also drank several cups of pure black coffee while he thought very deeply about a great many things. Finally, he got to his feet somewhat unsteadily and threw his stock of brandy bottles one by one into the canal. There was no answer to any problem in them. The only way was to face up to everything and attack a complex situation methodically and with a clear head. Far too many people relied on him: it would help no one if he went to pieces.

He went back to the bridge. Corcoran was nowhere on the site for which he was thankful. He was not sure he could bring himself to speak to the man, even professionally. Feeling somewhat guilty he thanked Hong for carrying on in his absence and set to work. With the coolies in a new willing mood a great deal was achieved before misty nightfall put an end to all activity.

But Mark's resolution to face his problems and attack them with a clear head was put to the test earlier than he had expected. Their little train had come up during the afternoon bringing the rails needed to re-lay track on the far side of the new bridge. With these supplies came the newspapers Mark had ordered to be sent up, and a packet of letters from his hotel. There was nothing of much interest except a large plain brown envelope addressed to him. What it contained seemed like the last straw. It was shocking and inexplicable, but it told him he would have to get to Shanghai as soon as possible. Yet how could he leave Corcoran in charge of a party of Chinese after what he had heard that day?

CHAPTER TEN

There was a martial air about Shanghai these days, thought Alexandra moodily as she walked back to her home just after breakfast one morning. She had gone out to buy paint she did not want, and declined a rickshaw because walking used up some of her surplus energy.

But the streets of the International Settlement were full of marching men making their way from the troopships alongside the jetties to their temporary encampments—men with pale faces and thick khaki uniforms who had been shipped straight out from England at a moment's notice. They were weighted down with equipment on their backs, had no proper quarters awaiting them, knew very little about the Chinese people, and were far from home. But they stared about them with sharp interest as they marched, exchanged laughing comments amongst themselves, and winked with saucy cheerfulness when they caught Alexandra's eye. The port seemed full of them: fresh detachments arrived each day. They were concentrated at the racecourse, in the godowns and the old Chinese amusement park—not ideal sites in a Shanghai winter climate.

Other troops arrived from Hong Kong, India and Singapore, while American marines poured in from their Far Eastern garrisons, and French troops arrived to defend the French Concession. NCOs and despatch riders roared back and forth on motorcycles, some taking a delight in terrifying the wheelbarrow men by riding straight at them and swerving at the very last minute. The rickshaws and curio shops were full of soldiers off duty, and every kind of refreshment bar was having a boom in trade once evening came. The hotels were full of officers who were quickly introduced into the various clubs in Shanghai as guest members, and Shanghai society threw open its doors to the military, as much to take advantage of the opportunity to see fresh faces and hear news of home as to provide recompense for what might lie before them.

All around the International Settlement barbed-wire barricades were going up, as well as fortified defence positions armed with artillery. All those gates leading from the Settlement were now manned by armed troops, and no one passed in or out without note being made of it. In case of attack it was essential to know if there were European civilians outside who would need to be rescued. Men of the Shanghai Volunteer Corps drilled and practised at the rifle range, liaising with the regular troops to provide expert knowledge on the area and the enemy. Most of them now wore their uniforms at their desks, ready for any call that might come.

Attitudes fell into two schools: the old die-hards of the Empire who did not believe the Chinese would dare to tamper with the friendship of the combined Western nations, and those who still remembered the siege of Peking and predicted another barbarous massacre of white people. There was much to support both views, but those in whose hands the defence of Shanghai rested prepared for the worst and hoped it would not come.

Alexandra viewed the militarisation with a feeling of unreality. She had lived amongst the Chinese all her life. Things had been the same year after year, and she could not think that it would really change. There would always be poverty, starvation, disease: there would always be avaricious merchants and moneylenders to encourage such things. There would also always be Western money and expertise struggling against tradition and ancient superstitions. She had read the newspapers, read about what had happened in Hankow. But that was a Chinese city occupied by the troops of a warlord. Shanghai was internationally owned. Surely this khaki invasion was not necessary?

As if to emphasise the new mood she encountered James Clitheroe in the hall of her home, dressed in the uniform of the SVC and ostentatiously armed with a pair of pistols. He was just leaving with a briefcase full of documents, and normally Alexandra would have made a teasing comment on the incongruity of the sight, but she just murmured a vague greeting in answer to his obvious enthusiasm at the sight of her, and continued up the stairs. Uniforms reminded her of Mark, and she had no wish to torment herself again.

She walked heavy-hearted into her studio to uncover the canvas of the Bridge of a Hundred Dragons. It was better than she had ever hoped: she was suffering now, without a doubt. For four days she had remained indoors seeking solace from her work. There seemed to be nothing else left. She had not wept over Mark, but that initial brave anger had died leaving her lifeless.

As for the night Lionel had taken his revenge of her, what little of it she remembered had killed 'Sandy' Mostyn forever. Of what use was it to fight for equality when the cause was hopeless? Brave and daring she might have been, defying convention at every turn and showing the world she was someone to be reckoned with but, when it came to the basic truth, her father had control over her until she came of age, Mark had exploited her undeniable biological longings, and Lionel had exposed her female weakness with absolute ease. 'Sandy' was a sham, 'Alex' was a romantic fool, Alexandra was a business accessory for the influential Garrard Mostyn. Who was left? A defeated recluse who had been shattered and humiliated by those she tried so hard to impress. It was a man's world, she knew and accepted that now.

The brave trappings of a modern woman in her wardrobe looked tawdry; her pride had gone. Those she had believed her friends had not noticed her absence. The one man she had loved paraded his mistress and bastard before the eyes of Shanghai at the same time as he made love to her. Her work was her only hope of keeping her head above water, even though the subject was such a painful one now. It was only iron determination not to go under that saved her from tears, recriminations, and hopelessness. This canvas could be the phoenix arising, the one good thing to emerge from this disastrous phase of her life. She concentrated completely on it, shutting out all else.

She had hardly positioned her easel and mixed her colours before there came a message to go downstairs where her father was waiting in his study to speak to her. It took her by surprise. Why had he not gone to the office by now? It was very unusual, especially in these days of uncertainty, for him to remain at home during the morning. Thinking of the scene she had just witnessed in the streets she wondered incredulously if Shanghai was under attack. Was that why Jimmy had been in uniform and armed?

Flinging off her smock she hurried down the staircase to the study where one look at her father persuaded her there was, indeed, some kind of emergency in the city. She crossed to him swiftly, apprehension sharpening her voice.

"Father, are we in danger?"

He looked back at her with such concentrated venom it halted her as suddenly as a blow across the face. His hand was shaking as he brought something from behind his back and held it out to her. His voice was that of a stranger as he said, "Your mother received this in her post this morning."

A wave of extreme coldness attacked her face, and spread slowly down her body as she stared at what he held—her last and vilest humiliation. The large photograph showed the interior of a cheap Chinese strip club populated by all the worst human flotsam to be found in Shanghai. In the centre of the picture was a European girl, her dress way up over her hips, sprawling drunkenly across a great brutish Lascar seaman, who was handling her bare breast. It sickened and revolted her, filled her with a shame that stripped her of the brave mantle of defiance she had first donned when a small girl had been carelessly pushed aside by the father she worshipped, fallen to cut herself, then been ordered away in the arms of her amah. She had mistakenly believed defiance would make her immune to rejection, but she stood there then with no protection, no defence, no shred of pride. It was as if this man she had never ceased trying to win back had become the Lascar stripping off her glad rags to expose her worthlessness to the world. She began to shake as she stood helplessly before him, trapped by the irrefutable vileness of that picture.

"With this . . . this *filth*," he went on with great difficulty, "was a written threat to distribute copies to every European household in Shanghai unless I subscribe twenty thousand pounds to the revolutionary cause."

Deep racking sobs started in the pit of her stomach, moved through to slice across her chest, then on to fill her throat so that her words jerked out in agonised phrases.

"It's . . . it's *terrible*. How could he do it? Dear God, I've known . . . known him for years. We . . . were fr . . . *friends*. How could he? How could he? How could *anyone* do a thing like . . . like this?"

"You little *slut!* You have been asking for something like this for a long time with your disgusting loose morals."

It was a nightmare she could no longer bear. To hear such words from him broke her apart. Reaching forward she clutched his arm desperately as tears burned their way across her cheeks.

"No, Father, *no*. *Please* . . . you don't understand."

He flung her off in a gesture of violent contempt. "I understand all too painfully that you have never hesitated to advertise your lack of moral values, your disregard for dignity, your contempt for convention. You publicly flaunted your body in defiance of modesty or decent standards of behaviour. I knew it would only be a matter of time before you sunk to frequenting such places. Well, you have now found your natural level in society . . . and you have broken your mother's heart in doing so."

Hurt beyond endurance she sunk to her knees on the floor and doubled up in an anguish of sobbing. "Don't say such cruel things. *Please*, Father, don't," she whispered against the palms of her hands covering her face. "You never understood it was the new vogue. All young people dressed and behaved like that. We all became *modern*. It was the thing to do . . . and *I* did it to . . . to . . ." Turning her face up to him in a last desperate appeal for understanding, she said, "Can't you see that I was trying to tell you that I was a *person*, an individual with feelings and hopes of my own that I wanted to share with you? I was . . . trying to tell you I wanted a father again, not a . . . not a . . ." Her words tailed off as she saw his expression. "*Please, please don't say such terrible things to me.*"

The photograph was flung to the floor so that it lay as irrefutable evidence of his condemnation. "When I see filth like that, what do you expect me to say? *What do you expect me to say?*"

"I think she expects you to say that you will listen to her explanation of something you cannot believe to be genuine," said a voice from the doorway. "That is what I have come up from Lu-Seng to tell her."

Mark was there—how she did not know—and offered a strength and refuge that overrode all else, yet she found she could not go to him. Her body ached, her head felt too heavy for her neck, and she trembled violently in the aftermath of shock. Next minute he was beside her, wrapping his own padded coat around her, as he drew her tenderly from her crumpled position on the floor into a close embrace against the comforting warmth of his body. She hardly heard her father's harsh demand to know what right Mark had to leave the bridge and walk uninvited into his house. Yet she heard Mark's equally harsh reply, and she clung to him.

"I make no excuse for walking in here, Mostyn. If you value your home as little as you appear to value your daughter, you plainly won't care who uses or abuses it. I might understand you if the pose of Victorian father were consistent, but your scathing and brutal condemnation of Alex's behaviour slips into professional exploitation when it suits your purpose. I was told how she was instructed to use her sexual attraction to bring me to heel that night, and it doesn't take much to guess it was not the first time it had happened. Your plan misfired badly. I didn't come to heel, but I do intend making Alex my wife as soon as such a move is feasible."

"The White Knight, Rawlings?" came the sneering comment. "Your somewhat sickening brand of nobility went out with Camelot. You'll change your mind when you've seen *that*."

He kicked the photograph toward Mark with the toe of his shoe, but Alexandra bent swiftly and threw it onto the fire. Mark must never see it.

"I haven't changed my mind," he continued with biting fury. "Whoever sent me a copy with a demand for money is vile and vicious. If you knew anything at all about this girl, you would be as certain as I am that that picture is not what it seems."

"I can tell you quite clearly what it is, Major. It is the outcome of a stupid and dangerous plan to coerce me into releasing you from the consequences of your arrogance in refusing to 'come to heel' as you put it. For the sum of seven hundred and fifty pounds she allied herself with a political group with Communist overtones, then thought she could end her membership when her purpose had been achieved. I warned her that she was outclassed and there could be serious repercussions, but she disregarded my words with her modern contempt for the wisdom of those with experience. *You* are to blame for this outrage, Rawlings, entirely to blame." His face working with anger, he went on, "Between you, you have put me in a position no one has succeeded in doing in all my years in China. My name is respected and trusted everywhere, my word is accepted by any organisation in the world. My reputation is untarnished by scandal of any kind." His voice rose to thundering proportions. *"I will not allow myself to be held to ransom by a parcel of Communist peasants. Do you understand that? Do you?"*

"Yes, I understand only too well, Mostyn," came the cold reply. "You are second only to God in your own eyes, and are afraid this might prevent your taking over the world when He gives up in despair. Men like you make me wonder what I fought for ten years ago." He began walking with Alexandra to a chair, where he lowered her into it before squatting on his haunches before her, his eyes darkened by shock. "Is it true that you deliberately tangled with such people, Alex?"

When she nodded, he seemed unable to say any more for a moment or two. Then he asked, "Had . . . had you no idea . . . did it never occur to you that all I have said about the Reds is true? I have fought these people, Alex, and know I have said several times in your presence that they are ruthless and cruel, that they spread the seeds of revolution and oppression of the people. Did none of it mean anything to you?" he ended in urgent concern.

Weeping had given way to utter exhaustion, and she looked back at him helplessly, feeling her cheeks stiff with drying tears. "It seemed the only way to help you. What *he* was doing was ruthless and cruel. That was all I considered."

He bowed his head, squeezing her hands in a tight grip for a while. When he looked up again his eyes seemed red rimmed in a face grown grey. "You had better tell me what happened—right from the beginning."

The nightmare was beginning to fade a little. Mark's presence formed a protective guard around her and, although she still felt unreal and in a limbo, he was there with her making it easy to speak of things that had been locked inside her too long. She forgot that other presence, the tall menacing figure by the hearth, as it all poured from her. Mark said nothing throughout her tale of how she had used Lionel's political fervour to gain her objective, then discovered he had a nasty side to his character when she told him she was giving up her membership.

"I lost my temper and told him he should help the Chinese by going into the Chinese City and scattering money for the beggars," she explained in a voice husky from weeping. "That was . . . that was why I made no protest when he drove there instead of going to Bunty Frobisher's. He threw the money: I helped him to do it. At least, I *suppose* it was money." She gripped Mark's hands. "It was very exciting. I thought he was . . . *apologising*, in some strange way. It went to my head. We drank champagne and scattered pieces of paper from each side of the car. It . . . it was heady, Mark. He was back as I'd always known him. He . . . he and D . . . Dot were my *friends*," she cried feeling the shock of Lionel's betrayal thick in her throat again. "We always had so much fun together. I thought it was like that again."

Mark nodded. "But this time it was different?"

"Yes. We laughed. Oh God," she said in despair, "how could I have been so gullible?"

"Because you thought you knew him."

She managed a dry derisory laugh. "We laughed, drank champagne and drove through those ghastly streets tossing notes into the darkness. I believed I was saving the poor of China through my wisdom," she said in a voice that wobbled. "That's very powerful stuff, you know."

It all came back to her then, but she did not flinch from Mark's gaze as she confessed that she had been too drunk to know where Lionel was taking her, and powerless to leave when something told her it was all wrong.

"I remember being afraid and feeling sick," she told him in a low voice. "But Lionel seemed to have vanished. Then I think I passed out. All I remember after that is being helped from his car and taken upstairs by Lai-Hi and my girl. Until just now I believed his only purpose had been personal revenge for the things I said in temper about his political motives. That is the only thing that arouses strong feelings in him, but even for that I could never forgive him. That he could be *so* vindictive, that he could send that picture with such an ultimatum, I still cannot accept." She begged with eyes and voice blurred with emotion. "Mark, is it possible to know someone so well, yet so little? I went to school with Dot. The Armitage house was like a second home. Why, . . . *why* would he do such a thing to me?"

His answer was of the utmost importance, and he appeared to sense this. Yet he spoke immediately, with confidence.

"He did it because he is weak. They recruit men like him and use their weakness for political gain. Your father was right to warn you. No one is allowed to escape the net once it is thrown. Armitage had no choice. You had made a fool of him before those whom he longed to impress. I have no doubt they pressurised him to seize the first opportunity to use you to hit out at a pillar of Shanghai society." He frowned. "That routine club photograph must have been a stroke of luck for his Bolshevik friends. That part of this affair will almost certainly have been taken out of his hands, although I suspect they were his which put a copy in an envelope sent up to me with my post from the hotel. His immaturity led him to think I would . . . ah well, it's not the first time I have taken on these people."

"Taking a party of Tsarist refugees across Russia will hardly have given you experience for *this*, Rawlings," said her father, reminding them both of his presence. "This is a matter of complex strategy. I have no intention of yielding to their demand, naturally. *No one* forces my hand, especially in such clumsy, brutish manner."

Looking at his slim, arrogant figure, the attractive silvering of fair hair at his temples, the fleshy petulant lips, Alexandra realised it had been useless to hope for so many years. Even in this, his concern was merely for his name and reputation.

"For once, I agree with you, Father," she told him tonelessly. "On no account must you give in to people like this. Let them send out those disgusting photographs. What society thinks of me no longer seems important. I don't care any more."

"I do," said Mark quietly. "I care deeply. So we must think carefully. There is no question of paying them off, neither is there any hope of getting from them the roll of film they must have bought from the strip club. However, we have to somehow counter their threat or they will continue to hold it over you."

All at once, Alexandra was forgotten as both men faced each other in common cause.

"The best method of defence in these cases, is attack," her father was saying. "It has never failed me yet, and I have had worse crises than this."

"Worse crises?" cried Mark. "What could be worse than a threat to your own daughter?" He slapped the back of a chair with a vicious hand. "Are you a father, or not?"

"I am first of all a man of great influence. As such, I have to consider the greater claim on me," said the smooth voice.

"*Bloody pious balderdash!*" exploded Mark. "The world would go on turning without you, Mostyn, but Alex could go under right now if you are not prepared to stand by her."

"Gird on thy sword?" sneered Garrard. "All right, Major, you are the great warrior. What is your solution to this?"

Mark considered for a moment, and Alexandra prayed he would meet the challenge. "Unlike you, I did not believe the evidence of that photograph," he began. "The only reason I thought it *must* be Alex was the manner in which it was sent to me. If I had been shown it under other circumstances I would have noted the strange resemblance to someone I knew, and no more. I give you credit for your swift condemnation to be based on the same reason—the cruel manner in which Mrs Mostyn should have been faced with such a picture." He cast her a sideways glance. "I really don't believe anyone who knows Alex and her background would believe she willingly frequents such places—even those who have seen her wildness at parties. There is a great difference between desperate high spirits and viciousness." He halted a moment, then went on deliberately. "If the photograph had been of a woman looking remarkably like Mrs Mostyn in an opium den taking the drug, would you have as readily believed that?"

Her father paled. "That remark betrays your total lack of breeding."

"It also reveals your total prejudice when it comes to your daughter, but it serves to make my point that something is only credible if you choose to believe it. That you did, and I did not is very enlightening, you must agree. It suggests that even if those pictures *were* distributed there is a strong possibility that the recipients might believe the girl bears a strong resemblance to Alexandra Mostyn, and no more."

"A possibility?" said Garrard harshly. "You profess to love my daughter, yet suggest gambling on a *possibility*?"

"You would, without a qualm . . . but I am suggesting that we turn it into a certainty by advance publicity."

"By . . . *what*?"

Mark gave a strained smile. "The power of the press—the men who have profited by Alex's escapades so richly in the past. It's time they did something in return. You know the owners of all the influential newspapers, Mostyn. It should be an easy matter to feed them with a story of Communist ploys. Along with the anti-foreign propaganda, the contrived strikes to disrupt the port, they are conducting a campaign to discredit foreign residents by simulating scandals and misconduct between the most influential members of Shanghai's European society. It is widely believed that forged letters and photographs are being circulated in certain quarters—that sort of thing," he explained. "I'll phone in the details myself if your henchmen can't be trusted to do it." He smiled to show his confidence. "It's a tried and trusted military manoeuvre, take my word for it. When the enemy is marching on a vital bridge in numbers of ten to one against you, you know you can't hold it. So you blow it up yourself. You have lost the bridge, but the enemy has also lost it . . . and there is always a chance to throw a pontoon over the river further upstream."

Alexandra was staring at Mark in much the same way her father was. It sounded so simple. Destroy their plan by rendering it useless to them. Could it possibly work? Then he turned to her to ask if she had seen anyone who knew her during the time she was with Lionel that evening.

"No, I don't think so. We were driving so fast . . . and my hat had fallen over my face," she said.

"What about since then? Have you mentioned it to anyone?" he asked urgently.

"I haven't been to parties, and no one has bothered to notice my absence," she added with bitterness.

"Thank God for that!" He swung round to Garrard. "Is there anywhere Alex can go for a week or two with someone who can be trusted to say whatever is necessary?"

"Our manager in Nanking has a very discreet wife."

"Discreet enough to say Alex was with her last week?"

"Dot knows I was here that day," cried Alexandra. "I spoke to her on the telephone."

Mark looked contemptuous. "Who would believe anything that girl said?" He thought a moment, then added, "What about the household servants?"

"I would entrust my life to them," said her father. "They have all been with us for years and are treated as part of the family."

"Which is more than Alex has ever been."

"I should stop firing your big guns, if I were you, Major," came the whiplash reply. "This whole messy business was brought about by Alexandra being forced to fight your battles for you. If this idea works it will be your conscience that is salved, not mine."

"You don't possess a conscience, Mostyn," said Mark levelly. "This idea will work, I guarantee, but all it will mean to you is twenty thousand pounds and your pride saved."

Garrard's face twisted into a bitter smile. "You know nothing of life in this country. It takes years to build up a trust in one, a reputation for genuine interest in the country, a name that is immediately accepted by Chinese all over the land. No, it is not *my* pride, Major, but that of all those of my countrymen who are able to remain here on the goodwill built up by me. Topple the ivory tower, and the rest fall with it. That was what they were hoping to do, you know. As I said before, I have to put the greater claim first."

"So Alex comes low on your list of priorities? In that case, you will put nothing in the way of my wish to marry her as soon as it can be arranged."

It seemed to be more than her father could take when Mark added, "After all, you will hardly miss her."

"You are ill-bred, vain, and singularly headstrong, Major," he said finally. "My daughter is shallow, selfish, and preposterously extravagant. I wish you luck of each other."

"Do I have your word on that?"

"Oh, yes," he said making for the door. "I shall not attempt to stop you. She'll not get a penny from me, of course, so I suggest you get back to that bridge and earn some money while you can. After this job you might find it difficult to get interesting work abroad."

The door closed behind him, and Alexandra saw the effort the morning had cost him written in Mark's face. Without a word she got up and went into his arms, his padded coat dropping from her shoulders onto the expensive carpet. For some while they stood silently, she finding comfort in his strength and the gentle way he stroked her hair.

"Do you really think it will work?" she asked against his pullover when she felt able to speak.

"Yes, of course. They would have sent a covering letter to suggest the girl in the picture was you. We are doing the same thing, in effect, by suggesting that it is not. People will see what they have been told to see. It'll work."

"And you, Mark, what do you see?" She held her breath waiting for his answer.

"I see a girl I love. That's all I shall ever see from now on."

She looked up, and he kissed her slowly and gently as if to mend the hurt she had suffered.

"Take me away soon," she whispered.

"I'll take you tomorrow, I think. If you are going down to Nanking for a bit it would be best if you came down on my train in the morning as far as Lu-Seng, then travel down the canal on my boat with Ah Wu to see that you are all right. That way, you're not likely to bump into people who know you, as you might on a Yangtze steamer."

"What about Lionel?"

He pulled her head back against his woollen pullover. "I think we can safely leave him to your father. The great Garrard Mostyn is not going to let a dangerous little pip-squeak like him run loose . . . and he is really in the best possible position to arrange professional and social downfall. My hands are tied by military law, I'm afraid. The most I could arrange would be to accidentally blow him up, but that would reflect on my professional competence and do my career no good at all. I couldn't risk that," he continued in the same light tone, "just as I am about to take on the responsibility of a wife." He tilted her chin up and kissed her again, more roughly this time. "It's high time someone took charge of you."

She let her glance wander over his square features, the obstinate smiling mouth, and eyes that inevitably betrayed him. She saw a man who truly loved her, someone who would defend her against the world, if necessary. He had seen that photograph and come to her at once. What had happened to her faith in him at the first setback?

"Mark, I don't really deserve your love," she whispered.

He put his fingers against her lips very gently. "Nobody ever *deserves* another person's love. It's something that happens between two people, whether they want it to or not. Mostly it works very well, but sometimes the obstacles are so great it becomes a source of pain . . . until it is eased by someone else." He took hold of one hand in both of his and studied her fingers as if trying to think of what to say next. Then he looked up at her. "Alex, I have just won from your father the right to marry you, but I think I should give you some idea of what you'd be taking on. If, after you have heard what I have to say, you want to change your mind, I'll accept your decision."

"Darling, *nothing* will change my mind," she said fervently.

He smiled abstractedly. "You really know nothing about me, except that I am eleven years older than you and rather hard up."

She suddenly guessed what he was about to tell her. It made her grateful and very happy that he should be so honest over something many men might try to keep hidden. Yet, when he began, it seemed she might have been wrong.

"I won't ask you to understand what happened in Russia. Only those of us who were there could ever do that. I just want you to listen and consider what I say in relation to our future together."

She drew him across to a leather sofa near the fire, and they sat together in the warmth from the flames. For a while he seemed lost in his own thoughts, and she made no attempt to prompt him, sensing that it would be wrong. Finally, he began speaking, but his gaze was on the fire and full of faraway days.

"Perhaps, as you once suggested, I should put it out of my mind, forget the things that happened then and concentrate on the present and the future." He turned, and she saw the honesty mingling with a plea for understanding in his expression. "I can't do that, Alex. It will always be a part of me, even though you have shown me it is possible to be happy again."

She put a hand over his, whispering, "Despite that photograph?"

"Despite *anything*," he assured her. "Who else but the most courageous, caring girl would have risked what you did for my sake? I love you very much, Alex." Hesitating briefly he plunged into his next sentence. "I also loved another courageous girl in 1919."

"I have always known that. Tell me about her. That is all I have ever wanted you to do, Mark."

He returned to his study of the leaping flames as he began to remove that veil over his mysterious past. "I was very young that summer —young, lonely, and badly shaken by the horrors of war. For a time I found all I sought in the wild countryside of Russia, but the horror began again when the train the Bolsheviks had guaranteed a safe pass was deliberately blown up with a mass of foreign troops aboard. Somehow I managed to crawl to the country estate of a man who was fighting in the north of the country. His wife and sister took me in and nursed me until the Red forces moved into the nearby village and we had to leave. I was still very ill, and they dressed me in peasant clothes and said I was the husband, who had been attacked by White soldiers and left for dead. As a result, they said, I was unable to speak."

His gaze shifted to the floor between his knees. "In the following few months I gradually became what I was supposed to be. When we spoke together it was in Russian; we ate peasant food and adopted their manners. Soon, I was confused about my identity, and deeply in love with the girl whose husband I purported to be. After a terrible morning when she was publicly stripped by Bolshevik brutes and almost raped, while I was forced to hide, we could hold back our feelings no longer. We became husband and wife." He angled his face toward Alexandra, and she was filled with compassion for what was written on it. "You notice I didn't say we became lovers. Reality and pretence had merged during those long days when night was marked by only an hour or two of half-light, and the wild bizarre aspect of what we were doing made anything seem possible. I guarded, protected and loved her as a husband; she tended and loved me as a wife."

"But you must have known it would have to end when you reached safety," she protested gently.

He swallowed and said with complete sincerity, "I think we believed that moment would never come, that each day would be our last. Toward the end, it may be that we even wanted that. It was as if we had lived our whole life span in those months together, and anything beyond it would be meaningless."

"Those years between now and then *have* been meaningless, haven't they?" she said with sudden discernment.

He turned away again, nodding slowly. "I suppose so. I have only made them productive because she begged me to, but I have been haunted by ignorance of her fate. All my enquiries led nowhere. Thousands disappeared without trace. So many were slaughtered in the most obscene and terrible manner there was no chance of identifying them. I have had waking and sleeping nightmares about her death, and impossible hopes for her survival."

She let silence hang between them for a while as she realised the past she had been fighting was more formidable than she had imagined. Then he continued.

"When Clitheroe met me off the ship he mentioned that there was a large White Russian community in Shanghai, and I was flooded with hope once more. I made enquiries in several bars and restaurants, then came on to dinner here. Your father revived the pain further by insisting on speaking of that period in my life, and you put salt in the wound by playing a song she often sang." He got to his feet and walked away, hands thrust into the pockets of his breeches, and shoulders hunched. "Yet the reawakening of my feelings for her taught me to love you, made me see they were blinding me to the full meaning of her words." He swung round and Alexandra saw the shadow of conflicting devotions on his face. "As we parted she said, '*You are young and have a future beyond this. Live it, my dearest.*'"

Alexandra felt the threat of returning tears as she realised her mother had been right to say a woman's weakness was often her greatest strength. The obligation to defend her had brought Mark here today; her need for a defender. All her precocious demands, her shock tactics, and her headstrong attacks on his sexual control had failed to draw from him what she had longed to know. Now, in her moment of greatest weakness, he was confessing without inhibitions. She realised then that women could always have equality if they used the gift of femininity with skill, understanding and thankfulness. It was their greatest weapon.

Mark was there before her, drawing her to her feet in a gesture of possession. "Alex, I have been a victim of my past for too long. Katya is dead, I know that now. Give me my future. I know she would want you to."

Lost for words she gazed back at him. *Katya*. His past love was dead! Who, then, was Marie Drozdova with a child of whom Mark was indisputably the father?

"Alex, what is it?" he asked in concern. "Nothing has been changed by what I've told you, has it? You knew all along there had been another woman somewhere in my life, surely."

"Yes . . . yes," she heard herself say with some hesitation. "I think I even guessed much of what you have just said, but I was not sure of the final outcome."

He took her hands and held them together in his enfolding clasp. "Even I did not know that until a short time ago," he said with a faint sigh. "My enquiries in Shanghai bore fruit. Katya's sister-in-law came to my hotel from the café she now owns in the city. When she escaped six years ago from Vladivostok she brought with her an infant boy. He is my son, Alex—mine and Katya's."

Swept with relief that he had confessed freely instead of forcing her to confront him with what she knew, Alexandra reached up and kissed him in gratitude.

"I've seen him, darling. He's a fine boy, and you must be proud of him. Before long he'll be proud of you, I'll make certain of that." She touched his mouth again with her own. "Don't look like that, Mark. Whatever my faults may be, refusing to rear another woman's child is not one of them. Every . . . everyone needs a father, and I shall see that he has the one he deserves. Your Katya would want me to do that, too."

He changed quite dramatically, drawing her against him and turning her light salutes on his mouth into a kiss of unbridled fierceness.

"I couldn't bear to lose you, Alex. I couldn't bear to lose love and happiness twice over."

"You won't, darling," she promised softly, even as she grew aware that confession had ceased and he was now holding back something he could not bring himself to reveal.

Marie's face was lit by a blaze of pleasure at his unexpected arrival at the café that afternoon, but Mark was thwarted in his intention by the presence in the parlour at the rear of the premises of a man as large as himself, probably ten years older, bearded, and with an undeniable air of breeding despite the fact that he was dressed in rough trousers and a thick woollen cardigan over a cloth waistcoat. Marie introduced Gregori Petrovich Galinkov, and they all spoke in French, the natural language of highborn Russians.

"You are the leader of those in Shanghai still fighting the Bolsheviks," said Mark remembering something Marie had told him, as he shook the man's hand. "I think you fight a lost cause, but I admire your courage."

Gregori's grip on his hand was fierce, and there was a familiar Slavic warmth in the man's wide smile as he responded. "It is an honour to meet a man whose courage *I* admire. Your name is known amongst those who stood against the Terror. You have become a hero of Russia; the story of your train is one of the legends of that time. It will be handed down from generation to generation." His smile widened even further. "In the telling, it will doubtless be exaggerated beyond belief, but your personal heroism can never be."

Acutely embarrassed by this fulsome national trait he had forgotten, Mark disengaged himself murmuring something about exaggeration being the key word. Reaction from the events of the morning, plus physical exhaustion, was making him light-headed and he longed to sit down. Marie must have sensed his weariness, for she indicated a chair and declared that she would fetch the samovar.

Gregori lowered himself into the seat facing Mark and took out a pipe, nodding at Marie's retreating back.

"Marie Fedorovna is a fine woman, from a family I have known all my life. She is the only member of it to survive and, if I have to lose her to another man, it must be to someone of your calibre." He lit a match and began to coax the tobacco into a glow. "The boy I have loved as my own son for two years, but it is right that he should have his real father. I would not argue with that." Puffing several times to establish his pipe, he leant back and went on. "All the same, I experience sadness that these two I dearly love will be on the far side of the world so that I may never see them. Must you take them from their friends and countrymen, *mon ami*? The boy has known no other life than this. He feels and thinks as a Russian. A stranger for a father, and a country of which he knows nothing—that is a great deal for a boy of such tender years to master."

Mark's slumbering anger flared once more at that. Not only had Marie confronted Alexandra with the boy in a manner that had shocked her into embarking on that intoxicated drive with Lionel that had had such dangerous results, it seemed she had indicated to this man that Michael's English father was about to marry her and bear them both back to his native land. She was taking the matter into her own hands, knowing he was powerless to do anything positive all the while he was working on the bridge. He had intended telling her of Alexandra's eagerness to adopt the boy as her own when they married. What Gregori had just said showed him Marie was as shrewd and determined as she had ever been; certainly unlikely to agree to his plan. For that matter, why had she not accepted the name and protection of this large Russian of aristocratic background? He had loved them both for two years, he had just indicated. Why, then, had such love been ignored?

Knowing it was out of the question to discuss the subject freely before he had confronted Marie, Mark controlled his anger.

"I am in Shanghai on detachment from Hong Kong. I have no permanent home in England."

"You have sold your estate?" asked the other in surprise.

"An army man lives where he is sent, you know that very well, Gregori Petrovich," hedged Mark, knowing full well the Russian imagined he was of equal rank to himself, with family estates and properties in England. Moving to safer ground he asked, "How many years did you continue to resist after your men mutinied? Such a distinguished regiment, Marie said, yet the soldiers were simple men easily swayed by bullies."

The large strong-looking man facing him had quick tears in his eyes as he shook his head. "I cannot speak of it—even now I cannot speak of it—without feeling shame. Mikov, a man with whom I would have trusted my life in battle, spat in my face as he clubbed me and left me for dead."

It was a story Mark had heard so many times whilst in Russia, and many officers had suffered brutal humiliating deaths at the hands of their men. Some had probably come close to earning such hatred due to their brutal arrogance in the past. Memory of those in his own small group flooded back, and he could even visualise their faces as they had regarded him with awe because of his attitude toward them. Used to addressing their officers as 'Excellency', they were equally used to receiving a kick or flick of a riding whip to accompany their orders. An English officer dressed as a peasant, who shared the food equally, consulted them when planning his next move, and shook hands with them on parting was a creature over whom they had marvelled.

Mark frowned. "When men are so desperate it is unwise to put trust in any of them alone. What so many of your officers forgot was that their men were humans with human weaknesses. War puts stresses on them they cannot withstand. I am sure you were not of that group, but you suffered because of them. The same thing is happening here. The Kuomintang claims to be marching to free the coolie of his yoke, but it carries another yoke ready to fit in place. When peasant marches against peasant the only really effective result is that the population is markedly decreased. Gregori Petrovich, what happened in Russia is about to happen in China, yet the world stands by."

"What can the world do, *mon ami*? It has decimated its own population in a four-year war. You fought a small battle with your train and emerged victorious . . . but the cause was lost, for all that."

Mark stared at him. "You say that when you are the leader of men dedicated to defeating the Red occupation of your country?"

Gregori shook his head again. "I think nothing I can do would end the occupation of my country. Like you, I fight one small battle against them, no more. We are a band of free men dedicated to the protection of our fellows in exile. There is a Soviet embassy here in Shanghai, and these people have long memories. There are still those fleeing from Russia and making their way here, as I did two years ago. They need friends, somewhere to live, a means of making a living—sometimes a new identity. That is what we do. My sabre rests in its scabbard now," he finished sadly.

"It's where they should all rest. The world would be a better place."

Gregori gave a gusting laugh. "No, no, *mon ami*, the world would use its fists, instead. Men must fight each other; they always have. You are an idealist."

"He always was," put in Marie as she entered with the samovar, and smiled in Mark's direction. "I remember the trait, my dear, as if it were yesterday."

With something of a shock Mark realised it was not only Michael who believed he was her true son. Everyone in Shanghai had been led to believe it, including Gregori. That meant everyone would also believe himself her former lover. Only then did he face the fact that Marie would never give the boy to Alexandra to rear, *never*. He took the tea from her, shaken by the alternatives facing him. His 'child of love' or his 'child-bride', he could not have both. Marie had been deadly serious when she had issued that ultimatum.

The door opened again and Michael entered carrying a school bag. His face broke into a smile when he saw Gregori, and he ran to the man to tell him in a flood of French about his lessons that afternoon. The big Russian ruffled the boy's curly hair in affection, but when Michael attempted to climb on his knee, his arms were gripped and he was turned to face Mark.

"We have a visitor, *mon petit*."

A blush covered the face so like his own, and the boy approached to give a small bow. "Excuse my bad manners, sir, I did not see you as I entered," he said in commendable English. "How very nice that you have come. Is the bridge finished?"

Mark shook his head, unable to think of anything save how proud Katya would be of their son. "Not quite, but it shouldn't be long now."

"I've been drawing some bridges while you have been away," came the shy confession. "Would you like to see them?"

"Er . . . yes, very much."

Dropping his school bag he ran to a side room, and Marie came to sit beside Mark, saying softly, "Be kind to him, won't you?"

With sheets of paper spread on the table before him, Mark realised why the request had been made. Michael had more enthusiasm than talent, as yet.

"Yes . . . I see," he commented with awkwardness. "Well, you have certainly put in some hard work on these."

With a small sigh Michael put alongside them the sketch Mark had left him at their first meeting. "Compared with yours, they're not really very good, are they?"

"Ah, I've been doing them for years and years, so mine ought to be better, don't you agree?" he said gently, taking the pencil from the boy's hand. "Look, this section here should go across to meet that one . . . and that curve should be convex rather than concave."

"I beg your pardon, sir?"

He smiled down into the earnest freckled face. "It should be an *outward* curve instead. As it is, the whole structure would collapse."

"Oh, goodness gracious!" exclaimed Michael, his English plainly having been taught him by a refined gentlewoman and sounding very quaint coming from his youthful lips.

For the next ten minutes or so, father and son leant over the table, heads together, while Mark explained how the scrambled mass of lines could be sorted out to look like something resembling a bridge. Michael watched him, totally absorbed.

"There," said Mark straightening up. "I think I'd be prepared to take a train over that one."

"Can you drive a train?" came the awed question.

"Not as well as a real engine-driver but, yes, I can take a train over a bridge when I've built it." He smiled, adding, "If it falls down when I'm crossing it, I have only myself to blame."

"As if it *would* fall down," said Michael with scornful confidence in his hero.

"Sometimes I'm forced to make them," he told the boy in sad tones. "You see, Michael, I'm a soldier as well as a bridge builder. If the enemy is approaching and there is no way of stopping them because their numbers are greater than ours, it sometimes means that a bridge has to be blown up to stop their advance."

"After all that work!" was the indignant comment. "I should think you feel very angry about that, sir."

"Very angry indeed," agreed Mark, thinking what an understatement that was.

"If I had spent all that time building a grand bridge, I'd refuse to blow it up," Michael decided firmly.

"A soldier has to obey orders, you know. Sometimes his orders make him very angry . . . or even very sad. He has no choice but to obey them. He has to go where he is sent, and do what he is told to do. At times, it means he has to leave behind those he loves," he added, thinking of a girl being led away from him while he stood between two of his fellow officers, knowing that moment would touch the rest of his life.

"You are my father, aren't you?" asked a quiet voice beside him, and Mark gazed back into eyes as brown as his own which were full of discovery.

"Your father?" he repeated, unprepared for the conclusions of a child's mind, the way he made observations on what he saw before him without complicating them with whys and wherefores, the unselfconsciousness with which he asked questions.

"You look just like me, don't you?" said the boy with frank confrontation. "And *Maman* has always said my father was a brave soldier who had to obey orders and leave us. Besides, my Russian name is Mikhail Markovich, which means Michael, son of Mark . . . and that's you, isn't it?"

"Yes . . . yes, that's me," agreed Mark fiercely proud of owning the fact, yet feeling the pain of Katya's loss as he claimed the child of their love for each other.

A delighted smile spread across the boy's face as he accepted the complications of life with the philosophy of the very young.

"How splendid! Now you've come back we can all live together, can't we?"

"Yes, *mon petit chou*, we can all live together now," Marie promised, taking Mark's hand in hers.

CHAPTER ELEVEN

Nanking had one of the largest foreign communities of any purely Chinese city, and within the seventy-foot encompassing wall that rose sheer from the marshy plain, past and present stood side by side. Beautiful old temples, shrines, palaces, and complex ornamental gateways remained as a symbol of centuries of rule by powerful and often cruel men of incredible learning. To mark modern progress there were excellent hospitals with up-to-date equipment, schools with a fine record of teaching, and a flourishing business community that made it one of the most important cities along the banks of the Yangtze. Nanking was also a busy and vital railway junction.

Before Christmas many had believed it would fall to the Kuomintang army, but further down the river the forward flow of the Nationalist troops had been halted by the Northerners, and they had wintered in Hankow. Now, they appeared to be heading overland direct for Shanghai. To take that port would be the finest laurel to wear in triumph.

When Alexandra had arrived a little over a week ago the Chinese population had been sullen and silent, afraid of their fate. There were many prosperous merchants, men of learning, respected families with valorous histories living in Nanking, all of whom feared the ruthless Communist policies advocated by Chiang Kai-Shek's Russian advisor, Michael Borodin. It would mean ruin and probable death for them if the city should fall into the hands of Red followers.

There were other men, lowly shopkeepers who made a meagre living and aspired to a couple of rooms over the premises in which their entire families made a home. They were wise enough to swing with the tide in this country of eternal conflict, but it did them no good. No matter which army marched through the city it ransacked such shops, emptying them of their stock and demanding money from the owners. To persuade obstinate men to fetch out their little cache of savings put aside for weddings and funerals, daughters were raped or relatives shot.

Then there was a third group—road sweepers, night-soil distributors, poverty-stricken farmers, stone breakers: the coolies. These people had been told the days of freedom and plenty were nigh, but they had not come in many hundreds of years and they could not believe it would happen now.

All these people had already suffered—not from the conquering army, but the defending one. Troops of the northern warlords had swept through the city like a grey ravening horde on their way to the place where the Kuomintang was being held in check, robbing and plundering as they went. Such acts did nothing to comfort the population of Nanking. Rather, it suggested that their 'defenders' were as much to be feared as any attackers.

Despite the air of gloom and unease the city still seemed like a refuge to the young girl who had suffered such disillusionment and distress. Travelling down to Lu-Seng on Mark's engine early in the morning had seemed like a wonderful adventure that brought them closer than ever before. She had seen the working side of the man she loved, seen things through his eyes as they rushed through the Chinese countryside, seen evidence of his professional knowledge.

The Bridge of a Hundred Dragons had been a terrible disappointment. With the images of her own painting firmly in her mind, the flat bridge of riveted steel sections looked unromantic and out of place on that Oriental marshland. Mark had laughed at her disappointment, not knowing of the existence of the painting yet, and pointed out that the 'Iron Beast' could not be expected to meander over wooden devil-bridges.

He was never far from her thoughts, whether she was driving through the streets of Nanking with her hostess, or sitting in the sheltered garden of the large Chinese-style house with her mother, idling the hours away in pale winter sunshine. Convinced he was still keeping something from her, despite his openness on that unforgettable morning, it stayed at the back of her mind as she tried to sort out her future and come to terms with Mark's past. The first was easier than the second, since she knew there was hope of shaping it herself. Those months in Russia she could do nothing about. That Katya would always be in Mark's heart she had to accept. A tragic memory was impossible to fight, and the boy would be there as a constant reminder. They would have their own children, and she would try desperately hard not to love them more than the little boy she had seen for no more than a moment. Children were an unknown breed to her, as yet, and she was worried over the problems of taking a boy of almost seven into her charge. Suppose he did not take to her? Was that the shadow over Mark's happiness: concern that his son and his youthful wife would be incompatible? After all, she had done little to persuade him she had a sense of responsibility for herself, much less a small boy. At that point in her thoughts she always vowed that her behaviour from then on would be so staid, everyone would realise she was a perfect stepmother.

Alice, who had joined them in Nanking two days after Alexandra's arrival, was worried and unhappy over the turn of events. She had come up on the regular steamer, making it known she was joining her daughter, who had been having a holiday with their Nanking manager. The story of the Communist attempts to discredit Europeans in Shanghai had duly appeared in the newspapers and, so far, there was no evidence that copies of the photograph had been distributed. It was early days, of course, but it seemed possible that Mark's plan was working. Alice was extremely grateful to him for helping them through a terrible situation, but she was full of doubts over the proposed marriage.

"My dear, if he has asked you to be his wife, I am certain he loves you, but look at the price you are expected to pay," she told Alexandra when sitting in the garden one morning. "All he can offer you is a spartan life waiting in cities all over the world while he builds bridges in isolated spots, or waiting in garrison towns while he is somewhere fighting a war. His obstinate nature will prevent his life ever running smoothly, and his son will be there to remind you that he once loved someone else he cannot now forget. Oh, I agree he has been very honest with you in saying that, but are you so sure you can live with a ghost?"

Alexandra had her answer ready. "Mother, you chose a husband who was wealthy, handsome, ambitious, and determined to make you one of the foremost hostesses in mercantile society. He had no past love, so far as I am aware, and I am your own child. Father could offer you everything, and your parents were delighted with the match, but did any of you ever bother to consider whether he actually loved you? Have you been happy all these years?"

Her mother looked at her wistfully. "Love—I wonder what that word really means! It certainly does not guarantee happiness. Many people have been made desperately sad by love, my dear, as your Mark will tell you."

"He will go on being desperately sad until I have helped him to recover," Alexandra said forcefully. "Mother, I think he has been unable to find consolation in any other woman since then . . . no, please don't look so shocked at my frankness on the subject. If I am to make you see how right this will be, you have to hear the facts. There's surely nothing 'modern and shocking' in being aware that men need to relieve their frustrations and tension with women who provide solace on business terms. It's my belief Mark has not done this, which has kept his feelings for Katya strongly alive. He has lived in the hope that she had survived and might miraculously enter his life again. Now he knows she is dead, and I think, in some way, that knowledge has released him from a bond of loyalty. Yes, the boy will be a constant reminder of that affair, but Mark himself admitted Michael bears no visible resemblance to Katya so, in time, I hope to create the family bond which will make the boy 'our' son, and thereby lessen the pull of the dead mother."

She sighed as she recognised the obstacles ahead. "Before he knew of Katya's death, before he knew he had a son by her, I had done what no woman since that time in Russia has been able to do—suggest to Mark that there was a chance of future happiness with someone else. He needs me, Mother, even more than I need him. With all my faults I have made him laugh again; despite my youth—maybe *because* of it—he has felt the fresh breeze of hope brush his cheeks. I am so utterly, totally the opposite of Katya, I believe I am his only hope of learning to live to the full again." Looking at her mother's doubtful expression, she smiled wryly. "I know, dear, but he has had too much earnestness and responsible thought. A little madcap nonsense is just what he needs . . . and I do love him most dreadfully. No man can suffer from that, surely."

"My fears have never been that *he* would suffer, you foolish child," said her mother with great affection. "You have always had a tremendous capacity for loving, and it has only been the lack of a suitable outlet that has made you behave so outrageously, at times. I knew that quite well. No doubt your Mark will be swamped with affection and devoted concern . . . but are you quite certain you will not suffer, and suffer very acutely, with what you are set on taking upon your shoulders?"

Alexandra bent to kiss her mother's cheek, saying with a certain amount of ruefulness, "He once told me I would never be an artist until I had suffered, dear. Think how brilliant I shall be with my brushes if your forecast comes true."

So mother and daughter enjoyed every moment of that last holiday together, gradually coming to terms with the inevitability of being separated before long. On the morning of the twelfth day in Nanking Alexandra awoke to a strange noise in the distance, and wondered why there should be thunder when the sky was so clear. Getting up from her bed she went to the window to look out across Lion Hill and the Yangtze beyond. Another bright clear day on its way, but the distant low rumbling continued like a storm in the offing.

Charles Maddox had gone to his office by the time the womenfolk sat down to breakfast in the stone-floored room on the south side of the house, and each of them remarked on the strange circumstance of the thunder, before going on to decide what to do that day. Jean Maddox was a hearty woman in her mid-thirties who loved having guests, but imagined she had to fill their every minute with excursions or occupations in order to be a good hostess. Even she could not have imagined how eventful that day was to prove to be. Whilst they were discussing the rival merits of a shopping expedition, a visit to Jean's dressmaker, or even a short trip on the small launch used by Charles and his staff, the telephone rang.

Alexandra and her mother were left at the table wondering how best to tell their hostess that they would far rather relax with a book or a sketch pad in the garden than do any of the things she suggested, when Jean came back into the room looking uncharacteristically worried.

"That was Charles," she said abruptly. "The thunder we heard was heavy artillery."

Alexandra looked at her in astonishment. "Guns? How could it be?"

Jean sat down heavily on her chair and looked at them both. "He said we were not to get alarmed, but there are all kinds of rumours flying around Nanking and people are panicking. Chinese are already trying to leave the city and are being stopped at the city gates by the soldiers."

"Whose soldiers?" asked Alice sharply.

"Oh, ours—I mean, the northern ones who have been here some weeks."

"Why should they stop people from leaving? What point does it serve?" asked Alexandra, feeling that the atmosphere of impending crisis had followed her to Nanking. A distant rumble, and everyone imagined soldiers with guns. The front was being held by northern soldiers a long way down river, and everyone knew the Kuomintang army was heading toward Shanghai now.

Jean Maddox shrugged. "You know how panic spreads so quickly. I suppose if they let a few out, the whole city will think there really is danger and start a stampede. That's why the soldiers are in the city—to keep control. The Chinese need to be organised. All the same," she added, "Charles suggests I go across to the British Consulate to get the truth. They are the only people likely to know that, at the moment."

"May I come with you?" asked Alexandra immediately. "Mother, you'll be all right here, won't you?"

Alice smiled gratefully. "Yes, my dear. If the sun continues to shine I shall get Lee-Su to push me into that sheltered corner of the garden to read my novel. It concerns a very stupid woman, but I must read on in the hope that she comes to her senses in the last chapter."

At the Consulate they found a great number of other English women all on the same errand, but all quite cheerful, which made nonsense of the rumbling that continued to be heard. Even so the secretary looked grave when he came to talk to them, and Alexandra had her first twinge of real apprehension. Surely there was no real danger here?

There was certainly a change in the situation that sounded most ominous. A number of the northern troops had been 'bought' by the Kuomintang—how many was not known—and the line of defence had broken. The Northerners were retreating toward Nanking, and the Nationalists were chasing on their heels. There was no immediate danger. It was confidently believed Nanking could be successfully defended once the retreating troops were back inside the city, and the worst thing that could happen would be to show panic. Still, it might be sensible if women with young children were to put together a few things ready for a possible short sojourn on one of the two warships presently standing in the Yangtze just off Nanking, he told them. No need to subject youngsters to unnecessary stress. He then added that it might also be wise for all the wives to make sure they had plenty of food in store, just in case supplies were held up for a while.

Feeling a little less cheerful then, some of the women bombarded him with questions which he adroitly avoided answering. To Alexandra, the things he did not say were more alarming than those he did, and she began to wonder if it would be better if she and her mother returned to Shanghai where her father would know what best to do. Alice Mostyn was an invalid in a chair, who could not escape in a hurry.

While she was thinking about that a young man appeared with a slip of paper which he gave to the secretary. It left Alexandra in a quandary when he read it, then looked up to say, "Ladies, I am sorry to tell you we have just received news that Nationalist troops are encamped on the outskirts of Shanghai, encircling the Chinese City which has been taken over by armed Communists of the Workers' Militia in anticipation of the arrival of Chiang Kai-Shek. There has been no attempt to attack or enter the foreign concessions and there is no immediate danger, although our troops are standing by." He forced a smile. "Business is being conducted as usual, as your husbands will confirm when they return from their offices. I suggest you all go home and ensure they have a good meal awaiting them. We shall keep you informed, of course, and the Consul suggests that it would be wisest for you all to remain in your homes. It makes things simpler if we know where to contact you."

The women dispersed in various frames of mind. Those with small children were plainly afraid for them. The childless ones claimed with great firmness that they were prepared to face anything at the side of their husbands.

"No armed coolie is going to chase *me* out of my home," declared one roundly. "Jack and I have lived in Borneo, Korea, Siam, and Japan, and our Eastern friends have wept when we left. I certainly don't intend to spoil a good record here."

Others, who had spent an entire lifetime in China, vowed there was no reason whatever to be afraid. The Chinese would not touch English civilians, they claimed. The bond of friendship went back too far for that. But Jean Maddox was worried about her invalid guest, and spoke of her to Alexandra as they got into the car ready to return.

"I think we should ask Charles's advice," she said. "I know Shanghai hardly seems safe now, but we have thousands of armed troops there—two to every one resident, I hear—and there are British and American ships in the harbour. Here, we have no means of defence except our husbands' revolvers."

"There are two warships standing off in the river," said Alexandra, trying not to worry. "Jean, how could this have happened? No one expected them to get anywhere near Shanghai yet. When one thinks of the terrain they have to cross between Hankow and Shanghai, it's . . . it's *incredible*. And how is it there are enough soldiers left in Hankow to break the line of defence and threaten a city as large as Nanking?"

Letting in the clutch, Jean Maddox said, "You heard Mr Keel. A lot of the Northerners have gone over to the other side and are now fighting their former comrades."

"That's terrible!"

Jean swung out into the road. "That's *life*, Alexandra. It is surprising what people will do for things they want. Look what our own young men did during the war, in order to keep Britain free. They are not cruel and barbarous, by nature, but they did the most terrible things for four years."

"Yes, I suppose they did," she reflected quietly, full of new thoughts of Mark that had been conjured up by Jean's words. Would she ever know what he endured during that period?

As they drove back through the city that morning the streets seemed totally Oriental and inhospitable. Alexandra missed the bustle of the International Settlement's white population, the many expensive cars outside the mercantile houses, the men in black bowlers and overcoats coming and going around the great banks. For the first time in her life she realised she was a stranger in China. Why had it never occurred to her before?

It was slow going, for progress was blocked by opposing streams of people pushing carts piled high with bundles, pots and pans, pieces of furniture. There was an outward flow of those making for the city gates, pushing against those who had been turned back by the soldiers determined to keep everyone within the city walls. Others tramped with babies in cotton slings upon their backs, or great bundles of possessions tied up in lengths of blue cloth. Old people stumbled along with the aid of a stick, those who had already been turned back having given up the struggle and commandeered a temporary home on a street corner where they ate rice bought from a street pedlar. Women hobbled along on tiny misshapen feet that had been bound since childhood, and toddlers wandered dazedly in the wake of their elders, tired and frightened, but facing it all with the resigned acceptance that was their inheritance from generations of oppression.

"See what panic does?" observed Jean crisply. "Poor devils, they have nowhere to go, but that marshland outside seems infinitely preferable to what they will suffer if the Kuomintang troops ever get inside the city."

To Alexandra there seemed little chance of that, for the streets were also swarming with the grey-uniformed men of the northern warlords, who looked tough enough to face anything. Yet they did not seem all that protective of those they would have soon to defend. The procession of would-be escapers was being abused and treated in a brutal manner by the troops, and she saw many instances where soldiers had stopped carts and were helping themselves to articles of clothing or things of value at bayonet-point.

"Jean, look!" she said indignantly.

"That's nothing to what they did when they went through on the way to the Front," was the matter-of-fact reply. "This isn't Shanghai, you know."

No, it certainly was not, thought Alexandra as they rounded the next corner and came upon something so dreadful she longed to be back home protected by those men in khaki she had seen marching from the troopships so short a time ago. Hanging from poles along both sides of the street were human heads, bloodstained and grotesque, as they gazed sightlessly on those who must take heed of the warning.

"Oh!" cried Alexandra as it dawned on her what they were. "Oh, how . . . *inhuman!*"

"But a powerful deterrent," came Jean's calm voice. "I doubt if I shall ever get used to the sight, but I now find I can drive along without looking at them, and if I concentrate hard on something else, they don't affect me one bit. Over the past couple of years we have had so many conquerors and changes of regime here, this way of purging the city of unwelcome elements has become all too habitual. These, today, are probably the victims of a renewed attack on anyone suspected of being a Communist sympathiser. They will have enough *outside* the walls before long, without another lot inside egging them on."

Finding Jean's impassive acceptance of something her own artistic sensitivity viewed with revulsion hard to understand, Alexandra remained silent, but was in danger of being sick as her hostess drove up to the house. Determined to show no signs of weakness before her mother she walked quickly through the devil-gates at the entrance and went to her room for smelling salts and a cool face-flannel on her brow.

The low rumble of guns could still be heard and, as she looked out across the Yangtze, it was comforting to see the two warships waiting there, guns pointing landward. She leaned against the window frame and saw them through blurred eyes. Out there were men from England—the mother country she had never seen. Back in Shanghai were those pale-faced soldiers who had instantly made themselves at home straight from the green island on which she had never stood. Like a bolt from the blue came an overwhelming longing to go there, to leave behind those with yellow faces, the smell of the noodle stalls, the wheelbarrow men, the garish nightclubs . . . the severed heads!

Charles Maddox had a great deal of news to impart when he returned home. Chiang Kai-Shek's troops were certainly encamped not far from Shanghai, but were making no attempt to enter the port despite the fact that the Communists had effected a complete take-over of the Chinese City. The foreign concession areas were being in no way threatened, and military leaders believed no attack would be made until the main force of the army moved forward—if then. Observers in Nanking believed Chiang Kai-Shek would wait for this other division of his army to take Nanking and advance up river and railway to Shanghai. The combined force would then make its next move.

"Shanghai is still safer than this city," he added. "Although the Consul thinks it is highly unlikely that foreign residents are in personal danger, it now seems certain that the Northerners are not intending to make a stand here. They're retreating through the city and out the other side. That's why the gates are closed to all those trying to leave. Troops are streaming through as fast as they can, and anyone not in their uniform is turned back in the approach roads. The cavalry, amongst them some White Russian mercenaries, have come in now from the advance positions to the south, so it looks as if the Kuomintang will be allowed to walk in unopposed."

"Perhaps that is the best thing for all these poor people," put in Alice. "If the revolutionaries are eventually going to take the city, it will spare the inhabitants the terror of a battle within the walls."

"Whatever happens, the people of Nanking are in for a rough time of it," said the railway manager, wiping the froth of cool beer from his moustache. "We must thank God we are British and divorced from it." He smiled at Alice. "But I have not yet told you the news that most concerns you, Mrs Mostyn. Your husband is on his way down from Shanghai to take you and Alexandra back. He feels it is best for you all to be together during these tense days."

Her mother had turned very faintly pink at such evidence of Garrard's concern, and Alexandra thought helplessly that the habit of a lifetime could not be changed. Alice Mostyn snatched at any evidence of a love she had believed in twenty years ago.

"Is it safe to travel at such a time?" asked the invalid.

"Oh, yes. He's coming on the evening express. There have been delays, but the trains are still getting through. The steamer service is practically nonexistent, however. After dinner, I'll go down to the junction and fetch him in the car. He already has a plan for your safe return, I believe."

So they ate dinner in civilised fashion, changing into evening clothes and chatting of generalities as if there were no sound of gunfire growing nearer and a scene of tragic pandemonium outside in the street. Although Alexandra put on an air of outward calm she could not forget those heads hanging in the street, nor the gunboats waiting on the river outside city walls that kept in anyone other than fleeing soldiers. Nor could she forget an isolated bridge near Lu-Seng. If only it were Mark who was coming tonight—coming to take her away into his permanent care.

When their host went off to meet Garrard, the atmosphere changed subtly. The three women sat drinking coffee and talking trivialities still, but there was a tension now and a sense of being vulnerable. It was then Alexandra realised that in times of trouble a woman always turned to a man, expecting strength and protection from him. She had done so with Mark when threatened by that photograph. At that moment, she had no desire to take command or prove her equality in any other way. Right then, she would willingly sacrifice all her modern principles for the sight of just one solid, reassuring Englishman.

The evening crawled past, and not one of them commented on the non-arrival of the men. Conversation lapsed, but silence was even more unnerving so they forced themselves to talk of anything but the present situation. Alexandra thought her mother looked pale and strained, the large violet-blue eyes full of fears. It must be terrible for a woman tied to a chair, she realised. To know one could not run away!

"Mother, the train must be delayed," she said, bringing the subject into the open, at last. "If there was anything else, Mr Maddox would have returned to tell us, by now."

Alice smiled. "Yes, dear, I know. One can't expect services to run normally at times like these. And we have got the trains. Those pitiful souls outside are intending to walk."

The din outside the windows had increased. Rumbling wheels, shouting, children crying, boots thumping in marching rhythm—even an occasional sound that could be a rifle shot. Then, thankfully, the sound of the car arriving.

"They're here!" she cried, and her relief was echoed in the faces of the two older women.

Jean stood up abruptly as her husband came in with two men —Garrard Mostyn and his assistant, James Clitheroe. "Charles, we were beginning to worry," she said in tones that betrayed the fact.

The manager looked tired. "Damn trains are being stopped all along the route by obstructions on the track. It plays hell with the schedules."

Garrard looked straight at his wife, ignoring Alexandra. "Are you all right, my dear?"

"Hello, Miss Mostyn," said the other new arrival hesitantly.

"Hello, Jimmy," she said with warmth. "You have no idea how glad we are to see you."

Then they were all talking at once. Alexandra marvelled at the changed atmosphere. Food and drink were brought for the two men from Shanghai who were hungry, and the ladies clustered around the table as they ate, all signs of formality abandoned.

"Now they are so near, Nationalist sympathisers from here to Shanghai are beginning to show their faces," said Garrard as he ate. "They are disrupting trains and blocking roads. At present, they're uprooting trees, dragging boulders onto the tracks, or jamming signals, but it won't be long before they start lifting out sections of rail altogether. Then we shall be in real trouble." He turned to Charles. "I doubt if we can maintain any kind of service much longer."

"No, sir. We've two expresses in Shanghai that have not even begun the journey down. You were lucky to get through at all."

"I know. The railways will be their first acquisition. That's how they have advanced faster than anyone imagined. Because they need the lines themselves they are not likely to blow up stretches of track or bridges, but once they seize the junction here they will control the entire delta network."

It was cold comfort to hear her father say they would not blow up bridges, for now it seemed that merely by being on the track Mark was endangered.

"Father, have the men at Lu-Seng been warned?" she asked, her voice very clear in the moment of silence.

He looked at her with cool uninterest. "My only concern is to remove your mother and you back to Shanghai. But in times of emergency, he takes his orders from the military, not me. He told me that from the very beginning," he added sourly. "I think you have forgotten he is a soldier, Alexandra. I presume he is able to cope with a simple situation without assistance."

She did not press the subject. Mark had taken a group of Russians —including the woman he loved—on an old engine across a barbarous landscape to safety. He was used to danger and threats to his life. Dear heaven, how had he lived through four whole years like tonight, only worse?

"We can't risk the train on the return journey," Garrard continued. "So I have formulated a plan that will suit our purposes admirably. At first light, we shall take the company launch downriver as far as Pu-San. Lancaster of the Warburton Group has a barge there ready to leave for Shanghai. The captain is a Portuguese who will willingly take us as passengers." He frowned. "It will not be very comfortable, Alice, but it will be perfectly safe. The captain has apparently been carrying opium for years up and down the river, and keeps all the officials happy in return for a trouble-free voyage." He looked at Charles Maddox. "Your wife is included in these arrangements, of course."

"Thank you, but I'll stay with Charles," said Jean immediately and firmly.

Garrard treated her to the look he reserved for stupid feminine obstructions to his plans, but merely said, "As you will. The main thing is to be ready to move the minute it grows light," he continued, looking at Alice and Alexandra. "With James in uniform and armed I think we can give the impression of some kind of military escort, and the guards on the gate will be tired and hungry at dawn. James and Charles with revolvers, plus a monetary bribe should do the trick," he finished.

Alice was looking more relaxed now and smiled at her husband's assistant with all her usual warmth. "It's very good of you to offer to take part in this rather bizarre adventure, James. We are all very grateful."

"That's quite all right, Mrs Mostyn. I'm very glad to have the chance to do something to repay your past kindness."

But he looked at Alexandra as he spoke, and she was forced to look away. She had been less than kind to him, in the past. Why did it take something like this to make her aware of so many things she had ignored in the days of her society antics? Mark had once told her dancing on table tops and smoking cigarettes was no substitute for suffering. His words were coming into their own with a vengeance just lately.

None of them expected to sleep, but the three women went obediently to their beds while the men made themselves as comfortable as they could in chairs, with their revolvers handy. Alexandra had packed the most important items of her own and her mother's luggage, in a small bag which they planned to take with them, and Jean had told her cook-boy to make some sandwiches for her guests to take first thing in the morning.

Alexandra lay in bed with the wooden shutters closed against the sound of gunfire as well as the cold, and thought about a great many things during that night. It was not the fevered pounding of a troubled mind: her brain seemed strangely full of a clarity that had arrived with the onset of danger. Past attitudes were sifted and put into perspective; past regrets and sadnesses no longer seemed to touch her. The alien streets outside did not seem real. She knew now her nineteen years in China had taught her very little about the Chinese people. It had always been 'them' and 'us' in Shanghai. Here, in Nanking, she could see that she was really 'them'. 'Us' were in England.

She awoke from half-slumber with a jerk that set her heart pounding. There was a loud frightening noise outside her door. No, it was just the telephone ringing! She looked at the clock. Only four a.m. Who could be ringing at this hour? Voices downstairs began an urgent discussion. Whatever was happening? Throwing on a wrap she went onto the landing that ran around the first floor leaving a square hall below. The men were standing together, unshaven and dishevelled from their night of vigil. Her father caught sight of her and beckoned her down. James was looking at her with a kind of hunger.

"Is something wrong?" she asked, standing on an Oriental rug because the stone floor was so cold.

"The launch has been taken by the soldiers. They have commandeered every craft they can lay their hands on. There is no hope of getting downriver now," Garrard told her. "We are making alternative arrangements."

Jean Maddox appeared, fully dressed, to hear the last part of that speech and hurried downstairs asking, "What alternative is there?"

Charles spoke quickly. "I'm taking Mr Mostyn down to the junction now to see what chance there is of getting to Pu-San by train. They might still pick up that barge."

"Be careful," she said, anxiety still obvious beneath her tone of nonchalance.

Her husband smiled reassuringly. "James will stay here. He is armed and can telephone the Consulate, if necessary. Some of the lines are still up, because we have just had that call from the jetty. But we've just tried to telephone Masters at the junction with no success. It's completely dead."

Garrard put his hand on Alexandra's arm and said gently, "Look after your mother. She is in an unenviable position, and I'm depending on you to help her."

"Of course," she said, surprised at his manner. But they were all behaving strangely. Jean Maddox was now holding her hand, for some reason, and James was quite unlike the fussy assistant in his new military role. He smiled without awkwardness and suggested that some tea would be welcome, which took their hostess off to the kitchen during the moment of her husband's departure with Garrard. But no sooner had the door closed behind the two men than she came running back.

"The servants have gone. There's nothing in their quarters, and the whole place is deserted. I told them to stay here in safety. We saw that terrible tragic procession yesterday," she told James almost in tears. "Whatever will become of them? They've been with me for years."

He just smiled reassuringly. "In times of crisis every person does what he feels he must. Perhaps they prefer to be with their own people." He hesitated, then asked, "Does that mean there will be no tea?"

Jean responded instinctively. "Dear me, no. I'm quite capable of making a pot of tea, even though I've had servants for years." She forced a smile. "Tea—the British stand-by in times of stress, wherever we might be."

Alexandra helped her mother to dress, then put her own clothes on. James was showing no signs of apprehension, but one man with a revolver would be little defence against a maddened mob. She now remembered the reports of attacks on foreign residents in Hankow, and longed for the return of the other two. They all drank tea, then their hostess cooked bacon and made toast, more for something to do than because they were hungry. Alexandra set the table for breakfast, and the women made a pretence at eating whilst James made a meal of the bacon.

Another hour dragged past and they decided to telephone the junction. But the line appeared to be still down, so they rang the Consulate instead, asking for news. It was worrying. The retreat was total and disastrous. The Northerners were in complete disarray as they rushed desperately through the city. Shops were being looted for food—the men were starving, it seemed—and those trying to leave with their meagre belongings were being attacked for the barrows they pushed, even the coats they wore. People in cars were not safe, for officers were taking them at gunpoint. Cavalrymen were fighting to retain their own horses, and troops had even been seen shooting each other for places in the boats plying across the Yangtze.

The Consul advised everyone to stay indoors with windows shuttered and gates bolted, since it was now immensely dangerous on the streets. There was no possibility of leaving the city by the gates or on the river, and the Kuomintang advance guard was already on the outskirts. When the enemy entered Nanking it was recommended that all foreign residents still keep to their houses and show no aggression to the revolutionary troops if they should appear on the premises. Conciliation was the best policy.

Charles Maddox and her father arrived back just at the point when Alexandra had run out of possible reasons for their continued absence. They were on foot and in a state of considerable dishevelment. Their car had been taken from them by several senior officers who had been fairly polite, but determined to have it. The pummelling they had received had been due to fighting their way back through the complete lawlessness and turmoil in the city. They saw many dead lying in the gutters, and lost children wandering sobbing through the heedless mob. They had not even reached the railway junction.

Everyone then accepted that the house was going to be their prison for a while, and during that day they watched from the upstairs windows the incredible departure of a panicking army—six people, each with his own thoughts, yet with a common prayer.

Alexandra helped Jean in the kitchen, glad of some task to take her mind off the clock slowly ticking away that day of unreality. Between preparing meals or something to drink she sat talking to James, and learnt more about him than she had ever known in the years he had worked for her father. From him, she discovered that he had been asked to make discreet enquiries into Lionel Armitage's activities, the clubs of which he was a member, and the societies to which he belonged.

"About time that young troublemaker received a cooler response from Shanghai society," was James's comment. "He is very unwise to upset your father, whatever it might have been. Of course, Mr Mostyn has not told me the cause of this latest incident—which must be something rather more intolerable than any other complaint he had against Armitage—but I suppose it must be some aspect of investment or banking procedure on which the young fool is digging in his heels." He smiled. "This is not a case of betraying a business confidence, Miss Mostyn, but I know he is a friend of yours and I thought I should warn you of your father's intentions. Friend or not, he really has been riding for a fall for a long time, you know, so don't be too sorry for him when he hits the ground with a bump."

Alexandra wisely remained silent: she hoped Lionel would land with a resounding crash!

Throughout that terrible day they had two sources of comfort: telephone contact with the Consulate and other British families similarly imprisoned all over Nanking, and the two gunboats watching over the city constantly in touch with the British and American Consuls by signal. James had been taught to read signals during his training with the Shanghai Volunteer Corps, and was able to tell them the heartening news that landing parties from the two ships would come ashore and take off all those who could get over the walls onto the marsh, if they should receive a signal for help. It was wonderful to know there was an escape route, their own armed forces preparing to take up arms on their behalf. No one let himself dwell on the height and thickness of those city walls.

It was toward evening when the Nationalists entered the southern gates of the city and caught the tail end of the retreating troops. Alexandra had never heard the sound of battle before, and it made her turn cold. Rattling machine-gun fire, single shots from rifles, great thuds from artillery outside the walls. Shouting, screaming, some human sounds she could not even identify. Running feet, roaring engines. Sobbing!

They had given up all pretence of enjoying an adventure that could not possibly last. This was real and deadly earnest. The men consulted together often, in low voices the women could not hear, until Alice said in clear steady tones, "We are not children, Garrard. I am sure we all appreciate that you are trying to spare us worry, but it is more worrying *not* to know what you are planning to do."

The other two men fell silent, but her father went across to the chair beside Alexandra and took Alice's hand. "My dear, we do not intrude upon your feminine plans for meals, do we? When there is anything definite to do we shall certainly tell you what we intend. Since none of us knows what is likely to happen out there, there is little point in making general decisions which will have to be altered hour by hour."

Night fell, and the noise of battle grew worse, perhaps because it could no longer be seen. They sat with the lights out fearing to attract attention from anyone bent on nocturnal madness. When troops ran out of control there was no knowing what they might do. So they counted the dark hours away around a meagre fire with no leaping flames to betray them, listening and waiting for any sound that might suggest danger in the midst of the battle. It raged around them—they heard bullets strike the wall once, and the rush of running feet outside the window—and the only comfort they had was the flashing signal-lamps from the gunboats. The telephone was now completely dead.

At some time during that night Alexandra noticed that Charles Maddox had his arm around Jean's shoulders, and her father was holding her mother's hand. Subconscious comfort! Without hesitation she slipped her hand into James Clitheroe's and saw his smile of pleasure in the faint glow from the fire. *Mutual comfort in times of stress.* How close to Mark she felt during that night. At a time when she was not even sure she would ever see him again, she came to terms with his past without reservations.

"They're signalling again," said Charles suddenly, and James went across to the window to decipher the message.

He seemed to take a long time over it, and Garrard said sharply, "Well . . . what do they say, man?"

James turned to face into the room, his figure just visible now in the pale light of dawn. "They have broken into two English homes down in the centre of the city," he said in monotones. "They demanded money, then shot one of the men. He's dead, I'm afraid. We are warned that these people are adopting a very definite anti-foreign line, and their officers are turning a blind eye to it."

No sooner had he finished speaking than there came a hammering on the door of the house, and Chinese voices demanding that it be opened. They all kept perfectly still, but Alexandra felt certain her heart could be heard thudding as far away as Shanghai. It pumped even faster and her legs turned to rubber when several loud cracks rang out and something flew through the door to strike the wall with metallic force.

"They're firing," said James hoarsely, reaching for his revolver.

"No, don't fire back," said her father sharply. "Go upstairs where they can't see you, and only fire if you really have to. You too, Charles. If they see I am unarmed with just three women they might take money and go."

Incredibly they did as he said. Alexandra saw the Garrard Mostyn who was used to having his word obeyed, the man who could think quickly and clearly in any situation, the man who had lived and prospered amongst those who now threatened his life. So, with two armed men hidden upstairs he called, in Chinese, to the men outside not to fire again and he would open the door. Alexandra and Jean stood each side of the invalid chair, holding hands for mutual comfort behind it.

They pushed their way in, three little men in green uniforms, with coarse evil faces, thrusting Garrard aside with their rifles. Dark cruel eyes looked all around the room, at the expensive polished furniture, the beautiful ornaments, the silver sports trophies. None of that was any use to them. They demanded food, and Jean hurried away to return with a cooked chicken, two cuts of ham and some fruit. They began tearing at it with animal savagery, the chicken dropping from their overfull mouths onto the lovely Oriental carpet. Garrard stood perfectly still as the soldiers advanced toward the women, and Alexandra was convinced the click of a revolver being cocked up on the landing could be heard for miles around. But their enemies were too busy stuffing food into their mouths, oversure in that house of three women and an unarmed silver-haired Englishman.

The tension grew unbearable when two of the soldiers, after looking Jean and Alexandra insolently up and down, began to pinch their arms as if they were choosing the plumpest poultry in a street market. The one touching Alexandra made a mumbled comment then guffawed so that little gobbets of chewed chicken spattered over her face. Then he began pinching her breast with cruel fingers, and she did not know how to stop herself from hitting him as memories of that Shanghai nightclub overcame all fear. Revulsed and trembling with anger, it was only her father's steely gaze over the man's head that kept her steady—that, and the presence of her helpless mother beside her.

Jean was suffering the same treatment, and Alexandra was terrified that Charles Maddox would lose his head and fire. If he did, they would all die from Nationalist bullets within seconds. At the moment, these men were insolent and aggressive, but not murderous. Then the third man shouted at Alice to stand up. He wanted his own white woman to humiliate. But she smiled—yes, actually smiled, Alexandra noted with astonishment—and answered in polite Chinese that she was unable to stand. Quite deliberately she pushed her chair forward and made an unusually clumsy business of trying to guide it across the room. The woman who had always courageously hidden her helplessness was now parading it before these crude peasants. It upset Alexandra more than the soldiers' vile assault, and she prayed for their ordeal to end.

Then, the soldiers were bowing before her mother, expressing their regret that she had been afflicted by devils, and announced their intention of leaving. She further softened them by remarking on what gentlemen they were after the uncouth Northerners who had been in the city so long, and it was in an almost friendly mood that they left. But the whole thing was nearly ruined when one came back in unexpectedly just as James and Charles were emerging from their hiding place upstairs. With bated breath Alexandra watched the soldier scoop up two silver tennis cups before running out with his booty, still unaware that anyone was on the landing.

Alexandra ran to Alice immediately and took her hand. "Mother, you were wonderful," she cried emotionally.

The violet-blue eyes were tear-bright. "No, dear, I suffered nothing. You and Jean were the wonderful ones."

But the Maddoxes were too engrossed in each other to hear, and James put an end to all confessions of relief by saying, "There's another signal from the ships. There might be more instructions."

They all stood waiting, envying him his ability to read what they were all anxious to know.

"By God, the American Consul and his party, isolated on the hill, are being attacked and fired upon by hostile troops who have ignored his diplomatic status!" He turned to them with a flush of anger darkening his face. "It's an outrage!"

"So it's every man for himself now," said Garrard with some of his disillusion after years of working with the Chinese very evident in his voice.

"The ships are now sending out landing parties to take us off," continued James, also affected by the betrayal of people he thought he knew and understood. "They warn that they are preparing to shell the city to cover our escape."

"How the hell do we escape? Over a seventy-foot wall down onto an extensive marsh—it's impossible!" snapped Garrard.

"The Carters!" cried Jean with inspiration, turning to her husband. "If we could get up the hill to their house and go through their garden, it would take us to the top of the wall."

Charles looked at the other two men. "Lower ourselves down on ropes—what do you think?"

"Have you got ropes?" asked James.

"Some—in the garden shed. I don't know about seventy feet of it, but there's some."

"We'll have to drop the rest of the way. It's soft marshy soil which will make it easier to land." Then he realised the drawback of the idea, and looked at his employer. "What do you think, sir?"

Garrard nodded. "We have no choice. Have you a strong cloth which would do to catch my wife in, Charles?"

"I've a tarpaulin."

"Just the thing. Let's get out of here right away."

Having something to do, at last, was marvellous. Alexandra fetched coats for herself and her mother, and tucked a rug around the invalid's knees. She gave no thought to the danger of what they were attempting to do. All her concern was for someone who was dependent on them all. That ship was out there waiting for them and they were going to get her mother on it. With that firmly in mind she would not think of anything else.

They were soon ready to leave. Thanking God that no other soldiers had come to the house before they could get away, Alexandra had forgotten that, for the Maddoxes, it meant abandoning a home and all their belongings collected over many years in the East. The sadness was written on their faces as they sighed and closed the door on an era in their lives.

But there was no time for lingering regrets once they were in the street. It was wild, uncontrolled pandemonium. They faced a tide of Chinese citizens rushing, rushing away from rape, looting, burning, and every kind of conquering depravity. Everyone was making for the gates—to get out, get away from the terrible trap inside the walls. They ran, shuffled, stumbled or trotted according to age and the burden they carried. They flowed blindly down the hill toward the gates, piling up in bewildered defeated crowds at the great closed wooden doors, knowing they were trapped, after all. The Kuomintang had finally come . . . and the great liberating army was as bad as every other that had marched through that city over the generations. Hope had gone: fear remained.

At first, it looked an impossible task to push uphill against the panic-maddened crowd, and Alexandra felt her legs start to tremble from the reaction to total fear. But the men were shouting to each other, undaunted and determined, forming a kind of battering ram with linked arms, and telling herself and Jean to push the invalid chair within the protection of the curve formed by them. Hardly able to think and responding instantly to their instructions she grabbed the chair alongside Jean, and they began their fight uphill—uphill to face a hazardous seventy-foot drop and a long trek across exposed marshland to the waiting boats. Those boats seemed an eternity away.

Yet, once they were in that crowd, she fought to go on. It was that or be swept away from all hope by the press of alien unpredictable creatures who had changed as suddenly as the wheelbarrow men that bright morning with Lionel. At the thought of him, she gritted her teeth and pushed on with even more determination.

They were swallowed up, completely engulfed in the mob. The three men were staggering backward, then putting their heads down to charge the oncoming flow with united strength so that they could move forward. Alexandra found herself gripping the handle of the chair with fingers that ached, as she and Jean tried to keep close behind them, fearful of losing contact. She was jostled and bumped by bundles on people's backs, and overladen carts as they passed too close. But, slowly, the men were winning. By shouting commands in Chinese and ruthlessly laying about them with the ropes, the downward tide was responding to authority and parting to flow each side of the little group before joining again.

Still they made slow progress, and were only halfway up the hill when a tremendous explosion rent the air, followed by a thud that made the earth tremble. Alexandra felt fear accelerate through her muscles, but James turned his head to shout, "It's all right, it's only the ships. They've started shelling."

The fleeing Chinese did not know what it was, however. They were further terrified by this new incomprehensible threat, and reacted accordingly. Under their renewed panic to get away, the three men were wrested apart. Garrard lost his balance and fell. The two younger men made a dive to pick him up from beneath the feet and wheels that crushed everything before them, and the women were left exposed to an overwhelming opposition that made allowance for nothing. Now, there was nothing but yellow faces tightly drawn with fear, eyes that already saw the shadow of terrors in store, pushing shuffling bodies in loose black suits that smelt of the hovels in which they lived.

The men had vanished from sight. The flowing mass had passed over them and swallowed them up. There was nothing to save the three women from being engulfed, also. Shattered, despairing, Alexandra was spurred into fresh action when the rug was snatched from her mother's knees by a young man screaming, "*Sha yang Kuei-tze!*"—kill the foreign devils!

Swinging to face Jean she yelled, "Turn the chair around. We'll *drag* it up."

With only fractional hesitation and a glance at the place where she had last seen her husband, Jean complied in the same desperate manner Alexandra had adopted.

From then on it was pure savage determination and the knowledge that it meant life or death that sent them struggling against the press of people. Never had Alexandra felt such violent and instinctive hatred against those who were trying to stop her from reaching safety. Gritting her teeth, she pushed forward dragging the chair and lashing out at everything in her way with her free arm and both feet. She was shouting, clawing and kicking, finding some kind of superhuman strength born of the need to protect her mother. The people were no longer people—just elements of human aggression. She pushed and punched, careless of the results so long as they moved another yard, another few steps.

Her hair became tangled, pulled by other desperate, clawing hands. Her face felt bruised and filthy from the odorous bundles and baskets that dragged across it. Her arms and legs ached, and she found she was crying for what she was being forced to do. All around her the din beat against her ears. Another great crash—another shell. Rifle fire. Screams and yells. Her own voice, hoarse and violent, using words that shocked her.

Her heart was thumping against her ribs, and there was hardly any breath left in her when she felt Jean pushing against her, forcing her to turn left into the driveway of a house.

"This is it," gasped Jean, as dirty and exhausted as she, then leant back against the wall momentarily, tears coursing down her cheeks. "I never thought I would ever have to behave toward people I have lived with and counted as my friends, as I have just done." Pushing herself forward with every intention of returning to the street, she added in awful tones, "May God forgive me, but if they have killed Charles I will choke as many of them as I can with my bare hands."

Instantly Alexandra caught her arms and held her back with all her remaining strength. "No, Jean, *no*!"

The other woman was crazed enough to fight back, and they wrestled for several minutes, both of them with tears flowing as a sign of their distress. Alexandra held on to Jean, knowing that to go out into the street again would mean certain death, and that knowledge made her as strong as the woman made powerful by grief for her husband. Sensing that she was slowly losing the battle, Alexandra made one last desperate bid to prevent a certain tragedy.

"*Jean*," she yelled above the din of exploding shells and a panic-stricken city, "if Charles is dead it's because he wanted to save you. Go out there, and you'll make his heroism pointless. Do you love him so little?"

Slowly Jean dropped her resistance, finally crumpling up to sob on Alexandra's shoulder. Swept with violent compassion for the woman who was witnessing the destruction of all she had held dear in life, Alexandra felt a sudden strange affinity with a woman in Russia who seven years before must have suffered in this same way—a woman who remained in Mark's heart and in a small boy who knew nothing of her existence.

At that point, miraculously, the three men stumbled into the driveway, cut and bleeding, but extremely relieved to find them all there. It was not the time for sentiment, however, just a great urgency to descend that wall and cross the marsh to the waiting boats. They ran past the side of the house, Charles taking his wife, and James catching Alexandra's arm. Her father was now pushing the chair. The house itself was deserted, or so it seemed until they reached the terrace at the back.

There, they came upon a man and woman lying dead, sprawling in attitudes of agony on the grass stretch leading to the wall. Alexandra put her hand to her mouth at the amount of blood everywhere, still wet, and recoiled instinctively as James forced her past them.

"Oh God, it's the Carters," whispered Jean brokenly. "How terrible—oh, how terrible!"

Charles hurried her on. "We can't do anything for them now," he said harshly. "I just hope whoever did this has moved on."

It was windy and bitterly cold up on the wall. Alexandra could see the boats way out on the edge of the marsh, and the little figures of the sailors walking about in readiness. She could also see the puffs of smoke from the ships as their great guns sent another shell to bombard the city's new occupiers. How far away they seemed! Would it be possible ever to reach those pin-dot figures?

Charles and James were swiftly tying the ropes together, then fastening the end to a stone. The men seemed completely in charge and never had she been so glad for them to be so.

"I'll go down first and test the drop," said James. "Then I can cover your descent with my revolver, if it should become necessary. I don't like the look of those figures coming along the top of the wall."

They were soldiers, still a long way off but running toward them with rifles.

"Get going, then," agreed Charles, and turned to Garrard, as James disappeared. "Look sir, I know how you feel, but it would be better if I took Mrs Mostyn down. I'm twenty years younger than you and tremendously fit. She'll stand a better chance with me."

It took Garrard no more than a moment. "All right. We must abandon the chair here, and we'll take turns carrying her over to the boats. You go down next, in that case."

Alice made no comment, just did whatever she was told. But it took a while to get her out of the chair and hanging on to Charles with her arms around his neck. As she could not grip with her legs, she faced him so that he could grip *her* with his legs if her arms could not stand the strain to the bottom. The tarpaulin thankfully was not needed as the rope reached almost to the ground, and James shouted up that he was ready to take the invalid. It seemed an age while the clinging pair inched their way down, and Alexandra tried not to look at the figures on the wall that were growing larger. They were firing at others crossing the marsh: other Britons and Americans making their difficult way to the boats.

Jean Maddox gripped the rope ready to follow her athletic husband down. Giving Alexandra a rather tense smile, she said, "I'll try not to take too long. I'd give anything for a skirt as short as yours right now."

Alexandra and her father were left alone at the top of the wall, with the soldiers less than four hundred yards away.

"Do you think we'll manage it, Father?" she asked as casually as she could.

He looked back at her frankly. "All your life you have defied everyone who has crossed your path. I cannot see you letting these male brutes stop you from doing what you are determined upon."

Before she knew it she was smiling at him, danger and the whole dramatic situation giving her a sudden appreciation of the unshakable assurance of a man who was seeing the evidence of the beginning of the end of the colonial giants like himself.

"How well you know me, after all," she said. "After fighting so hard for emancipation, I shan't allow a few men in silly uniforms to stop me reaching those ships."

A shout, then it was her turn to go down that rope, first dangling in space, then spinning round and around, bumping hard against the grey stone wall, and dropping in sickening lurches. She dared not look up. The soldiers were shouting, firing at them as they drew within range. The thought of her father in danger at the top slackened her hold too quickly. She dropped, feeling the rope burning her hands as she plummeted. Wincing with pain she loosed her hold automatically, and so practically fell into James's waiting arms as he shouted up to Garrard. The rifle shots intensified. She could see the soldiers clearly now. They were aiming at her father just starting down the wall, and her nerves jumped as James and Charles began firing back.

"No, save your bullets," cried James, almost at once. "They are still out of range."

So they all stood helplessly watching Garrard descend slowly, slowly, while bullets struck the wall around him sending sharp granite chips flying. But, by the time he was safely down, the enemies were almost at the top of the wall and within range. Shots began to fly all around them as they started to struggle across the great width of marsh. The sailors were coming to meet them, firing their rifles, too, and shells still screamed overhead. James had his arms around Alexandra and Jean, while Garrard and Charles formed a 'chair' of crossed arms to carry the invalid. The cracking of shots was deafening, and Alexandra was so intent on moving forward across the difficult marshy terrain, it was only on the second of her father's commands that she caught that note of urgency.

"*Go on*, I say. Go to your wife, man!"

Alexandra glanced over her shoulder. Her father was taking Alice into his arms and urging Charles away, shouting in sharp tones, "*Go to your wife, I say!*"

Then Charles was stumbling forward in a dazed manner to take Jean's arm. But only as her father shifted Alice into his sole hold did Alexandra notice the strange limpness of her mother's figure. Alarmed, she twisted to go back, but James pushed her on, holding her tightly with his arm. She saw how ashen her father's face had become, how frighteningly shadowed with anger as he began to drop back under the weight of the burden he now carried alone. Then, a pale shaft of morning sun caught them both, and she saw the dark hole in her mother's temple, the tiny trickle of blood that had already dried in the wind.

"*Mother!*" she screamed, and tried to run back, not believing what she saw, not accepting the implication of that still figure. In that exchange of shots how *could* one have found the most vulnerable mark? Twisting free of James's hold she staggered back to grip the hand now hanging loosely.

"*Mother!* Oh no, oh no," she moaned, trying to cradle the fair head against her breast.

"James, for God's sake get her to that ship. Take her, I tell you! *Do as I say!*" The voice was harsh, familiar, a tone she had heard so many times in the past when she had displeased him.

Her arms were gripped, but she fought. "No, no, Jimmy. *Please!*" But she was being dragged away, dragged further and further toward the sailors, while the lonely walking figure carrying his burden dropped further and further back. Her hair was sticking to her face, obscuring her vision as she turned her head again and again, looking back at those who had left her alone. Time and again she pleaded with James to release her, but he led her inexorably onward with a face that was white and set, as he ignored her tears and pleas.

The thud of heavy guns was deafening now, and the crack of rifles increased as more soldiers appeared on top of the wall.

All around her there were others, stumbling and straining toward those ships. Others carried burdens—young children who were afraid even to cry—and some walked bowed down in sadness at the betrayal of those they believed they had reached through a lifetime of barriers.

When she was almost within grasp of the brawny nautical arms waiting to assist them into the boats, Alexandra saw her father fall and lie still in the middle of the marsh. James seemed as frozen as she, for he stood for a moment with the smell of the river all around them and the walls of Nanking wreathed in smoke.

"Oh God," he murmured. "After all he had done, what a way to end!"

Then he was handing her to a huge man with a beard and merry eyes, and the boat began to rock on the water as it pulled away leaving several still shapes on that lonely marsh. The eyes of all those on board were turned toward the smitten city for as long as possible. With tears drying on her cheeks, Alexandra kept her gaze on those two bodies lying so closely together. If this had been the end of an era for the Maddoxes, it was the end of a lifetime for her.

CHAPTER TWELVE

The bridge was finished. On a mist-shrouded morning, to the complete lack of interest of the coolies, and with no spark of personal pride or pleasure, Mark prepared to take an engine across and back to test his construction. It was a mere formality. Since he had inspected every rivet and nut and bolt as the days had passed, and supervised every stage of growth, he knew the bridge would stand for as long as it was needed. But he was the engineer and obliged to check stress and strain under a slow-moving weight.

He stood on the footplate of the little engine waiting for the steam-pressure gauge to indicate that he could get underway, and stared morosely ahead to where the bridge vanished into the mist as it crossed the water.

"This'll scare the living daylights out of those hundred bloody dragons," he muttered to himself. "If they're lurking on the opposite bank, they've got a shock coming."

He tapped the gauge lightly, then unwound the brake ready to move off. The silence was rent by a shrill blast of the whistle, which he did for the hell of it, followed by the slowly accelerating puffs as the engine began rolling along the re-laid track toward the bridge. From his position high up on the embankment Mark looked down on the canal. The coolies were all squatting on their boat, arguing noisily, paying no attention to the engine. As far as they were concerned, it had been a long session of hauling and hammering. The sense of having created something of infinite worth would not touch their prosaic minds.

At such a moment, he had expected that Corcoran might have shown some interest, but he was nowhere to be seen. Since their fight he had been as silent as Mark, the few words they had been obliged to exchange in order to get the work done had been brusque, hostile, and strictly to the point. Thank God the job was over, thought Mark once again. As he took the engine slowly over the last few yards of track to where the canal bank fell away to the water, he saw a solitary figure watching, and a reluctant smile broke across his face. He leaned from the cabin to wave a greeting.

"Here goes, Hong," he shouted. "If I really am meant to drown in this canal, this is their last chance!"

Hong waved back, grinning. "No, Major, the devils ride in the machine with you."

His voice floated up faintly in the thick mist, and the changing noise of the wheels as they ran onto the bridge drowned anything else he might have said. Next minute, Mark was out on the bridge surrounded by mist that was at its thickest over the water, seemingly in a world of his own. It was an eerie sensation running slowly forward into a grey obscurity, with only a few yards ahead visible. It was easy to see how simple coolie minds could imagine all kinds of fearsome beasts waiting to take revenge for past deeds.

He shivered and turned up the collar of his greatcoat. Since he had returned from Shanghai with Alexandra on his train, he had been in uniform all the time. The military authorities with whom he was obliged to keep in contact had dictated that he should continue his work on the bridge now it was so near completion, but had insisted that he obey the wartime ruling now in force for all military personnel to display their identity and rank at all times. Mark felt it a little absurd in the middle of a marsh, but recognised the wisdom of the ruling and complied. His khaki greatcoat was considerably warmer, anyway, and he would be back to army duties in a day or two.

The muffled sound of the wheels suggested that the engine had reached the end of the bridge and was running out onto the far bank. He leant from the cab and saw water lapping against the upward slope leading to the new stretch of track that linked up with the original line that had led to the ill-fated first bridge. The mist hid it now, but it was still there, two single spans with nothing to join them together across the canal. He smiled grimly. The dragons had won that battle. The victory here was his. The bridge was sturdy, functional and perfect. He had just proved the facts.

He went on along the far side until the new curving track met the old. Everything was fine. He stopped the engine and prepared to reverse. All that remained was to clear up the site, load the equipment, and pay off the coolies. Tomorrow morning he could shake from his boots the dust of the Lu-Seng district along with its myths, superstitions, and Corcoran's perverted rape of virgins. There had been nothing for him here but distrust and disillusionment. Force of habit made him return just as slowly across the new structure, listening for any sound that suggested all was not well. The scene was exactly as he had left it. Hong was still on the bank, grinning at his reappearance. The remainder were in their boats. But Hong climbed up the embankment and strolled along beside the slowing engine until it stopped, and Mark jumped down.

He smiled at the Chinese foreman. "It's a good bridge. You did an excellent job."

Hong shrugged with nonchalant pleasure. "It was your skill, Major."

Mark put a hand on the man's shoulder in a gesture of gratitude for his example of something approaching co-operation on a project that had been fraught with trouble.

"There were no dragons to be seen," he began laughingly, then his hand dropped with instant reaction to the place where his revolver should be. But, of course, he was not wearing it, and all he could do was stand in immobile disbelief as more and more armed ragged soldiers materialised out of the mist and surrounded them, rifles lowered menacingly. It was a scene he knew so well, but in a place where it could not possibly happen. The Kuomintang was in Hankow, surely?

"Who the hell are they, Hong?" he asked under his breath, trying to regiment his thoughts. "What do they want?"

There was no time for an answer. Pandemonium broke out as further crowds of soldiers arrived and ran down the banks of the canal to the boats moored there. Everyone began shouting in rapid Chinese which was undeniably aggressive. The coolies wailed like banshees as they were dragged up to the railway track, some trying to kneel and beg for mercy even as they were being beaten with rifle butts. The whole place had gone mad where it had been silent a moment before. Grey-uniformed men swarmed everywhere like vicious angry ants, coming and going in the mist so that it was impossible to tell just how many there really were.

Mark did not dare move, there were too many rifles pointing at him. Several of his captors shouted angrily, but he had no idea what they said. It certainly was not Mandarin they spoke. Then Hong began reasoning with them, waving his arms in excitable gestures, as they did, while Mark watched dozens of them clambering into the boats—his own included—shouting and fighting each other in chaotic selfishness as they clung to any empty space. He had never seen anything like it before in all his experience of combat. Then, as others jumped and jostled to get onto the overcrowded boats, several volleys of shots rang out. Bodies dropped into the water and there was an immediate deadly scramble for the vacant places. Dazed and shocked by the lightning attack, Mark could only stand by helplessly as his own boat suffered the same treatment. But he started forward involuntarily when he saw Ah Wu, whose voluble defence of ownership of the boat reached his ears, smashed over the head with a rifle butt and tossed into the canal by a fat bully. His captors immediately closed in, but made no attempt to touch him, which seemed strange in face of all that was going on around him.

Anger and sadness at the killing of his loyal servant made Mark long to hit back, and he turned to Hong in vicious mood. "Is this your famous Kuomintang—liberators of the coolie?" he flung at him.

"No, Major, they are soldiers of the northern warlords," came the taut answer. "They have lost Nanking and are running away. I advise you to make no further movements. Your English uniform makes them cautious, but they are afraid and will shoot if you cause trouble. All they want is the boats and supplies. They have said they will also take the train. The Kuomintang soldiers are coming after them and they are afraid."

He said the last words with contempt in his voice, but Mark was no longer listening. *They have lost Nanking*. How could they have done? How could the situation have changed so rapidly? What had happened to the vast defending army? Dear God, Alexandra was in that city! His mind churned with all he had heard of the attacks on white foreigners by troops out of control—rape and murder by sadistic men thirsting for revenge. The things they could do to a woman were unfaceable. He felt sick with helplessness. It was happening all over again. First Katya now Alexandra. How could he stand there doing nothing?

On the point of lunging recklessly at the surrounding soldiers he was halted by the sight of a fresh batch of figures emerging from the mist, figures brandishing any kind of weapon they could find and looking far more dangerous than the desperate, fleeing soldiers. Mark immediately recognised the villagers of Lu-Seng, taking advantage of the presence of overwhelming numbers to seek revenge. He had no chance after that. Those same men who had watched for him to drown in the canal seized him, and the soldiers who had been guarding him ran off to clamber onto the engine or the various trucks that were now being hitched onto it. It was clear that all the troops had wanted was a means of getaway. The villagers of Lu-Seng wanted a third Englishman to appease the dragons.

Mark's hands were tugged behind his back and tightly bound with rope, while a knife was held at his throat by one of his erstwhile coolies with hatred in his eyes. There was no discussion between the villagers. It was as if it had all been planned step by step before they arrived on the scene, and that silent aggression was the most unnerving part of the attack that had come out of the greyness that morning. Buffeted and pushed along in the midst of his captors, Mark was forced toward the canal feeling utterly defeated. Had he endured a savage war and a revolution to fall victim to ethnic superstition? He had never done these people any harm, yet their distrust of men who built bridges plus their treatment by another of his race truly marked him as one of the hated 'foreign devils'. He could not believe his life would shortly end. After all he had endured, to die this way just as he had found a chance of happiness! Yet Alexandra might now also be dead, victim of those amongst whom she had lived her short life.

He began to pray as he stumbled along; pray that death would be swift and merciful. The Chinese were barbarous killers, and he was haunted anew by the atrocities he had witnessed in Russia. He knew a terrible fear that was an echo of what he had felt so constantly in France; a reminder of the dread that had lived with him on that flight across Russia. There was a chilling din now over the mist-laden area. The shouting and squabbling of soldiers grew louder as boats began to pull away from the banks, so overladen two of them instantly began to sink. Up on the track there was complete confusion as some of the troops urged the driver to set the train in motion, while others threatened him with their rifles to stop him from leaving before they were all on. The hiss of steam grew louder and all the trucks banged together with a ringing stutter of sound that added to the hue and cry.

Suddenly, the men surrounding Mark began to shout, starting forward angrily and waving their arms. Hamish Corcoran had been dragged from the cabin of his boat by soldiers who were manhandling him onto the bank. Several villagers ran forward gesticulating, and whatever they were shouting caught the attention of the troops. They stopped and looked up. Within minutes a bargain was made. Corcoran was thrown to the ground and stripped to his underclothes. His leather boots, thick shirt and pullovers plus the plaid coat were snatched and handed over in exchange for the man himself. The soldiers immediately fought each other for the clothes, falling into the water or pushing each other in as the boat drew away leaving struggling half-drowned men swimming desperately for the far bank in the hope of getting on the train after it had crossed the bridge. The engine was already on the first span making heavy weather under the load it was now pulling, and those who had not been fortunate enough to climb on were running behind begging for a hand to help them up, and being offered none.

Mark stood captive, watching the departure of a retreating army which swept everything away with it. Five minutes later, the previously cluttered work-site was empty and deserted. Every boat had vanished into the mist. Of the train there was nothing but the distant muffled sound of a puffing engine. All that was left were a few dead soldiers mown down by the train, and a flotilla of corpses in the canal, amongst them Ah Wu, who had been diligent, loyal and proud of his work with the British Army.

Yet, there was no time to dwell on such things, because those left behind were impatient. Mark was brutally dragged up the track leading to the bridge, where another group of villagers had taken Corcoran, also with his hands tied behind his back. He looked a pathetic sight dressed only in long woollen underwear in the bitterly cold atmosphere. Mark could just see his face. Written there was the knowledge of what awaited him. In the ashen, sunken mask of his face and eyes grown black with shock was dread of the moment of reckoning. He knew there would be no mercy shown him.

Mark's heart hammered against his ribs. What, in God's name, was about to happen? The hammering of his heart increased when Corcoran was pulled forward and a long rope was tied around his body beneath his armpits. Were they planning to drag him behind a horse or something similar? The Scot began shouting at his captors, swearing and kicking at them with his bare feet, until one man swung at his legs with a crowbar, cracking his shins and sending him sprawling with a cry of agony.

Everything happened very quickly then. One of the Chinese shinned up the tripod that had been erected beside the bridge while they were working on it, and flung the rope over the pulley until the end snaked to the ground where his friends awaited. Mark swallowed painfully as he watched. They could not be planning to hang them both, or the rope would have been around Corcoran's neck. The truth soon became horrifyingly clear when the Scot was hauled up on the pulley until he was dangling as high as he could go. Then, those holding the rope simply let it go so that he crashed down onto the ground below with a great thud. He was instantly hauled up again and dropped in the same fashion, with another sickening thud.

"*Christ*," breathed Mark as the hideous torture was repeated with longer intervals between, so that the battered, bleeding man was dangling at the top of the tripod in his agony never knowing when he would drop again. Corcoran's screams rang across, freezing Mark's blood in his veins with the knowledge that it would soon be his turn to dangle there waiting for merciful death. He felt nausea rise in his stomach, and sweat broke on his body as the noise of agonised cries and those obscene thuds filled his ears.

Closing his eyes did nothing to help, yet when he opened them again there seemed to be no more than a bloody bundle of pulp on the end of the rope. The savage ritual had served its purpose, but when the remains of Corcoran had been lowered and the battered head struck from the body to be carried in triumph back to the women of the village,

Mark began to pray, as he had never before prayed, for the gift of courage. In his room in Hong Kong was a medal given to mark his heroism but, at that moment, he was weak with fearfulness, near to complete collapse. He thought desperately of all those he had seen face death in the past, and tried to draw courage from them. Yet it was the thought of a lovely young girl who had walked away from him to face an unknown fate, knowing the child of their love was growing within her, that made him suddenly calm. *Katya*! She had gone into the dangerous streets to search for food for their son, and died. He must display the same courage now, for her sake and for Michael, who had claimed him as his father and would expect him to live up to his heroic image.

Someone began speaking fast—a sudden normal voice after horror. It broke Mark's concentration, and he turned his head sharply. He had forgotten about Hong. Had he been there all the time? A violent argument broke out as the rope was pulled from the tripod by two of the younger villagers, and it continued as his own arms were seized and he was marched down the embankment to where the boats had been moored. It was then he realised what fate had been planned for him all along. A third Englishman had to be drowned in that canal to satisfy the hundred dragons, and it *would* be him, after all.

Stumbling along on legs weakened by what he had just witnessed Mark could only breathe his thankfulness that he had been spared the torment Corcoran had suffered . . . torment the villagers had extracted in return for the fear and depravity they had suffered at his hands. Drowning would surely be quicker, and his body left whole after death?

The whole group stopped as Hong stood between them and the water in an attitude of defiance, his round face full of mobile expression, his words flowing fast and furiously. Many times he pointed at their captive, touched the greatcoat and boots in deliberate manner, and Mark decided that a bargain was being made over who should have his clothes. The altercation went on for a long time, and all he could see were the bodies already floating on that muddy surface.

It seemed to be settled when they untied his wrists and began pulling off his uniform in sudden silence after the fierce exchange. They stripped him naked to the waist, then pulled off his boots and socks, leaving him only in the khaki breeches. Then, they tied his wrists and ankles with rope so that he was entirely helpless. He had to submit, or be hacked to pieces with farm implements . . . and he would no longer need the clothes, anyway. How long did it take to drown, he wondered? How would it feel to be in the water and unable to move arms and legs? What an ironical death for a man who had won countless trophies for swimming!

Hong came to stand before him looking sad, but resigned. "There is nothing more I can do, Major," he said. "They wish very much to kill you, and it has taken me a long time to show them that it would be wrong to do so. I have argued with them that you are a good man who has done them no harm, but they now have a hatred of all white men who swarm over our country and ignore our customs and rituals. They have been told how China has been robbed of all its wealth to fill the pockets of foreign devils."

Even in that situation Mark could not let this pass. "Have they also been told that 'foreign devils' have built hospitals and schools—provided life-giving industry? Can't they see that even this railway has helped to make China rich? Without us they could not have done it."

"Without them, neither could you," said Hong without rancour.

Strangely calm now, Mark looked back at the man who was such a mixture and shook his head. "It doesn't work, does it? You have adopted Western Christianity and many of our ways, but you are a man of the East, Hong. Nothing will ever change that. Those who eventually run your 'new China' will have to decide which they want to be, and forsake the other, or this will happen all over again."

Hong looked even sadder. "Yes, I am a man of the East, Major, which is why I understand these people. I think your countrymen never will. I regret very much that there is this difference between us; because I have much admiration for you. It has been possible for me to persuade them not to kill you . . . but that is all I have been able to do."

His words sounded infinitely ominous, not in the least comforting. If they did not intend killing him, what . . . ? With dread thoughts of mutilation and maiming rushing back into his head, Mark's earlier fear returned.

"What are they going to do, Hong?" he asked sharply. "Why have they stripped me in this manner?"

With a quick instruction to a man laying hands on the captive, Hong stepped nearer. "They wished to throw you into the water to appease the dragons, in the hope that their persecution will stop. I have told them that you are a warrior—the reincarnation of that ancient man who was betrayed and slain. I have said that if they kill you the dragons will descend on them without mercy. They have not seen you in uniform before, Major, and they are full of uncertainties now. Most of them believe that you are the returned spirit of the warrior, but others are doubtful that the spirit would return as a foreign devil. I have also said that you went beneath the water in your devil-suit and came up unharmed, that you built the bridge and climbed over it many times, and the dragons have not harmed you because you are the Warrior."

He shrugged as he had done on so many occasions when explaining the complex behaviour of his countrymen. "They are worried. There is much to show that you are the Warrior, and much to show that you are not. They do not want to believe it, yet are afraid to ignore the possibility. They do not know what will anger the dragons most—to kill you, or let you go free. So they will let the dragons themselves decide." He shrugged again. "It is our way, Major. What is to happen will happen, and I can do no more."

The conversation had gone on too long for the villagers, who took hold of Mark and dragged him down to the water by the bridge. Then, those men, who were used to toiling all day under heavy loads, manhandled him across the lower structure that supported the first section until his feet rested on a broad girder just at water level, and his face was pressed against an angled upright. Lashing his legs tightly to the upright, they released his hands from behind his back, pulled his arms above his head to their fullest extent and lashed his wrists to a crossbeam. It happened so suddenly, and he was so full of apprehension over what they were doing, they had all climbed back to the bank before Mark realised the true horror of what lay ahead of him. Far better to have been thrown in and allowed to drown!

By twisting his head so that his cheek was against the upright, he could see them on the bank folding his clothes into a pile with his boots standing beside them, in case he really was that ancient warrior and the dragons released him. Then they all left the spot without a backward glance—all, that is, except Hong, who seemed torn by indecision. With pulse thudding, Mark shouted at him, trying to delay the only man in the world who could help him now.

"Hong, for God's sake! I don't stand a chance like this. You know that."

"There is nothing more I can do," came the sad but firm reply.

"You can't just walk away and leave me to die slowly," he roared, already feeling the bite of marshland cold on his bare torso, and the freezing water lapping over his feet. It was impossible to move, and the pull on his arms was already painful. "You don't believe this mumbo jumbo about dragons," he added desperately as Hong made to walk away. "You're a Christian, Hong. You believe in compassion."

The Chinese foreman was halfway up the embankment when he turned to shake his head. "It is better to leave some things for a greater power to decide. That is the same in any religion, Major. I cannot interfere with this decision. The village of Lu-Seng would lose face, if I did. It is our way, you see."

He walked off into the mist in the direction of Lu-Seng, and Mark was soon alone firmly lashed to the Bridge of a Hundred Dragons. The floating corpses at his feet were macabre company for his forthcoming ordeal.

In Shanghai there was prolonged tension. Within the International Settlement and the French Concession there were armed troops watching and waiting behind the barbed-wire topping on the barricades along the perimeters.

Outside in the Chinese City, the Communist grip was already felt as Red workers patrolled the streets wearing military armbands and carrying weapons more worthy of a museum. The Chinese citizens of Shanghai were already suffering: the daily toll of murders in the name of the People's Revolution increased at an alarming rate, and those who inhabited the poor hovels along the swampy Yangtze delta found their miserable lives made even worse by oppression.

Further out still lay the Kuomintang army, threatening the great port yet making no attempt to attack or join up with the self-styled 'militia' which had seized the Chinese City.

It was a period of uneasy waiting. The Shanghai Communists were impatient for the advance that would seize the entire port and chase the foreigners from China's shores, and they grew restless and angry as the days passed without a sign of troops on the skyline. The Europeans inside their barricades longed for the excuse to open fire on those making an unprovoked attack; their fingers itched to avenge the deaths at Nanking of helpless civilians.

The events at the Chinese City had shocked and outraged the Western nations, who had issued a violent protest to Chiang Kai-Shek but were determined to go to any lengths if such aggression were shown to any single European again. There was a vast army of the world's best fighting men assembled in Shanghai, and if it meant a bloodbath to bring it home to the Kuomintang, then so be it. Not only would the Chinese be facing troops who outclassed them in every way, they would be up against men who had a score to settle.

The Nanking attacks had echoed Peking twenty-seven years earlier, for not only had Europeans been assaulted and killed, but both the British and American Consuls had been openly attacked and forced to flee for their lives to the protecting gunboats. Diplomatic liaisons had been disregarded, and a complete breakdown in international understanding seemed inevitable.

The death of Garrard Mostyn and his invalid wife shook the mercantile and social nucleus of Shanghai very badly. Apart from outrage at the murders, the fabric of European trade grew flimsier through his loss.

Mostyn flair, dedication and foresight had played a tremendous part in the success of Anglo-Chinese co-operation in many essential areas —notably the railways—and Mostyn wealth had financed projects from horse racing to homes for lepers. Fellow financiers had depended on him; Chinese of intelligence had trusted him as much as they would ever trust an Englishman. He had devoted his life to Chinese affairs and had achieved where a great many men had failed. He had made a vast fortune in China, but had helped to make Shanghai one of the greatest international trading cities in the world.

His death was felt all over the globe: share prices fell, small businesses began to founder, and financiers started a wary quadrille with their eyes on each other's partners. The Mostyn heiress was a wild and irresponsible girl of nineteen, well known for extravagance and said to be emancipated to the point of disaster. Anything could happen!

So, in the days following the fall of Nanking there was more than military anxiety in Shanghai. The two gunboats had brought the survivors and the bodies of those who had been killed back up the Yangtze, and a diplomatic row was raging over the affair. In reply to Western protest against attacks on their nationals, the Kuomintang leaders launched a counter-protest which accused the British and Americans of unprovoked hostilities by firing shells at a Chinese city—shells that had killed innocent residents of Nanking.

This was answered with a long list of those Europeans who had been killed or assaulted by the conquering army since it left Canton, plus a reminder of Chiang Kai-Shek's personal assurance that all foreign residents and their property would be unharmed. The answer to that was the usual one. It was not us! The attacks, in particular the one at Nanking, were blamed on the Communist element in the Kuomintang, which had been persuaded by Soviet advisors to perpetrate such attacks in order to discredit Chiang Kai-Shek in the eyes of the western world.

The correspondence continued and, if Chiang Kai-Shek were to be believed, it would seem that his policies and those of the Communists were surprisingly branching in different directions, so that he was becoming very disenchanted with his Russian allies. In fact, there were strong indications that the two factions might soon fall out. That was if Chiang Kai-Shek were to be believed. By most Europeans he was not.

There were others in Shanghai whose motives were kept secret from others. One was Gregori Petrovich Galinkov, former White Russian officer and leader of the refugee community in the city which had plans of its own afoot. So, while diplomatic notes flew back and forth and international financiers waited anxiously for indications on the stock exchange, and while rival factions plotted and schemed and the massive military reinforcements stood with rifles at the ready behind their barricades, the fate of a young British major out on a swampy marsh near Lu-Seng was of no concern to anyone save those whose future rested in his hands. What was the life of one soldier pledged to give it for the sake of his country, against the continuance of Western influence in China? Bridge builders were easily come by. East-West goodwill had been hard won, with the blood of many.

CHAPTER THIRTEEN

Mark was no stranger to pain, yet as the long hours passed he found it was solitude that made his present ordeal almost unendurable. He had been wounded more than once during the war and again in Russia, when he had nearly died. But there had been comrades, nurses, hospital beds in cool quiet wards. At the Bridge of a Hundred Dragons there were none of these, and the villagers' belief that the mythical beasts would effect a rescue of the man tied to the bridge if he was, in truth, the reincarnation of that long-ago warrior, was not one that put any hope in Mark's breast. He knew he was a slowly dying man . . . and Hong had known it when he had just walked away disclaiming further responsibility.

During the first hour he had searched his brain for ways of freeing himself, lacerating his wrists as he jerked impotently at the ropes binding them to the girder above his head, bruising his body as he sought to twist away from the cold steel against which he was pressed, and cracking his knees as he tried to hang by his bound hands whilst inching his feet so that the rope around them rubbed against the sharp edge of the angle-iron. He had known all along that his situation was completely hopeless, and the only thing he had succeeded in doing was to increase the agony of his upstretched arms and expend energy he would need if he should be rescued.

During the second hour he acknowledged that there *was* no one to rescue him. The only people who would bother to cut him down were his own countrymen, and they were all in Shanghai. With that firmly established, panic overtook him, a feeling of hysterical desperation at the thought of the hours ahead, dying slowly and quite alone in that hostile spot where he would never be discovered by his own people and given Christian burial. Even in the vast carnage of war men struggled to do that for their dead comrades.

The freezing water of the corpse-strewn canal lapped over his bare feet so that they were soon completely numb, and the bitter temperature of a day on which the mist did not lift had him shaking violently and painfully in helpless spasms as his half-naked body rapidly succumbed to the cold. There was no way he could stimulate his bloodstream. His ankles were firmly lashed to the girder; if he twisted or bent his body the pull on his arms was increased. As it was, he had to stretch to the limit to ease the lacerations around his wrists, and the excruciating ache in his torso forced him to cry out for release, for someone to take mercy on him before he went crazy with pain. It throbbed through him with increasing force, and the violent convulsions of his slowly freezing body combined with it to send him to the fringes of delirium, which was the only escape from the hours ahead.

He hung there in a place that had become a hazy grey no-man's-land, and travelled in the realms of his past. Faces he had long forgotten paraded in front of him in the pale mask of death; landscapes of unimaginable destruction and desolation stretched before him as seas of mud. It was bitterly cold, standing knee-deep in icy water waiting for star shells to illuminate the night enough to creep beneath the barbed wire and place charges in the forward trenches they were about to abandon to the enemy. The ground was frozen hard with layers of ice as he dug, heart in mouth, to remove mines before an advance due at dawn; the freezing water lapped around his feet as he worked under fire to throw a pontoon bridge over a river red with blood.

Then he was beneath a bridge waiting for darkness to come so that he could steal a train. The train he was on blew up, and he was in agony resembling the fires and torments of hell. He was crawling, crawling, crawling. There was a feminine face above him, a face of great dignified beauty and passion. *Katya*. She had come for him, come to ease his suffering, tend his open wounds, tip warm sustaining broth between his stiff lips. All the time she touched his brow with gentle hands, begging him to hold on to life for her sake. Where was Katya now? He longed for her. There had been tears on her cheeks as she had walked away from him, and they were now on his as he realised she would never return. He tried to speak her name as he saw her body lying in that street in Vladivostok, but no sound came from his lips so stiff and cold. Was he already dead? If so, Katya would be waiting for him there.

Suddenly, she was standing in the hazy distance beckoning him, but they would not let him go to her. The Red soldiers held him back, pulling his arms from their sockets as they laughed at his helplessness. One lifted his rifle, and Katya fell to the ground where, even during her death throes, they stripped her body and tried to rape her. He screamed, and managed to run to her. As he looked down at the girl lying so still, he saw she had a different face—rounder, with red, red lips and eyes so large and blue they promised him anything he wanted. She was smiling, but he then realised that smile was fixed in death. They had killed her in Nanking and were sending out photographs of her being stripped naked in Shanghai. He *must* get those photographs. When he tried to run his captors finally tore his arms off. The world turned dark with his blood and agony.

Are you my father? Are you my father? A voice was repeating the question over and over again, until the darkness became grey and mysterious. Mark could not see the boy, although he must be nearby. He could not answer; must not answer. If he claimed his son he must take into his bed a woman he did not love, who would send him into the street for food and let him die. He must not answer the young voice with the truth. Yet, if he did not, he would be denying Katya; he would be denying her love and sacrifice. Straining his eyes to see Michael, the grey blur beneath him swum with floating shapes that drifted back and forth like lifeless swimmers. Then he saw the boy in the distance, small and sturdy, exactly like himself. When the child drew near, however, Mark grew deeply afraid, for he had a face which was Chinese and full of menace.

Alexandra began to cry, saying he was not a true son because he looked nothing like his father. She refused to marry him if he brought the boy into her home; Marie refused to marry him if he did not. The Chinese Michael brought a host of his countrymen to seize Alexandra in anger, because she would not take the boy as her own. Seizing her they tied her to a rope on a tripod and pounded her until she was no more than a bloody bundle. When they made to strike her head from her body, Mark screamed at them to stop. They returned to torture him, instead, and his moans grew louder and louder until he dropped into blackness again.

It must have been a long time later that he realised all pain and fear had gone, and that he felt at peace. He was not certain he still possessed a body. A curious happiness took hold of him as he realised he was about to join all those who had passed from his life leaving him to carry the burden for them all these years. He had done his best; no man could be expected to do more. Now he could cross that final boundary where they would welcome him, and he could rest, at last. Already he could hear his Russian friends. They were shouting. *"Posmostrite! Posmostrite! Bozhe moy, anglichanin!"* Look, look! My God, an Englishman!

A distant clanging began in his ears that muffled what they were saying, and he was afraid they were going away from him—escaping him in death as they had in life. Then one of his eyelids was opening again against his will. A faint blurry image appeared for a moment, but the bearded face he saw belonged to a stranger.

They were all around him now, saying all manner of strange things.

"Zhivyot!"—he is alive. *"Veryovka"*—the rope. *"Skoro!"*—quickly! *"Chto eto takoi?"*—what is it all about?

His peaceful entry into the realms beyond was shattered by shouting voices and the ringing of metal. They kept on asking him questions, but he could not form any answers. It was not possible to think. Why did they not leave him alone? He seemed to be floating in space, then, and the sound grew fainter and fainter. But eyelids were again pushed up ruthlessly, and the faces hung above him, this time. He could not understand what was happening. All he wanted was to sleep. If only they would let his eyes close.

Some liquid filled his mouth until he choked. But it was followed by more and more until he swallowed painfully, and felt it setting his throat on fire. Their faces vanished from above him, and he thankfully lowered his lids. But sleep was still denied him as blows seemed to rain upon his face, and a sensation of tossing and turning invaded him to such an extent he tried to protest. All that came from his lips was a faint croak, and it heralded more of the fiery liquid which he was forced to swallow. There were more blows on his face which made him drag up his eyelids in order to see his assailant, but the action cost Mark dear. With a great shout the bearded man began subjecting him to a sadistic attack on the whole of his body, which he was newly aware of in the gradual return from his peaceful, semiconscious state.

From then on it became clear that his ordeal was by no means over, for a new set of tormentors now had hold of him. Helpless in their hands, he was pummelled and rubbed, his limbs bent and stretched, bent and stretched without mercy until the slight tingle he began to feel multiplied into an agony so great he could not stand it. Fighting them, struggling to be free of their hold, he was merely told, *"Eto budet uzhasno"*—it *will* be terrible!

Their torture continued and intensified. There were daggers of red-hot pain in his arms and back that set him crying aloud, *"Bolit, bolit!"*—it hurts! Those words—clear words from a throat and jaw now ruthlessly forced into action—caused tremendous excitement amongst the men surrounding him, and they began smiling, calling him *tovarishch*—comrade. But their cruelty to him continued and grew even worse.

They dragged him up and forced him forward between two of them, and when he simply hung from their shoulders they seized his legs and made him move them in a walking motion, which put hot daggers in them, also. He pleaded loudly with them to put an end to him quickly, struggled to get away from them, cursed their never-ending Red terror. But back and forth they marched him, ignoring his moans and violent oaths, repeating steadily, *"Eto budet uzhasno!"*—it *will* be terrible!

Yet, gradually, his involuntary moans died away. Gradually, it seemed to him there was encouragement rather than sadism in their treatment of him. Gradually, he returned to the land of the living.

Only then did they have mercy on him and lead him across to a fire which they had lit on the embankment beside the bridge. His eyes stayed open now, and the leaden weight in his head had lifted. The pain in his racked body was now bearable; full awareness had returned. Glancing across to the bridge Mark saw his former bonds hanging severed from the girders, and knew he had been on the point of ending his life a short time ago. The hundred dragons had left it almost too late to save their Warrior!

They wrapped him in blankets taken from their horses, and gave him some kind of hot soup to drink from a tin cup such as he had seen in Russia seven years ago—a soldier's cup. He knew now they had saved his life, but just slumped where they had set him down and sipped from the cup they held to his lips. They had dressed him in his uniform that had been left in a pile on the canal bank, and his exhausted brain told him that these men were no Reds, after all. Russian cavalry—White Russian mercenaries—probably part of that same force that had appeared from the mist earlier that day. The greyness had not lifted so it was difficult to tell what hour of the day it now was. How long had he been tied to that bridge?

He began to shake from head to foot, and they wrapped more rugs around him, but he did not hasten to return to the problems and burdens of a life he believed he had surrendered. He was not, after all, to be reunited with those he had thought so near, and the immense sadness of that denial led him to bury his face in the rough blankets like a man hiding from the truth.

The Russians were in jovial mood. Their conversation finally penetrated his bewildered brain to make some sense. Their saddlebags were filled with everything they had seized during the successful looting of shops and hotels in Nanking. They had food galore, spirits and wines, spare padded coats, and plenty of blankets. Since they were cavalry troops they had left their getaway until the last minute and taken advantage of the brief pause between retreating troops and the occupying army. Now, they were heading north to join one of the generals in the Shantung district to continue the fight.

The bearded man came across to give Mark more soup, then left him in peace to drink it while he joined his men to study a map. He was shocked when he heard them speak of Shanghai being invested by the

Kuomintang. How had they got there so quickly—and were the British now in on the war? With thoughts of Red atrocities in that civilised port, he reluctantly faced the fact that life would have to carry on from the point it had reached when the villagers of Lu-Seng had tied him to the bridge. He put down the tin cup and said faintly, *"Spasibo, tovarishchi"* —thank you, my friends.

They turned immediately and crowded round him, asking who had tied him to the bridge and why. How was it that he spoke such good Russian, they asked enthusiastically. Then they apologised for putting him through such agony.

"We have had much experience of men freezing to death in our country," said the bearded one who had slapped Mark's face to keep him awake, and who appeared to be the group's captain. "When men reach the stage you had reached all they wish to do is die. All pain has gone by then, and they fight against facing more. When the body begins to grow warm again it is the most terrible agony, but it must be endured if the man is to stay alive. We also had to return a flow of blood to your arms and legs, which must have been additional torture after the way they had been tied. It is cruel and ruthless, my friend, but it works and saves the man's life. Now it is safe enough for you to sleep, if you wish."

"I can't sleep," said Mark. "I have been listening to all you have been saying. I must get back to Shanghai."

While they squatted around him he told them, in Russian that flowed easily, about the bridge he had built and how they had been overrun by the soldiers, who had taken all the boats and the train. His details of the killing of Corcoran left them unmoved, but the bizarre practice of leaving a man's life in the hands of mythical beasts had them marvelling at the Chinese fondness for handing over responsibility to one or other of their numerous gods and devils.

Mark tried to smile at their leader, but could not quite manage it. "You and your men don't look in the least like a hundred dragons, but I'm bloody thankful you came along when you did, Captain."

The man jumped to his feet, and executed a little bow. "Alexei Feodorovich Glukov. *Rad staratsya*—glad to be of service, Major . . . ?"

"Mark Rawlings, Royal Engineers."

Captain Glukov hesitated, stared hard at him, then frowned. "I have heard of a man with that name. It is said . . ." He broke off as an incredulous smile broke across his face. "You speak Russian; you are an engineer. You are he—the one who took a train up the captured line to freedom?"

"Yes, but . . . good lord, how did you come to hear about that?"

Mark never knew the answer, for the excitable Glukov gripped his hand and began pumping it up and down while he told his men they had just rescued one of the great heroes of their last desperate stand against the Bolsheviks. After that, they all seemed to forget his weak state and bombarded him with questions that again had him exhausted and muddled.

Captain Glukov soon spotted the fact, however, and called a halt to the questions, saying in a kindly tone, "You must sleep, sir. It is quite safe for you to do so now."

It was tempting, but Mark shook his head with an effort. "No, I have to get to Shanghai," he said, forgetting why but knowing it was important.

After a moment, Glukov agreed. "Yes, of course. I have a map over here, sir. If you'd like to come across we can decide on your best route. It will be on foot, of course, now your boats and train have been taken."

"Well, I might pick up a boat somewhere," he replied vaguely, only just realising his position. He pushed aside the blankets in order to get up. He was on his feet for no longer than a count of two, then his legs folded beneath him and he fell heavily at Glukov's feet.

Rolling over painfully he looked up at Glukov. "All right, Captain. Point taken—sleep it is."

He was helped to his feet and led to where a pile of blankets made an inviting bed beside the fire, and it was only the strong arms of the supporting Russians that prevented him from falling again. The incident had frightened him, and he lay weak and shaking wondering how he was ever going to make a journey of around one hundred and eighty miles without any means of transport through countryside seething with revolutionary troops.

He closed his eyes. Better think about it after he had slept. The last thing he remembered was Glukov saying jokingly, "I suppose you could always hang on to a passing train. There is one coming through here tomorrow on its way to Shanghai but, unfortunately, it will be full of Kuomintang troops."

When Mark awoke night had fallen, and it took him a while to recall all that had happened as he lay looking at a fire blazing merrily on the bank. The flames cast orange lights on the canal, highlighting the bodies that still floated on the sluggish water. A returning memory of that nightmare experience when he was tied to the bridge had him shaking and bathed in sweat. If the Russian cavalry had not followed the railway, knowing the network of canals and tributaries could only be crossed on those bridges, his body would now be hanging there stiff and frozen, a victim of the suspicious hatred of 'foreign devils' that dated back many years.

He tried to move and grunted with pain. His entire body felt as if it had been stretched on the rack—a comparable experience, he felt—and he hardly had the will to leave his blankets. But at the back of his mind was a voice telling him he must get to Shanghai.

When they saw he was awake the soldiers roused their captain, who strode across to look at Mark with a grin.

"So, *now* you are ready to walk to Shanghai, Major?"

Mark gave a faint smile. "I must live up to that exaggerated reputation circulating around your people. I can't look much like the hero of those tales, right now."

Glukov squatted beside him, very serious suddenly. "My friend, it was only because you are a strong man that you survived. I thought we were too late. The angels had you by one hand, you know."

"Yes, I know. At the time, I wanted to go with them. There are so many I hoped to see again."

Captain Glukov looked at the ground between his bent knees. "Have we not all thought that, at some time?" Then he smiled at Mark in complete understanding. "But we have so much still to achieve, hey? I have been looking at my map, and there is only one thing to be done. You ride, of course?"

Mark frowned. "A horse, you mean? I'm not an expert, but I can stay in the saddle. Why?"

"Our paths lie together for some miles, then we head north. We will take you as far as the village of Maw-Yan. Then I fear you must continue alone. We plan to leave at dawn, which will be about two hours from now."

"You risk staying here so long?" asked Mark staggered at how long he had slept. "The soldiers who took my boats and train were in a hell of a hurry—spoke of Kuomintang troops on their heels."

Glukov spread his hands in a dismissive gesture. "Coolie soldiers! What can one expect? They were also infantry." He smiled broadly showing large teeth. "We are skilled horsemen, Major, from central Russia. No army overtakes *us*." He twisted to sit beside Mark, one knee upbent casually as he leant on it. "The men now in Nanking are in no hurry to leave the comforts of a city, but when they do they will use the trains and steamers. There is little chance that they will swarm over this terrible marsh when they have control of railway and river. They might be stupid in many ways, but when it comes to their own skins it is a different matter. When it suits *them* to travel on the train the 'devil-machine' is perfectly acceptable and in no way offends the dragons." He wagged his head. "A most incomprehensible creature, the Chinaman."

Gradually, Mark had been collecting his thoughts and pulling away from the horrors of the previous day, and now he asked, with some sharpness, about the fall of Nanking and how it came to be surrendered so easily. He listened to the Russian's words with growing despair at how swiftly the revolutionary army seemed to be taking over China. Then he was jolted by words that had him sitting up swiftly while he questioned Glukov with growing heat.

"You mean, they actually attacked the foreign settlements?"

Glukov shrugged. "There are no foreign settlements, as such, but they certainly attacked the oil tanks and European businesses. Of course, I do not know exactly what happened because," he grinned broadly, "I and my men were taking what we could and leaving rather hastily. But we saw them tearing down flags and crying, 'Kill the foreign devils!'" He snapped his fingers in a return of memory. "Yes, one of my men heard it said that the British Consul was attacked, and some English people shot, their women raped. It might be exaggerated, but an American and a British gunboat began shelling the city from their moorings in the river." His smile flashed on again. "That was when we decided it would be wiser to leave."

He was silent a moment, his smile fading. Then his hand fell on Mark's shoulder. "This has saddened you, my friend."

He nodded, unable to speak for a moment. "I . . . I had a . . . friend there. God knows what has happened to her."

"I am sorry. It would have been better for me to remain silent. You see, it happens here just as it did in my own country. Who is there who will stop them?" he finished bitterly.

Mark was away on thoughts of his own, staring at the ground oblivious of all else but the fear that the Reds had taken Alexandra just as surely as they had taken Katya and her husband's brothers. When Glukov got to his feet and quietly moved away he was remembering the last words Alexandra had said, the way she had looked as she had gone off on the small boat with Ah Wu. He remembered that terrible photograph and how Mostyn had reduced her to complete wretchedness by the time he had arrived at their house. She had rushed to cling to him as her only hope, although she had already suffered the shock of meeting Marie and Michael in his hotel. Oh God, he had promised that morning to look after her from then on. Was it now too late?

For a long time he sat, full of hatred for those who had taken from him anyone he had truly loved, and echoing through his mind the whole time were Glukov's words: "Who will stop them?" He sat on even when the first glimmerings of revenge grew and increased until he was filled with the need for action. He sat on trying to rationalise something that threatened to rule his heart rather than his head, trying to put passion in the right perspective alongside cohesive professional thought. Only when he was calmer and ready to put thoughts into words did he struggle to his feet and walk unsteadily across to Glukov.

"Major, will you have a draught of brandy—with the courtesy of one of the best hotels in Nanking?" asked Glukov with a laugh, holding out a bottle.

Mark took it and drank. "Thanks. I'm sworn off the stuff, at present, but I needed that. You had better take another pull, because what I am about to ask you is going to be something of a shock." He handed the bottle back. "Do I remember your saying something about a train passing through here in the morning—a train loaded with Kuomintang troops?"

With the bottle almost to his lips, Glukov lowered it again. "That is what we heard, yes. That is the shock?"

Mark shook his head. "I want to send that train into the canal off a broken bridge."

The Russian stared at him. "Yes, I need the brandy." Tipping his head back he took several long gulps, then wiped his mouth with the back of his hand as he looked at Mark to see if he had heard aright. "So, you will send this train off a broken bridge? How is it possible?"

"I can't do it alone. I need the help of your men. The job is simple enough, but it takes a lot of manual labour."

Glukov handed him the bottle once more, and indicated a straw-filled sack a few feet away. "Explain to me what this is, and I will then consider."

Both men settled on the sack and there, in that spot he had grown to know so well, Mark outlined what he wanted from his Russian rescuers. As he spoke, he could not keep his gaze from the ropes hanging from the bridge, nor the floating bodies, black against the fire-reddened water. The stillness of the mist-shrouded nocturnal swamp was all around them, and he thought only of his chance to hit back at the Reds who had struck at everything dear to him. Greater issues were forgotten: this was his personal revenge for those who could no longer fight the evil.

"The old bridge is still standing, but with the two centre spans missing," he concluded. "All that is needed is for the track to be lifted and re-laid back on the original sleepers—we didn't bother to take them up. Any train on this line will then run straight onto the old bridge and into the canal."

"Mmm," mused Glukov. "Why not destroy the new bridge?"

"Oh, no," Mark said with great firmness. "I have just built it and have no intention of destroying it again; and unless you have explosives and charges with you, which I doubt, there is no certain way of making that bridge go beneath the weight of a train. I built it to avoid just that." He took another swig at the brandy and passed it back to Glukov. "Well, what do you think?"

Grey eyes met his over the neck of the bottle, and they sparkled with the light of battle that was now filling him.

"I think you are, in truth, the man who took a train through the forests of Russia, my friend."

"You'll do it?" he asked urgently.

"We shall do it. *Bozhe moy*, we shall do it!"

Mark let out his breath slowly, in thankfulness. "Now all we must hope is that your information concerning the train is correct."

"The troops were all assembling at the railway station, and Manski heard them grumbling at having to sleep there ready to board the morning train." Glukov grinned. "They must have been regular soldiers or they would have ignored their orders and rushed to join the looting and rape enjoyed by their brothers-in-arms who broke ranks."

Mark looked at his watch. "We should get started. It will soon be dawn. As we have no idea what time the train is liable to pass through here we must be ready by first light. If luck is on our side it will come early, while the mist is still thick. There'll be no chance of the driver seeing what lies ahead, then."

Glukov's men might have looked a wild, rough band, but they were not afraid of hard work and plainly admired their leader to the extent of doing anything he asked of them. Compared with English sappers they were volatile, noisy, and undisciplined, but enthusiasm made up for lack of organisation and the work went well once they began on it.

The most difficult part was trying to see what they were doing. They made flambeaux to stick in the ground all along the embankment, but the smoke from the burning torches only thickened the obscurity caused by the mist. Mark thought to himself grimly that the villagers of Lu-Seng would be terrified if they could see this battery of moving lights in the middle of the haunted marsh. The hundred dragons coming to take their revenge on the frozen body of Mark Rawlings, perhaps?

There were crowbars left lying around, but all Mark's personal equipment had gone along with the clothes and money that had been in his boat. It was as well that the marks made by the old track were still clear enough to be seen when studied at close quarters, for it made the re-laying of lengths of rail easier and quicker.

The night wore on. Mark had forgotten how much of the track they had been forced to take up, or else the darkness suggested it was more than it really was. The Russians worked hard but cheerfully. They were excited about what was to happen in the morning, and he realised they were savage, brutal men. They would hardly be mercenaries, otherwise.

For his own part, he was tense, but there was no sense of excitement. It was something he just *had* to do, and he went about directing the work with a cold authority that ruled out any thought of the fact that *he* had virtually become a mercenary. So far as he knew, the British army was not at war with the Kuomintang—but it might well be up in Shanghai, by now.

So, throughout the rest of the short period of darkness, he was driven by personal vengeance and large doses of brandy. It was a combination of the two that kept him on his feet at a time when he hardly knew what he was doing.

The job was not finished when the first indications of approaching daylight could be seen, although the mist remained as thick as ever. Mark was glad of that last fact, but he urged the Russians on with anxiety sharpening his voice. This act of revenge had become a crusade, a crucial point in his life. It had become symbolic, in some way. In the mood of pagan unreality inspired by that place and all that had happened there, Mark felt his reprieve from death would only become final when the train crashed into the canal and he left the spot exactly as he had first come upon it. If he failed, the hundred dragons would have triumphed, after all.

So feverish did he become, Captain Glukov remonstrated with him and suggested he took a rest while he and his men completed the work. It was the wrong time to propose such a thing, and the Russian received a vivid demonstration of what had earned an unknown Englishman a place in those legends that always emerged from wars and revolutions. He wisely refrained from further interference after that, and Mark willed himself to stay on his feet for as long as he must.

It was fully light by the time everything was done, and their anxiety did a complete about face. Now, they began to fret because the train did *not* come. The two officers walked out onto the old bridge and stood at the point where the track ended above twenty feet of water. It looked as eerie and alien as it had ever done. Mark shivered—not so much with the cold, but at the passing of ghosts.

"It will be an awesome sight," said Glukov quietly. "What you have planned is a magnificent revenge. Your friend in Nanking must mean a great deal to you."

Mark nodded slowly. "It is for all of them, you know . . . all of them."

They struck camp and loaded the horses, ready to ride off the minute the train plunged into the water. Mark had been loaned a horse by a man of slight build who intended to share a mount with another light rider. The fire was smothered, then they all crossed the new bridge and began their wait on the far bank. Everyone grew increasingly anxious. It had been light for more than an hour. Surely the train would come soon! They lounged against their horses, smoking cigars they had looted from Nanking, too restless to talk. Captain Glukov was anxious to be off. Magnificent riders or not, he did not want his men to run into Nationalist troops who might have moved north by other means.

Mark began to doubt that a train had ever been detailed to travel by this line, but Manski, when questioned, was quite definite about what he had heard. He had been a soldier for many years and knew the wisdom of learning the route an advancing army was planning to take. Why else had he risked his life creeping around Nanking rail junction? The train was definitely leaving early this morning for the northern outskirts of Shanghai, and this was the only line that would take it there. Mark had to trust the man, and told Glukov to go on without him. He had a personal need to see the outcome of their work, but the Russians should not risk staying longer. They did, of course, but tension mounted as the minutes ticked by.

Another hour passed and brought a new anxiety. There was a slight thinning of the mist that allowed a pale haze of sunlight to penetrate and make visibility easier. Now, the waiting men could just see the old bridge in the distance, and the track leading to it.

"*Oh, hell!*" exclaimed Mark under his breath, as he realised the engine driver would have more chance of seeing the break in the bridge and stopping in time. Unless that train came soon the whole plan would be ruined. All it would do was halt their progress for as long as it took them to put the rails back again—and vengeance would laugh in Mark's face. His heart began to thud as time dragged on, and his vision was so erratic he imagined a dozen trains in the distance where there were none. The morning remained silent as the mist dissolved into no more than a wispy layer, blurring the brilliance of the sun in a clear sky.

Then it was there, a faint rumble in the distance and a singing in the rails that was not a figment of his imagination. He turned his head sharply and signalled to Glukov, who told his men to mount and steady their horses. Mark gripped the steel structure of his own bridge as he fixed his gaze on the distant rails. The mist was only patchy now, leaving whole areas of clear visibility. Suppose the driver stopped in time? Suppose the engine simply derailed on the hastily laid track leaving himself and his Russian friends exposed to machine-gun fire from Kuomintang troops in the trucks? His heart lurched. Suppose . . . oh God, suppose this was *not* a troop train but one full of poor people fleeing from Nanking?

It was too late to do anything. Out of the hazy distance there had appeared the huge, round, black smoke-box, the dark-green fender and scarlet wheels of the engine, its bronze-coloured buffers catching a shaft of sunlight, its funnel belching out smoke in loud, laboured puffs. Clearly, it was hauling a heavy load. It ran into mist, leaving just the rhythmic puffs and the hiss of escaping steam to prove it was still there, then emerged again, startlingly near and already entering the long curve that led to the bridge. It was going well. The driver had worked up a steady speed over a distance of some miles and was plainly loath to slow unless the curve was too sharp.

The morning was now full of puffing, clattering, and thumping as the huge engine advanced toward the bridge with its long, long line of trucks rattling along behind it, full of soldiers crammed tightly inside and even braving the cold on the roofs of the covered ones. The Oriental habit of overcrowding had never been more evident. The faces of the soldiers were quite clear as the train passed—faces beneath the uniform caps of the revolutionary army, faces that moved in mobile expressions as they laughed and talked together, unaware of disaster ahead. The red flag of revolution fluttered from the engine and rear truck—the flag that meant only one thing to Mark at that moment.

Well into the curve now, the train entered another patch of mist. Mark strained his eyes in an attempt to follow its progress, in vain. But it was suddenly out in the open again a mere twenty yards from the bridge and still forging ahead. His heartbeat increased until it seemed to be keeping time with the smoke escaping noisily from the funnel. Fifteen yards . . . ten yards. The air was filled with a terrible screaming sound as the engine was subjected to pressures it could not withstand. Nothing would stop its onward progress now, and the driver jumped from the cab just as the front wheels ran onto the first span of the broken bridge. The engine went roaring out into space before tipping and plunging nose-first into the canal.

What followed was inevitable. The momentum carried each of the trucks on to pile up one after the other in a twisted, tangled, disintegrating mountain of wreckage and screaming men that relentlessly increased until it could take no more, and the last trucks simply crashed into each other and split asunder as they derailed on the bridge approaches. There was a terrifying mixture of splintering wood, shrieking steel and tortured humanity which together made up a sound Mark would never forget. It seemed as if the train were still moving even then, for the ghastly mound in the canal shifted and settled continuously. Water rose in great spouts up over the bank where the boats had once been moored, and steam rose with a deafening hiss over the whole area.

The morning atmosphere of the vast marshland was suddenly split asunder as a tremendous explosion erupted from the canal. Rising above the whole scene appeared a great mushroom of wreckage and bodies tossed up by the force of the disintegrating smoke-box and piled ammunition. Tongues of flame issued from the water itself, and a second explosion had just rocked the ground when the first section of that ill-fated bridge folded up and collapsed beneath the weight of debris crashing down upon it.

A hand fell upon Mark's shoulder. "Come, it is time we rode off."

He thought he knew the man, so he went with him and swung into the saddle of a horse awaiting nearby. But he was icy cold and could not turn his head away from the sight down by the canal. When the others moved off, his horse went, too, racing along the embankment beside the railway track until it branched off onto a dyke leading between paddy fields. Mark let the horse take him, but still his head remained turned in the direction of the canal until the waterway disappeared into the misty distance. They rode at breakneck speed that added to the wildness of his mind. Clinging to the horse as it pounded along beside its fellow beasts, Mark travelled in realms of dangerous darkness as he relived what he had just witnessed. It brought a return of other similar sights in countries far from there.

They left the dyke and swept through a village—a collection of poor mud huts beside a stagnant pond. The mood that was on him possessed him completely until he saw them, one after the other—the bodies of men, women and children sprawled in attitudes of death along the crude track that led from the village and out onto the wild marshland again.

"Ha, my friend, it is a day for vengeance, is it not?" said a voice beside him. "While you slept, my men came here to Lu-Seng. These people will never again tie a man to a bridge and leave him to die."

Mark stared at the man and saw someone from yet another barbarous, alien country. He looked around at his fellow riders: bearded, strong, savage, and ruled by attitudes bred from years of oppression and slaughter in another land as wild and vast as this.

Free of the village the horses raced madly and dangerously along the

narrow dyke through the marshy wilderness. Mark swayed in the saddle as he raced with them, wild warriors of long ago, fleeing from dragons—the red dragons that would now roam over this area.

CHAPTER FOURTEEN

The funerals had been harrowing, but shock had made them seem abstract and unreal. The procession of sympathisers had seemed just as unreal, which had allowed Alexandra to face Dot and Mrs Armitage with the same unemotional politeness she had used toward high-powered diplomats and businessmen.

There had been long bewildering sessions with shareholders' committees and chairmen of boards of directors. The bank manager and family solicitor had wanted documents signed and a multitude of facts to enable them to organise her life until everything was settled. Apart from some bequests to Chinese institutions, charities, and to the household servants who had worked for the Mostyns so well and faithfully throughout their years in China, Alexandra inherited the massive Mostyn fortune, which was to be held in trust until she came of age, or married with the full approval of her trustees. These men had visited her full of kindly sympathy and promises that she would not find them unreasonable. She had not mentioned her unofficial engagement to Mark. It did not seem relevant, somehow, when she was not even sure she would ever see him again.

Tragedy had left her numb. She lived day by day, getting through the long hours by losing herself in her painting. She would neither hope nor despair over Mark. She had learnt that what was meant to happen would happen, and that she was as vulnerable as anyone else. Her belief that tragedy only hit others had been shattered: her faith in optimism lost. For now, she would get through the hours as best she could and leave the future where it belonged.

Surprisingly, out of the vast circle of people she had once considered her friends, it was James Clitheroe whom she welcomed and depended upon at a time when others were turned away by Lai-Hi. He seemed to have grown stronger through the experience, and Alexandra wondered why she had ever laughed at him. Quiet, familiar and intimately concerned with all the business problems that followed the death of so notable a man as Garrard Mostyn, James was her one prop as the numbness wore off and grieving took possession of her. Without him she would have felt completely alone—that girl 'Sandy' who had once believed she held the world on a string.

When she heard voices in the hall one afternoon Alexandra left the sad task of folding all her mother's clothes into boxes, and went to the top of the stairs expecting to find James awaiting her. The visitor was a tall woman in a full-length blue coat with a matching toque on her upswept fair hair. As Marie Drozdova watched her descend the stairs Alexandra felt the shock of her presence there. If the news was bad she must bear it with the dignity shown by the aristocratic Russian.

"Good afternoon," she greeted quietly on reaching the foot of the stairs. "Please come through to the sitting room. Lai-Hi, bring a tray to us."

Leading the way down the shallow steps into the room where a fire brightened the sombre light of the day, Alexandra indicated a settee.

"Please sit down. Tea will be here shortly."

Her guest settled on the large mint-green seat, loosening her coat to reveal a heavy silk blouse and long skirt of serviceable wool. "I read of your sad loss and came with my condolences."

"How kind of you," she replied levelly, knowing it was a polite lie. Sitting in an armchair she realised the skirt of her own dress of cream crushed-velvet was well above her knees and causing disapproval in the other woman. "You clearly wonder why I am not in traditional black. My father would have regarded mourning garb as hypocritical of me. My mother was an exceptional person who never allowed the tragedy of her illness to banish her love of colour and beauty." Her throat began to tighten as she saw again that hole in her mother's temple, and that limp body as her father had struggled across the marsh. "She would not have wished me to dress in funereal black for her, whatever convention decrees."

"Sometimes it is impossible to obey convention," came the grave pronouncement. "My father was torn asunder by crazed workers outside the Winter Palace in 1905. Alexei was killed fighting in the northern forests, where the snows would have quickly covered his body. The two brothers he placed in my charge when he went to war were betrayed, executed, and thrown into a communal grave near Vladivostok. Alexei's wife was shot in a narrow street, and her body was taken off on a cart with others who had been gunned down that morning. They are still in Russia while I am here in exile. I think there is no convention that covers such circumstances, Miss Mostyn."

Realising how truly formidable her adversary would be, Alexandra said with genuine sympathy, "It is terrible enough to lose one's entire family, but to lose them in such manner . . ."

"That is why I presumed to call upon you. I know what it is like when those one loves are murdered by Reds. I felt it created a link between us . . . in addition to the other one."

Lai-Hi arrived with the tea-tray at that point, and Alexandra fitted a cigarette into her holder while the boy poured tea into delicate cups. Smoking always soothed her, and this time the business gave her something to do to cover the necessary silence following that last remark. However, after Lai-Hi had departed, she decided to force the issue.

"Have you any news of Mark?"

The other woman looked up sharply. "No, have you?"

She shook her head. "My father's assistant has tried to find out what is happening down there at Lu-Seng, but it's virtually impossible. Lines of communication are down, and all the Europeans are heading up to Shanghai. Although it hardly seems safe here any longer. We know the Kuomintang has command of the entire rail network through the Yangtze delta, and anyone still down there has to make his way here by some other means. I suppose there is something comforting about being with one's own people when danger threatens, but the tension is growing unbearable. I wish that great army gathered outside Shanghai would attack and end this awful waiting."

"Why do you not leave the city, Miss Mostyn?" asked Marie, drinking her tea gracefully. "There are ships galore taking those who wish to go."

"My father's affairs have yet to be settled," said Alexandra, then took a draw at her cigarette before blowing out smoke slowly. "Why don't you leave, Mrs Roskova?"

Marie's eyes flashed, vivid in her pale face, as she lowered her cup and saucer to the table. "I have reverted to my family name. My husband has been dead for some years."

"So Mark told me."

"I see. What else has he told you?"

"Everything—including the fact that the boy you confronted me with is not your own son, as you meant me to believe."

It took Marie a moment or two to assimilate the implications of that, but she was still very poised as she said, "Mark claims he is not, that is all."

"I believe his claim, Miss Drozdova."

A faint smile touched the strong haughty face. "You are very young, Miss Mostyn, and Mark is not in the least like the men of your set. After several brief meetings you think you know him? I suspect you have been overwhelmed by his adherence to some qualities that have been lost in this modern age. He has a strong sense of responsibility, and a tendency to champion those who are victims of circumstance. Living side by side with him in primitive conditions for many months, it was possible to know him very well. Believe me, under almost impossible stress a man will do many things he may afterward regret or deny."

Unable to control her anger Alexandra stood up and went across to crush out her cigarette in the onyx tray, saying, "Are you implying that he was your lover whilst he also played husband to your sister-in-law? Dear me, I wonder he found the time to fight for your lives, steal a train and cross half Russia with the enemy in hot pursuit." She swung round furiously. "How dare you insult him with such a suggestion after all he did for you!"

Marie rose to challenge her. "You think it an insult to suggest he could find consolation with me?" she asked in biting tones. "What do you imagine he would find with you? You are a child of this bewildered, unstable age, who would give nothing and demand all. Take a long look in any mirror, Miss Mostyn, and you will see what you are—a spoiled darling of a gaudy society. Now you have control of enormous wealth you will squander it on the pleasures that are the mainstay of your existence, until you sink lower and lower into the mire of your selfishness. Is it your wish to take Mark down with you?"

"You begin to sound like my late father," she exclaimed with a brittle laugh. "That means you would never understand my wishes for Mark even if I felt obliged to list them for you." She lit another cigarette with deliberation, giving herself time to think. Then she looked across at the woman on the other side of the room. "So far, I'm not exactly clear what your wishes for Mark can be."

"Are you not? Are you really not? I wish him to be a father to his son."

"We share that wish. I have already told him I will happily rear the boy."

Marie began to laugh. "*You*? You will happily rear the boy? I told you to look in a mirror, Miss Mostyn. You will then understand my mirth." Her face grew serious. "Do you think I would give Michael to any other woman, much less a heedless superficial *girl*? He is my child," she cried in passionate tones. "I have nursed him, defended him, taught him. *He is mine*. I shall never be parted from him. Mark knows that. He knows, and must make his choice when he returns."

Alexandra sat slowly on the edge of a nearby chair as she realised what he had kept back from her at the end of his confession that morning. It kept her silent for some moments, then she looked up. "How cruel you are!"

"*Life* is cruel. My entire family has been taken from me."

"So has mine."

"But you have extreme youth, a wide circle of friends, and great wealth. All I have is Michael. He is a clever child who is sensitive to moods. Right now he is uncertain and confused. Ever since Mark admitted to being his father the boy has been asking that we should all live together now. It is the most sensible answer, you must agree. I am of Mark's generation, and know him intimately. During those months in Russia it was impossible not to discover the basic man he is. I have seen him in every mood. I know his strengths and weaknesses . . . and his passions. I helped to nurse him when he was helpless; to wash his body and dress his wounds. I understand him as you never could. Apart from that, there is no argument against the natural pride of a father for his child. If you could see them together you would admit the undeniable bond."

"Not necessarily," she replied, still quietened by that which Mark had felt unable to tell her. "My father had no pride whatever in his child, and Mark has lived in ignorance of the boy for seven years. Isn't your maternal instinct making too much of several brief meetings between two strangers?"

"Isn't your sexual instinct making too much of virtually the same thing?" came the crushing response. "Mark has always been unsophisticated where women are concerned. He is momentarily dazzled by your novelty, that is all. There is no substance in your relationship to hold it together for long, but a son is a man's son for as long as he lives."

Alexandra stood up again to meet her opponent on equal terms. "What we are really talking about this afternoon is who has the greater claim to Mark, aren't we?"

"Are we?" The Slavic face was full of challenge.

Flinging the cigarette into the fireplace, she said with a feeling of growing desperation, "Our scores are equal on several counts. We are both alone in the world, and we have both suffered from violent attack under wartime conditions. I will allow that my experience in Nanking in no way equalled what you must have suffered seven years ago, but it was enough to qualify for that tendency of Mark's to champion victims of circumstance you mentioned a short while ago." Getting to her point as fast as she could, Alexandra moved restlessly back to the chair and gripped it. "Of course, you have his child, but I can give him others and over a longer period of time than you because I am considerably younger. However, nowhere, absolutely *nowhere* in this conversation this afternoon has there been any account taken of love," she cried. "He is not a fur coat, an antique vase, an old master to be squabbled over; he is a man who has suffered and inherited unhappiness from the past. Don't you think it is more a question of whom he loves than of what we two women want?"

Marie looked back with a dignity that betrayed her past ancestry. "Your 'list of qualifications' is not only insulting, it shows your complete immaturity. There is only one woman Mark will ever love, and she is dead. Whatever he has shown toward you, it cannot be love. You were not there in Russia to see them together, as I did. You did not see him as she walked away to die in those streets he was ordered to leave. You did not see him three weeks ago when I told him how she had died. All these years he has tortured himself by imagining all manner of depravity, hoping, even, that she was still alive so that he could claim her again. When I gave him proof that she really was dead, it was as if it had happened only yesterday. I know love for Katya will always rule him. I know and will accept it. Could you?"

As she stood there before her mature, controlled adversary, those few months she had known Mark seemed to flash before Alexandra's eyes to reveal a whole procession of moments when he had been possessed by his past. She had only to play a Russian song on the piano, and he grew still and distant. She had only to ask what had happened there, and he walked out on her from a restaurant. A woman from that past arrived with his son, and there had been lies and broken meetings. Even when he had asked her to marry him, he had made a full confession including the words: "*You have told me to put it all behind me, but I cannot do that.*"

Marie was picking up her handbag. "I am part of that time he spent with her. I shared the experience. When he is with me it brings her closer. He can speak of her to me and know I will understand. There is no one else left who will listen or care."

It lent a strange emphasis to the statement when Lai-Hi appeared at that moment to announce the arrival of James Clitheroe—the man who had shared her own experience and to whom she now felt closely drawn. In view of this, Alexandra made the necessary introductions in abstracted manner, and was thankful when Marie Drozdova left the house almost immediately.

James followed Alexandra back into the sitting room and looked at her in concern when she asked if he would like a drink.

"Are you all right? You look very pale."

She forced a smile. "Yes, Jimmy, I'm fine."

He turned down the offer of a drink and asked, "Who was that? Russian, wasn't she?"

"Yes. She's an old friend of Mark's. She called to ask if I had any news of him. I told her we still didn't know what has happened down at Lu-Seng."

He drew nearer, his round face troubled. "I'm afraid we do, Alexandra."

It was amazing how calmly she faced what might be coming. "I see. Is he dead?"

He took her arm and led her to a chair, then sat opposite her looking very protective in the uniform he wore constantly these troubled days. Picking up her hand in a gesture of comfort, he said, "The Kuomintang troops have advanced from Nanking and overrun the whole Yangtze area. One of our railway staff members who had recently arrived here on a small steamer says a military train crashed into the canal over an unfinished bridge near Lu-Seng. The death toll was terrible due to the explosion of the ammunition being carried on the train. The entire population of the village was shot or stabbed to death, and the only survivors of the whole affair are some soldiers who have wandered into scattered villages to tell the tale." He pressed her hand. "I'm sorry, dear," he said in an awkward attempt at affection. "So dreadfully sorry."

She stared at him, hearing Marie's last words which had destroyed her hopes with finality. "He'll be happy now," she murmured as if seeing everything clearly for the first time in her life. "He is with her again. That was all he really wanted, to be with her again."

"Major Rawlings, we are now approaching Shanghai."

Mark returned from the corridors of ancient China to see a calm wrinkled face with a beard, smiling gently at him.

"God has been with us," said the missionary. "I trust you will remember to thank him, my boy."

Thinking of Hong's last words as he had walked away on a morning that now seemed so long ago, Mark replied, "It is better to leave some decisions to a greater power, so I have been told."

The elderly churchman nodded. "You certainly did that, from what I could make of your story. I hope you are going to continue that way by getting yourself to a doctor as soon as possible. During these past three days I have consulted the Almighty about you, and He has not let either of us down. But now you are within reach of a hospital I suggest we allow medical science to take over."

At Mark's listless nod, he continued on a serious note. "Young man, you were half dead when we took you up in this boat. If you do not give me your word that you will go straight to an army doctor, I shall take matters into my own hands. Do you wish to surrender your life after having fought so hard for it out on that marshy plain? You are very ill. It does not take a great intelligence to see that."

Mark took his time thinking of an answer. If Alexandra had been killed in Nanking, he was not certain he wanted to continue for another twoscore years—maybe more. The prospect did not seem attractive without her. Drifting away on a tide of thoughts he went over those days—even now he was not certain how many—during which he had been filled with a burning need to reach his own people, to reach civilisation as he knew it, and know he was no longer alone. It was not possible to put things into chronological order, because one day had seemed very like another and he had been ill for some of the time.

For two days he had ridden with the Russians. He had fallen repeatedly from the horse at the end of that first day, and they had wrapped him in rugs, fed him with hot soup from their camp fire, broken his fever with the experience of men from the plains. During the second day they had carried him in a litter, and begged him to continue with them when they reached the village where their routes diverted. But after the night's bivouac he had bidden them a grateful farewell and struck off across the paddy fields toward Shanghai.

The period that had followed had been an echo of days he had known in France. Walking, walking, walking in the knowledge that to stop would mean certain death. Hunger, bitter cold, mud over the tops of his boots . . . fear! Hiding until the sound of marching enemy feet had passed. Stealing food from those who needed it as much as he, sleeping in muddy holes in the ground, vomiting after a meal of raw fish and strange roots.

There had been occasional rides in bullock carts driven by incurious, impassive men in black with plaited saucer hats, and one on an ass that had moved slowly beneath its burden until it collapsed and gave up. Once, he had awoken to find women above him with pitchforks. But it was fear of his uniform, and once they realised he was in no state to attempt rape they had given him rice and a strange hot liquid that had made him so punch-drunk he had staggered boldly off to demand passage in a sampan, careless of who might be in the vicinity.

The sampan had taken him down the narrow tributary to meet a broad waterway. There, the boatman—or woman, he had never discovered which—had given him a gold-toothed grin and said, "Yangtze."

Reaching the great yellow river had not been the piece of good fortune he had initially thought, since steamers full of troops were passing up it. Somehow finding the will to continue he had remained in hiding on the banks, waiting for Chinese barges because they would be safer vessels in which to attempt to reach Shanghai. After successfully travelling in one until it moored some miles down river, he had waited a whole day for another. That time he had been unlucky. Pushing his way beneath the tarpaulins he had found large numbers of Northern troops fleeing from the Kuomintang and in no mood to share the cramped space with a lone stranger. Within minutes Mark had been pushed over the side in mid-river, where he was forced to swim across the choppy, craft-filled waterway in clothes that dragged him down.

It had been at that point that a tiny battered motor-launch almost ran him down, and he had then been hauled aboard in a state of collapse by a man speaking English. He now remembered little of the rest of that day save the sight of the barge from which he had been thrown, drifting aimlessly and on fire, the fleeing troops lying torn and bleeding after a machine-gun attack by their enemies. The vision haunted him almost as much as that of the ropes dangling from his bridge. In his worst moments he could see the body of Mark Rawlings in both those visions.

The English missionary had escaped from a lonely mission outside Nanking. Thanks to the basic medical knowledge of his calling Mark was still alive on the third day, and sufficiently rational to hold a conversation with his saviour. Shanghai was in sight: he had achieved his goal against all odds. Yet he was aware of a strange reluctance to arrive in that city, to find the answer to a question which had tormented him since hearing of the fall of Nanking. The missionary confirmed the story of attacks on the Europeans, but knew no details of casualties.

The journey he had just made had seemed so very long—indeed, Mark felt he had been on a journey of immense magnitude since he was seventeen-and-a-half—and he was tired, utterly tired. So tired he did not want to face the problem of his future. Better by far, to go on drifting in this boat forever, and never see what awaited him on the banks of the river. Perhaps the dragons *had* claimed him. The prospect of roaming that plain with them forevermore was vastly attractive—roaming and looking down on life being played out below, a life that could no longer touch him.

"Major, do I have your word?"

The question surprised him and he frowned. The man had asked that days ago . . . or had it been just now? He looked up from the old cane chair in which he was lying, and saw concern on a face that had the lines of age and frugality upon it.

"When I have discovered what has happened to . . . my friends who were in Nanking, then I'll go to a doctor, I promise. You have done so much for me. I'm deeply grateful."

"You don't sound too certain of that," said the other gently.

Mark looked back at him for a moment, lost in other thoughts. "I . . . don't I?"

Pale eyes smiled into his with perfect understanding. "We all have doubts, my boy, but if you have come this far, it would be pointless not to go on."

Somehow Mark knew he did not refer to his journey from Lu-Seng to Shanghai. He nodded wearily. "Yes, I suppose so."

They ran in to some shallow steps on the waterfront, and the boat was tied up. Mark was frightened by his initial inability to walk, but after an effort managed to get up the steps, and by the time they were stopped by a British armed guard on the jetty he was moving reasonably well.

"Excuse me, sir, but would you mind telling me where you've come from?" challenged the corporal, casting a suspicious eye over Mark's filthy uniform.

"The river," he snapped in reply. Having decided to face what lay on the banks of the river, he now wanted the answer fast. "Is there an officer on duty here?"

"No, sir, just me and another corporal, turn and turn about," came the response to the voice of undoubted authority. "Can I be of help at all?"

Mark glared at the blunt red-cheeked face in the fading light of afternoon, and realised it was good to see such a face after so many Chinese ones. He relaxed and spoke normally. "Perhaps. Where can I get information about the British people who were in Nanking?"

The soldier pursed his lips. "Been away a long time, haven't you, sir? Well, some have gone on to Hong Kong, others are still here. Did you have friends there, sir?"

"Yes."

"Well, there was some casualties, I'm afraid, but most of them got away on the gunboats. A terrible business it was, though."

There was a movement beside him, and the missionary said, "I think Major Rawlings wants to see the casualty list, wherever that may be."

The corporal blinked at the strangely-dressed, bearded man, who could have been Neptune himself. "If they was English I can tell you the names. But I don't remember the Frogs or the Eyeties—I mean, the French or Italians, sir."

"The name is Mostyn."

The man's eyes bulged. "*Mostyn?* Oh, blimey, sir, they was both shot whilst crossing to the boats—him and her, sir."

"*Him?*" queried Mark, confused and upset.

"Garrard Mostyn, sir. It's caused a terrible shindig what with him being such a high-up in Shanghai affairs. It's been in all the papers, with a full report on his life. And his wife was crippled, too. He was trying to carry her to safety when they both got shot by Reds up on the city walls . . . are you all right, sir?" he finished in quick concern.

Mark thought the jetty was rocking, but it must have been those days in the boat which had given him such a weird sensation just then. Through dry lips he managed to ask, "What about their daughter —Miss Mostyn?"

The soldier looked more cheerful. "Oh, she got away safely on the boats, with the people she'd been staying with down there. Come into a tidy fortune, she has . . . but I always say, what's the good of having money if someone has to die before you get it?"

Mark walked away without another word, down the stone jetty with his feet moving automatically as he fixed his eyes on the taxi rank by the gates. His companion forgotten and deserted, he sat in the taxi staring at streets he seemed to have left so very long ago.

Lights were flooding them and there were people everywhere, people like himself who lived in a civilised, straightforward manner, people who were clean and well fed, and who dressed smartly. Men were raising their hats at passing ladies. The women smiled and nodded, elegant in furs and jaunty, close-fitting hats. Their faces were pretty and pink-lipped. Children were walking beside their mothers—children with pale, alert faces, dressed in sailor suits or velvet-collared coats and warm woollen stockings. Military men were saluting each other as they walked smartly along in uniforms with creases down the trousers, and polished buttons that caught the light. An officer was helping a lady from a car, with a hand beneath her elbow in gallant fashion. Two soldiers were going along in a rickshaw and waving cheerfully at two more passing in the opposite direction. Couples were foxtrotting inside a large hotel famous for its tea-dances. The sound of the music floated into the street, reminding him that he had walked away from Alexandra during one of those tea-dances. Would it have been better if he had stayed away? Would it have been better if he had died on that bridge and joined those he had lost long ago?

Leaving the doorman to pay the taxi driver Mark walked into his hotel seeing no one but a tall blonde woman from his past, and a small boy whose looks denied Katya as surely as the truth of her death. The man behind the desk hesitated before handing over the key of one of the best rooms to the creature standing before him, but did so eventually when Mark grabbed his sleeve and demanded it immediately. The lift up to the first floor was empty, and he met no one in the corridor as he made the difficult journey to his room. Once inside the door it seemed cold and hostile. Where was Ah Wu with his cheery smile, warm loyalty and quaint form of friendship? Of course, he was floating in the canal, stiff and bloated, smiling no more.

Catching sight of movement Mark swung round sharply in fear. In the room with him was a tall filthy creature with gaunt face, dull staring eyes with no little wildness in them, and a thick matted beard. Stumbling toward the mirror Mark slowly stretched out his arms. Around his wrists were deep festering scars where he had hung from a bridge while a hundred dragons had decided his fate. Staring at those terrible scars he sunk slowly onto the bed, and put his head into his hands. Next moment, his shoulders began to heave, and the fingers covering his eyes grew wet.

By early evening Mark was ready to go out. He had sent a boy for a razor, hairbrush, toothpaste—all the personal things he had lost with his boat—and he had forced himself to eat a light meal. Then he had telephoned the Mostyn house and told Lai-Hi he would call on Miss Mostyn within half an hour. He had not wanted to speak to Alexandra then. What could he say into a small black telephone horn? Until they met face to face he had no idea how he would need to approach her. The murder of her parents would have shattered her, and the experience of flight from Nanking must surely have left her drastically changed. Until they met in the privacy of her home, he could not analyse the new situation between them. The only thing about which he was absolutely certain was that he wanted to hold her against him for a long, long time, and revel in the fact that she was alive and real. The problems, the difficulties would have to wait.

The man behind the desk recognised him now he had clean clothes and no beard but, as he took Mark's key to hang on the numbered hook, he said, "Major Rawlings, a note was delivered for you a few minutes ago. I was about to send a boy to your room with it."

Mark took it quickly, certain it was from Alexandra to change their rendezvous. After he had read the brief message his brain seemed clearer than it had been for days, his sense of purpose well defined. This was something he understood. There were no mythical beasts tied up in this, just Reds, and he knew exactly how *their* minds worked.

Walking from the hotel he stepped into a taxi, telling the driver to take him to the cement manufacturer where Gregori Petrovich Galinkov worked as a lorry driver. He was the only man in Shanghai who might have some idea where their old and unforgiving enemies would be holding his son hostage, for a sum in excess of that which Mark had refused to pay for the photographs of Alexandra. This time, however, the challenge was more deadly. If Mark did not pay, he knew he would never see Michael alive again—or Marie, who had gone in pursuit of the boy everyone believed was her own. Her maternal deception had put Michael in the greatest danger. The Bolsheviks had vowed to kill every member of the Drozdov family, and counted the boy as such. In fact, he had no blood tie with them.

In a state of cold deadly purpose Mark questioned the men at the cement factory until he was directed to a large shed at the rear, where he was told the Russian was loading his lorry with sacks. In old clothes, with a sack across his shoulders to take the rub, Gregori little resembled a former cavalry officer of the fine regiment which had mutinied, but he still looked strong, fierce and full of inner pride that shone through any humiliation he might feel at what he was forced to do. Catching sight of Mark, he left what he was doing to hurry to him.

"*Mon ami*, you have returned as I knew you would," he cried seizing one of his lacerated hands in a close grip. But the heartiness faded swiftly as he absorbed the words rapped out in economical style, like a military communiqué.

"They have taken Michael and Marie. I had been back no more than four hours, so they acted swiftly. They claim to want a ransom, but we know they will never let them go." He handed the other man the note, as he went on, "They have added my name to their list now, so there is no question of doing as they say and approaching them openly. You must have some idea where they would hide hostages down in the Chinese City, some knowledge of their operational centres."

Gregori looked up then from reading the note, his eyes ablaze with passion. "*Bozhe moy*, we must get them out of there! This very night there is to be an attack on the Chinese City. Chiang Kai-Shek's troops are coming in under cover of darkness to massacre the Reds."

CHAPTER FIFTEEN

Mark had done it before, in France—sailed up a river under cover of darkness unsure of the odds against him, ignorant of the terrain ahead, and knowing it was a race against time that depended solely on him. That wartime mission had been to blow up a vital bridge; this was to save the life of his son and a woman he now realised still had a claim on him. He had promised, seven years ago, to save her from the Reds. That promise still held.

There was less than two hours to go before the attack was due to start. Mark stood in the small boat with Gregori and five of his henchmen, watching the bright lights of the mercantile port slip away as they headed past the short riverfront area of the French Concession, out to the darker stretch where lay the Chinese City with its rabbit-warren of lanes and complexity of hovels. A man could hide out there forever, and never be found. Within ninety-eight minutes that place would be a death trap. The rumours of Chiang Kai-Shek's disenchantment with his Communist brothers had been true, and he was about to make the break with true Oriental savagery. With the aid of the gangs that controlled Shanghai's rich playground of vice, he had planned for his troops to enter the Chinese City overnight and take control from the Communists presently holding it. They were to make that control certain by killing them all.

Officials in the Kuomintang army had passed on the warning to spies in the Chinese City. They had wisely left the area for the International Settlement, and rejoined their fellows with the news of the longed-for revenge. There were some Chinese who refused to leave, preferring to see for themselves every bloody detail of the massacre. These men who lived in the Chinese City knew everything that went on in that festering suburb. It was from one of these men that Gregori hoped to receive information about the whereabouts of a white woman and small boy.

Both men knew this Chinese was their only real hope, yet Mark knew he could never turn around and sail away even if the source of information proved negative. To come upon them by chance would be a million to one, but he would scour that area inch by inch, if necessary, until he found them. The wind had freshened making the water very choppy. The boat danced as it was rowed with difficulty toward a rickety, single-plank jetty in a mud bank. Mark shivered and turned up the collar of his coat. It was a wild night, in every sense of the word.

As a British officer his first duty should have been to inform his own authorities what was planned for tonight. The sounds of battle outside the military barricades might well suggest an all-out attack on the Concessions, but it was possible those in high places had been given a hint of the truth and chose to turn a blind eye. Whatever the case, Mark Rawlings, Royal Engineers, had spent the past few months as a bridge builder, underwater diver, engine driver, chaser of contractors, mediator in Anglo-Chinese quarrels, and political pawn for mercantile diplomats. One more night away from the military demands of his rank would make no difference. Tonight, he was simply a father trying to save the life of his son. The fact that he wore a British army greatcoat was only because it was now the only one he possessed.

Those thoughts were abandoned as the boat neared the bank, and one of Gregori's Russians jumped into the water to wade toward a figure just visible in the darkness. They conversed in Chinese dialect for some while, their voices swelling and fading as the wind took them. Mark watched with tenseness filling his chilled bones, and wondered if the large man so outwardly calm beside him was feeling the same desperate anxiety as himself, waiting for the outcome of that strange nocturnal meeting.

After the initial passion, Gregori had become wholly dedicated to the purpose of the night. Rarely had Mark engaged in any action with a man who so completely partnered him. There was unspoken acknowledgement of command to whoever was most suited to take it. The Russian knew his men and the set-up in Shanghai. Mark was content to let him run this part of their quest, yet knew Gregori would comply with his own decisions when it came to seizing Marie and Michael. At that thought, his anxiety increased. Pray God, they would not be too late!

The Russian was being hauled back into the wildly-rocking boat, and the passive, plate-hatted coolie at the helm set the bows toward open river once more. Dripping wet, the man related what their Chinese ally had said. As he listened, fire ran through Mark's veins to set him aching for action.

A small white boy had been taken to a disused godown on the extremities of the Chinese City just as it was getting dark. A woman had gone there several hours ago. Nothing had been seen of them since.

There were two guards on the door, and across the narrow way was one of the guard-posts of the Communist Militia, where there could be up to thirty armed men eating and sleeping.

Their informant suggested that their only hope was to follow the narrow tributary two miles further on, and attack the godown from the river side. The building stood on stilts in the water and had a broken door which had been used as a loading hatch in better days. If the boat were taken up there, it would be possible to enter the building with the maximum surprise and without alerting the men in the guard-post opposite.

It sounded possible: Mark decided it must be a certainty. Silently he shook hands with Gregori, the gesture being a token of mutual congratulation and an affirmation of comradeship in whatever lay ahead.

Hope ran high, and time became vitally important. Mark had now automatically assumed command of the operation and chafed at the progress of the boat under the sole propulsion of an ancient, puttering engine. The choppiness of the river did much to restrict their speed, and made it necessary to weave between the huge ocean-going junks that rode the river, often without navigation lights to avoid the notice of customs officials and river police. In this part of the Yangtze, away from the giant wharves and light-studded jetties of the main port, all manner of illicit trading and activities were conducted. It was a fool or a very brave man who ventured here during the hours of darkness, when the trade that had made the fortunes of many a taipan was in full swing.

An hour had already passed since they had set off and, even when they entered the tributary, Mark was certain there would be any number of godowns on stilts in the water. They were a common feature of Chinese trade. It would take time to locate the right one, and they now had no longer than three quarters of an hour. He asked sharply if the man could move a bit faster, but the answer came back that the engine might give up altogether if put under further strain. He fell silent, head hunched into his shoulders, as the cold ate into him and his confidence began to wane. It no longer seemed as easy as he had imagined. The bitterly cold wind buffeted him and aroused some confusion in his mind as to where he was. He seemed to be drifting away from his sense of purpose. Taking hold of himself he forced his thoughts back to Michael and Marie, knowing in his heart it was a slim chance that they were still alive, that they were still in the same place, or that he could get them safely out.

He wondered yet again if he should have gone to the authorities, but knew it would have been pointless. Official red tape, the present emergency situation, diplomatic procedures, all would have ruled out instant action. No, he had done the right thing to take matters into his own hands. If he failed to save them, he would not care what disciplinary action the military took against him. If he was killed by the Reds it would not matter to him if tonight's events began a diplomatic row. If he carried it off and returned with them both, he would defend his right to act as he had done, and to hell with the outcome.

Gregori was suddenly beside him. "Bad news, my friend. The boatman says that dead ahead of us lies a sampan colony. It will be necessary to head out to mid-river to get around it. The tributary we need lies just the other side of it, but it will take at least half an hour to get around the sampans."

"*Half an hour!*" Mark swung round to look at the coolie faintly visible in the light of the one swinging lantern. "He's lying. He's a riverman and as fickle as they come," he exploded. "He is working for the Reds."

The Russian put a hand on his arm. "Steady, steady! He is one of our own men. Trust him." His long fingers gripped Mark's forearm. "We must face the fact that there is no way we can get to them before the attack is due to start," he said with quiet sadness. "This godown is on the extremity of the area. We must hope that the attack will not spread that far until after we can arrive."

He answered savagely. "This godown is right opposite a Red guard-post, remember?"

"One must continue to hope."

"I don't," returned Mark in the same mood. "Hope never got me anywhere. The only way we are going to save those two is by getting there quickly . . . and I could *swim* faster than this bloody awful, broken-down vessel."

He did not hear Gregori's reply, or anything else for the next few minutes. His wild words had filled his mind with an even wilder consideration. It was impossible, suicidal in his present weak state. It was a chance that would never come off, a risk so great only a madman would contemplate it. Yet, he had only to think of that small square face gazing up at him, asking him to talk about bridges, he had only to remember Marie telling him gently how Katya and her brothers had died, to push aside all negatives and start thinking fast.

He turned to Gregori. "How far ahead are the sampans?"

"Half a mile. Why?"

"Tell the boatman to keep going as he is," ordered Mark. "I want him to get right up there to those boats and as near the shore as possible."

In the darkness their translator peered from man to man, uncertain who was truly in command at that stage. Mark saw Gregori's hesitation and asked with brisk impatience, "Do you trust me or not?"

There was a fractional pause, then the deep voice said, "The man who took Alexei Drozdov's family to safety and offered his life for them, I would trust with anything."

"Thank you. Then tell the boatman to do what I said."

While this was being done, Mark gave Gregori the explanation he deserved. That ability to think calmly in a crisis which made him a first-class leader, now set him outlining his proposal clearly and concisely to the man he depended upon for help. Facing each other in the cockleshell boat in a biting wind that whistled around their ears, he told Gregori the most important piece of information first, without emotion or bombast.

"I am an extraordinarily good swimmer—I mean really top class, take my word for it. I'm going to have a crack at swimming under those sampans to the tributary. Once there, I'll try to locate the godown where they are held. When I see what the situation is, I'll either get them out and remain in hiding there until you come up with the boat, or I'll create some kind of diversion which will delay action." When Gregori remained silent, he added, "It is a chance which must be taken, and I am best qualified to take it. Not only that, Michael is *my* son."

"And Marie Fedorovna?"

"We were never lovers."

Gregori took in the implications of that comment, but merely said, "You must explain that at a later time, *mon ami*. It is of the greatest importance to me. However, what you propose is very dangerous. You are in no condition to walk far, much less swim. I agree that if it were possible to swim beneath those boats a man could reach them before the fighting breaks out, but I am too familiar with the sight of a man on the brink of complete collapse not to know you have reached that stage. You might be the best swimmer in the world, but right now you will never do it."

"Have you no other objections?" asked Mark harshly.

"A great many . . . but if I voice them will it stop you?"

"No."

Gregori's teeth showed in a wide smile, "The stories I have heard concerning you are undoubtedly true."

"Knowing your countrymen, I'll wager they are not," said Mark unemotionally, all his thought on what he was facing. "If I should not be at the godown when you arrive, you'll carry on without me, of course."

"Of course."

Mark nodded. "Good. We understand each other . . . on every point, I think?"

The other man looked at him through the darkness. "They will both be safe in my hands. You need have no fears for them, I promise."

Making no further response to that enigmatic statement, Mark set about explaining to the others what he was planning to do, and made several requests. Firstly, he was completely unarmed and asked for a knife, which was the most suitable weapon for what he had in mind. A Russian gave him one without hesitation. Then he checked that his own watch was correct with Gregori's. That done he made one appeal to them: that they should do nothing on arrival at the godown until they had checked that he was definitely not there.

"It would be fatal if I was in the midst of a stealthy rescue when you all rushed in alerting the guards," he said crisply. "I know you are all longing to take pot shots at the Reds, but leave that to the Kuomintang, will you? Neither I nor Gregori Petrovich wish to advertise what we are doing tonight. I might be arrested and all of you deported to Siberia, if the truth gets out."

From then on he concentrated on what lay ahead. It was amazing how dense darkness could be in the middle of a river, but he could now see a faint glow ahead from the lanterns hung on the sampans, and realised they were drawing near. Now it was upon him, he viewed the prospect with revulsion. Sampan colonies were best avoided by those who did not live there. Chinese boat-people were very individual, aggressive and suspicious. They lived in huge floating villages in the most primitive conditions and defied strangers to intrude upon their lives.

The boats housed entire families who lived out their lives on the decks. They housed poultry, pigs, and wild dogs that fought each other and defended their owner's boat without discrimination. The sampans formed a complete bobbing carpet on the water which served as dustbin, sewer and graveyard. The garbage from a sampan colony usually floated on the water for several hundred yards beyond its limits, and the water within the colony itself was thick with refuse, filth and occasional rotting carcases. Girl babies were very often dropped over the sides of the boats at birth, the pathetic little corpses drifting for days beneath the boats to appear finally out in mid-river or washed up on the muddy banks. Then there were gang killings, suicides and other gruesome evidence of life at its most elemental level, all to be found in the vicinity of the many clusters of boats that clung along the coast of China.

Sampan colonies could be quite small or could cover enormous areas with hundreds upon hundreds of canopied boats interwoven with planked walkways. Mark's coolie boatman could give him no idea of the size of this one. "Big," he said—which could mean anything. Even so, as they drew nearer and nearer to those pale bobbing lights, Mark looked at them with misgivings. It was true he was a superb swimmer, but he was far better on the surface than under water. If the colony were one of the really large ones he was taking on an enormous task. The need to come up for air frequently would expose him to the danger of being seen by the Chinese, who were liable to do anything from hitting him on the head with a boathook to knifing him. Then there was the danger of losing his bearings completely. Beneath an almost solid spread of boats he could swim for a long time in circles and never find a way out unless he could surface and look for landmarks. He would not let his mind dwell on what that dark water beneath the colony would contain.

As it was, when their boatman cut the engine and doused the lantern to allow a silent, unobserved approach to the sampans, Mark felt his stomach begin to crawl at the thought of what lay ahead of him. A sampan colony never sleeps, and there seemed to be as much clamour and movement as one saw at daytime. He looked out over the never-ending shapes of the hooded boats that appeared distorted as the lanterns threw shifting light over them, and wondered how he would summon the courage to go over the side into the water and dive beneath, never knowing if he would come out again.

Their small vessel surged nearer, and Gregori turned to him in some concern. "You are sure about this, my friend?"

"Not now that I see it," he replied with his usual honesty. "But I still think I must try it. If I fail, you will still do what you can without me. If it comes off, there's a ninety per cent better chance of getting them away."

"All that is true. Good luck, Markov."

His heart jumped at the sound of the name Katya had always used. "Why do you call me that?" he demanded sharply.

Gregori gripped his hand. "That is how you are known among my people—Markov, the engine driver."

Still shaken, he tried to sound lighthearted. "After this, it will be Markov, the merman—I hope."

Wasting no more time he pulled off his boots, the greatcoat and pullovers, then dropped over the side of the boat into the icy black water, thinking of Katya and that last desperate attempt he had made to foil the Reds. Markov, the engine driver. Would she think him as stubborn and foolish to attempt this swim as she had when he took that train off along an unknown track?

"*Spokoinoi nochi*," came a soft call from Gregori in the boat, completing Mark's return to that other time, and he swam away from the dark shadow on the water knowing he was taking this risk as much for those who had gone as for those who were presently in danger. It gave him renewed confidence, banished the revulsion he had felt on first seeing the sampans.

It was immediately apparent that there was a strong current running that night. It dragged him toward mid-river, and he adjusted his crawl to counter it even as he recognised that beneath the surface the pull of a current was less obvious and there was every chance he would drift off course. His best hope, once he was under the boats, was to veer all the time to the right and try to keep in touch with the shore. With this in mind, he headed for the river bank, swimming parallel with the first boats of the colony but out of range of their dim lights.

He was dismayed to discover within a few minutes of entering the water that he felt ready for a rest. He had known he was in a fairly weak state after his escape from Lu-Seng, but fervour had given him false strength whilst he had been with the others. Now, the physical effort of swimming against a strong current seemed to be more than he could manage. Panic seized him momentarily. He stood no chance at all beneath those boats. Why not climb ashore and go overland to the godown? The reason was the same one that had stopped them all from doing it. The Reds were patrolling the shore and all the lanes. No, the only way was by water . . . and the moment had come. His feet had just scraped against rocks, a certain indication that he was as close to the bank as he dare go. It was under the boats now, whether he wanted to or not.

Swallowing his revulsion he swung round toward the nearest sampan and changed to breaststroke as he neared it. From his surface level he looked up at the rotting boat with its woven rattan hood illuminated by a wick in a saucer of grease, which was shaded from the wind by an old tin with a hole cut in it. There were voices shouting at each other, voices that reminded him of the villagers of Lu-Seng as they had tied him to the bridge. It was only as he put up his feet to dive down beneath the boats that it occurred to him that he might very well drown after all. Had the hundred dragons let him go at Lu-Seng only to extract vengeance this way?

He had not guessed it would be so terrifying. There was total blackness and the water around him was full of things that touched and slithered against him. The old claustrophobic fear seized him immediately; his lungs felt near to bursting. Floundering, thrashing about like a novice, he tried to surface and found a solid roof of boat bottoms above his head. The blood began to pound in his temples, and all rational thought flew. All he could think of was the need to get up to the air, and he fought to find a gap in the layer of wood that kept him down: fought like a man possessed. Weakness invaded his limbs. He clawed at the water like a man who had never been at ease in that element.

Suddenly, he was up and gasping in air with great sobbing breaths, clinging to a rope hanging there and shaking with the immense cold. But, with oxygen in his lungs and something to cling to, he grew calmer and more rational. The first thing that struck him was that he had been fortunate in surfacing between two boats which apparently had sleeping occupants, for no faces looked over the sides having been disturbed by his frantic splashing to arrive there. His second deduction was that he was a fool to have started a swim such as this without due thought. He was an expert—why did he not act like one?

Conscious of the minutes passing he took the wise step of regulating his breathing and doing what he should have done before. *Think*, he told himself. Think like a man who is perfectly capable of making this swim, not like a child who has just lost his water wings. So he did just that as he clung to the rope with two wooden hulls shifting on the surface each side of his head and threatening to crush it between them.

The boats were all roughly the same size, so there would be gaps like the one he had found where the prows and sterns all met. Due to the movement of the water the boats shifted, altering the width of the gaps, but they *were* there at fairly regular intervals, and all he had to do was form a pattern of the number of strokes between each intake of air. After one or two attempts it should be possible to gauge his need to breathe to correspond with the gaps, then progress steadily and with confidence. As for the things in the water that brushed against him, he must either shut his mind to what they might be, or dive deeper to avoid them. His third fear, that he might lose his way and be swimming forever beneath the floating village must be banished from his mind completely. It was a defeatist attitude, and Mark Rawlings was a fighter. As for the facts that he was already frozen and exhausted . . . !

"I am an extraordinarily good swimmer," he had told Gregori, so it was time he set about proving it. Taking a deep breath he released the rope and sunk beneath the surface once more. He counted twenty strokes, then tried to surface, but he had to search awhile for the right place. This time, he came up gently, which was just as well since voices were clear just above the gunwale of the boat on his left. He took in air and went down again.

After several more attempts he found it was possible to do as he had imagined, and regulated his progress so that he had a regular supply of air with the minimum number of halts. Often the 'breathing holes', as he came to think of them, were indicated by a faint lightening of the water where lanterns or candlelight threw reflections. So that part of the business had been conquered. It was not so easy to ignore the floating rubbish, however, and since he would not use up time by diving deeper, he found it increasingly unpleasant as slimy objects dragged across his face or clung to his legs. It took a strong dose of willpower not to start imagining what they might be.

It did not help when he came up once eye to eye with a child about to empty a bowl of rubbish on him. He sincerely hoped the fright the child received at seeing a white face appear from under the sea would take away any inclination to do what he had intended doing. It did, but the child let out such a cry, Mark had to submerge again swiftly before taking in adequate air.

All the time he worried about where he was. He seemed to have been swimming for a long, long while, and still the boats lay above him. Bearing all the time to the right he began to wonder if he was swimming in circles and would never emerge on the far side of the colony. He tried not to admit that he was getting slower, that his arms and legs were moving sluggishly, that the cold was making him numb to the point of losing all sense of progress. He was a superb swimmer when fit. The task he had set himself was demanding more than he was capable of giving, at the moment.

Time passed, and still the boats were there above him. Lethargy was winning the battle, and he began to wonder why he was there at all. His head felt as if it was being squeezed in a clamp. His pulse began to thud throughout his body, and the need to go up for air did not seem as urgent, all of a sudden. He was in a diving suit under the bridge, wasn't he? Ah Wu would be working the air pump. He need not go up to breathe.

Then, he was caught, wrapped around by something that held him down and grew heavier and heavier. He struggled, but was caught even more firmly as he was borne inexorably downward.

The dreamy sense of unreality vanished, the sensation of swimming forever in a misty underworld had gone. As he fought, sharpness of thought returned and, with it, a reserve of energy. It was a fishing net that was taking him down to the river bed, but that fact also told him that he must now be free of the sampans and out in the open river, and it made him come alive and alert in a flash. Fumbling for the knife stuck in his belt, he dragged it out and began blindly hacking at the entangling threads around his ankles, knowing that he must free himself before lack of oxygen and water pressure rendered him unconscious. Time, time, time! Every minute was vital. If there was open river above him, the tributary must be there . . . and up that tributary were Marie and Michael.

In hacking at the net he slashed the side of his right calf and felt a sharp pain from the cut. But that foot was now free and he continued to attack the next, wielding the knife in the total darkness of the icy water. Recognising the danger signals in his chest and head, Mark thrust desperately at the mesh around his left foot, kicking wildly at the weighted cords.

It stubbornly clung in a tangle that would not fall away and, only when the pain in his chest grew too great to withstand, did he succumb to the inevitable. But the last great effort he had made must have done the trick, for the next thing he knew he was bobbing up into a world of darkness that heaved up and down on the swell of waves, and as he rose on the crest of each one, he saw the clustered lights of the sampans behind him.

Unable to do more than just float on his back while the pain in head and chest slowly diminished in the fresh air, he found himself almost laughing with relief. He had done it! He had swum beneath that blockade of boats and come up just where he had hoped he would. He *was* a bloody merman!

The congratulations did not last long. He was drifting away from the shore, away from the tributary. Rolling over he began a slow crawl against the pull of the current. Exhausted though he was, it was easy swimming after the underwater session he had been through. Within a few minutes he had settled into a steady pace that his natural skill enabled even a weakened man to maintain.

Fifteen minutes had passed whilst he had been beneath the boat colony, and there was no way of knowing how far up the tributary the godown was located. Mark prayed it would be near the mouth because he was not certain how long he could keep up the progress he was now making. Even a born fighter knew when he was on a losing streak. But it was much easier once inside the tributary. It was narrow and deep, but the pull against the current was greatly diminished. In fact, it was so still and quiet, Mark was certain the faintest splash could be heard from the banks. There were occasional boats moored, but they appeared to be strangely deserted, as if the owners knew what was to happen there very shortly.

The old godowns, of which there were many, stood on stilts in the water to enable boats to moor against them. It suggested to Mark that there was only a deep channel through the centre of shelved banks. He made a note of the fact. It might be possible to hide beneath the godown in the shallow water until Gregori came up with the boat. Some of the old storehouses he passed by without stopping, for they were no more than a pile of rotting timbers that would collapse in a strong wind. But by others he lingered, clinging to the stilts and listening for any sounds from above. The whole area seemed empty of people.

When he rounded a bend in the river there was no doubt that he had found his goal. Up on the right bank was a scattering of lights indicating some kind of thoroughfare, and the riverside buildings were sturdier in a stretch where the tributary widened. Plainly the first reaches had silted up, and trade had been moved accordingly. The Chinese did not dredge: they adapted to circumstances.

It could not have been easier. There was only one godown where light shone through the splintered wood, and it was from that direction that the sound of voices reached Mark. The soldiers changing guard? His arms and legs had grown so heavy he could hardly move them at will, and he swam wearily to the stilts asking himself how he expected to achieve anything now that he was there. He had lost the knife during the struggle to free himself of the fishing net, and it seemed ludicrous for one unarmed, exhausted man to attempt a rescue from beneath the guard of an uncertain number who would certainly have weapons of some kind.

He dragged himself from the water to stand on the cross-spars of the stilts, turning his mind quickly from an instant memory of being tied, arms above his head, to that bridge at Lu-Seng. He could see how simple it might have been to bring up a boat containing half-a-dozen armed men who could burst in and take out a woman and a child without much difficulty. He wondered momentarily if it would be better to wait for the others, then realised that the planned attack was due to begin in six minutes. He had experienced surprise night attack: it was uncontrolled and bloody. Men shot their own comrades by mistake, killed those attempting to surrender, went in fear every step of the way. When such an attack was between men of the same race and supposed allies, the resultant chaos would be even worse. A woman with a child would stand no chance in that. No, he could not afford to wait for the others. With that in mind he seized a spar above his head and began to climb up toward the broken loading-door on the river side of the godown. His sodden shirt and trousers weighed him down, and he had to dash his hand over his eyes to clear the water that ran from his hair.

Now he could hear voices, one of them Marie's, speaking in an angry Russian interchange. Thank God she was still alive. Translating their conversation gave him information that there were several men in the place with her. Then, as he pulled himself up over the ledge of the godown floor, he heard another voice, and recognised it with a rush of renewed anger. Lionel Armitage was being forced to play a deeper game than he had ever imagined when he had embarked on a liaison with men he did not understand.

Standing on the narrow ledge that ran all round the wooden shack Mark looked through one of the many cracks in the wall. The scene aroused mixed emotions—relief that Michael and Marie were quite unharmed physically, but dismay at the sight of three Russians armed with revolvers, and two Chinese with the red armbands of the Communist Militia standing at the open door with rifles. Beyond them he could see a little of the rough track outside and the lights on the pitted facade of the wooden building opposite, which he guessed was the guard-post. He was totally outnumbered, which meant his only hope was to wait for the attack to begin, then act instantly in the subsequent confusion. The one advantage he had was that he was the only man amongst them who was expecting it and would be able to think straight when all hell broke loose.

Knowing all attention would be drawn to the guard-post, he would have to attempt an escape into the river. Normally he would be perfectly capable of supporting a woman and a child in the water for a considerable time, but his strength had suffered drastically from that swim and he had just discovered he was losing a lot of blood from the gash he had inflicted on his right leg with the knife. All in all, he was not much of a rescue party. Clinging to the wooden wall he watched the scene being played out inside, burning to burst in and snatch up the pale-faced, frightened little boy in the corner before he was terrified by the imminent all-out attack. Suppose a stray bullet should find him, as it had found his mother? There would be nothing left of Katya, or a love that had risen above the horror all around them during that distant summer.

His gaze moved to Marie, holding the boy against her side for protection and full of ashen-faced courage as she faced those she considered as no more than peasants, still, as they recited a list of her supposed crimes against the Soviets. The pointless ritual merely salved their consciences when they finally executed their victims.

"I am a Drozdov," she was saying with passion, "and nothing you can do will ever alter the fact. By killing my young brothers you made them into martyrs and heroes of all free Russians. You have not the intelligence to see that it is greater to die for one's country than to kill for it. You are peasants, and will remain so. If you kill me and my son, the name Drozdov will become a legend. An entire family to die for a great cause! A defenceless woman lured to a hovel in a filthy backstreet by the kidnap of her son. One female and a small boy challenged by three men with guns and their Oriental allies with rifles. How mighty are the liberators of the Russian people!" she sneered. "After seven years you are still afraid of one Drozdov! You are nothing. You will always be *nothing*," she spat at them.

One of the men stepped forward and dealt her a resounding slap across the cheek, yet even as Mark felt himself moving forward she retaliated. Her slap was equally vicious and left as red a mark on her assailant's face as there was on hers. He looked stunned as she cried, "*Merzavets!* Keep thy hands off me," in the old Tsarist style of speech to underlings.

Lionel, standing back with a sheaf of papers in his hand, stepped forward at that point and said, in English, "It was my understanding that we brought them here to force Rawlings to give money to the revolutionary cause, and to get from her the list of names of those led by Galinkov. Hitting her is not only undignified, it is getting us nowhere."

One Russian rounded on him. "She will not give us the names until the child has been released, she vows."

"Then release him," shouted Lionel betraying his nervousness. "I have been standing here for three hours while you've been conducting negotiations in a language I don't understand. If that is her condition for betraying her countrymen, then for God's sake comply with it. That poor little blighter looks terrified and probably hasn't eaten for hours. Give him to me to take back to Shanghai, then this whole distasteful business can be over and done with."

The second Russian glared at him. "You are a fool who has no notion of the meaning of revolution." Pointing to Michael hunched now on a box in the corner, he went on, "You are the same as him, with wits to match. The Drozdov woman has more spirit than you." He swung the butt of his revolver to thud against the side of Lionel's head, which sent the slimly-built young banker staggering backward to fall against the far wall.

Turning back to Marie, the man broke into Russian again. "You will give us those names or we shall throw the boy into the river."

"If my son is harmed I shall never give you the names," she cried passionately. "I told you that right at the start. Only when I have proof that he is safely with his father in Shanghai will I consider your demands." The first hint of fear crept into her voice as she began to plead with him. "Release the boy. He has done nothing to you or your vile regime."

"He is a Drozdov."

"No . . . no, he is not," came her low-voiced confession. "His mother is dead."

Just as Mark told himself she had gained nothing by telling the truth, since Katya's family had been as much enemies of the Bolsheviks as her own, he heard with astonishment her next statement.

"The woman was shot by White Russian soldiers as she fought for food at the market. They left the child she carried in her arms to die, there in the street. I am a woman. To me a child is innocent of all sin. I picked the boy up and kept him as my own."

The man before her sneered. "Was this Rawlings a stud stallion that he fathered children of peasant women of the revolution whilst he also served two high-bred mares of the Tsar as he crossed the country? He is an enemy of the people, and he is the undoubted father of this child. It does not matter who the mother is."

Desperate now, Marie cried, "Yes, he is the father! That makes this child a British national. Harm him, and you will have the British government in full cry . . . a vastly different prospect from that of a defeated exiled regime. *Think*," she urged with heat. "What can you possibly gain from taking the life of this boy . . . and what can you *lose*? Release him. He cannot help your cause, but he can harm it considerably if his people turn against you. They have only very reluctantly acknowledged your existence. It would take very little to persuade them you are, indeed, the uncouth peasants they believed you to be when they fought on our side seven years ago.

The man laughed boisterously. "The small boy of one Englishman! You think they would take issue with us over one soldier's bastard?"

Mark heard that with such a rush of anger he was hard put to control the urge to reveal his presence there and then yet, even as he forced himself to stay silent, he knew why Marie would never hand the child over to Alexandra. She would give her life for Michael, just as he was preparing to do.

"Bastard or not, the father is not merely a soldier. He is a hero of the war against our common enemy, Germany. He has friends in high places, and is pledged to marry the Mostyn heiress." She turned to Lionel, breaking into English. "Take my son to Alexandra Mostyn. She will pay whatever you ask, and will keep him safe."

Lionel, holding his handkerchief to his bleeding temple, looked at the man who had clubbed him. "What do you say?" he asked in a voice that had grown higher and more nervous than ever. "Miss Mostyn will pay more than Rawlings. He hasn't a bean of his own . . . and the little chap will be safely out of all this. I swear I'll return with the money as soon as . . ."

"Shut up!" ordered the third Russian. "You are here to do as you are told, without question."

"Yes, but . . ."

"When they tell you to kill the boy after getting the money, will you do it?" cried Marie. "Did you really not know that was what they had planned when you took him as he returned from school? Do you think this is all an exciting game? They are right, you have no notion what revolution is and how long reprisals continue because they are afraid of those they have overthrown."

The Englishman had a greyish tinge to his face by now, and tried to summon up bravado by strutting over to her. Mark well remembered him on the ship from Hong Kong, and knew the youngster finally realised his bombast had been no more than hot air.

"I understood all this was merely to gain money for their cause and to stamp out a group of reactionaries in Shanghai. I don't know half of what has been going on here, but I think it has been going on too long. Someone has to make a decision," he declared in wobbly tones. "I'm taking this boy back where he belongs. What you do after that is not my affair. I shall have fulfilled my part of the whole business."

By way of reply, the third Russian raised his revolver and pulled the trigger. At point-blank range death was immediate, and Lionel's body fell at Marie's feet. She had seen death too often to be affected, but Michael began to scream with terror. The first Russian snatched him up to silence him, and Marie flew at him like a tigress defending her young, seizing the child and thrusting him behind her for protection. She had forgotten the third man was there. He tucked the boy under his arm, holding his revolver to his head as a warning.

Marie was now acting instinctively, her calmness flown in the face of Michael's danger. The whole situation had grown explosive and unpredictable as she grappled with one of the men holding her back. Mark looked desperately at his watch and realised the expected attack had not begun at the appointed hour. He could wait no longer, and did the only thing he could.

"Everyone stand perfectly still," he ordered in Russian, moving to stand at the broken loading-door so that his head and shoulders were visible to those inside. "I will shoot the first person who moves," he added sharply.

The unexpectedness of his appearance in so unlikely a place halted each one in the old store, as they stared at him in various degrees of shock. Mark knew it would not last for long.

"Marie, come over here," he said, willing her to obey his orders implicitly, as she had finally done seven years before, after initial resistance to him.

He had forgotten that she was now a mother, and she made the fatal mistake of putting emotion first. Rushing for Michael, she was seized by one of the men, who held her against him, pointing out to Mark that he could only shoot one of them before the other two killed him and their helpless prisoners. His advantage entirely lost, Mark reverted to desperate means.

"I will strike a bargain with you," he said. "My life for their freedom. Surely Mark Rawlings committed more crimes against your revolutionaries seven years ago than this woman and a small boy who was not even there." Wondering frantically what had happened to delay the planned attack, he added quickly, "I have also recently caused the deaths of a great number of your Chinese allies by sending their train into a canal. I'm still fighting against your cause. I shall continue to do so all the time I live." Unsure how much longer they would believe he held a gun behind that broken door, Mark looked at the face of his son whose dark eyes were fixed on him with burning, fevered hope. When he looked at Marie she revealed that same hope in her eyes. Dear God, what could he do?

"I have a boat waiting," he said then, with the bold pretence that he held all the aces. "Let them both come over here to me. Once they are safely away I'll throw in my gun, and you can read out *my* list of crimes against the People's Republic."

It was no bargain, and they knew it, but his bluff was never called because there was the sudden deafening rattle of rifle fire mixed with the unmistakable cries of battle outside in the lane. As the only person there who had been expecting it, Mark acted with speed and purpose.

Kicking in the flimsy door he ran to Marie shouting, "Get out to the river. There's a boat coming!"

Then he went on past her to the man still holding Michael under his arm, although with his revolver now pointing in the direction of the lane outside. Caught between two unexpected situations, he went over beneath Mark's assault, losing his hold on the boy as well as the gun, which slid across the floor. Staggering to retain his balance, Mark seized Michael's arm and, protecting him with his own body, rushed with him to the large gap where the door had been. Two steps from it there was a loud stutter of machine-gun fire and Mark felt two thumps in his right thigh. No longer able to stay upright he fell forward with his face only inches from the projecting edge of the godown floor. With his right cheek pressed hard against the wood he could just see Marie already on the outer ledge, clutching Michael to her.

"Get below," he gasped through the pain every breath brought. "Gregori has . . . a boat. Go. *Go!*" he commanded. "It should be here at any moment . . . down below this place. Take the boy away from here."

"Mark . . ." she began, then turned and urged Michael along the same narrow ledge he had used until they were out of his sight.

He rolled his head around to look out beyond the street door where the three Russians lay dead, also shot by the Chinese who had no wish to be taken over by a new set of 'foreign devils'. The two guards were sprawled at the entrance, stabbed to death by their own bayonets which had been thrown contemptuously beside them by those who had their own ideas on liberating the coolie.

The air was full of screams and shouts of triumph as Nationalist killed Communist, with all the sectarian, geographical, and linguistic prejudices adding savagery to the racial barbarity. Across the road, the guard-post had been set on fire with the soldiers all locked inside. Mark could hear their shrieks and saw human torches leaping from windows to their death. The red flare of the fire lit the inside of the godown and touched on the body of Lionel Armitage, that youngster who had said on the ship from Hong Kong that sometimes revolution was the only way. His killer had been right to say Lionel had no idea what revolution was. The blond socialite who had partnered Alexandra in a mad table-top dance had been betrayed by those whom he found he could not, after all, serve in the total manner they demanded.

Then it was that Mark realised the fire had spread across the road to catch the roof of the godown, and the red flare was no longer a mere reflection. He thought of those two clinging to the stilts down below and knew they would be caught in the flames before long. Gripping the edges of the hatchway he pulled himself slowly forward until he was hanging headfirst over the ledge with the water below already gleaming with the bronze of fire. The wounds in his limbs were creating agony, and it was no longer possible to move his right leg at will. Yet he *had* to get into the river, and gave the extra pull on the last handhold of the wooden building before dropping like a stone to hit the surface with a smack that seemed to break his body apart. The shock of cold water kept his brain alert, and he called to Marie to get into the river before the roof of the godown, which was well ablaze by now, fell down upon them. He could see her, clutching Michael against her, outlined by the reddish light that now illuminated the tributary.

"Come on . . . *jump*!" he gasped, keeping afloat through sheer natural skill.

They leapt together and vanished beneath the surface. He got to them somehow by the time they came up spluttering, and they both clung to him, supported by his iron determination and strong arms that could conquer the water as they saw the godown crumble and fall into the river with a loud hiss and a cloud of smoke.

Mark knew he could not hold them for long, and decided to head for the opposite bank a matter of yards away. Marie did her best to flounder along with his help, but he held tightly to his son as he turned onto his back to propel himself to the shore. Michael had grown rigid with the shock of all he had been through, and Mark was saddened by the thought that the boy looked destined for a life as full of violence and disillusion as his own had been. Not yet seven, and he was experiencing revolution. Not yet seven, and he was realising what it meant to have Russian blood in his veins. He clutched the little drenched body against him, as he realised it was all starting again. There had been happiness, like a bright shaft of sunlight breaking through black clouds, but all there would ever be for Mark Rawlings was battle and blood and fire . . . and pain. Every limb, every inch of his body was afire with it now, yet he knew he had to go on, on, on. There would never be peace, freedom; not for him.

Reaching a shelving, silted bank he dragged himself and those with him onto it and up to the dyke running along the top. He could not think why it was so important to be there, and there was a terrible red glow of fire everywhere. Staccato rifle-shots sounded nearby. No, it must be firecrackers, of course, to celebrate the New Year. He had been caught out like that before. It was New Year, and there was a lovely girl with red hair promising him a life without pain and fear. Now she was dead; they had raped and killed her in Nanking . . . or was it Vladivostok? There was a woman beside him sobbing. He had crawled for hours from the carnage of that train, and she would make him her husband and look after him. If only she would stop crying! Something that felt like a tiny hand was stroking his face, yet it brought him no comfort from the agony growing within him.

In the midst of trying to remember whether they were in Ypres or had moved on during the night, he heard deep voices all around him speaking in Russian. They had come to untie him from the bridge. He knew it was too late; they could not save him now. The hundred dragons had wanted a third Englishman to die in the water, and they would have their way. He would go with them to where all those he had lost were waiting. *She* would be there, although he could no longer recall her name.

CHAPTER SIXTEEN

The massacre of over two hundred Communists in Shanghai by the secret design of Chiang Kai-Shek was only the start of the purification of the revolutionary army to solely Nationalist policies. The purge spread all over China, where Soviet adherents were murdered, Russian Communist strongholds attacked, and those advisers from China's vast neighbour, who had sought to extend its frontiers, fled back to Moscow. The greatest merger ever planned had failed: China adhered to its unbroken policy of resisting 'foreign devils' whoever they might be.

The Western world was astonished, but relieved. That 'evil Communist Chiang Kai-Shek" was turning out to be not such a bad fellow, after all. A united Russo-Chinese landmass in the East would have been disastrous, but the Chinese revolutionary leader had upset the Russians so badly there was little chance of it ever happening. The Western powers were prepared to grant concessions and give a little ground to the man who had shown such good sense.

Shanghai was left an open port. The foreign concessions were never attacked by the Kuomintang army which left the Yangtze delta and swept north. There was a great deal of speculation, naturally. Rumour had it that large sums of money were handed over to Chiang Kai-Shek by wealthy Chinese and foreign merchants to ensure the safety of the port. It was also said that the man known as 'The Green Dragon' who controlled all the gangs, the vice and illicit trading, the clubs and brothels in Shanghai, had pledged his vast network of thugs to work in Chiang Kai-Shek's interests whenever called upon, in return for a blind eye turned toward those things condemned by Nationalist aims. Whatever the truth, life in Shanghai continued as it had done before the emergency.

Many people argued that Chiang Kai-Shek knew on which side his bread was buttered, and could not afford to lose the trade with the rest of the world while his country was still so deperately poor. For that reason he had bypassed Shanghai in his conquest of China. But the question to which no one knew the answer was whether the Kuomintang would have attempted to overrun and take the

Concessions if that vast force of the world's best fighting troops had not been sent out to defend it. In this instance, had a bloodless victory been won by quick thinking and the formidable reputation of those pale-faced men who had been rushed to Shanghai from their homelands? If the Chinese General knew, he remained inscrutable on the subject.

The emergency seemed to be over, but it had taught a strong lesson. Plans were made to establish a permanent garrison in the area. The history of China being what it was, there was no guarantee that friend Chiang Kai-Shek would remain in power for long.

The incident at Nanking began to fade in the minds of all except those who had been there. It had been perpetrated by Communists set on discrediting the Nationalists and their leader in the eyes of the West. It had been a small band of violent anti-foreign agitators. It had been local ruffians bent on revenge. All kinds of excuses were forthcoming, and a diplomatic exchange of official regrets seemed the best way of ending the matter, under the new circumstances. Once more, barbarity and the violation of treaties and promises were tolerated for the sake of the vital trade and political dabblings in a country renowned for duplicity.

Another incident that created interest for a day or two was the terrible accident near the village of Lu-Seng. Stories gradually reached Shanghai of how a troop train had taken a branch line to reach the northern extremities of the port, unaware that it was not open to trains. Details of the first accident only four months before were reported in the newspapers, together with the fact that the new bridge had had to be re-sited further up the canal due to Chinese superstitions of *fung shui*. This would seem to be borne out now. From what could be deduced, local Nationalist sympathisers had reported the new bridge completely rebuilt, but had failed to inform their comrades that the track had not been re-laid. In consequence, the train had run straight onto the broken first bridge in the thick mist and resulted in one of the worst accidents recorded on the line in that area.

Reports went on to state that the young British army engineer who had been in charge of the rebuilding of the bridge had been captured by Chinese soldiers, brutalised, and left for dead, whilst his assistant engineer, a Scot who had spent most of his life amongst the Chinese people, had also been killed when retreating soldiers took, at gun point, all the boats and equipment, leaving twenty dead coolies in the canal.

Major Mark Rawlings had made an amazing solo journey on foot from Lu-Seng to Shanghai, where he had finally collapsed. He was now very ill in a temporary military hospital set up during the emergency. He was, as yet, unable to give the full story of what had happened at the bridge, or of the long journey he had made with two machine-gun bullets in his leg. Doctors said his condition was critical, but only to be expected, in the circumstances.

The story was talked about in Shanghai clubs and hotels for several days, then forgotten. Hardly anyone in the city knew this Major Rawlings, and he was just another casualty of the whole peculiar business of what was really going on in China at the moment. Besides, he was a soldier and must expect to be shot at and beaten up. What was more shocking and titillating were the stories of church missions being burnt to the ground and nuns being raped. That really set the cloche hats quivering over the teacups—that, and the juicy scandal in the Armitage family.

Young Lionel had been found shot, together with three Soviet Russians, down in the Chinese City beside a guard-post of the Red militia. He had always been known as a socialist with peculiar notions about the working classes that did not equate with his own style of living. Now, it appeared he had been some kind of Communist and—the word was whispered behind gloved hands—a *traitor*. Everyone in Shanghai now knew that an investigation was already being conducted into his activities at the time of his death, and the truth was gradually coming out. The members of his clubs now recalled incidents to his discredit. An accusation of cheating at bridge, which had been disproved at the time, now seemed more likely to have been true. Tardy payment of subscriptions, rather paltry donations to gifts for retiring members, and some scathing remarks at the annual dinner were seen in a new light with this revelation. The bank was looking into various transactions he had handled with Russian merchants. Mrs Armitage and Dot were known to be returning to England. It was only servants' gossip, for no one had called on them since the news broke, but a senior clerk at one of the large shipping offices had confirmed that passages were booked on a future sailing. All in all, Shanghai society thought it the best thing. Mrs Armitage was a nice enough woman, but the girl Dot had always been completely brainless. People began to speculate on the possibility of eccentricity in the family. *Eccentricity* was the kinder word, in view of the fact that poor Cecelia Armitage had just buried her son barely two years after her husband.

There was only brief reference to the fact that it had been widely believed that Lionel Armitage would make a match with the Mostyn girl the minute she came of age, for the topic was of small interest now. The escapades of that pair, which had once shocked them all, had been forgotten in the light of greater events, and even apprehension about the future of the Mostyn heiress had died. In the hands of capable directors confidence in Mostyn projects had been mainly restored. The girl herself was rarely seen, these days.

The story that would really have set Shanghai by the ears was unlikely ever to be told. Mark had been in a state of utter collapse when the military authorities had been called out to a place on the outskirts of the Settlement that housed a group of White Russian refugees. They said they had found the Englishman wandering in a daze and had taken him inside, where he collapsed. He had lost blood from a deep cut on his right calf and appeared to have two bullets lodged in his thigh, so they sent for help.

He was on the danger list for two weeks, showing neither signs of sinking nor of improving. Then, at last, his system showed some response to treatment and the wounds began to heal. Unfortunately, he fell an almost immediate victim to fever which pulled him down again and took a long time to break; but the doctors were extremely worried about the state of his mind, even when he made physical improvement. He seemed to wander continuously in nightmares and fantasies, either babbling a lot of nonsense about dragons, and dogs with no heads, or staring at the ceiling lost in a world he did not want to share.

A military doctor of vast experience was called in from Hong Kong, and he recognised symptoms very similar to those of shell-shock cases he had treated during the war. Enquiries were made into the patient's record, and it appeared he was a war hero with an unusually complex set of experiences behind him. It was then they realised he was the man who had been out at Lu-Seng building a bridge, and tried to guess at what he had been through before he had collapsed in Shanghai. The receptionist at the hotel had stated that Major Rawlings had simply turned up late one afternoon in a filthy state, sent for toilet articles, then gone out again taking no notice of anyone and with a very odd expression on his face.

Whatever the truth, there was no doubt in medical minds that the young officer was dangerously near a complete mental breakdown. In his fits of delirium he muttered an endless mixture of names, speaking in French and Russian as well as English. A linguist was called in to translate, but none of it made much sense to anyone. A notable German psychiatrist resident in Shanghai was consulted, but he could only conclude that Major Rawlings appeared to be seeking an identity. He was unable to say how long it would take, and whether he would ever emerge from the strange world in which he presently wandered. He added that no matter a man's strength and personality, he could only take so much, and their patient appeared to have experienced more in his thirty years than most normal people could endure.

The staff caring for him solved the mystery of some of the names he cried during his most fevered spells. Marie was the woman who constantly called at the hospital to enquire after him. Michael was her young son. When the army doctor asked her into his office one day when she called, she was able to throw light on some of the other names. Katya had been her sister-in-law; Konrad and Volodya her brothers. When she related the full story of what had happened in 1919, the medical man began to realise the extent of the complexity of his patient's former life. When he set eyes on the boy Michael, he began pondering even harder on the past of the man who might never have a future.

Marie could not throw any light on Mark's obsession with dragons, and the military machine began making enquiries into whether Major Rawlings had been 'chasing the dragon'—smoking opium. He had a reputation as a hard drinker, but there was nothing to suggest he took quantities of the drug of the East. His other source of great fear—the Reds—was more easily explainable, especially after Marie told of that summer in Russia. It also seemed possible he had suffered some kind of torture by Communists recently, for there were festering scars around his wrists and ankles which were conducive with the bite of ropes tied very tightly.

The true state of his health was kept from the press, who sought a story from the man who had made such a journey from the site of the disaster bridge. Whilst the army would have been only too happy to have a wounded hero praised to the skies in the newspapers, a man cracking under mental strain was no credit to the military, or the British image abroad.

Suddenly, there was a dramatic change in him. The dragons were forgotten, and instead it was a lion that made him extremely agitated—a lion and a man called Alex, for whom he kept calling. The experts were further baffled. They could find no trace of a man called Alex in his past, nor any connection with lions. He worsened, and they decided a risk must be taken in a bid to save his sanity. Four weeks after he had entered the hospital they allowed Marie into his room, warning her she might find him confused, listless and even hostile. They instructed her to ask no questions about what he had been doing, but to chat about everyday things in the hope that he might volunteer confidences to her he would not make to hospital staff or strangers. A doctor stood just outside, ready to tend an emergency and listening to what was said.

Mark looked at her with a frown. She had not been there a moment ago, he was certain. He knew her, but could not remember her name. Because of that, he said nothing, just stared at her thinking how sad she looked. Everyone looked sad. He was not surprised, really. Sitting on the chair beside the bed, the woman put her hand over his as it lay on the coverlet.

"I have come every day," she told him, "but they would not let me see you."

Did he look terrible, he wondered. Had they dropped him from that tripod, after all? Could he have been bounced into pulp and still lived?

"I brought some flowers," the woman went on. "The nurse is placing them in water to put beside your bed." When he said nothing she went on, "I was speaking to your doctor just now. He says they will be sending you home to England for a long holiday just as soon as you are well enough to travel. We will stay in the country, my dear, where it is green and peaceful; where there is nothing but flowers. We will go somewhere quiet, just the three of us, and walk in the hills, beside rivers, and through fields of wild poppies."

"There were poppies in Flanders," he said, seeing them very clearly. "We trod them all down with our muddy boots, and dug them over to make graves."

It appeared to upset her. "Mark, that was so long ago. You must forget that now."

They all said that. "Someone has to remember, or they'll start all over again."

"No," she told him close to tears. "All that is over now."

"It'll never be over. Each time I look at you I know that," he told her, realising now who she was. "They will never give up. You saw that. You saw that they go on killing and killing until there is no one left. They killed Lionel, and they would have killed you and Michael. There's no one left to stop them. I can't send them all into the canal," he added desperately.

Marie was taking something from her bag, as if she had not heard what he had said. Then he realised he had not said it, only thought it. He seemed to do that a lot lately.

"Your son sent you this," said Marie holding out a scrap of paper. "It's a drawing of a cathedral. He says you told him he might build something bigger than a bridge one day."

"People are never what they seem to be, are they?" he mused, thinking about a bridge he had built. "Hong just walked away and left me there. Even in the war we would not have done that to a man. I thought we had understanding and respect for each other . . . but he walked away and left me there for the dragons to decide."

"I know, my dear," she said soothingly, just the way the nurses did. They all acted like that—quiet voices, gentle nods—agreeing with everything he said. Yet he knew they did not understand, did not really care. They had asked him questions, kept him locked up in a room nobody visited. They had given him pills and potions, put sterilised hands on his brow, and tut-tutted when he grew angry. Grave expressions, sad sentences, tear-filled eyes. Loss and pain, that was all there ever was. People were torn from him as if they were limbs—the agony was equal to that. Was there no hope, no happiness, no love anywhere? He was certain he had experienced it once, for a very short while, but there were always soldiers coming to turn everything into mud and blood.

All at once he realised he was crying, and it was a great relief. The tears ran freely; the sobs built up inside his chest until they burst from him in a great agony of sound The woman with him moved swiftly to sit on the bed, wrapping her arms around him and rocking back and forth as if she, too, were sobbing.

"So much . . . you have done so much," she whispered in thick tones. "Rest now, Markov, please rest."

At the sound of that special name, he broke down completely, clinging to her like a man seizing hold of the last remnants of hope. Shaking convulsively he began to tell her of the hundred dragons that had entered and possessed him. His voice sounded louder and louder in his own ears, and others seemed to have appeared in that lonely place. Nothing could stop him now, however, and he clung to the woman who called him Markov, while he shouted so loudly the dragons all began to slip away in a final acknowledgement of defeat.

During the following two days Mark gave the doctors all he was prepared to tell them of his activities. Realising that Gregori had saved him from military punishment by saying he had been found wandering in a dazed state in Shanghai, he kept quiet about the true events of that fatal night, saying the bullets in his thigh had been the result of machine-gunning by Kuomintang troops on a barge in which he had hidden. Of the bridge at Lu-Seng he said only that he had been rescued by White Russians, leaving the presumption that the villagers had been killed by Chinese troops to stand. When he was told of the crash into the canal, Mark listened in silence. If it were ever revealed that a British officer was responsible for killing Chinese soldiers—especially now the Kuomintang was viewed in a more kindly light—it would be the end of him and the start of a fresh diplomatic row.

Now he had emerged from the state of mental confusion which had been the cause of such concern, they told him that the emergency was over. The railway track had been reconnected to his new bridge at

Lu-Seng by a party of coolies, and trains were running normally over it. There was nothing to keep him in Shanghai now, they said, and extended sick-leave had been granted him as soon as he was able to sail for England.

He had been out of bed several times, and promptly fallen over. His right leg was very stiff, and the prolonged period of fever had made him weak, but he was growing restless and practised walking when the nurses were not there.

He saw Marie each day—often with Michael, who spoke of the events of that night as if it had been a story he once read or a dream he had had. Thankfully, his childish mind soon rejected the fear and horror in favour of the pretence that it had never really happened. Gregori was once allowed in to see him. He gripped Mark's hand in friendship and called him 'Markov, the merman' in a private joke.

Marie's visits broke the monotony of the days, Michael chatted so continuously it took his mind off other things, and Gregori always sent messages regarding the chasing of Reds from China, but Mark could only think of one thing. He had apparently been in hospital for over a month, yet there was no mention of Alexandra. Telephone messages were always given to him promptly, as were letters. But there was no word from her at all. She knew he was back from Lu-Seng because he had telephoned the house that evening. There had also been a colourful and imaginative account of his escape in the newspapers.

A whole month, and she had done nothing. He brooded about it all the time, reading into the silence any number of meanings. Either the doctors were deliberately keeping her away—they were an eccentric bunch, in his opinion—or they would not tell him the truth. After all, it had only been a soldier on the jetty who had said she escaped when her parents had been killed. Mark had seen no official confirmation of the facts. As for Lai-Hi, he had probably pretended to take a message over the telephone because he was too upset to say the whole family was dead. The Chinese were like that. *It is our way*. Would he ever forget Hong saying that as he walked off leaving him to slow agonising death?

Mark brooded more and more as the days passed into a week, and still there was no news of the girl he had hoped to marry. He distrusted everyone around him, and said as little as possible to any of them, vowing he would not give the doctors the opportunity to lie to him by asking to see Alexandra. All the time he wondered if she had been killed along with her mother and father, but would not ask because he could not bear it to be true. Something held him back from facing anything more. He would rather go on forever not knowing, just so long as nobody came to him and said, 'She's dead', as they had with Katya.

The deterioration in his progress prompted the arrival of a hearty nurse to jolly him out of it. He swore at her and said he preferred being alone. Another one came, young and very pretty, bringing him letters which he made no attempt to read. She tried very hard.

"Oh, this is from your mother," she exclaimed, and began reading it out to him. "'Dear Mark, I hope this reaches you because I've just had yours saying you are going to Shanghai to build a bridge. You and your bridges! I could do with you at home right now. Nora's lost the baby and been very ill. I don't know which way to turn for the means to pay the doctor's bill. It's all right for you out there in foreign parts doing what you want to do and not caring. . . .'"

The girl broke off and looked at him with genuine sympathy. "I'm sorry, Major. I'm sure you don't want to hear that right now, do you?"

He swallowed. "Not really." She seemed nicer than the last brisk woman, so he said desperately, "You're a girl. If you lost both your parents in an accident, how would you feel? I mean, would you shut yourself away and forget everyone you ever knew?"

She looked at him cautiously, then frowned. "Perhaps, for a while, but then I'd want to feel there was someone left I could care for."

It made him feel worse. "Yes, that's what I would have thought."

After a moment she said, "Girls vary, you know. What I would do under such circumstances is not necessarily what anyone else would do." She got to her feet and walked over to the cupboard. "Don't you think you've enough to worry about without thinking of other people's tragedies?"

He glared at her then. "Come away from that cupboard. I won't take any more bloody pills."

"I wasn't going to give you any," she said calmly, taking out a large box.

"I don't want to play dominoes, either."

"Well, I do, and you're the only person in this hospital good enough to try to beat me. Come on, it's better than more pills, isn't it?"

"Go to hell," he snapped.

"No, you're the one who is bent on going there," she said softly as she tipped the black oblongs onto a board beside his locker. "I'm here to try and stop you. Please let me."

In the middle of the following morning he was sitting up and staring out of the window when the door opened and she stood there dressed entirely in black. Despite the evidence of mourning, it was the most wonderful thing that had happened to him for weeks. So wonderful he could think of nothing to say.

Alexandra also seemed to be struck dumb, for she stared at him with eyes full of shock. The nurse who had ushered her in broke the silence by saying briskly, "If this doesn't prove you are the most pampered patient in this hospital, Major Rawlings, nothing will. No one else is allowed visitors out of specified hours." She smiled at Alexandra. "The doctor has just been on his rounds, so we won't be discovered breaking the rules, Miss Mostyn."

She went out and shut the door, but Alexandra stayed where she was on the other side of the room, staring at him as if she had seen a ghost. All of a sudden, Mark had a terrible fear of something happening all over again, and he spoke fast to prevent it.

"I knew you'd come as soon as you felt like facing the world again, Alex. I heard about your parents, and I've been so worried about you. I should have been there to help you."

She came across to him then, pale and very serious. "You were forbidden visitors, at first. I had no idea you would still be in here when I came back."

There was something very wrong about what they were doing. They were treating each other like strangers, and he seemed powerless to change the situation because of her distant attitude.

"When you got back?" he questioned, longing to hold her in his arms, longing to feel her warmth melting the chill inside him, longing to tell her she was the only thing in his life now.

"I've been to Hong Kong for two weeks arranging for an exhibition of my work. It will be held just before I leave for England."

He was back in Vladivostok with a girl dressed in peasant clothes, and the words he burned to say would not come because she was acting as if they had never kissed, laughed together, pledged their lives to each other. This one had no husband, no country to demand loyalty from her. This one was free to love just him, yet she was acting as if she had no heart. He could not believe it.

Alexandra began unwrapping the parcel she held in her hands. It contained a canvas done in oils and, when she held it out to him, there was sadness but great determination in her eyes.

"It's entitled *The Bridge of a Hundred Dragons*. You inspired it, Mark, and I'm very grateful. It has turned out to be the passport to the career I've always wanted. You told me I had to suffer in order to be a good artist. You were right."

The picture was misty, haunting and unforgettable. He looked back at her, freezing up inside at what was happening. "Yes, I was right."

"I'm now exceedingly wealthy and free to go where I belong," she went on breezily. "I never want to see China again. From now on I shall travel to all the great art-centres of Europe, learning from the acknowledged masters and gaining experience of a world other than the one in which I have been living." She gave a brief brittle laugh. "No struggling pauper in a garret, me! My father was determined I'd never disgrace the Mostyn name, so I'll do the whole thing in style."

Mark looked at the sweet curve of her cheek, a little tauter, perhaps, and at the absurd bow mouth which was now slightly paler than scarlet. How eagerly and boldly she had returned his kisses; how brokenly she had clung to him when confronted with those photographs. How warmly she had sworn to rear his son as her own, and follow him wherever he was sent. How determinedly she had forced her father to settle that debt; how recklessly she had made him see that the future could be bright and wonderful.

"Alex, what are you trying to say?" he asked thickly.

She sat on the chair beside the bed, and now he knew he was losing her he loved her more than his life.

"Mark," she began with a suggestion of difficulty, "things have changed. I'm free of Father's selfish restrictions. I no longer have a compulsion to give a mother the love and friendship she should have had from her husband. I'm *free*, darling. The Mostyn fortune is mine, and there's so much I want to see and do. I could have died with them on that marsh. I didn't, and I can't fritter away that reprieve. I want to *live*, to justify being allowed to survive when others did not."

He reached forward and took her hand. "Don't you think I have felt that way ever since I saw the first man die at my side? I tried to explain it once, but you told me I should forget and find happiness. I did, Alex. Are you going to snatch it away from me?"

She smiled brightly, withdrawing her hand. "You are a wonderful champion of damsels in distress, sweetie, but I can stand on my own feet now. Tragedy has made me less selfish. I clung to you for support, but you belong in a world where girls who dance on tables don't deserve to be."

"Let me be the judge of that," he said, the huskiness in his throat making it difficult to speak at all.

She got quickly to her feet and indicated the hospital room. "You can't make sane judgements in a place like this." Walking to stand at the bottom of the bed she gripped the rail with black-gloved hands. "When you asked me to marry you, you also said you could never forget Katya and those months in Russia. I now understand that, Mark . . . but I can't live in your past. Marie can. She loves you, and so does your son. You belong with them."

There seemed to be nothing he could say or do. Trapped in a hospital bed and completely devastated by the calm, reasoned way she had destroyed his defences, he could only face the fact that the second woman he had loved was now walking away from him, choosing to follow a star that seemed brighter than all he had to offer.

She was at the door preparing to leave. "You are a wonderful person, Mark. They will make you happy, and if you teach your son to be like you, you will have done one of the greatest things in life. Bless you."

The door closed behind her, and there was nothing to suggest she had ever been there except a piece of brown paper and a painting of a crooked devil-bridge, a ghostly warrior, and a hundred dragons rising from the mist.

He had a bad day after that, and they turned Marie away when she arrived to see him. That night he had a return of the nightmares and fantasies, throwing himself about in the bed and shouting out in fear of dragons who had returned to claim him. He awoke bathed in sweat and exhausted, but reasonably calm. His doctor gave orders that no one was to be allowed to see him save Marie and his son, who had always had a calming effect on him. The nurse who had secretly let the wealthy Mostyn girl visit the patient was given a severe reprimand, and reminded that rules were made for a reason and the results of her disobedience to them should be patently obvious. She retired in tears.

When Marie arrived Mark greeted her quietly, letting her do the talking while he studied her. She was very striking, with an old-fashioned dignity found only in older women these days. He sensed that her feelings for him had deepened slightly since the night he had rescued them. *A wonderful champion of damsels in distress*. Their gratitude could easily be mistaken for love, he knew that too well now. As a wife she would bring him nothing but credit. Her breeding was evident, her intelligence and education equal to any rank he might attain. Then there was Michael. That boy was her anchor, as she had been his. As long as she had Michael she had her past and the family she had lost. Yet she had no kinship with the child. He was Katya's and his own. As long as he had Michael he would have his past and the love he had lost. What of the time when the boy grew, spread his wings, left to make his own life as the young Mark had? What of the pair left together with only the past to bind them until death brought separation? Would they grow old with nothing between them but the ghosts of those they had lost?

He began to feel panic rising, feel the onset of those things which had beset him over the past weeks. His temples began to thud with his pulse-beat, and waves of giddiness swept over him. Marie sat smiling at him while a procession of soldiers marched past behind her—soldiers with no faces and blood-spattered uniforms. Then, over her shoulder, he saw Katya saying goodbye to him. *You are young and have a future beyond this. Live it, my dearest.* She had walked away knowing their child was growing in her. She had walked away with their son, wanting him to be Russian, and leaving the father to go to his own people.

Shutting his eyes he tried to control the giddiness, the feeling of overwhelming panic it brought. He felt as helpless as when Hong had walked away leaving him tied hand and foot to that bridge. He would never get away from the sadness and tragedy of the past. There would never be happiness for him; just a long parade of heavy years to be endured until he could bid them farewell.

"I'm sorry, but visiting hour is over," said a clear voice, and Mark opened his eyes to see the nurse at the door. Thankful for the interruption just when he feared he would do something uncontrollable, he watched Marie turn to Michael and say fondly, "Come along, *mon petit chou*, we must leave now. Gather up your paper and pencils."

The nurse smiled at Mark. "He's very good compared with most of the young visitors. He never complains when it's time to go."

When Michael approached the bed to say goodbye, Mark caught himself putting out his hand to ruffle the dark curls so like his own. "That bridge today was the best ever."

The small freckled face looked up at him with seriousness. "Do you mind if we draw boats next time? Gregori Petrovich came in a splendid boat to fetch us that night. It was the most exciting adventure, and he was very brave. You were sleeping, but I could draw the boat for you. I think I might be a sailor when I grow up. Would you mind that?"

"Michael," he began gently, "it won't always be like this, you know. I'm a soldier, and once I'm back on my feet things will be different."

The boy nodded. "I know. You'll have orders you must obey, and you'll go away again." He smiled up at Marie who was putting the drawing materials away in her bag. "But Mother will always be there . . . and Gregori Petrovich will come and see us as often as he can. We'll be all right."

A great artist I'm going to be, thought Alexandra in despair, throwing down her brush and storming from her room. Ever since her visit to the hospital the previous day all inspiration had vanished. The desire to paint had disappeared. She felt she never wanted to paint again. Downstairs in the sitting room she fitted a cigarette into the jade holder and lit it, but the action did nothing to calm her. There was a terrible ache in her heart and throat that would not go, and she walked up and down the room that held so many memories feeling it grow even worse.

In this room she had been instructed to seduce a stubborn young officer into abandoning his integrity over an official report. In this room he had shown her his opinion of girls who tried to be emancipated. In this same room she had been confronted with the humiliating shame of her folly, and he had saved her from it. In this room he had confessed his past and vowed to make her his future. In this same room he had kept secret the conditions under which that woman would give him his son. In this room Marie Drozdova had broken her with that knowledge.

Throwing the cigarette on the fire she looked around her. The shipping agents were coming shortly to pack everything. Within a few weeks she would be on a ship bound for the motherland she had never seen. All this would be behind her. She was off to a new life and an artistic career. She would be an independent woman flouting convention and all the old established ideas of female subservience: a rich, eccentric Bohemian who was patroness to brilliant penniless young painters. They would conduct passionate *affaires* with her until they needed her no longer, and she would fill her house with people of sensitive, aesthetic and gifted natures.

Putting her arm along the mantelshelf she rested her forehead against it and closed her eyes against that image. It no longer seemed beckoning and attractive. All it conjured up was a life of unbearable loneliness in the midst of the frantic fantasy worlds of those who would use her wealth and influence—even her body—to gain their own ends. Was that all Alexandra Mostyn could ever expect? Would she go from a father who saw her as no more than an accessory to success, to a whole succession of others in the same mould? Was there no one person who wanted just a girl who had a burning urge to live life to the full, even if she made mistakes along the way? Was there no one person who could recognise defiance as courage, daring as exuberance, independence as eagerness? Was there really no one who recognised that in a world of suffering, tragedy and depression, optimism was bubbling within her seeking an outlet?

Oh Mark, came the inward cry as she faced again the fact that she had found that one person, and yesterday put him from her future. That great love of his life, Katya, must have been a very courageous woman to walk away from him after they had lived as husband and wife for six months. Alexandra had discovered nobility was a virtue she did not possess, when the moment for it had come. Saying goodbye to Mark had broken her so completely there was no joy in freedom or artistic fulfilment now. What a price to pay for setting him free from an intolerable choice. If Marie had not shown her that she should, the fact had been brought home all too clearly when Mark had returned from that bridge to Shanghai in the most incredible manner, telephoned Lai-Hi to say he would be there within half an hour, then failed to come.

Having been told only hours beforehand that he was almost certainly dead—killed in the slaughter at Lu-Seng—she had been frantic to see him and had castigated Lai-Hi for allowing him to ring off without speaking to her. As time had passed she had grown more desperate, especially when a call to his hotel revealed that he had left the premises some time before. She had stayed up all night, distracted and fearful, praying that he would contact her to set her mind at rest. *Anything* could have happened to him. That he had eventually been found, dazed and badly wounded, wandering in an area where White Russians lived removed any lingering doubts in Alexandra's mind. When in need of help and comfort he had gone in search of those people who were so closely linked with his past, not to a girl who had forced her way into his life offering no more than champagne bubbles and reckless optimism.

Her many calls to the hospital had been met with noncommittal statements on his condition, and the information that he was allowed no visitors. It was then she realised the time was right to walk out of his life and let him go to those who would make him happiest. She had accepted the invitation to go to Hong Kong for the exhibition, knowing she was avoiding the actual moment of farewell. It had shaken her to discover he was still in the hospital when she returned, and it had taken her several days to pluck up the necessary courage to release him from the burden of a promise he had made to her when under pressure.

The scene had been carefully planned by her, to the extent of wearing deepest mourning, which she had felt would prevent Mark from attempting to prolong the meeting. She had been shocked at his appearance, which had undermined her determination badly, and deeply disturbed at his reaction to her farewell. No one had prepared her for the extent of his illness, which had made her feel that what she was doing was more than cruel, under the circumstances. The scene had been so carefully rehearsed it had played itself out in spite of her shock, and she had had to tell herself constantly that he would be happiest with Marie and his son in order to banish the expression of frightening desolation that had been on his face as she walked away. All desire to telephone the hospital had had to be ruthlessly crushed in the past twenty-four hours. Further contact would merely bring more unhappiness. The break must be clean and final.

Walking moodily to the table, she had just lit another cigarette when the doorbell jangled in the distance. "I'm not at home to *anyone*, Lai-Hi," she called to the boy, who shuffled past bowed down by the tragic deaths of those he had served for so long, and by the imminent departure of a girl he had watched grow from a baby. With all else that was happening in China it was more than he could take.

Moving back to the fireplace Alexandra realised she did not want the cigarette and had just thrown it on the fire when she heard movement in the room. Looking up irritably, guessing that Lai-Hi had disregarded or not heard her instructions, her heart missed a beat, then raced painfully.

"Mark!"

He stood at the top of the few steps, holding the rail, dressed carelessly in a shirt and trousers. Dark eyes in a pale, sunken face stared at her across the elegant room.

"What are you doing here?" she cried, starting forward and wondering how on earth she would get through another conversation with him. "Has the hospital discharged you?"

"No, I walked out when no one was looking." He came down into the room looking as if he would fold up at every step.

She had no idea what to do when they reached each other. There was something about his expression that seemed to defy her to take his arm, support him, or lead him to a chair, as she longed to do.

"You shouldn't have come out like that without letting them know," she managed to say in something approaching a brisk tone. "You have been very ill for some time."

"I had to come. You might not have come to me."

Something warned her not to silence him; some sixth sense kept her standing perfectly still before him while he said what he had been desperate enough to struggle there to say.

"Alex, you can paint . . . I promise," he began in a strange, unsteady voice. "You can do all you want to do. You can smoke cigarettes and wear skirts as short as you like. You can even dance on tables, if you feel you must, but don't walk out on me." He seized one of her hands in his own that were shaking. "*Please*, don't walk out on me."

His words left her shattered. He had always been so strong, so determined, so self-assured. He had protected and defended her against a man others normally surrendered to, and held on to his own integrity in the face of devastating attacks. He had shown her the true values of life, and taught her the unselfishness of devotion. Now he was standing before her, pleading with a new kind of frightening desperation that suggested his survival was in her hands. It was more than she could stand.

"I thought it was what you wanted," she whispered.

He appeared to have difficulty in speaking at all, but finally said, "What I want . . . is you. I want your . . . your gaiety and optimism. I want your crazy feminine in . . . independence. I want your audacious, generous brand of loving. I . . . Oh God, Alex, I want *you* . . . and if you walk away from me now, I think I'll . . . I'll . . ."

She went into his arms because she could bear to hear no more. Moved to tears by this evidence of the power of a woman to make or break a man as strong as he, she held him very close while he rode out the anguish that had driven him to her. How very right her mother had been to say a woman's weakness was very often her greatest strength.

After a while she coaxed Mark to a chair, where he sank back visibly exhausted but much calmer. He was still clinging to one of her hands, but in those dark eyes there was now a faint flicker of life and on his face was a softer kind of yearning. Sinking to the floor at his feet she looked up at him with the love she no longer needed to deny.

"Mark, what will you do about your son?"

"I'll leave him with the mother and environment he knows. He accepts that I have duties that take me away from him, but I shall want to see him when I can. Marie will not deny me that, and if she should marry—as I think she might eventually do—the man in question will prove an admirable father to a boy born and raised as a Russian. Katya will understand that."

She had to ask it, even then. "What of Katya?"

He looked back at her without guile. "I loved her deeply. I can never forget her . . . but I see that it is time for me to say a final goodbye. The past is over, and I desperately want you to be my future, Alex. Say that you will."

Curling her fingers round his she smiled through her emotion. "Yes, darling, I'll be your everything, if that's what you really want."

His tense body relaxed, and whatever had been lurking in the recesses of his mind ready to take possession of him seemed to gradually slip away as they gazed at each other. Then he put up a weary hand to touch her vivid hair.

"You are like a bright flame springing up from the embers of my life."

She leant forward and kissed him full on the mouth before whispering, "Sweetie, together we shall set the whole world on fire, I promise."